F CHR
Christopher, Jaysen
$19.00

Judgment Day

A "Kaylyn Vale" Mystery

by Jaysen Christopher

PITTSBURGH, PENNSYLVANIA 15238

The contents of this work including, but not limited to, the accuracy of events, people, and places depicted; opinions expressed; permission to use previously published materials included; and any advice given or actions advocated are solely the responsibility of the author, who assumes all liability for said work and indemnifies the publisher against any claims stemming from publication of the work.

JUDGMENT DAY is a work of fiction, set in a fictional place, and as such is solely the product of the author's imagination. Any resemblance to any person living or dead is unintended and purely coincidental.

All Rights Reserved
Copyright © 2015 by Jaysen Christopher

No part of this book may be reproduced or transmitted, downloaded, distributed, reverse engineered, or stored in or introduced into any information storage and retrieval system, in any form or by any means, including photocopying and recording, whether electronic or mechanical, now known or hereinafter invented without permission in writing from the publisher.

RoseDog Books
585 Alpha Drive
Suite 103
Pittsburgh, PA 15238
Visit our website at *www.rosedogbookstore.com*

ISBN: 978-1-4809-6651-2
eISBN: 978-1-4809-6628-4

For Susan

"Family is not *necessarily* a matter of blood."
—Wade Ashbery

CHAPTER ONE—August

I don't have many friends anymore; it is not a word I use lightly, and working for "The Company" hasn't helped. A friend is the one running *into* the burning building to get you, while everyone else is running *away*. As I said, it is *not* a word I use lightly. The people who *do* know me, however, will tell you that I am more than a little bit crazy, and I agree. They will also tell you that I don't know even know my own mind, which is untrue, by the way; they'll tell you that I don't know evil from good, or whether or not I'm gay or straight. What I am is a thirty-four year old woman trying to find her place in the world—a task large enough for anyone, let alone someone who has been a contractor for "The Company", a soldier, and a private investigator…all before her thirty-fifth birthday. I've also been employed as a mercenary, but that's a story for another day.

There's an ancient Chinese curse that goes something like this: *May you live an interesting life.*

And to tell you the truth my life up to this point has been anything *but* uninteresting.

As I said, I'm thirty-four, and I'm self-employed. I resigned from "The Company" late last year after taking part in a rescue mission in Afghanistan, which I will tell you about later on, and

I am the sole-proprietor and only employee of the "Kaylyn Vale Agency".

I'm a private investigator, but don't come to me to find out if your husband is cheating on you or if your wife is fooling around with the pool-boy. Sitting in motel parking lots and digging through trash cans isn't my style—but if someone's trying to kill you, or if the police can't solve a crime, I'm certainly the girl you want to see.

People tell me I'm beautiful, but I actually think a better word would be…*different*. I stand five-foot-seven in my bare feet, and I weigh a hundred and eighteen pounds… I'm not too modest to say that most of my weight is pure muscle, although I'm not exactly flat-chested, either. I have long dark hair (not *quite* to the middle of my back), which I usually wear in a pony-tail, although I am not too vain to cut it *short* when I'm involved in something where long hair could be a liability. I also have very blue, very *strange* eyes—lovers tell me that it's an odd color that actually glows in the dark, but when I look in the mirror they actually seem *other-than-human*, like I'm one of those chicks who are into colored contact lenses and unnatural shades. All I can tell you is that the color hasn't been enhanced, and that I see *extremely* well in the dark.

I mentioned lovers—so I might as well get into my sexuality a bit. First of all, please understand that I don't like labels. I like *men*, but I occasionally sleep with other women if someone turns me on. People would call me bi-sexual, but, again, I don't like labels—I'll go to bed with a woman because of *who* she is…not *what* she is, and if you can't wrap your brain around that, too bad.

In the end, all I'm trying to do is find someone with whom I can feel connected. There *was* one guy, and it had something to do with my stint in Afghanistan, but of course he was married. I felt bad about it afterward, but it was really very sweet. He was there for me when I needed him to be, and what the hell…his wife was banging another chick at the time (don't worry; I'll get to that in a while). All I can tell you is that anyone who knows what it's like to be lonely will probably understand all that—if you don't, you're luckier than most.

I never had much of a real mother (and, no—I don't want to talk about it), but the crazy broad my Dad was shacking up with at the time stabbed him, and then I got abused by my step-brother for the next year or so—until I put him in the hospital. I developed quite young, and not just my boobs, either. I am extremely fit, and possessed of an uncommon strength that I seem to have been born with. I'm not telling you this for any reason except to help you understand how my mind works; in short, is someone gives me a firecracker; I'll give *them* a hand-grenade.

It's just the way I am. I've never bothered anyone, but if you plan on hurting *me*, make sure your health insurance is all paid up.

I'll get to the story of The Judgment Day Killer shortly, but you'll need a little more background before I do…so please be patient. After I put that little pervert in the hospital (and yes, I fucked him up *good*, especially considering I was just a kid at the time), I got sent to a foster home, where my new "parents" taught me martial arts. I got in a lot of fights in school, and by the time I was eighteen I was on my fifth foster family—that's when "The Company" recruited me and paid for my schooling. I can't tell you much about my time with them, but it was bad enough that I eventually wanted to do something on my own—especially after Afghanistan.

Like I said, I'm more than a little bit crazy, but despite the fact that I have a big heart and actually cry at "chick-flicks", I am not in the shit business—I don't *give* anyone shit and I don't *take* any…it's as simple as that, and you have to understand that to hear my story.

I also have a baby-face, or so I've been told, and really sensuous lips that let me get away with almost anything. Hey, I didn't *make* the world—I only *live* in this shithole and I am not above using whatever tools Mother Nature gave me.

At any rate, it was three-o'clock in the morning when my phone rang, and I wasn't too happy.

"Vale," I mumbled, reaching for the water bottle on my night-stand.

"Hey, Lynn—it's me, Bobby."

'Bobby' was Detective First Class Robert L. Spinelli of the Rhode Island State Police. "It's my week for girls, Spinner. What do you want?"

"Christ, you sound like shit, Vale."

"Usually do at three o'clock in the morning. What do you want, Bobby? And this better be good."

"We've got a hot one, and my boss, not to mention the Governor, called the State Department and…"

"Let me guess, Bobby—they recommended *me*." I took a sip of water and swore to myself, knowing I'd never get back to sleep. "And I'm not interested."

"Look, Lynn, no one's asking you to come out of retirement. This is just…well, we're up against it, and we could really use your help."

I took a deep breath. Spinner was a decent enough guy, and usually wouldn't ask someone for a cup of water—even if he was on fire. I decided to be gracious—something I'm usually not very good at.

"Care to tell me about it?"

"Not over the phone, Lynn."

I sighed. "I *hate* this cloak and dagger shit, Bobby—it's why I got out in the first place."

"Look, Lynn—I know how you feel, but this isn't coming from me. The Governor…the fucking *Governor*, for Christ's sake, called the damn State Department. I *had* to call you."

"I'm involved in a case right now, Bobby, and I'm up to my ears as it is. Can't you call Ross?" Ross was a codename, the guy I worked for in Afghanistan. Right out a Tom Clancy novel.

"Who do you think got the State Department to *take* the call, Lynn? Jesus."

The curtains were blowing gently into the window, and the breeze was soft, the kind of summer night you hope for if you have someone to share it with. My clock now read three-ten, and my water bottle was empty and I had to pee. If I wasn't about to prance into the bathroom in my pink pajamas the whole thing would have reminded me of a Humphrey Bogart movie.

I rubbed my face with one hand as I stumbled to the bathroom. "If I'm going to meet you at this ungodly hour, Spinner, you have to give me *something*, for Christ's sake." I squished the phone between my ear and my shoulder, dropped my drawers and sat down on the toilet. I was more awake now, and *pissed*, if you'll excuse the expression.

"We've got a dead judge, here, Lynn."

"Then give the guy a medal and let me go back to sleep, Bobby."

"God, I hate to bring this up, but—"

Judgment Day

"Don't you dare, Robert! Don't you *dare* bring up that shit about some dirty cop who got banged out!" That, too, was part of the whole Afghanistan thing. I didn't do that one, but I know who did, and Bobby ran *serious* interference for me. See why I don't like having "friends"?

"Your other car a *broom*, Lynn? Fuck! You've done more for me that I've ever done for you. All I'm saying is this is bad, *real* bad, and I hate telling you details if you're just gonna blow me off!"

"Oh." That got to me, it really did. I got up and threw a face cloth in the sink, turned on the hot water and wiped my face with my free hand. "I'm sorry. Tell me what you gotta tell me. I promise to come down, take a look, and then decide if I'm in. Fair enough?"

"I guess it'll have to be, Lynn, but not a word to anyone or they'll have my balls on a stick."

Bobby was an ex-Navy Seal, and as tough as they come, except for maybe a guy like Wade Ashbery (Afghanistan) and I didn't like hearing the fear in his voice.

"Ok, ok! I'm in—but I'm not doing this for free."

"Wouldn't ask you to."

I tossed the face cloth into the sink, pulled my top off with one hand, and stumbled back to the bedroom to get dressed.

"Well, *tell* me for God's sake, so I can get dressed already!"

"The killer left a note, Lynn—this is personal with him, and we're afraid there'll be more."

"Any demands?" Now, I was *really* interested, and fully awake... despite the fact that I couldn't get my bra on with one hand and had to squish the phone against my shoulder again.

"None—he's just playing with us."

"There's more, isn't there, Bobby? I can tell."

Spinelli sighed. "The dead guy is the second judge in two months, Lynn."

"Give me the address, Bobby—I'll be there as soon as I can."

He gave it to me and I hung up, knowing he was right to be scared. I could already picture what the newspapers would do with this—*The Judge a Day Killer*, *Judgment Day*, stuff like that. I got dressed: black slacks, black boots, black shirt—and 9mm Glock—the Kaylyn Vale wardrobe collection.

I got in my Mustang, thinking I should probably have my head examined.

• • •

I live in Farmington, a little borough nestled between Barrington and Riverside, so it didn't take me long to get to the big house up by the Barrington Country Club, especially at three-thirty in the morning. Many of you are probably familiar with the *Broken Heroes* series, written by the *Pulitzer Prize*-winning editor of the *Providence Times*, Clair Sacchetti, under a pen name—if you are, you'll already know about my involvement in the Ashbery case, and my last trip overseas. If you're not, it tends to get pretty lively around here, especially for such a small area of Rhode Island.

The house on Royal Crescent Drive was huge, and overlooked the water. The front lawn could have been used for a golf course, and there were cop-cars all over the place. The coroner's wagon was in the driveway, back doors open, and there were two local cops on the front steps, watching me as I parked on the edge of the lawn. As I've said, I have a great figure—I'm not bragging, I just work hard at it, and I tend to wear tight clothes, because when people are distracted, it gives me an edge. I've found that pretty, confident women can get away with almost anything, and not just with men, either—like the old song says, *the girls get dressed up for each other*.

I got out, fished out my I.D. case, and walked right up to them. As I got closer to the front door, the lamp-light revealed that the two cops were quite young, a guy and a girl. They looked like kids to me, probably right out of the academy. The male cop couldn't seem to take his eyes off me, so I addressed myself to the female officer.

"Kaylyn Vale," I said, handing her my I.D. "Detective Spinelli called me."

The woman looked at my identification, sniffed, and handed it back with a frown on her face. She was kind of *butchy*, and probably pissed that her partner was drooling over me.

"Second floor, and down the hall to the right," she said.

"Thanks," I mumbled, and stuffed the little wallet into my pocket. The team from the coroner's office was standing at the bottom of the stairs as I went in, looking tired and bored.

"Hey, Tony," I said to the older of the two. "How's business?"

"Always picking up," he quipped, nodding at the empty stretcher. "Glad you're here, Lynn—been a long night."

That one pulled a chuckle out of me. "I'll see if I can get Spinner to move a little faster," I promised as I started up the stairs. There were crime scene units all over the place dusting for fingerprints, and uniformed cops in the hall. I nodded to them as I entered the bedroom, thinking that being a judge must pay pretty well.

"Who ordered the pizza?" I said to Spinelli's back as I went in.

The body was on the floor, with a line drawn around it. It looked like a single shot to the head had done the job, and there was a lot of blood on the beige carpet because head wounds tend to bleed a lot.

"Sure took your time getting here, Vale," Spinelli said. Bobby was maybe six-foot-one, forty-two or three, thin, with dark hair and a bald spot. I met his eyes, which, at this hour of the morning looked like rusty nails in an old wooden door.

"Next time I'll come in my pajamas," I said as I looked around the room. I had taken a quick look at the front door when I'd come in, and there hadn't seemed to be any signs of forced entry, but the killer could have come in a window or used the back door. I squatted down by the body, and caught Spinner looking at my ass as I did so. I turned my head and gave him a look, and the prick actually blushed. I returned my attention to the dead judge, and did a quick survey without actually touching him. "Mmmm. Single shot, .32 or a .38—no exit wound. Capped him, what? Around two maybe?"

"Neighbors said they heard a single gunshot at quarter of, actually."

I stood up and went to the window, which was open, and moved the curtains aside with a pen. The screen was down and locked, and there were no marks on the sill. I turned around. "The guy come in the back door, Bobby?"

Spinelli nodded. "Used a pick. They're dusting it right now."

"They won't find anything."

"Why not?"

"Because this guy is *good* and because you were right to be worried—this was anything *but* random; it was an assassination—the guy didn't even *try* to make it look like robbery."

"I didn't call you cause I'm *stupid*, Lynn—I just want you to give the crime scene the once-over in case I *missed* anything."

"There's a *Rolex* on the bureau, and some cash." I walked over and slid the judge's wallet off the folded wad of bills with my pen. "Looks like at least three hundred dollars here." I looked around the room. "Laptop, *Kindle Fire, Bose Acoustic Wave*—shit, Bobby, *that's* worth a grand by itself." I walked over to the doorway after judging the angle of the shot. "Killer stood here, took him out with one shot to the head. Waited till he turned around by the looks of it—wanted him to see it coming. You said he left a note?"

Spinelli nodded, walked over to the open laptop on the desk, and hit the space bar with his own pen. A *Word* document appeared, with a single line of text:

"*For in the way you judge, you will be judged.*"

"Matthew 7:2," I mumbled, after peering at it. I straightened back up and took out my notebook.

"Didn't know you were the religious type, Vale, I'm impressed."

"Don't be—I speak Arabic, too; doesn't make me a Muslim."

Spinelli chuckled. "I'm shutting up now."

"Smart boy. You say this judge was the second?"

"Yup."

"What's his name?"

"Unger, F.," Spinelli said, taking out and looking at his own notebook.

"Please don't tell me his first name was Felix."

"Frederick," Spinelli said with another chuckle.

"And the first victim?"

"Jordan, Paul."

I wrote that down, and squatted by Judge Unger again. He seemed to be about sixty, austere-looking, a fair-skinned man. He was overweight, but not overly so. I stood back up. "What kind of note did the killer leave with the first body?"

"Another Bible quote—maybe I should just give you Chapter and Verse, see how smart you really are," Bobby said with a smirk.

"I dare you," I said, holding my pen ready over my notebook.
"Genesis 1:5."

I wrote while I said it out loud: " '*And there was evening and there was morning—the first day.*' "

"Holy *shit*," Spinelli said.

I smirked. "Gotta learn to piss in the tall grass if you want to play with the big dogs," I said. "And by-the-way, it might not really *be* 'Holy shit.' Could be something he's using to throw us off."

"Didn't mean it that way."

"I know you didn't." I frowned. "Today is August 21st," I said, thinking out loud. "Assuming he really died after midnight." I wrote that down. "When did the first judge get killed?"

Spinelli again went to his notebook. "July 10th."

I wrote that down, too. "Mmmm."

"What?"

"I don't know—something's clicking with me, but I can't quite put my finger on it." I looked up. "You're *sure* the two are connected?"

"The first message was also written on the judge's computer."

"Okay." This was really starting to bother me, and Spinelli picked up on it.

"What?' he asked again.

"If the two *are* connected, this guy's just getting started."

"I think so, too, Lynn—that stuff about the 'first day' and all, but I wanted *your* opinion as well."

"Anything taken at the first scene?"

"Nothing, why?"

I shrugged. "I hate to tell you this, Bobby, but they'll be more, and the only way to stop him is to figure out some kind of a pattern."

"I don't see any way to do that, not with what we have so far. Do you?"

"No, not really," I said, but something was bothering me, like one of those itches you get that you can't seem to scratch away. I closed my notebook. "Send me both Murder Books, Bobby, as soon as you can."

"I can email them."

"Good. And the sooner the better."

"How come?"

"Because I don't know how much time we've got until this guy does it again."

• • •

My office is in a little strip mall on Old Town Road, about a mile from the Ashbery Dairy Farm—I know I said I'd tell you about them, and I will. It's a small office, nothing impressive, but to paraphrase Sherlock Holmes, I never try to inspire confidence in anyone but myself. There was a *Cumberland Farms* store right next door, a chiropractor's office, a *Fed-Ex* joint, a hair-dresser and the local post office—all very convenient. My office was at the end of the strip, near the woods. There used to be a photo shop kiosk out in the lot, but they took it down—life in the digital age, I guess.

Anyway, it was just after five o'clock when I drove by, and I knew I wouldn't be able to sleep, so I pulled in, went inside, and pulled up the shades. Despite the convenience store, I'm quite fond of those little K-cups, so I made myself some coffee and sat down to enter my notes into a data base. The email from Spinner was already there, and I entered all *that* stuff, too. That nagging itch was driving me out of my mind, now—if you've ever tried to think of an actor's name or something like that, and couldn't quite get it, you'll know what I'm talking about.

First I looked at the dates—July 10th; August 21st. Nothing. Then I looked at the names: Jordan, Unger. Again, nothing. I looked at the first two letters in each name: J and U. I *should* have seen it right then, but I didn't, and all I can say is that I was over-tired and still had that other case on my mind. Then I looked up the quotes from Scripture and read each Chapter. The killer or killers had jumped from Genesis to the Gospel and even though the part about judging others was clear enough, again—nothing. I sighed, and sat back.

Then I got out a pen and wrote the two names on a piece of paper.

I transposed the letters, moved them around like a crypto-quote, and, again, got nothing for my trouble. By this time I was yawning and had just about talked myself into taking a nap on my couch, when I heard a car pull up outside. The August sun was bright, though, and there was a terrific glare—five-fifty-nine by this time—and I couldn't make out the car, so I went back to my notes.

I've been investigating crimes for a long while, now, and I'm something of an expert, especially since I've killed more than one person myself. There's *always* a pattern with serial killers—and I believed we were dealing with one now. The whole thing about two dead judges *screamed* ex-con or someone else wronged by the judicial system, but even in a small state like Rhode Island, where would I start?

"Start with the recent cases of each judge, dummy," I actually said out loud, and made a note to check that with Spinelli.

I had just finished jotting it down when the little bell over my door rang and Samantha Ashbery came in.

I usually don't mind interruptions—but at *6 A.M.?* Not good.

Samantha is by far the most beautiful woman I have ever seen. And I'm not the only person who thinks so. She resembles the actress Lyndsy Fonseca, and has an *incredible* body. Sam is the wife of the guy I slept with in Afghanistan, and, oh, what the hell—let me tell you a little bit about that story right now and get it out of the way.

Those of you who read *Broken Heroes* already know about Wade Ashbery and his wife, the former Samantha Vianna—for those of you who *haven't* read about it, here it is in a nutshell: The story I'm telling you right *now* takes place a little over a year after I came back from Afghanistan, but Wade and Sam's story actually goes back a few years further than that, and the two are connected.

Wade had just come back from overseas when his wife, Janice, was killed by a drunk driver. She was pregnant with their first child at the time. Wade was already suffering from PTSD, and when he saw Sam getting slapped around in a parking lot one day—by a drunk... he stopped it. The two fell in love and began an affair. The problem was, Sam lied to Wade about her age, and when he started seeing her he was twenty-five and she was only sixteen. The whole thing blew up in their faces when Sam's step-father (the same drunk who had slapped her around), tried to rape her. The guy ended up killing his ex-wife, shots were fired, and the drunk was killed. The cops barged in, shot *Sam* for Christ's sake—and Wade, a highly decorated Force-Recon Marine, took them out. There's a lot more to this, but I don't want to get too far away from *this* story. They took off together, and Wade eventually faked his own death and went back to Afghanistan, where he was working for that guy Ross I told you about earlier, rescuing MIA's. Sam didn't know that he was dead, however, and Wade didn't know that she was pregnant when he left the country to protect her. He came back when he found out, stood trial—and believe it or not, they were exonerated. Shortly after that he went back to Afghanistan, and that was the mission where I came to *know* him, if you'll pardon the expression.

"Hey, you," I said, as Sam came in. "You're up early."

"Life on a farm," she said with a smile that almost quite worked. "You're up kind of early yourself."

"Couldn't sleep. Got a case here that's bothering me, a real puzzle; I thought I'd take a crack at it while it was quiet."

Sam looked down at my word jumbles. "I'm pretty good at that stuff—let me know if you need help with it."

"I'll do that. Want some coffee?" I asked, standing up and tossing my pen on the desk.

"Uh, sure. Thanks."

As I've said, Samantha is *gorgeous*. She's got rich honey-wheat-colored hair, beautiful green eyes, and keeps herself in fantastic shape. She studies martial arts, and to tell you the truth she's also become something of a celebrity for her work as a writer. Because of what happened to her and her husband, she writes mostly about social justice and human rights—altogether, a formidable package.

"Cream and sugar?"

"Please."

I gave it to her and sat back down, picking up my own cup. We stared at each other for a moment, and to tell you the truth, and despite the fact that she was about ten years younger than me at the time; I was as attracted to *her* as I ever was to her husband.

"What's on your mind, Sam?" I asked, sipping my coffee and looking at her over the rim of the cup. "Please don't tell me you need an investigator—not after everything else you've been through."

"Oh, no—nothing like that." Sam was wearing a sleeveless tank-top that showed off how toned her arms were; there was a little tattoo of a butterfly on her arm with her husband's name on it, and she was wearing shorts that would have caused an accident if she walked down the street wearing them. "I just have a question."

Being who and what I am—I thought I knew what it was, so I prepared myself for the worst.

"Shoot."

"Something's been on my mind since Wade came back from Afghanistan," she said, "and I thought I'd just come right out and say it."

"Let me guess," I said, deciding to take the bull by the horns. "You want to know if I slept with your husband."

Sam's green eyes were like shards of bright glass, and I had to be careful not to make her an enemy.

"Did you?" she asked quietly.

It's been said that I am a *great* liar, and that I have no conscience. The first part is true. Sam, however, had a reputation for getting to the truth—she's a writer after all, but I'm good at what I do and confident enough to use the tools at my disposal.

"Why would you ask me something like that?"

"Why did *you* know I was going to ask it?" she countered.

"Seriously, Sam? It's six o'clock in the morning and you knew I was alone here." I wrapped my hands around my cup and met her eyes. "Besides, you and I are more alike than you can imagine."

"Did you?" she repeated.

"No," I said, lying straight out, but I was a little pissed at her direct approach, not that I didn't admire it, because she was sleeping with her girlfriend, Jennifer, when I went to bed with Wade. It's true that she started the affair when she thought Wade was dead, but she didn't break it off when he came home, either. If *that* doesn't work for you—I don't kiss and tell.

"Look, Lynn—we're both adults and you know damn well that I'm not exactly an angel myself. I know *something* happened between you two. Woman to woman, you on the level?"

Samantha's eyes were gorgeous, piercing and dangerous. I didn't *like* lying to her, but I have my own code of ethics and I wasn't about to rat out her husband. Attorney Dante Graviani, now *Judge* Graviani, brought me on board in the Ashbery case when Sam and Dante's wife, the noted journalist Clair Sacchetti, were run off the road by dirty cops. I knew that Samantha's own step-father had tried to rape her, and more than once, so I used that to get her to understand where I was coming from.

"I had issues similar to what you went through with your step-father, Sammy. Only it went a lot further and lasted over a year—when I was just a kid."

"I'm sorry, Lynn. I didn't know."

"I had a meltdown over there. Wade came in one night to go over the mission protocols for the next day, and found me crying. I broke down and asked him to hold me. If you consider *that* cheating, I'm sorry." I wanted to tell her that if I had my choice between the two of them, *she'd* be the one I'd hit on, but I held my tongue—I'd done enough damage as it was and I really liked Samantha—a lot.

"Ok," she said and got up. "Thanks for the coffee."

I stopped her when she reached the door.

"Sam?"

Her hand was on the doorknob but she didn't turn around. "Yeah?"

"Why didn't you ask *Wade* about this?"

Samantha turned. Not only was she beautiful and strong—she was extremely intelligent and wise beyond her years.

"I did, but he's not a very good liar, Lynn." She met my eyes. "I'll see you around."

The fatigue was a living thing by this time, and my head was swimming. I went to the window and watched Sam pull away in her Jeep. Then I turned the "Be Back Soon" sign face up in the glass door, pulled the shades and sat down on the couch. Five minutes later I was out like a light.

• • •

I woke up at eleven-fifty-five, feeling more refreshed than I had any right to be. I went into the back, took a quick shower, and changed, putting on some jeans, my *Nike* running shoes and a sleeveless yellow blouse. I went back to my notes, read them over quickly, and sent Spinelli an email, asking for the recent cases of each dead judge. I thought for a moment, and then added that I wanted him to go back at least five years. Knowing *that* would take a while, I thought about my next move.

This was definitely the work of someone who had been wronged by the judicial system, or *thought* he had…he or *she*, I thought, reminding myself not to take anything for granted, so the best place to ask for information about an ex-con…is another ex-con. I hadn't been kidding when I'd told Spinner to give the guy a medal. Our judicial system is all screwed up, and it's more about careers, elections and job creation than it is about true justice. No one cares about the law anymore; all they care about is feeding The Prison Industrial Complex; thinking about that, I realized that our killer could be just about anyone.

"Fucking needle in a haystack," I mumbled as I started the Mustang and let it idle. I've always been fond of *The Pony*, and mine was anything but street-legal. The engine was balanced and blue-printed, with police-grade brakes and transmission, bullet-proof windows and heavy-duty *Cooper* tires. I liked the sound of it gurgling through the dual exhaust as it warmed up, and I popped in an Art Pepper CD while I sat there thinking about another cup of coffee.

I *love* jazz, and Pepper is a favorite of mine. Listening to him calmed me and helped me to think, and as I put the car in reverse I suddenly knew where I had to go. Old Art was working his way through *Blues in The Night* as I hit the *Dunkin Donuts* drive-through, and I ordered two large, hot coffees with extra cream and extra sugar.

"Two large hots, extra-extra," the girl repeated. "Anything else?"

"Yeah—give me a half-dozen plain donuts, will you?"

"Drive up," she said, and five minutes later I was on my way.

The coffee smelled *good* and I popped one open, taking a big sip and dying for a cigarette. I know it's supposed to be taboo for a health-nut like me to smoke, but, what the hell—I like it, even though I *do* try to control myself. There was a pack of *Winston Lights* in the glove compartment, and I decided that *one* wouldn't hurt.

When I got to Roger Williams Lane, I called David Redman on his cell phone just to make sure he was home. He still worked full time as the mechanic out at the old Becker ranch where he lived, but he also volunteered down at *Second Starts*, a jobs-program for ex-cons, and I didn't want to waste my time if he was out. He picked up on the first ring.

"Hey, Beautiful," he said, and it made me smile. If he knew it was me, it also meant he had my number programed into his phone; I'm a girly-girl at heart, and I was flattered—sue me.

"Hey yourself, Handsome—got a minute for an old friend?"

"I'm up to my ass in a valve job, here, Lynn, but I was just about to take a coffee break. Sure, come on up."

"I'll actually be there in five minutes, Dave—and I've got coffee and donuts *with* me."

"My kind of girl," he said, and again it made me smile. "You know where to find me."

David Redman was a black man in his sixties who had done ten years in the state prison up in Walpole, Massachusetts, for killing a guy in a bar fight who had gotten rough with his date. If *I* was his kind of girl, he was certainly *my* kind of guy. Remember when I got mad at Spinelli, thinking he was reminding me of the dirty cop who got roughed up? Well, *David* was the one who actually did that—used a baseball bat on the cop who ran Sam and Clair off the road, and damn near killed him; Dave is an old friend of the Ashbery's, and like a father to Wade. He and I had met when Dante brought me in on the case—and we hit it off from the start. I drove right up to the garage, and he came out to greet me, opening my door with a smile.

"Here," I said, handing him the tray with the coffee and donuts, "make yourself useful."

I got out, and he gave me a kiss on the cheek. "Damn, girl—you get any prettier, someone's gonna put a frame around you!"

"Look who's talking," I said, "you get younger every time I see you! What's your secret?"

"Hard work and more hard work, young lady."

Judgment Day

Dave had always reminded me of a young Morgan Freeman, and had the most amazing smile. He was upbeat and positive; you'd never know from looking at him that he had done a *dime* in one of the most violent prison systems in North America.

"Well, aren't you going to invite a lady in?"

"Right this way, Ma'am," he said, bowing and showing the way.

I laughed, and followed him in. His kitchen was large and well-kept, and Danny (Dante) and I, had spent more than one evening at his table after the case, sharing war stories, as it were. I felt comfortable here, as if I was family, and in a way, I guess I am—in our world, the world most people rarely see, friendships are like gold. We sat down, and he lit a cigarette as he took the top from one of the cups.

"Smoke if you got 'em," he said.

We drank some coffee, ate a donut each, and smoked while we caught up. After a while he sat back and looked at me.

"So, what's on your mind, Lynn?"

I made a face, because I knew this wouldn't go over well.

"The State Police brought me in on a bad one, David," I said, crushing my cigarette out in his ash tray. "I have a question or two, and I'll need you to keep what we say strictly between you and me."

"You got that," he said, and I smiled. People on the outside always say, *You've got it*, but *You got that*, is prison lingo, and always said with a bit of an edge.

"Been two Superior Court judges murdered in a little over a month, Dave. Killer's been leaving notes, too. There's going to be more, and I need to get a handle on the guy who's doing it."

David broke another donut in half and chewed for a moment. "How can I help?"

"Well, this is delicate," I began, knowing that Dave, being an ex-con, wouldn't rat anyone out. I had to make him see that this was bad for all ex-cons, everywhere, if I was going to gain his support. "We figure the perp must be an ex-con, someone fucked over by the system, you know, but if we don't stop him, he's going to keep doing this, and it'll seriously make it harder for all the guys out on the street who are trying to do the right thing."

"Don't play me, Kaylyn—I invented it."

"Sorry," I said, and meant it.

"You need my help, just spit it out, kiddo."

"Alright—here it is in a nutshell: do you know anyone, or have you heard of anyone, who's been running his mouth about offing judges? I know this is hard for you, David, but it really is in everyone's best interest if we nab this jerk."

David looked at me for so long that I knew I'd disappointed him. Ratting someone out is the worst thing any con can do, and once a con, always a con. He cleared his throat then and made a face.

"I've never knocked on anyone before, Lynn," David said, employing even more prison lingo, "but if this guy is really doing what you say he's doing, then you're right—if it continues, it'll only make the suits clamp down on parole, probation, everything." He sat back and laced his fingers together behind his head. "I don't like doing this, but I'm with you on this one, because it undermines everything we're trying to do at the *Second Starts* center." He cleared his throat again. "Alright, I'll ask around, see what I can find out—but, not a word to anyone, or you and me…we're done."

"Not a word, Dave, I promise—and thanks!"

"Don't thank me, Kaylyn—this rubs me the wrong way, but wrong is wrong. Incidentally, have you called Danny and told *him* about this?"

"Wow," I mumbled, "I hadn't even thought of that." Danny had been appointed to the bench shortly after the Ashbery trial. He was not only Clair Sacchetti's husband and a good guy—we had a little history, and David and I were both very fond of him. "I think he's still in *probate* court, Dave, but yeah, I'll give him a heads up. Doesn't hurt to be careful."

"Why haven't we heard about this in the papers?" David wanted to know.

"They're lying to the media, Dave, but eventually someone on the force will sing. They passed the first one off as a heart attack, and last night as a robbery."

"Who's working you on this?"

"Spinner. Bob Spinelli."

David Redman nodded. "Ok. I hate to admit it, but as far as cops go, he's all right." He stood up and stretched. "Look, I gotta get back to work," he said, and I knew I'd worn out my welcome. "Don't let me down on this, Lynn—don't even tell Spinner, you dig?"

"I'd never hurt you, Dave—you're like a brother to me. The guy last night didn't have any family, but the other guy had a wife and kids. We need to stop this, and I didn't know who else to turn to."

"As long as we understand each other," he said.

"Perfectly," I answered, meeting his eyes and knowing that I'd just lost a little credibility with him but also knowing he'd eventually come around once he realized he was doing the right thing.

Eventually.

CHAPTER TWO—September

In *The Maltese Falcon*, Humphrey Bogart says that he doesn't mind a little bit of trouble, or words to that effect, but in the ten days following the conversation I'd had with David Redman, ten days when I didn't hear a *word* from him, I began to think I'd bitten off more than I could chew. It wasn't just trouble I was afraid of, but losing a friend, something I could hardly afford. Cons have a code of honor that prohibit them from squealing on anyone, and despite the circumstances, I was starting to think I'd put too severe a strain on our friendship. As I've said, I don't use the word, *friend*, lightly, and I didn't want to lose one as good as Dave.

September First brought the promise of an early fall, and for that I was glad, because I'd just about had it with the heat and high humidity, so when David called me at ten o'clock in the morning, I was grateful in more ways than one. I was out jogging on Old Town Road, heading back to the office when my cell phone rang; I fished it out of my shorts and answered gladly, trying to catch my breath.

"Do I even want to *know* what you're doing, Vale?" he asked, obviously referring to the fact that I was gasping for air.

"Get your mind out of the gutter, old man!"

"Why? To leave more room for dirty young chickens like yourself?"

There was a hitch in my side, and I slowed to a walk, holding a hand on my hip. "I was jogging. What's going on?' I added carefully.

"The part you ordered for your Mustang came in," he said. "You wanna come by here? I can install it for you."

If David was worried about talking plainly on the phone, and didn't even want to meet at a restaurant, I figured he had something pretty good. At least, I hoped he did.

"I'm all sweaty. Can you give me an hour?"

"Maybe I *like* sweaty woman, Vale—just hop in the car, will you? I got a ton of work to catch up on."

"Ok, pal, but don't say I didn't warn you."

"Seriously, Vale? Don't threaten *me* with a good time! My last Bunkie went two-ninety, and stunk like the fish pier on Gull's Point!"

"I'll be right up," I said, and jogged over to the car. As I was getting in, Samantha Ashbery drove by and gave me the once-over. She didn't look at me with any malice, it was more like she was checking me out and it kind of turned me on. She gave me a little smile, and I returned it, and as I got in the car I saw that she was still looking at me in the rearview mirror.

"Careful, Chicky," I mumbled as I slipped the key into the ignition. "That's trouble you don't need." All the same, she had made me more than a little bit interested—just with that one little look, and not for the first time, I wondered what it would be like to kiss her. I've told you that she looks like Lyndsy Fonseca, and she does, but she's got lips like Scarlett Johansson, and hitting on another woman isn't like picking up a guy; with a woman, it's all about the looks you share, and more about what you don't say than about what you do—ok, so I'm a horn-ball—so what?

"Focus, Vale—focus!" I growled, and drove to the Becker place, trying not to think. I got there while David was taking a spark plug out of a pickup truck, frowning at it as if it were to blame for all the trouble in the world.

"That the part you ordered for me?"

David tossed the fouled plug into a trash barrel, and took a new one from the box on the bench. "You're a smart ass, Vale—anyone ever tell you that?"

A million snide remarks came to mind, but I held my tongue as David looked around and then fished a crumpled piece of paper from the top-right hand pocket of his overalls.

"Here, don't ever say I didn't do anything for you."

"Thanks, David, I began, and knew it was a mistake as soon as I opened my mouth.

"DON'T," he snarled, "thank me for being a lowlife. Just take your sweaty, sweet little ass out of here and do what you gotta do."

"Ok," I mumbled, stuffing the slip of paper into my shorts without so much as looking at it. "Ok," I repeated, just to have something to say.

I turned around and left, because he was at the bench, looking for something. His voice stopped me as I got to the open door.

"Kaylyn?"

"Uh-huh?" I said, turning my head.

"I love you like you was my own kid, but don't ever ask me to do anything like that ever again. Ever."

"I won't," I promised, and went back to the car, sure that I had lost one of the best friends I've ever had.

• • •

Spinelli met me that night at the little coffee and ice-cream shop up at Barrington Point, not three-hundred yards from where Judge Unger had been murdered.

He looked at the three names I had given him, retyped on a sheet of paper with some notes I had prepared for him, and tucked it into his own notebook.

"I'll check these out. Don't suppose it would do any good to ask where you got them?"

"You know better than that."

"I guess I do, but we can't go around guarding every single judge, so I thought it would be helpful to know where this came from."

"All you need to know is that all three of those guys have been shooting their mouths off about capping judges, Bobby—and one of them might actually be innocent."

"Seriously?" He took the folded sheet of paper out again. "Which one?"

"The second one on the list. Worthington."

"Worthington, Kyle." He tapped his lips with his pen. "I'll pull his jacket. What's his beef?"

"Convicted sex offender. Claims he didn't do it. Ran a tattoo parlor down in Bristol with his wife—a real flake, that one. They were into threesomes—he and his wife and some chick who worked for them. One night, his wife and the other girl, with all the evidence right there between her legs and down her throat, went down to the police station and filed a rape charge. The two of them got everything when he went away—house, bank account, and the business by itself was doing close to half a mil a year. His wife was drunk one night and let it slip in some bar that she had set him up, but the Appeal's Court shot it down as 'hear-say'—did ten years."

"And he blames the trial judge?"

"That would be my first guess, Bobby, but we've gotta start thinking about the Appellate Court now, too. If this guy's really innocent, and I think he is, doing a dime in the slammer could have caused him to snap. That sex offender shit; it's big business, and an easy card for any wife to play when she wants a divorce."

"I know. Got a friend of mine whose wife said he was molesting the kids. Totally bogus charges. Sad." For the first time, I realized that he looked a little like the actor, Jason Statham.

"Focus, Bobby—how do you want to do this?"

"Ok, we'll put men on both his trial judge and the Appellate Panel, but we really should stake *him* out, too, Worthington, I mean."

"I'd watch the other two guys, as well—I wrote down what they were pissed about, but both of them are lowlifes, a pimp and a small-time drug dealer…both of them probably full of shit and just talking tough." I bit my lip. "But you never know…"

"You want in on the stake-out?"

"I don't feel like baby-sitting any judges, but I'll take Worthington. Can you give me some back-up?"

"How about me?"

"Isn't your wife gonna get pissed—you spending so much time with a girl like me?" I smiled sweetly. "I don't exactly have the best reputation."

"Probably thank you if she thought you were doing me, Vale—woman thinks sex is just for making babies. Why do you think I'm so thin? I *run* off all my excess, uh, energy."

I giggled. Sometimes I do—not a woman's laugh, but a real schoolgirl giggle. I just can't seem to help it.

"What time do you want to meet?"

"Let's see: what have we got here? Three ex-cons and three trial judges; the three on Worthington's Appellate Panel make six judges altogether. Christ, Lynn, this is like whistling past the graveyard! Do you have any idea how many judges we have in this state?"

"What time?" I pressed, knowing that, if I let him run on like this, he'd get himself all worked up.

"Why don't you and I take the night shift, say midnight to six or so, considering both victims got it between those hours?"

"Sounds like a plan," I said, happy that I called Danny right after talking to David. It was true that we couldn't watch every damn judge in the state, but we had to start *someplace*, didn't we? "That reminds me—did you pull the cases on the dead judges?" That wasn't going to *prevent* anything, but it just might point us towards the shooter.

"That's going to take a while, Lynn. Jesus, for all we know, this guy's throwing darts at the *Lawyer's Weekly* and picking his judges *that* way. Christ, what a mess!"

"I've got an idea," I said, finishing my coffee and fighting with myself over the urge to light another cigarette. "What if we just focus on *criminal* trial judges? It'll narrow the field, and maybe we'll see something that way." I frowned. "I don't know, just thinking out loud."

"No, that's probably a good idea." He made a note and put the little book back in his pocket. "What time is it?"

"Almost seven."

"Why don't we both go home and rest for a while? Worthington lives in Warren, so it won't take us long to get there. There's a *Food Mart* on the corner of his street. Used to be a *Mister Donut* there, too. I think it's a burger joint now."

"It's a *Wendy's*, and I know right where you mean." I got up and put my cell phone in my pocket. "Meet you there, at, what? Eleven?"

"I'm tempted to say earlier, but we both need the rest. Eleven it is."

"This could take a while, Bobby, and I don't just mean tonight." I bit my lip. "We still don't know when, let alone where."

"Don't forget *who*, either!"

I laughed. "It's either that or let the bad guys win. *Tale e' la vita*," I added.

"You Italian, Vale?'

"Half. My mother was Lebanese, or so I'm told."

"Wow. Remind me not to piss *you* off. What's that mean?"

"*Such is our life*, roughly translated. See you tonight, Bobby."

• • •

My office was closer to where I had to meet Bobby, so I stopped there, rather than go home. Believe it or not, I saw Sam Ashbery jogging on Old Town Road, heading back to her place, and, unable to help myself, I waved. She gave me a thumb's-up and kept going, and then I swore to myself. I live in the same town as that girl, and haven't seen her three times in a year—now, all of a sudden, I see her three times in the same week. I've always believed that people who are interested in each other are on the same wavelength, so I didn't think too much of it, except to say that even her running bra couldn't hide the way she jiggled. I got hot all of a sudden, and put on the a/c, thinking I needed my head examined.

There was a message on my machine, but the number was blocked. I played it and recognized David's voice right away.

"We're cool, Chicky, don't sweat it."

I played it again, feeling better after doing so, and took my shirt off after locking the door and pulling down the shades. I got on the couch and tried to get comfortable, thinking, that, if this went on much longer, I was going to have to sub-contract out my other case, at least for the time being. I wanted to go over my notes on this whole judge thing, too, but I was tired and ended up lying down. I set my alarm for quarter of eleven, and fell asleep almost instantly.

● ● ●

The alarm never went off because I woke up on my own at ten-thirty. I made coffee, washed my face, got dressed and went out. *Dunkin Donuts* was on the way, so I stopped there and got two large coffees, thinking it would help to keep us awake. Bobby was already in the parking lot when I got there, so I left my car at *Wendy's* and got into his unmarked *Crown Vic* with the coffee tray.

"Now, *that's* what I call a partner!" he said with a smile, taking one of the cups. "Thanks, Lynn."

"Don't mention it."

"I'll buy tomorrow."

"Whatever."

Bobby turned his head in the middle of trying to take a sip of coffee, and almost spilled it. "What's the matter?"

"I don't know. This guy, Worthington, he's been shooting his mouth off about this stuff, but if a guy was really doing something like this, wouldn't he keep his mouth *shut*?"

"You thinking we've got the wrong guy?"

"No, it's a good lead and came from a reliable source, but there's something bothering me and I can't quite figure it out."

"Well, you said it yourself, Lynn—we have to start somewhere." He drank some coffee. "And this guy's as good a place to start as any." Bobby put his cup down in the little holder between the seats and started the car. "Just because he's gotten away with two murders doesn't mean he's smart, Lynn. I pulled his jacket." He reached into the back seat and handed me a folder. "Here, check this out while I drive over there."

Worthington was apparently a "whiner"—I've never been wrongly convicted of a crime, so I don't know what that feels like, but if it were me, and I really didn't do it, I would have been more diligent about my appeals instead of doing the jailhouse lawyer thing. Maybe I even would have tried to publish some articles, too. Hire an investigator. I don't know. Written to the Legislature, built some support. All this guy had done was get in fights, argue with the prison staff and shoot his mouth off about how rotten and unfair the system was. There was even a copy of a letter he had written to the parole board, real radical stuff, skating right up the edge of threatening language and stopping just short of it.

"Maybe you're right, Bobby." I studied Worthington's face. Thin, haggard, receding blond hair. Looked to be about thirty-nine or forty—and a loser. "Maybe he's just not too bright."

"You know, I take that back. Look at Tim McVeigh, or maybe even the Unabomber. Both very bright guys. Hell, in Kaczynski's case, his damn I.Q. was off the charts. Both of them still nuts, though, writing manifestos and leaving all kinds of evidence." He glanced at me for a moment as he turned onto Worthington's street. "You can be bright and not have any common sense, you know, or so damn arrogant that it becomes a liability. Don't sweat it; I think we're on to something here."

"We'll see," I told him, and put the folder in the back seat.

We parked at the end of the street the first night, watching the little apartment building where Worthington lived, and got nothing for our trouble but stiff necks and sore backs. The second night was no better—hell; Worthington actually shut his television off at eleven-fifteen, judging by the lack of flickering lights in his window. The next day, the Third, I insisted we take *my* car, and park at the other end of the street.

"That damn Ford of yours couldn't look any more like a cop car if it had a shield painted on it," I told Bobby.

And that night, the Third, we got something at a quarter to twelve.

Worthington came out the front door carrying a ten-speed bike. I'm not kidding you. A fucking bike ride at midnight.

"That him?" Bobby asked.

"Yeah, that's him. No! Stay down! He's coming this way!"

Worthington got to the curb, pointed the bike in our direction, looked up and down the street and headed right for us. We were both slouched down low as he passed, looking neither left nor right, and I was sure he hadn't seen us.

"Get out and behind that tree!" I snarled at Bobby, who knew I had already pulled the bulb in the overhead light. "See which way he goes! I'll turn around!"

Bobby jumped out, ducked low, and got behind the big Maple right beside the car. I started the Mustang, leaving the lights off, and swung it in a tight arc, coming to a halt exactly where Spinelli was hiding.

He got back in and pointed. "He took a right on Cherry Street!"

"Damn," I said, just sitting there with the engine gurgling.

"What's the problem?"

"I can't just barrel-ass down there, Bobby—even with the lights off! He'll make us for sure."

"So what are you thinking?"

"I was going to give it a minute, but now I'm thinking maybe we should drive down to the next cross street, the one running parallel to Cherry."

"That's Oak Street."

"Ok. We can park at the end, and watch as he comes down."

"Do it."

We had studied the maps of the area diligently, and unless he pulled into someone's driveway we'd be able to see him when he got to Poplar Street. I suppose the city planners thought it was cute to name all the streets in this neighborhood after trees, but it was damn confusing and pissed me off.

The Mustang was *fast*, and I got there quickly, taking the turn on those big *Cooper* tires without a sound. Bobby had already alerted the local cops about our activity in the area, but I was hoping that we didn't run into some eager-beaver rookie, looking for joy-riders in fast cars. When I got to the end of the cross-street, Worthington barreled through the intersection without even slowing down and continued down Cherry Street. I waited a minute, and then took the turn, stopping when I turned left onto Cherry. Worthington had those little reflector lights on the back of his bike and we could see him pretty well because the street was well-lit. Bobby got on the phone and called in another unit, asking for someone to go to the apartment building and let us know if he went back there in case we lost him.

"Now what?" he said.

"I can't just *follow* him, Spinner. We'll blow our cover."

"Even with the headlights off?"

"Bobby, the fucking street's lit up like a damn Christmas Tree!"

"I've got an idea."

Worthington was still visible on Cherry, heading down to the Parkway. "Let's hear it."

"Back out, and take Myrtle; it runs parallel to Cherry, and we can keep an eye on him through the yards."

I did as he suggested, and we saw him after a hundred yards or so, still on Cherry but pedaling slower now, like he was looking for something. Worthington got to the intersection at the Parkway, turned right, and started riding along the river. I pulled onto the Parkway myself, and pulled over. He was now a good quarter of a mile ahead of us, so I pulled out and followed. He took another right onto Dogwood Lane, and stopped in that little park near the playground. He got off the bike, and just sat there on one of the benches.

"Now what?" Bobby asked.

"Let's wait and see."

After fifteen minutes Worthington got back on his bike and started up the next street on the left.

"What's up there?" I asked Bobby.

"That's Elm Street. It's a cul-de-sac."

"Ok, let me get down there."

"Careful, Vale—I don't want to spook him."

I nodded and let the car roll down the incline. Bobby was looking up Elm Street, and touched my shoulder without looking at me. "Hang here for a minute, Lynn. He's turning around."

Worthington came flying down the hill, and turned back onto the Parkway without even looking at us. We watched for a minute or two, and saw him turn left back onto Cherry Street.

"I know—Myrtle again," I told Spinelli, and turned around. We followed him the same way we had on the way down, and watched as he went back to his building.

Bobby got on the phone again as I pulled over.

"Don't approach him," he told the other unit.

We saw Worthington go back in his building, and we both let out a breath.

"You thinking what I'm thinking?" I asked.

"Yeah—we need to find out how many judges live in the area."

"Know what, Bobby? We should have already *done* that."

• • •

We used a rental car the next night, September Fourth, a nondescript dark blue Honda with Massachusetts plates. Turns out there were *three* judges living in the area—a woman on the probate-and-family bench, a retired Federal Circuit Court judge, and a Superior Court judge by the name of Robert Donato, who lived—you guessed it, on Elm Street.

We put a unit on Donato, and sat once more by Worthington's apartment, and again, Worthington left his building, this time at eleven-o-five. He was wearing a running suit this time, and carrying a backpack, which he pulled on as he began to jog.

"Right," I said, "that's not *too* suspicious, is it?"

"Maybe he's going camping," Spinelli suggested.

"Funny," I said, and gave him a look. "We'll, Bobby, this is your game—how do you want to play it?"

"Can you run, Vale?"

"Well, I haven't run all the fat off of me like you have," I answered, lifting up both boobs with the palms of my hands, "but I can keep up with you if I have to."

Bobby laughed. "I wish my wife had *fat* like yours, Kaylyn. Come on, let's do this."

We got out, and without talking, started off. I took the right and Bobby took the left, and I was glad I'd had the foresight to wear my *Nike's*. Bobby sprinted ahead—he was clearly the better runner—and went on ahead to the road I had taken last night. I turned onto Cherry, and after a few minutes, got into a good rhythm. I like to run, but I prefer hiking or working out in the gym. Running gives you too much time to think, and I'm the kind of person who's better off not dwelling on certain things. I'd been rescued, I suppose, by "The Company", but they *use* girls like me as *assets*, people no one will miss. They teach you to kill and tell you you're a Patriot, but I was never comfortable doing it and I see the faces of the people I've killed when I have too much down-time. It didn't seem to bother me as much when we were on a ground mission, like we had been in Afghanistan, or even the time I spent as a mercenary. Rescuing prisoners-of-war or kidnapped children somehow makes taking a human life more palatable, at least it does to me, but even though I've killed people, it isn't really me, and if I had my life to live over again I suppose I'd do it differently. I'm well aware that I come off like a cold-hearted bitch, and a loose woman, too, I guess, but most of that is just posturing and hides a wounded spirit; it also brings high-priced jobs and makes it easier to deal with the enemy. Trust me, if I acted like *Pollyanna*, no one would ever hire me, and I'm doing a lot of good doing what I'm doing now, trying to make up for my sins, as it were. We all lose our way in life, sooner or later, but I was on the right track now, or so I thought, and to tell you the truth, if I met the right person I'd be more than happy to settle down and live a normal life—if there is such a thing.

At any rate, I was able to clear my mind by the time I got to the Parkway, and settled down into the run, legs churning, arms pumping, controlling my breathing to conserve energy. I could just make Worthington out ahead, but instead of going up the hill to Elm Street, he veered off and started running up the hill over-looking the river—a hill that looked down on Elm Street.

Bobby was just behind me, on the other side of the Parkway, and I knew he was thinking the same thing I was—that the hill would make an excellent vantage point for a sniper. I increased my pace enough to keep the target in sight, but not enough to get too close…or so I thought.

Bobby had given me one of those portable two-ways that double as a phone, too. He chirped me, and I looked at the screen. There was a short text: KEEP HIM IN SIGHT. When I looked up again, Worthington was standing right in front of me and knocked me out cold with one punch.

• • •

When I came to, the world was as bright as daylight, and for a second I figured I'd been out all night. But as I sat up, feeling like I'd kissed a truck, Bobby put a hand on me and kept me down.

"Did we get him?" I asked, realizing now that the brightness came from Klieg-lights.

"Yeah—we got him," Bobby said with a snarl, "but not before he took Donato out."

I swore, and felt the tears burning on my cheeks, but it was nothing new—just another failure in my miserable loser life.

• • •

Kaylyn Vale, was, of course, invited to the de-briefing, but I wasn't really paying too much attention to the details. The gist of it went like this: after cold-cocking me, Worthington had quickly assembled his rifle, a .30-.30 with a high-powered scope, and shot Donato in the back of his head as he sat in his hot tub on Elm Street. I felt like shit about it, but they had taken him alive, finding another quote from Scripture on his person, a quote he had never had a chance to enter into anyone's computer—this time, from James 2:13:

For judgment will be merciless to one who has shown no mercy.

The fact that Donato had been naked in the hot tub with his best friend's wife (his own wife was a sales-rep who was on a business trip at the time), didn't bother me as much as what Worthington had to say. According to *him*, and we checked it out, Donato had a reputation for going WELL over the sentencing guidelines, even where it wasn't warranted, and once, just last year, had actually overturned the Not Guilty verdict on the jury in a trial he had presided over.

A real compassionate guy, that Donato.

A week later, Worthington was found hanging by his bed sheets in a cell in the maximum security wing of the prison where he was being held. I had my own thoughts about *that*, but it didn't matter—the killer was dead, it was all over and we could all get on with our lives.

That's what I thought, anyway—but once again, I was wrong.

• • •

I got up on the morning of the Fourteenth and decided I'd go for a run. I was back on my own case, and had caught up on all the loose ends, and I simply wanted to relax before the work day.

We had gotten Worthington by pure, blind dumb luck, and wouldn't have had a *clue*, if it hadn't been for David Redman. And no, I wasn't insensitive enough to call and thank him.

Anyway, it was over, even though the papers made a big deal out of it—so big, in fact, that there was talk of Bob Spinelli being promoted. I had let him take all the credit for the information which had led us to the killer, mostly to protect David but also because such things don't mean *shit* to me, and he passed it off as coming from a "confidential paid informant"—something that pleased Dave to no end, I'm sure, since he only knew Spinelli by reputation and had no connection with him whatsoever.

Pure, blind dumb luck; still, it could have been a lot worse, or so I thought.

Do you remember what I said earlier about people who are *into* each other being on the same wavelength? Well, that on-the-same-page *mojo* was working again that morning when I left my apartment. I actually have a lovely place overlooking the river, and there are running trails leading up into the conservation land right behind where I live. Nice view, well kept, lots of shade, quiet. But what did I do *that* morning? I drove to my office already dressed in my black *Under Armour* shorts, gray *Champion* running bra and a black, French-cut *Elevate* workout tee. I also wanted to try out my new, brown, *Merrell* running shoes. Too many brand names for you? Sue me. Tough as I'm supposed to be, I am a *chick*, for God's sake, and shopping makes me feel better when I'm depressed. I should probably start wearing more feminine colors, but something always stops me from buying stuff like that, and I always end up with earth-tones. I suppose my therapist would have a field day with that, but it is what it is.

Anyway, just as I left the parking lot, guess who ran up right beside me, looking like a fucking *goddess* in cut-off jeans, sleeveless pink *City Sports* top and plain old *Reeboks?* You guessed it—Samantha Ashbery.

See what I mean about the same wave-length? Either that or she was stalking me, and I gave that serious thought later, as things turned out.

It was weird, but I guess she probably thought it was weird, too, or maybe not, because she slowed to a jog and turned her pretty face towards me with a smile. As attracted to that girl as I am, I *hate* her, too. She was maybe twenty-three at the time, and had already had two kids, and she *still* looked seventeen! I mean, the broad must *bleach* her frigging teeth, and her hair was—well, let's just say that if her writing career ever falters she can sell *Pantene*, no problem. I won't even *mention* her figure (ok, her breasts literally *defy* gravity), but her skin was positively radiant; yup, I hated her and wanted to *do* her, both at the same time.

"Want a partner?"

Again, being Kaylyn Vale caused a million snide remarks to pop up in my head. Instead, I nodded and said, "Sure."

We jogged down Old Town Road at an easy pace, and I could tell she had slowed down just to match me. An odd thought came to me as we ran—in all the time I've been running, since I was fifteen years old, I had never done so with a partner, a sad realization for a person as lonely as I am.

"You do this every day?" she asked.

"Most days," I admitted, "although I prefer to go to the gym."

"Really? Where do you go?"

"I study Krav Maga down at *Frederick's*," I told her, having heard that she was into martial arts as well. I didn't mention the Black Belt I hold in Tae Kwon Do.

"No way!" She smiled, and although I couldn't see her gorgeous green eyes behind the shades, I could tell that she was amused; not being able to see her eyes somehow made her even more alluring, and again, I reminded myself to be careful. "I studied that, too, when I was living in Boston. I'm into Aikido now." We ran for another minute in silence after that, and then she added: "Maybe we could spar some time?"

"Sure thing," I said. Sam was my size, maybe an inch or two shorter, and solidly built. Her shoulders and arms were toned and well-muscled, and I suddenly got as turned on by the idea of fighting with her as getting her into bed. I started to sweat, and it had nothing to do with the temperature.

"Hey, by the way—congratulations on that whole judge thing! That was awesome, Kaylyn!"

I turned my head again, unsure if she was *playing* with me, *interested* in me, looking for equal time because she knew I'd slept with Wade, or just being flirty.

"Yeah. Thanks. Truth is, we lucked out. That was a tough one."

"Really, why?"

I thought about it and then decided to lighten up. Maybe she was just as lonely as I was—and besides, it had already hit the papers.

"You may have read that the killer was leaving messages at the scenes," I admitted, "but we were also looking for a pattern based on the judge's last names, the days of the month, or in the quotes themselves."

"Is that what you were working on that day when I came in?"

"Yeah—why?"

"Not always good to just look at the first letters of the last names. Sometimes it's more complicated, or an acronym or maybe even a whole word."

"You seem to know a lot about it." Damn, I wish I could have seen her eyes!

"I told you—I'm good at that stuff. It's just the way my brain works, Lynn. I like puzzles and I've been reading mysteries since I was a kid."

"Ever try writing one?"

"I'm actually thinking about that right now, as a matter of fact. Just started an outline."

"Good for you," I said, and meant it.

"You ever get anything like that again, call me—I'd like to help."

Ok, she was definitely hitting on me now. As I said earlier, it isn't about what you say with another woman—it's about making a connection, about putting yourself in a favorable position with the girl you're interested in, and about the long looks and tender, hesitant touches. She laid a hand on my shoulder right then as we ran, almost as if she were reading my mind and her touch sent a shiver through me. "Seriously," she added.

"All right," I told her, not trusting my voice.

"Can you tell me about the pattern you were looking at?"

"I suppose so. I was thinking maybe the judges' names were going to spell something out."

"What were they?" Sam asked, as we turned onto Riverside Drive and headed down towards the ball field.

"Jordan, Unger and Donato," I said, after a second of hesitation.

Sam laughed. "That's easy!"

"I'm glad *you* think so!"

"You don't see it?" she asked, pulling off her sunglasses and staring at me. Sam tucked the shades into the little pouch that I suppose also carried her phone and waited for me to answer—but I was lost in those beautiful green eyes.

"No," I admitted.

"J-U-D, Kaylyn!"

"So what?" I was getting a little annoyed now at her enthusiasm, and I thought her interest was a little weird, too.

"Judges!" she exclaimed. "For my money he was spelling out the word 'judges'! You didn't *see* that?"

"Why would he tell us that if he was already *killing* judges, Sam? It doesn't make sense. What was he hoping to gain?"

"Maybe he was just an arrogant bastard," she said as we ran onto the ball field. "Or maybe he was spelling something else. I don't know." She paused. "Maybe he was just lonely—sometimes, being lonely can make a person do crazy things, you know."

We did a lap around the track without talking and then she asked me if I wanted some water. We ran over to the hotdog vender that's always there in the summer, and she bought two bottles of water while I collapsed on a bench.

"Here," she said, holding one out and looking at me oddly. It wouldn't dawn on me until much later how strange it was that she figured that out so quickly when Bobby and I hadn't even *seen* it.

"Thanks," I said, gasping for breath.

"You smoke, Kaylyn?" she asked, sitting beside me and taking the cap off her bottle. I was really getting pissed now at all the personal questions.

"Yeah, but not too much, why?"

"It's affecting your wind, that's why."

"I seem to remember seeing you with a smoke a time or two," I said defensively.

"Hey, relax!' she said with a totally winning smile. "I do—but only five a day. And never near the kids. One with coffee in the morning, one after lunch, one after my snack in the afternoon, again after supper, and right before I go to bed."

"Jesus—I wish *I* had that kind of control."

Sam studied me for so long that at first I wanted to smack her and then I wanted to grab her by the back of the neck and put my tongue in her mouth. "For real, Lynn, I'm thinking you could do anything you put your mind to." She reached out then and moved a lock of my hair away from my face, tucking it behind my ear, and if I wasn't sure about what she wanted from me *before*—I was now.

Still, something about all this was weird, so I decided to play it cool and maybe ask her a few questions to get her off balance. I cleared my throat after I took a sip of water.

"Hey, I'm just curious, you ever seen your girlfriend Jennifer anymore?"

Sam never took her eyes off of me the whole time she was tilting her head back to gulp her water. If she knew I was aware of the affair the two of them had had, she showed no sign of it. She shook her head, and the way the ponytail swished made my toes curl.

"Nope—she's an old married lady now. Put on some weight, too." She giggled and I decided that, if she gave me half a chance, I would definitely try to get her into bed.

"That's too bad—she had an awesome figure."

"I noticed that once or twice myself," Sam said quietly, letting me know with her eyes what we were both thinking. "Anyway, she's really into her husband."

"That's not necessarily a bad thing," I said, just to toy with her a little.

Samantha shrugged. "I suppose."

"You miss her?"

Again Sam studied me for longer than I was comfortable with. "Uh-huh—a lot."

And there it is, I thought.

"And what about you? *You're* an old married lady, now, too."

"I suppose I am," she said, and laughed lightly.

"You don't make it sound very exciting."

Samantha made a face. "I'm bored, I guess. I write; I take care of the kids. Wade's always working." She stopped suddenly and shrugged.

"No need to be bored *all* the time," I said very quietly, looking directly into her eyes. "Not if you're discrete about it." I was hoping to come off like an older woman giving a younger girl advice, but to my own ears it sounded creepy.

Just then a young woman ran by on the track, a transplanted, long-legged very pretty California blonde.

"Oh, I'd never cheat on my husband."

We were both looking at the blonde, who was really very sexy.

"But you miss Jenny," I said, taking a chance.

"I don't think it's the same with another woman, do you?" Sam said without a moment's hesitation, tearing her eyes away from the other girl, and admitting the affair to me, all in one breath and without actually putting it into words.

All I could think of was some comedian imitating Bill Clinton—*eating ain't cheating*, but what came out of my mouth was: "No, I *don't* think it's the same."

Sam looked down at her water bottle, with a look that suggested she wanted to share something.

"What is it?" I asked.

"Huh, nothing."

"I think we're kinda becoming friends here, Sam," I said. "You can tell me anything."

"You really didn't sleep with Wade?" she asked suddenly, dashing all my hopes about getting into her pants.

"No I didn't," I said in a harsher tone than I intended, "and please don't ask me that again." I finished my water with an annoying habit I have—namely, making the plastic bottle cave in from sucking the water down.

"Ouch!" Sam said, and squeezed her thighs together. "I hope you don't do that to the guys you date!"

I *wanted* to get mad at her, but it made me laugh, and I actually had to spit some of it out. "You should see what I do to the *girls!*"

Samantha started to say something, blushed and then closed her mouth. She got up, tossed her bottle into the trash can, and looked down at me. "Bet I can beat you back to the town line," she said.

"I bet you can't," I told her, wondering if this sort of thing qualified as Lesbian Foreplay.

CHAPTER THREE—October

Do any of you remember the Rwandan genocide of the early nineteen-nineties? An estimated one-million people were killed, mostly by machete and in other, equally gruesome ways, when the Hutu's decided to cleanse themselves of the Tutsi Tribe. It started in 1994 when an airplane full of diplomas was shot down while trying to land in Kigali, killing everyone on board. The genocidal killings began the next day, including what the World Court would eventually come to call, the use of War Rape. It was horrible, perverse, and absolutely insane, and I was actually there a year or so later, on my first ground mission. I was just a kid myself, and still reeling from being raped by my stepbrother, seeing my father killed and being passed from foster home to foster home. I won't even get into what being abandoned by my mother had done to me; it's enough for you to know that I was, and I suppose I still am, a very angry person.

    The mission I was part of called for us to extract a dozen young girls who had been abducted from a Missionary School by a guerilla group. All of them had been beaten and repeatedly raped, including an ambassador's daughter, who had been attending the school as part of an exchange program. By the time we got there, at least six of those poor kids had actually been sold into slavery, and we were supposed to get them back—at least that was the *cover* for the mission, at any rate. I learned much later that the *real* reason we were there was to assassinate the leader of the guerillas—which was my very first lesson in international policy, at least as far as "The Company" was concerned.

All Kaylyn Vale knew was that the oldest of these girls was twelve—the *oldest*, and at the time all I cared about was getting them out of there. I had killed a man a year before as part of my training, a guy who, I was told, was guilty of treason, so I at least knew that I was capable of pulling the trigger. In Rwanda, however, I learned that I could actually *enjoy* taking a human life.

The team I was with entered the village at midnight, and took out almost all of the guerillas. Then we fanned out to look for the kids. I found a young girl tied to a cot in one of the tents, and as I was cutting her loose, one of the rebels came in and tackled me. He outweighed me by at least a hundred and fifty pounds, and I had my hands full fighting with him, so I took out the .45 I was carrying and shot him in the face. You've probably seen stuff like that in the movies, but real life isn't a movie. The guy's head literally *exploded*, and then, in a rage, I emptied the rest of the clip into him. I picked the girl up and ran, and that night I cried myself to sleep, not because I had killed someone, but because I hadn't gotten there in time to save the kid from contracting HIV. *Other* things happened over there, but I'll get to that later.

You needed to hear all that to understand something about me, because I'm not sure I've done a very good job up to this point explaining exactly just why I am what I am. Deep down, I'm really not a very violent person. I've hardened myself because if I ever allowed myself to feel what I'm really feeling, I wouldn't even be able to function. Dave Redman had once explained it to me like this: "People hear the term 'hardened con', and think that means the guy is nuts," he had told me one night over a few beers. "But what it really means is that you shut off your feelings to keep from *going* nuts." I am proud, too, of the fact that David likes to introduce me as, "My friend, Kaylyn, who can drink one more beer than I can," but even Dave doesn't really know me. All I can tell you is that, if you've ever seen a group of cruel school children steal a weaker kid's hat and toss it around in a circle while he runs around trying to get it, I'm the one who walks up to the biggest kid and, after punching him in the face, tells him to give the hat back. So I'm not really any kind of a superhero or anything, I'm just the girl who learned that it's easier to punch the big guy in the face than run around the circle trying to get my hat back.

It was October First and the weather was *awesome*: cool, crisp, dry and somehow *clean*. I had finished the case I was working on and was in the process of cleaning up my files, when I came across my notes for the Worthington case. Almost a month had passed since I'd last spoke to David, and despite the voice mail he had left, I was worried that our friendship had been strained. I also hadn't seen or even *heard* from Sam, and I have to admit I was feeling a bit lonely and more than a little bit bored. If you've ever been betrayed or abandoned, there's always a nagging ache in the pit of your stomach and in your heart, and a little voice in your head that constantly reminds you how very alone you really are. I *do* have friends, but they expect me to be the Kaylyn Vale I show to the world at large—confident, full of energy, happy with myself...and absolutely full of shit. It's exhausting to have to pretend to be something that you're not, and even though I would have loved for someone to call and ask me to go get a pizza, I was somehow more comfortable sitting here attending my own little 'pity-party'. Being lonely is a horrible thing, and I've learned to deal with it by staying busy. I didn't feel like going out and I didn't have a case at the moment except for a guy who had hired me to do a little digging into the activities of a woman who worked in his Accounts Payable Department, so I was intrigued by my notes.

That sort of attention to detail, that work ethic, and strict adherence to discipline keeps me in great shape, makes me good at what I do...and more often than not, gets me into trouble. Maybe it's because I've never gotten to ask my mother why she left us, or have never really dealt with why my step-brother just had to go and abuse me, but I sometimes obsess about things. It's like what the kids today call an *ear-wig* when referring to a song that you just can't get out of your head, but I just can't seem to let certain things go, and even though it makes me a good detective it also makes me very hard to live with. Sherlock Holmes used a seven-percent solution of cocaine when he was bored...Kaylyn Vale ruminates. I seriously think I'd be better off with a drug habit.

Still, this thing about Worthington *bothered* me, and even though it was over, I still had that nagging little itch. The first two murders had been committed with a .32 caliber revolver, at close range, just before the quotes were left on both computers. The third one was done with a high-powered rifle and a scope—why? You're probably wondering why I gave a shit, but like I said, I was bored, and as I sat there lonely and miserable, I looked around my office. It's actually kind of nice. The furniture is very expensive, including the couch I'm so fond of, and I have five movie posters on my walls, nicely framed: *The Maltese Falcon*, *The Big Sleep*, *Dark Passage*, *To Have and Have Not*, and *Key Largo*. All perfectly fine posters to hang in the office of a private investigator, I suppose. At home I have three in my living room—*From Here To Eternity*, *The Bodyguard*, and *Nights in Rodanthe*...and as I sat there, trying to let go of the notes from the Worthington case, wanting to *delete* them, in fact, I realized that all of those films have one thing in common: all of them are about lonely and broken people, desperate to make a connection with someone, people who would give anything to have someone to hold...someone to hold *them*, perhaps.

"Let it go, Kaylyn," I actually said out loud, wondering what my therapist, Dr. Erica Brown, would have to say about what was running through my head.

The first two murders had been meticulously planned and executed, if you'll pardon the expression...the third was sloppy, rushed and unprofessional—almost as if it had been committed by an entirely different person. Had Worthington been a copycat? Was the third murder even *connected* to the other two? Were the letters J-U and D, as Sam had pointed out, perhaps spelling something? And if so—what? Did Worthington have any family? What did we really know about him after all? Was this really over, and why did I care so much?

I bit my lower lip, suddenly feeling like I wanted to cry. How pitiful was I to be sitting here worrying about this when the killer was dead? And he had, by-the-way, I reminded myself, that quote from Scripture in his pocket.

"That's enough," I mumbled, and picked up the phone. I dialed Erica's cell, and she picked up on the third ring.

"Dr. Brown."

"Hi, Erica, Kaylyn Vale."

"How are you, Kaylyn? Did I miss an appointment? My secretary's on vacation and I'm a little out of sorts without her."

"I'm fine, and no, you didn't, but I was wondering if perhaps you'd had a cancellation this week?"

"Is everything all right, Kaylyn?"

"Well, there *is* something I'd like to talk about."

"As it happens, I actually have a cancelation at two o'clock today. Does that work for you?"

"Yes it does, thank you." I glanced at my watch, which I wear with the face on the inside of my wrist. "I'll see you in a couple of hours, then."

"Kaylyn—*is* everything all right? You sound a little…strained."

"Work is a bit overwhelming just now," I lied. "That's all."

"Ok, then—see you at two."

I hung up and just sat there; I needed help—I figured that part out for myself, but how could I get proper treatment when half the things that were bothering me were classified?

• • •

The parking lot of the medical building where Dr. Brown had her office was jammed packed when I pulled in at a quarter to two, so I ended up with a bit of a walk. I didn't mind, though, because the exercise took the edge off a bit. I took the stairs two at a time all the way to the sixth floor, and when I got to her office it was empty. Her inner door was closed and I could hear muffled voices, so I knew she was still in session. There were magazines, but I didn't feel like reading, so I just sat there trying to relax with a *National Geographic* open and unread in my lap. When she opened the door at five-past-two and ushered out an overweight, fortyish woman with an awful perm who looked like she'd been crying, I did my best to at least *pretend* that I was interested in an article about mountain climbing.

"Come right in, Kaylyn. Sorry I'm running a little late."

"If five minutes is your idea of 'late', Doc—you're my kind of girl."

She smiled, closed the door behind us, and sat down on one of the two little sofas she has, one facing the other with a tiny coffee table between them. I'd been coming here for over a year, and I had never seen her sit behind her desk. I liked that about her.

Erica Brown was in her mid-fifties, but could have easily passed for forty. She was thin—a jogger herself—with short dark hair and a soft voice.

"So, what brings you here between sessions, Lynn?"

"I'm not sure," I said, which caused her to raise an eyebrow. "At first I thought it was the last case I was working on; now I'm not so sure."

"I read about that in the papers. The police were very positive in their remarks concerning you, saying that your advice and assistance was invaluable—is there more to the story?"

"No, it's a closed case, Erica, but now that it's over I can't help but feel like I'm waiting for the other shoe to drop." She remained silent, which was how she worked, knowing that if she remained quiet long enough I'd find a way to spill what was bothering me. I shrugged. "I'm always at my best while I'm in the game," I heard myself saying, "but when it's over, that's when I start feeling anxious." Before I knew it I was spilling my guts, telling her all about my feelings for Sam, my loneliness and my grief over losing my father and what had been done to me as a child. It was nothing new—she'd heard it all before (except for that part about Samantha), and when I was done talking I sat back, feeling better but like I hadn't actually accomplished anything.

Erica waited a minute more, and then sighed. "We've been through this all before, Lynn, and I *still* think you should be on some kind of medication." She held up a hand to ward off an argument because that was a bone of contention between us. "But putting that aside, all I can do here is employ a very non-medical term and tell you that you're a 'control-freak', and that you're too hard on yourself. You're suffering from a severe form of post-traumatic stress disorder, which, as you know, is a condition in which one's life has been disrupted by a severe traumatic experience of the past. In your case—several of them.

"A person who has experienced severe trauma: war, combat, natural disaster, physical or sexual abuse, or witnessed violence, such as murder or physical abuse, may display one or more of the following symptoms: Reliving the event with repeated flashbacks or recurring dreams of the event, or perhaps being haunted by a single image. Impatience. Outbursts of anger. Intense distress if exposed to anything even *resembling* the event…look, I know you can't tell me about your work with the government, but I also suppose it doesn't matter where this came from. You've never dealt with your mother leaving you, and whether you see it this way or not, your father leaving you as well. You have been in combat, been sexually abused and live in a world with constant danger which is triggering the past events, or at least the feelings they represent, over and over again. If you want my advice and I'm talking to you now as a friend and not as a therapist, get out of it and try to do something else—you've served your country and very well, based on what I know of you. What you need, Lynn, is what all of us need; to love, and to be loved, to be in a stable, nurturing relationship, because, quite frankly, I can't help you if you keep doing the very thing which is causing the problems in the first place."

We talked for the rest of the hour, but in the end I knew she was right—and I wasn't willing to do what I needed to do—namely, give up my work. In the final analysis, the only one who could help me was…*me*, but I couldn't give up what I do without giving up who I am.

I also knew that I wouldn't be coming back here again.

"And here's something for you to think about," Erica added as we were wrapping things up. "And I hesitate to mention this because I am *not* an advocate of extra-marital affairs…but if you really think this other woman is pursuing you, pursuing a relationship beyond the physical, I mean, then certainly explore the possibilities. You're an intelligent, caring and very beautiful woman, Lynn, but you need to give yourself permission to love again—I can't do it for you."

I thanked her and stood up.

"And one last thing," Dr. Brown told me as I took out my car keys. "Just because you feel paranoid, just because you feel like something bad is going to happen, doesn't necessarily mean that it *won't*."

• • •

The rest of the week was actually pretty boring, but I did the best with what I had, working on the embezzlement case, going to the gym, and even reconnecting with an old friend from High School, who I happened to bump into at *Shopper's World*. I hadn't seen Cheryl Raleigh since my senior prom, and although we exchanged numbers and made tentative plans to have lunch sometime soon, I knew I'd never call her. Too much water over the damn and no way to talk about even half of it. I debated calling Sam and asking her to have dinner with me, but as Erica had said, and despite the mistakes I'd made in my life, I wasn't really fond of cheaters, either, and didn't want to be one again.

On the evening of the Sixth, I found myself alone in my apartment with a take-out pizza and a glass of white wine, watching *Casablanca* on some retro channel. It got over at eleven, and I went to bed, tired, but unable to get comfortable. I was still tossing and turning when my phone rang at one o'clock in the morning.

"Kaylyn Vale," I said, picking up on the first ring.

"Kaylyn, Bobby. It happened again."

"What happened again, Spinner?" I asked, even as that cold tendril of fear slithered through my intestines like a snake.

"Someone killed another judge."

• • •

"*There is only one lawgiver*," I read on the screen of Rebecca Gregory's open laptop, "*and one Judge, the one who is able to save and destroy. But you—who are YOU to judge your neighbor?*"

"The Book of James," I said, standing up straight and taking off the latex gloves. "Chapter Four, I'd guess—don't know the verse."

"Verse 12," Bobby said, glancing at his notebook.

I closed my eyes and nodded, able to think only of Samantha, and not for the reasons you might think. Sam had told me that the killer was spelling out the word, J-U-D-G-E-S...and it now certainly seemed that way. Jordan, Unger, Donato and now Gregory. It was too big to ignore, and I shared it with Spinelli.

"Jesus, Lynn! Are you seriously telling me we're going to have to guard every judge whose last name begins with the letter 'E'? There must be *dozens* of them, and *when*, exactly are we supposed to start guarding them and for how long? Where are we even going to *get* that kind of manpower?"

"I honestly don't know, Bobby, but we can't ignore this." I looked at the dead body of Judge Gregory, shot point blank in the face with what looked like a .32 caliber bullet. We were back to the pattern of the first two murders, and again I knew we had missed something with Worthington. "I only know I'm right, and that there must be another clue as to *when*—something in the quotes, perhaps, I don't know."

Spinelli swore, and shook his head.

"Do you still have the file on Worthington, Bobby?"

"Yeah, it's in my car—why?"

"Let me look at it first and then I'll tell you what I'm thinking."

We were standing outside as the coroner's unit took out the body. I had the file open on the hood, but couldn't find what I was hoping to find.

"What, exactly, are you looking for?" he asked me.

"I was hoping that Worthington would have relatives. But he's an orphan. Parents died in a car crash when he was eleven. He had a sister, too, but it says here that she was an embassy employee, killed in a bombing in Beirut five years ago." I shook my head. "Nothing."

"Christ, Lynn—this will be national news in an hour! What are we going to do?"

"You guys got any cadets handy? Or even in the local forces? If you do, have them pull the cases of each judge that's been murdered, and start looking for correlations—I'm telling you, there's a connection…even if you have to go back five years." Something else was bothering me, too, and I just couldn't put my finger on it.

"Ok, I'll get on that right away. What are you going to do?"

"The killer is telling us ahead of time, Bobby, telling us *when* if nothing else—I'm sure of it, and I'm going to put everything else aside until I find out what it is!"

• • •

This time, my apartment was closer, so I went home, downed a glass of wine and got back into bed, knowing that the answer was staring me in the face and that only a good night's sleep would help me to find it. I woke up at nine-thirty and drove to the office, opening up the big folding table I have and putting all my notebooks on it, along with some pens and a pad of paper. Then I got a power-strip out of the supply closet and moved my laptop over. I sat down with my cell phone and an ash tray at my right hand, and began making notes on the legal pad.

> *Jordan, Paul—July 10th, Genesis 1:5—.32 caliber pistol*
> *Unger, Frederick—August 21st (I'm brought in on the case), Matthew 7:2—.32 caliber pistol*
> *Donato, Robert—September 4th, James 2:13—.30-30 rifle w/ scope**
> *Gregory, Rebecca—October 7th, James 4:12—.32 caliber pistol*

"He used *James*, twice," I mused. And then I decided to write down the judge's ages:

Jordan—59
Unger—62
Donato—49
Gregory—55

"What else?" I said out loud as I got up and made a cup of coffee.

I sat back down and made a note to get a good bible with a study guide and a concordance. I could have looked on line for that stuff, but I've never been a fan of toggling back and forth.

Then I looked at the dates again, wondering if there was a clue there. Again nothing came to me.

I picked up my phone and dialed Bobby's number, lighting a cigarette while I waited for him to pick up. He didn't, so I left a message.

"It's me, Spinner—any chance you can get me those files on the four judges? I'll come and get them or you can send them over by courier. I'm at the office. Thanks."

Three men and one woman, I wrote.

Then I wrote down the four passages from scripture, one from the Old Testament, one from The Gospel and two from the Book of James... all of them about judgment except for the first, which seemed self-explanatory. I looked up at the little asterisk I'd made beside Donato, because I still had odd thoughts about that one. And then, in a brain-storm, I called Ross.

He didn't pick up either, so I left him a message too, asking him to call me back. As I told you earlier, 'Ross' is a codename of a government contractor who works for the State Department. He's also tied in with the Diplomatic Security Services, and has enough money to hire his own armies—hence the codename, after the billionaire, Ross Perot.

I wanted more information on this Worthington guy, and more specifically, on his dead sister who had supposedly worked as an embassy envoy. Embassy employees are almost always tied in with one agency or other, and are often working undercover. I didn't know what I was digging for, but I still had that damn itch.

By noontime I was pissed off, had a stiff back and wanted some lunch. I closed up shop and went to the mall, where I picked up a copy of *Strong's Concordance*—"Strong's Exhaustive Concordance of the Bible", generally known as *Strong's Concordance*, is a concordance of the *King James Bible* that was constructed under the direction of Dr. James Strong and first published in 1890. It was and is THE definitive work on the Bible...and then it hit me: what if the version of the Bible we were using made a difference?

"No, dummy—he's writing the quotes out for us."

"Excuse me?" the woman in the isle at the religious store said to me.

"Huh? Oh, just thinking out loud." I smiled, hoping I didn't look like a ghoul. "Sorry."

The woman moved away, and I didn't blame her. I opened the concordance and checked that it had, in this edition, cross-references to the other versions. I closed it, brought it to the check-out counter and then went to have lunch. I was sitting in the Food Court eating a small order of Bourbon Chicken when my phone rang. Naturally, I assumed it was Bobby and I answered without looking at the screen.

"Thanks for getting back to me so quickly, shit-for-brains," I said.

"Nice to talk to you, too, Kaylyn Vale," a cultured male voice said—Ross. I cringed, but Wade Ashbery and I had actually rescued his kidnapped daughter a year ago in Afghanistan, even though it's *still* not a good idea to swear at billionaires.

"Oh, sorry, Ross—I thought you were someone else."

Ross chuckled. "Apparently. What can I do for you, Ms. Vale?"

I told him and he said he'd get right on it.

"That guy, "he said, "the one killing those judges?"

"What about him?"

"Have you considered giving him a medal instead?"

He hung up before I could tell him that I had said the very same thing, and my phone rang in my hand before I could put it down. This time I looked at the name.

"Hey, Bobby."

"I got your message and we're working on it, but here's a little something for you to play with in the meantime: all of our dead judges *do* have something in common, Nancy." That was his nickname for me: *Nancy Drew*.

"Gonna tell me or let me guess?"

"All of them have a least one case where it was obvious that the defendant was innocent, and in Evidentiary Hearings, *still* refused to overturn their own verdicts, *despite* evidence of actual evidence or even where the law was violated."

It wasn't much, but at least now I had a motive to work with. Maybe Ross was right—maybe we *should* have been handing out medals.

• • •

The rest of the month went by quickly, and even though Bobby had listened to me and put guards on all the judges with a last name beginning with the letter 'E'—turns out there were six of them—I still couldn't rid myself of that awful feeling that I was missing something that was right under my nose, and when the killer struck again, this time on November the Fifth, I knew I needed help and knew exactly where to get it.

CHAPTER FOUR—November

"You are therefore without excuse, O man, whoever you are who sit in judgment..."

Edwards, John—November 5th, Romans 2:1—.32 caliber pistol

It was ten o'clock in the morning on a gray November 6th, and I was in my office again, sitting at the folding table and feeling like shit. I threw my pen down after making the above notations, and added his age: 57. I'd been here since nine, and hadn't slept well, and decided to make good on the promise I'd made to myself earlier.

Samantha Ashbery answered on the third ring.

"Hey, Kaylyn—what's up?"

Again I smiled, as I had with David—I'd given Sam my card well over a year ago, and it felt good to know that she had entered it into her phone. I've found that arrogant people, and I have to admit that I am among their number, are often hiding a wide streak of insecurity.

"I need help, Sam. Is your offer still good?"

"Sure is, and I should really apologize, too."

"What for?" I asked, confused.

"For not calling you after that last one, *Gregory* I think it was. I *wanted* to call, but I figured you'd call *me* if you really wanted help. What can I do?"

"For starters—can you put a day aside this week and come down to my office?"

"I'm actually free right now, Lynn. My Mother-in-Law took the kids to The Roger William's Zoo, and Wade has football practice tonight—again." I'd forgotten that he was coaching down at the High School. "Trust me; no one will miss me until at *least* six o'clock."

"Uh, great then—and Sam?'

"Yeah?"

"Not a word to anyone."

"You *got* that," she said, and once more I smiled. Girl had spent *way* too much time with David Redman over the years and occasionally sounded like an ex-con. "Need anything?"

"Pound of twenties would be nice."

"Huh?"

"Just kidding—no, I'm good." I hesitated. "No, scratch that. You got a laptop?"

"Sure do."

"Bring it—I only have the one here in the office."

"Not a problem. I'll be there in twenty minutes."

Sam hung up and I went into the bathroom to brush my teeth, knowing that I really *did* need her help, but probably had ulterior motives floating just below the surface. I could have hired an assistant, the University of Rhode Island was *full* of criminal justice undergrads for example, but I had called Sam, not just because of her research abilities and knowledge of the Law, but because I had a thing for her.

"Who *are* you?' I asked the girl in the mirror as I rinsed out my toothbrush. The answer was a solitary, scared woman, heading alone with "forty" breathing right down her neck, and I was petrified of ending up dying without a real friend, someone I could share things with. Picking a married woman probably wasn't the brightest idea I had ever had, but, then again, I've spent my whole life letting my emotions rule me and couldn't seem to find a way to stop doing it.

"Focus on the case, *Nancy*," I growled, and spit out the last of the *Scope* I'd used to rinse my mouth. As an after-thought, I hit myself with a little bit of Warm-Vanilla-Sugar body spray, because, whatever perfume Sam used, always smelled like vanilla to me.

I told you, didn't I, that, at heart, I'm a real girly-girl?

Samantha arrived thirty-five minutes after we had talked, carrying a tray from *Dunkie's*, with two large coffees and two blueberry muffins; her laptop was in a bag and slung over one shoulder. She was wearing jeans and a nice top, and her hair was in a ponytail. With her round, John Lennon-style glasses, she looked like a college kid. As usual, she smelled like vanilla.

"Sorry I'm late—drive-through was *mobbed!*"

"Beautiful research assistants bearing muffins need never apologize to an old lady like me, Sam."

"*Old*," she scoffed. "You're so pretty it hurts." She wasn't looking at me when she said it, so I assumed she hadn't seen me blush. "Where can I plug this in?" she asked, and then, seeing the power-strip, said, "Never mind."

We both sat down and cracked open the coffee. "Thanks for coming, Sam, but first things first—I'll need to put you on the payroll for this."

"I don't need any money," she said, sounding a little put off.

"I know you don't, but the only legal way I can tell you about all of this is if you're an operative in my employee—in fact, if we stay on this thing long enough, we'll see about getting you licensed. In the meantime, my own ticket will cover you, and everything we discuss… everything…is protected by the same sort of privileged communication as lawyers and their clients—got it?"

"Got it," she said, and nodded.

"I'm serious—you can't tell *anyone*, or we'll both wind up in the shit, ok?"

"Not a problem." She looked me right in the eyes and added: "I know how to keep a secret, Lynn."

"Ok," I said, and had to clear my throat. "Here it is then."

I told her the whole story, starting with Jordan back in July, before the State Police brought me in, and ended with Edwards. Sam nodded, looking at the charts I'd made the whole time I'd been talking. She had her face in both hands with her elbows on the table, looking down at the data, when I got up and went over and pulled down the shades and locked the door.

"Not hitting on you or anything," I said, trying to sound funny, "but I don't want anyone else to see this."

"Too bad," she mumbled, joking back, I supposed, but really concentrating on what was in front of her.

Then I broke out all of the files Bobby had sent over, including the cases where all five of the judges to this point, had refused to overturn convictions where they blatantly knew they had been wrong... or the law had been violated.

"I've written a ton of articles on this kind of thing, Lynn."

Sam had published literally *dozens* of articles on the unfairness of the system, calling it an 'Illegitimate child of The Prison Industrial Complex'.

"And I've read all of them. Why do you think you're here?"

Sam started to say something, and her lips curled like she had something clever to say, and then she just nodded.

"I was right, you know."

"About what?"

We'd been playing innuendo and *double-entendre* since we first met, and it sometimes got a little tricky talking with her.

"Whoever this is—he's spelling out the word, JUDGES."

"I think so, too, but there are nine judges with their last names ending in 'S', and the State Police are going to have their hands full watching all of them, especially with what the newspapers are doing to them—which isn't helping. Also, there's the question of when—which is really why you're here, because I can't rid myself of the feeling that he's leaving us clues, but I keep drawing a blank."

"Have you studied the Scripture quotes?"

"And the dates and the names and the *cases*—until I'm blue in the face...and there's something else, something I haven't even told the police yet."

Sam raised an eyebrow. "Well, clue me in."

"Never mind the letters of the last name of each judge—look at the *months*."

Sam did so, and a moment later looked up, startled. "July, August, September, October and November," she said. "Jason!"

I nodded. "And I don't believe in coincidences."

"Neither do I."

We worked until five-fifteen, and then I decided to wrap it up. My head was spinning and I was dead tired. It was already starting to get dark, especially since it was so cloudy, and neither one of us, I suppose, had noticed how subtly romantic the single lamp seemed to be. I stood up, and looked down at her. She had a pencil in her mouth, and I had to clear my throat again.

"Why don't we call it a day, and start fresh again tomorrow?"

"All right," she agreed, stretching her back, which accentuated the fullness of her breasts. Again, I had to turn away. "I should probably get home anyway."

She bumped right into me when she got up, and we laughed, and then, with our faces only a few inches apart, I put my hands on her shoulders, and just looked at her.

"What?" she asked in a very soft voice.

"I was wondering what you'd do if I tried to kiss you," I whispered.

"I'd probably let you."

"*Probably?*"

"I might *slap* you, too," she said with a smirk.

"Either works for me, actually," I mumbled, and touched my lips to hers. We kissed for a moment, and then she slipped the tip of her tongue into my mouth, making my knees wobble. We'd been looking at each other all day long, and it was intense after waiting and looking and wondering.

And of course, just then her phone rang.

We kept kissing and then she broke off. "I have to get this, Lynn—the kids, you know?"

I nodded. I wouldn't have respected her if she hadn't.

"Hi, Marie," she said, and listened. "Ok, I'll be right there."

"My daughter threw up. Probably full of ice-cream and God knows what else." She grabbed her cigarettes and her keys and then just stood there looking at me. "I'll be back tomorrow," she said.

"I'll be here, Sam," I answered softly.

"How much is it, by the way?"

"How much is what?"

"A pound of twenties—how much money is it?"

"I could tell you," I said, "but then I'd have to kill you."

She smiled as she left, and then I started crying, realizing just how pathetic I was.

By the way—a pound of twenties? It's about six grand.

• • •

Out in the car, I popped in my Art Pepper CD and selected *Winter Moon*. I drove slowly because my head was spinning with all the thoughts in my head. I could still feel Samantha's sweet, soft lips on mine, but I was also still being nagged by that awful feeling that I was missing something. I was tired but keyed up, too—ever feel like that? I firmly believe that people who have been abused are always trying to prove, at least to themselves, that they're not broken. It doesn't matter what kind of abuse it was; being dehumanized makes you angry, and I suddenly felt an odd sort of kinship with the killer. Oh, I didn't approve of what he was doing, but can you imagine being sent to prison for something you didn't even do?

When I got to my apartment I was literally beside myself—filled with my desire for Samantha and driven by an unsettling nervous energy that made me want to keep working on the case. I've never been the sort of girl who can—hell, there's no delicate way to say this—*pleasure* herself, but I needed release, so I ended up doing pushups, four sets of 25 with my feet on the coffee table and my hands on the floor. I took four *Advil* and two decongestants when I was through, and went to bed, hoping the pills would help me to sleep but not leave me groggy in the morning.

It was nine-thirty A. M. when I got to the office, and there was an email from Ross on my computer:

KV—RW was a spook.

Ross was too careful to be more specific, but I understood him perfectly. Remember that I wanted information about Kyle Worthington's sister, Rebekka? That I was suspicious of her status as a mere embassy worker? Well, *spook* is a term we use in "The Company"—it means she was a spy, and most likely, an assassin.

Not knowing what to do with that, especially since she was dead, I added the information to my data base and then went to check my voice mail. There were three calls on my machine—two dealing with cases I had on hold, and one from David Redman, who sounded a little drunk, telling me how sorry he was to have acted so *pissy* about getting me the information I had asked him for, especially in light of all that had happened since, and assuring me that he was available if I needed him for anything else.

Listening to the message brought tears to my eyes, and I didn't want to be crying when Sam got here so I made some coffee and took it to the folding table. I took a fresh legal pad and made three separate columns—one with the dates of each murder; the months; and the quotes. On another sheet of paper I made two more columns—one with all the names, and the other with their ages, hoping that I would see something if I looked at the information differently. Comparing it to the spreadsheet Sam had printed out I saw that I had made a mistake. In my head I had thought that Judge Gregory was murdered on the Sixth of October. I don't know why I had written it that way, but she had been killed after midnight, making the correct date the *Seventh*. And in that fraction of a second, I made the connection that had been staring me in the face all this time.

'Gregory' had seven letters in it, and she had been murdered on the 7th. All of a sudden my heart was pounding and I felt like I was on speed. I went back to the beginning and checked them all. 'Jordan' had six letters in it and had been killed on the…10th. Damn! I was so sure that I had been right, but it didn't match up! I stared at it, angry and with my hands shaking; willing myself to see what I *knew* was there. So I started over. 'Jordan'. I sat there staring at that word and then, in a fit of anger-driven inspiration, I wrote out the entire alphabet from A to Z. 'Jordan'. I looked at it some more. J. Judge Jordan had been killed on the tenth of July. July was the seventh month. Did that have anything to do with it? I looked at the rest of the names. No. Ok, J was the tenth letter of the alphabet…and he had been killed on…the 10th! My heart was beating out of my chest now and I started sweating. Unger. U was the twenty-first letter of the alphabet and he had been killed on the…21st! I had it now, and I couldn't have stopped if the room was on fire. Donato. D was the fourth letter of the alphabet and he had been killed on the 4h! Gregory—G was the seventh letter! It had nothing to do with the months! It had to do with the days! Edwards—E is the fifth letter, and he'd been murdered on the 5th!

It still didn't tell us *who*, because we still didn't understand the pattern of the word the killer was spelling out, but if Sam was right, and the killer was spelling the word JUDGES, then there would be one more murder and now we had to guard every judge with the letter S, and on the 19th of December.

"I've got you now, you son-of-a-bitch!" I snarled and then I got up and started pacing. But what if the killer was already done? What if the word had been JUDGE? No S? What if he was spelling something else? Or using more than one word?

I collapsed on the couch and started crying because of the frustration, the feelings I had for Sam, the guilt of not being good enough to save these people and the guilt I felt about going to bed with Wade last year when I respected his wife so very much, now that I really knew her.

Samantha came in while I was sitting there blubbering like a five-year-old, because I had neglected to lock the door. She quickly put down the tray of coffee and donuts she was carrying and came over to the couch and sat down beside me.

"Kaylyn," she said, and put an arm around me, giving me a glimpse of how good a mother she must be, "what's wrong?"

"I figured it out," I sobbed, "but it's still no good."

"Figured what out, honey? You're not making sense."

Sam rubbed my back and held me while I got control of myself, and when she leaned forward to look in my eyes I almost kissed her again, but it was exactly the same thing I had done to her husband, so I started crying again. When I finally calmed down, I told her what I had discovered, and then she sat back, looking stunned.

"You're right," she agreed. "It only works if we know what the killer is really trying to spell."

"And there's something else," I said, knowing that I would never be able to live with myself if I didn't come clean.

Sam pushed the hair out of my eyes and wiped my face with a tissue. "Tell me, Kaylyn."

"It's about Wade," I began, and then she shut me up with a kiss. "I know," she said quietly. "I just wanted you to admit it."

All I could do was look at her. "You *knew?*"

"Of course I knew."

"Then why aren't you beating the shit out of me right now?"

Samantha shrugged, and then wiped away another tear with her thumb. "When it happened with Wade…were you crying, like you are now?"

Again, all I could do was look at her and nod. And then I managed, "I'm sorry, Sam! God, I'm so sorry!" And then I buried my head in my hands and started crying all over again. Samantha let it go on for a moment and then pulled me back by one shoulder so I would sit up.

"Kaylyn," she said. "Kaylyn, look at me!"

I did it, but it wasn't easy.

"Wade and me…we fix people. We fixed each other and we fixed Jenn, and in a way, we fixed her husband Bobby, too, I suppose, by breaking it off with Jenn. Wade was there for you when you needed him to be, and I wasn't able to stop seeing Jennifer, and he was hurt." She sighed. "How can I hate you when I was still in love with another woman at the time?"

Sam told me the whole story then, about how she had begun the affair with Jenny when she thought Wade was dead, and didn't want to just kick her to the curb when Wade came home. Her solution had been complicated, to say the least, creating some very complex dynamics between the three of them, but I was suddenly aware of the fact that she was much more mature, and much more open-minded, than I had given her credit for.

"If you knew," I said, "then why are you even *here?*"

"At first," she admitted, "I just wanted to get at the truth, but as we continued to see each other, I began to…feel something for you. My life with Wade has been very complicated, to say the least, and now all I'm doing is trying to find myself. How can I with-hold forgiveness for you and my husband when I wasn't able to give myself totally to him because of Jennifer? I need a friend, Lynn, and you were right—you and I? We *are* a lot alike. This doesn't change anything. I still want to work with you."

"But *why*, Sam?"

"Why not?" She sat back and sighed, looking for a moment as if she might cry herself. "I was in *love* with Jennifer, Lynn. Do you understand that? It wasn't like we were just sleeping together. And because of that, I had to divide my emotions between the two of them. I'm not sure that Wade has ever really been able to grasp that, and he deals with it by teaching and coaching and staying busy. We love each other, and we have a good life, but he's whole and I'm not. I can't just be his wife, Kaylyn, I have to be *Sam*, too, and doing this, with you… maybe this is just what I need, you know?" She shrugged. "Does that make sense?"

"And what about these feelings you have for me?" I dared to ask.

Samantha looked at me for a long, long time. And then she slipped a hand along my cheek and into my hair and pulled me close for the sweetest, softest kiss I have ever had. She was smiling when she broke it off.

"I'll make a deal with you," she said, "because I'm not sure where my marriage is going. Wade *says* he forgives me, but he's deeply hurt. I *loved* Jennifer, and I couldn't break it off with her, but I am *not* a cheater—I thought he was dead, for Christ's sake!" Her beautiful green eyes glistened with tears. "Let's finish this case together, and if I find that my relationship with Wade *is* beyond repair, you and I will still be there. As for right now, I need a good friend, don't you?"

"What kind of friend am I to have done what I did to you?'

"Did you do that to *hurt* me, Lynn?"

"You know I didn't."

"Then the kind of friend you are is a *broken* one and maybe we can fix each other."

"That's it? That's all you have to *say* about this, after what I did?"

"*Everyone* makes mistakes, Kaylyn Vale, but I only want to be friends with someone who can admit that."

• • •

Judgment Day

Samantha's rationalization would come back to haunt me in the days and weeks to come, but for now, I knew she was right. We needed each other just now, maybe for different reasons, but that didn't change anything.

After taking another shower, because I really needed to relax and get control of myself, I came back out and we got back to work.

Sam had put the Art Pepper CD in my *Bose* system while I was in the shower, and *The Prisoner* was playing when I came out. "Wade and I *love* that guy," she told me. She had also made a list of everything we needed to do. The first thing on her to-do list was to call Spinelli and give him everything we had come up with, which I told her I would do after lunch.

"And the second thing," she said, tapping her list with a pinky, "is to ask the State Police about ex-cons with the first name of Jason." If you remember, we had figured out that the months involved—July, August, September, October and November, spelled out the name 'Jason'. Since we were working on *months* now, we decided to have Spinelli check anyone with the name of Jason, whose last name began with the letter D...for December.

"Finally," she said, "if you have any contacts left in your old line of work, then you need to get all the information you can on this Rebekka Worthington." (By my old line of work she meant "The Company"). Like me, Sam didn't like how the Donato murder had gone down. "What else?' she asked, looking up at me.

I sat down next to her, because I had been reading the list over her shoulder, and even though I had put on a clean sweatshirt, I hadn't bothered with my bra, and my right breast touched her bare arm because she was wearing only a T-shirt. There was a zippered hoodie on the back of her chair, with *Chug Moo Do Academy* written on it and the little martial arts symbol for *Yin* and *Yang*. Our eyes met, and I knew she was going to kiss me again, and then she sat back and picked up her coffee cup. Still, I could feel the desire baking off of her—mostly because I felt it in *myself*—and I knew we would end up on the couch together before the day was out. It turned out that I was wrong about that, but at that moment the heat between us was a living, breathing thing...and then it was gone, so I sat back.

"Let's see," I said and had to clear my throat. "That leaves reading the Bible concordance on the Scripture quotes, and, if we're *going* with the word, JUDGES, it means that the letter 'S' is next, and we'll need to find out how many judges that is." Turns out there were only three, which surprised me because S is such a common letter for last names, but Rhode Island is, after all, a very small state. I made a note for Spinelli.

"We're leaving something out," Sam said with a sigh.

"I keep feeling that way, too, but are we really, or does it just *feel* that way?" I bit my fingernails for a moment, apparently driving Sam crazy, because she pulled my hand away from my mouth.

"Stop that!" she said.

"Yes, Mother," I answered, and we laughed.

"Oh, I know," Sam said. "The date! If it's an S, then the next murder will occur on the 19th of December."

"Unless he's finished."

"Doesn't feel that way to me. What about you?"

"No," I admitted. I added that to my list for the police. We worked until twelve-thirty, going over and over the quotes from scripture. It felt good to know that the first letter of each last name correlated to the day on which the murder occurred, but the quotes left us both blank.

"I'll call Spinelli," I told her, "and then we'll grab some lunch. Sound good?"

"I can eat," Sam admitted, but she had that damn pencil in her mouth again and was still looking at the concordance. Watching her nibble on the pencil, all I could think of was the boys in the library in the Stephen King film, *Christine*, drooling over Alexandra Paul, who did the same thing while *she* was reading.

"What?" she said, realizing that I was staring at her.

I decided to be honest. "I was just thinking how very lucky your girlfriend Jenny was, and maybe how stupid she is."

Sam blushed, and got to her feet. "You're killing me," she said, but I knew she was flattered. "Come on, I'm buying."

"Boss's prerogative," I told her. "Oh that reminds me. While we're out, I want to have a key to the office made for you, and I want you to apply for a gun license."

"I already have one," Sam told me, meeting my eyes. "Dad was a lifetime NRA member and taught me to shoot when I was a kid. I own a snub-nose .38, and I know how to use it, too."

If I remembered correctly, the cop in the Ashbery case, as well as her step-father, had both been killed with a .38. I shuddered, wondering just how much of an accident those killings had really been. "Ok—start carrying it, then."

"I've had it on my person every single time you've ever seen me, Lynn," Sam told me, drilling me with her bright emerald eyes. I thought of that little pouch she always wore when she jogged, and again a chill ran through me.

"Oh. Ok then."

"Do me a favor though, before we go out?"

"Name it," I said, being the hopeless romantic I am.

"Put a *bra* on, will you? You go out looking like *that* you're going to cause an accident."

I remember smiling. At least she had noticed.

• • •

We got back to the office at two, having lingered over coffee and going to get the key made at the hardware store, and when we sat down again, we both admitted that the nagging feeling that we were missing something was still there.

Spinelli had been *very* upbeat about the information we had provided, and given me an "Atta-Girl" that really picked me up. I still hadn't told him about hiring Sam, though; I wanted to do that in person.

"All right," I began, looking at all the data, "let's see what we can see."

We worked until five again, going over everything we had, but other than what we had already come up with, we couldn't see a damn thing.

"Well," Sam said and stretched, "let's just hope we're right about the S. If we are, then it gives us more than enough time to see if there are any clues in the quotes."

Just then my phone rang. "It's Spinelli," I told Sam. "Hi, Bobby. Oh, good. Really? That's all? Ok. Huh? No. You don't need my permission...and you're welcome." I hung up.

"What was that all about?"

"You believe there are only three judges with a last name ending in S?"

"Thank God we're the smallest state."

I didn't think God had anything to do with this, but I didn't want to burden anyone else with the nature of my skepticism. "Tomorrow, we'll start going through those cases."

"Sounds good," Sam said and got up.

We stood there looking at each other.

"Thanks, Sam," I finally said. "For everything."

"Just don't ever lie to me, Kaylyn, and I'll be the best friend you ever had,"

I met her eyes, taking that as an invitation. "*How* good?" I said in a husky voice and kissed her.

Sam allowed it until I got a little frisky with my hands, and then she grabbed both wrists, gently but firmly. "I meant what I said, Lynn. I can't do this now, as much as I'd like to. I won't be a cheat, and we made a deal, remember?"

I touched her face. "If you want me," I whispered, "I'll be there. No matter what."

Sam pressed her forehead against mine and closed her eyes. "Me, too," she said, and then she was gone.

I stood there all alone, knowing that at least she was a woman of her word. Over time, I'd come to question almost everything else about her, but for now, all I wanted was to go home and get into bed, I was hungry, but I've eaten most of the meals in my life alone, and I just couldn't do it again tonight. The *Bose* system was in *constant* mode, and the Art Pepper CD was still playing. As I went to shut it off, I realized that *The Prisoner* was on again.

• • •

The next morning I was in the office by eight, and I called and left a message for an old friend at "The Company", asking her to call me back. And then I checked my answering machine, discovering that there was a call from the journalist, Clair Sacchetti-Graviani. Clair is the wife of Judge Dante (Danny) Graviani, and a very good friend of the Ashbery's. I hadn't heard from her since Wade Ashbery's trial, so naturally I was intrigued.

She answered on the first ring.

"Clair Sacchetti," she said.

"Hi, Clair—Kaylyn Vale."

"Oh, hi, Lynn. Thanks for getting back to me so quickly."

"Not a problem. What's going on?"

"I got a note in the mail yesterday, late, that I think you might be interested in, and I'd like to meet with you."

"What about?" I asked, although I had a good idea.

"It has to do with the case you're currently working on, and I'm wondering if we could talk about it in person."

"If it's what I *think* it is, Clair, then we'd better meet somewhere in private." I was working on a very high profile case, after all, and couldn't be seen going to the office of a *Pulitzer-Prize* winning journalist. Likewise, I couldn't have her coming *here*, either.

"I agree; where would you like to meet?"

I thought about that for a moment, and then I cleared my throat. "Confidentially, Clair, I've just taken on a research assistant to help me with this case. I'm sure she'd let us meet at her place."

"Oh, I didn't know that. Who is it, if you don't mind me asking?"

"Samantha Ashbery," I answered without hesitation.

There was a moment of silence, but if Clair was surprised by the information, it didn't show in her voice. "Good choice, Lynn—they don't come much smarter than Sam, or any tougher, either."

"I've noticed that myself," I told her and chuckled, although I *could* have added, *any prettier, either*. Sam also had an IQ north of 150, but I'm sure Clair already knew that. "What time is good for you?"

"I'm clear after noon, Lynn. Why don't I give you my cell number and you can call me back after you check with Sam?"

"What is it?" I asked, grabbing a pen. I wrote it down, thanked her and hung up. I checked the clock, dialed Sam, and got her as she was leaving the house.

"What's up, pal?" she asked.

"I got a call from Clair Sacchetti this morning, and she says she has information about the case for us. Can we meet at *your* house, Sam? I don't want to be seen going to her office and I don't want her coming *here*, either."

"Jesus, Lynn! Sounds serious. Of course we can meet here. What time?"

"Noon, or a little after, if that's all right with you?"

"Sure. Why don't we do this?" I could tell she was looking at her watch. "It's not even eight-thirty yet, and I was just going to bring the kids next door to Marie, but why don't I stay *here* this morning? It'll give me a little more time with the kids, and I can make lunch for us."

Marie was her mother-in-law, and I knew she had agreed to watch the children during the day now that Sam was working. "You're a good man, Sister."

"*The Maltese Falcon*," Sam said. "1941."

My jaw dropped. Literally. Quoting movies and guessing the titles was a game I had played with her husband while we were on that rescue mission in Afghanistan that I told you about earlier. Not for the first time, and certainly not for the last, I wondered what kind of game she was playing with *me*. "Uh, right," I said, because she had caught me off guard. "I've got enough to keep me busy. I'll see you in a couple of hours."

After I hung up, I just sat there, wondering what I had gotten myself into. I had slept with her husband, after all, and despite the fact that she seemed ok with that, and had explained why, I was uneasy. Obviously, she was very open-minded about sex. Her 'solution' to the problem of her and Jenny and Wade had involved morphing their relationship into a threesome; still, why would she then pursue a friendship, even a limited partnership, with yours truly? I didn't have time to ponder it, though, because just then my phone rang.

"Kaylyn Vale."

"Do you still have the phone?" a female voice asked. It was my old partner from "The Company", Ashley Vaughn.

"I do," I said, without embellishment.

"Then call me back."

The satellite phone had a secure link, and had been on my desk, on the charger, since I had 'retired'. I dialed Ashley's line and waited for it to cycle through.

"Calling on my *desk* phone, Kaylyn? Seriously?"

"Sorry, Ash. But we *are* old friends, you know."

"Didn't mean to be snippy—you know how it is around here. What's up?"

"I need some information on an *asset*, Rebekka Worthington, killed in Lebanon five years ago."

I heard her typing, and, after a moment, she said: "Killed in a bombing at the embassy five years ago, as you said. Wait, this is strange."

My P.I. intuition was on full alert with just those four little words. "What?"

"Well—hang on; I want to close out of this." Ashley was quiet for a moment. "Ok, she completed several assignments for us, but they're all listed as *need-to-know*."

"Huh. But her death was verified?"

"Absolutely. Tell me, Lynn—does this have to do with the case you're involved in? It's been all over the news."

"Her brother, now deceased, was the shooter on at least *one* of the killings, Ash—but now that the killer is at it again…"

"Got it. Anything else I can do for you while we're ruining my career?"

"No," I laughed, "except maybe let me buy you lunch next time you're in town."

"Me? Come to Rhode Island? In your dreams, girlfriend!"

We chatted for a few minutes, promising to stay in touch—you know how that is—and then I rang off.

Just then my cell phone rang again. Bobby. I told him about Sam, and he didn't see an issue with it. "The way you two have come up with the thing about the days and the letters is awesome, Lynn. Just keep her out of the 'field', at least until she gets licensed."

"Not a problem. So you're ok with this?"

"Sure—I even took a detail or two when we were guarding her house during the trial. She's a great kid."

"I think so, too," I said, and made a mental note to drill Bobby later if I needed any more information about her. We hung up, and I sat there remembering how the State Police had been ordered by the Trial Judge in the Ashbery case to guard them because of all the crooked cops in the Farmington Police department, and the fact that a cop had actually run Sam and Clair off the road. I also recalled a case, a few years back, where certain members of the Farmington Police had actually kidnapped and literally tortured, a man on the Sex Offender Registry—so I made another note to see if Kyle Worthington had ever lived there. I now had so many notes that my *notes* had notes, and then I remembered to call Clair to firm up the lunch date.

It was nine-twenty by this time, and I needed another cup of coffee. I'd been here since eight, and I hadn't done a damn thing, so I got out the Scripture quotes and looked at them. The Book of Genesis—Moses; Matthew—by a disciple; James/James—another disciple; Romans, written by the Apostle Paul. All about what I had, by this time, privately come to think of as Divine Commands against judging others. I worked until 11:45, got nothing for my efforts except for a sour stomach, and drove to Sam's. Clair's car was in the driveway, and there was plenty of room, so I followed suit. Sam's Jeep was there, but Wade's pickup was not—so I assumed he was at school. I walked up the steps to the back porch, and knocked on the door.

The Ashbery home was located on the property of the Ashbery Dairy Farm, and adjacent to the main house, a rambling old Victorian large enough to accommodate an army. Wade and Sam had their own driveway, garage and yard, and enough privacy to make living next door to relatives a workable enterprise. Sam yelled for me to come in, and I did so, putting the six pack of *IBC* root beer I had brought, on the kitchen table.

The other two women were standing by the counter drinking coffee. Clair shook my hand, but Sam surprised me by giving me a hug. I just looked at her, a bit embarrassed, and then managed a smile.

An Art Pepper CD was playing softly on the stereo system, reminding me that she and Wade 'Love that guy', as she had put it. The track was *Over The Rainbow*, and I immediately got drawn into the soft and melancholy lyricism, the pure anguish of the performance, which somehow brought to mind the harrowing life Art Pepper had lived.

I hadn't been in prison, as Pepper had—at least not yet—but I understood loneliness all too well.

"Well," Sam said. "You two hungry, or should we look at what Clair brought first?"

"I can eat," I admitted, "but I'm rather curious about that note, Clair."

Clair made a face, but it was more about the subject matter than at what I had suggested.

We all sat down, and Clair took out an inter-office envelope. "I opened the mail without knowing what it was, obviously," she said, "so I'm sure I tainted whatever evidence the police could have found."

"If it's what I think it is, Clair, I'd bet a kidney that there aren't any fingerprints on it anyway."

Clair raised an eyebrow, and slid it across to me without a word.

Dear Ms. Sacchetti—we're sending this to you *because you are the only journalist we are aware of who can convincingly lay claim to any form of integrity, and whatever happens, we want the record to reflect what we're doing—and why.*

The justice system in America has far more to do with careers, elections and selling newspapers than with getting to the truth, and it's time for anyone who calls himself an American to take back what it ours—namely, Constitutional Safeguards and actual Due Process.

For decades now, judges have been—not impartial observers—but an integral part of the prosecution. Guilt or innocence no longer matters, only feeding the already bloated Prison Industrial Complex.

We're far from finished with our sacred work, Ms. Sacchetti, so when you show this to the police, as you must, please make them aware that we are only doing what we've been forced to do.

The note had been typed on a single sheet of copy paper, and was unsigned. I closed my eyes, read it again, and passed it to Sam.

The thing that struck me most was the use of the word, "we", reaffirming what I had thought all along—that we were dealing with more than one person.

Sam put the note down, looking like someone had struck her.

"Holy shit," she said softly.

"What?" Clair asked, although I already knew what she meant.

"This could have come from any one of the articles I've written myself!"

I chuckled. "Good thing you've got me for an alibi."

"Oh, we've got jokes, huh, Lynn?" Sam snapped, but the smile on her face reached her eyes and I knew we were ok.

Clair was studying both of us, her pretty eyes flickering back and forth. "Either of you get the use of the word, 'we'?"

"First *I* knew of it," I said, and without even looking at Sam I knew Clair had caught the lie, even though she didn't say anything. To cover myself, I quickly added: "What struck me most was the literate tone. This is anything but some random nut, Ladies—assuming it really *is* from the killer—or killers. If it is, we're dealing with someone who views themselves as a Patriot, and is willing to die for their cause." I pursed my lips. "Not good."

"I understand that you to have to keep certain things close to the vest," Clair said, "but the note came to me, and when this is over, I expect an exclusive from the two of you, in exchange for sharing this and anything else that might come along."

"Not a problem," I told Clair, and put the note back in the envelope. "We need to turn this over to the police as soon as we can." I looked at Clair. "Would you like me to handle that?"

Clair nodded. "Well," I said," why don't we eat, and then I'll call Spinelli—better for all of us if we go through him."

Everyone agreed, and we hashed it out while we ate, breaking up our little party about an hour later. I told Sam to stay home the rest of the day, assured Clair that I'd be in touch, and called Spinner when I got back to the office, asking him to come by at the end of his shift. Then I made a copy of the note and stuck it in a desk drawer. I sat down at my computer after that and went to Sam's website, where most of her articles on social justice and human rights were posted. One, in particular, gave me the chills:

THEM—By Samantha Ashbery

When we dehumanize a person, or a group of people, collectively, it becomes easy to oppress them, monitor them… . concentrate them; it becomes easy to punish them, simply because we tell ourselves, they're not like us. Especially those accused of crimes, more to the point, the one person out of a thousand that causes our lawmakers to legislate by the lowest common denominator.

As a practical matter, however, does any right-thinking person believe that, locking the barn door, after the horse is gone, actually prevents the horse from leaving?

Sounds funny, but that's just what our elected officials do, every time they legislate in response to the media – they're locking the barn door after the horse is gone.

Why?

Because those laws made in response to media pressure, usually aimed at those people (the ones who aren't really people at all), are not, in fact, about preventing crime, or punishing criminals – they're not even about public safety…it is, in actuality, about them, the lawmakers, making laws that erode civil liberties simply to win elections by looking tough-on-crime; it's about jobs.

But evolving standards of decency dictate that the tax-payers deserve better. It demands public safety and the humane "correction" of those who break the law. It demands, that, we don't become the "monsters" (those people) we say we have the right to punish.

In a letter to a local wrongly-convicted man, Human Rights advocate, Rev. Jonathan Dressher, said: "There is viciousness over nothing, and ignorance of evil disguised as righteousness; what they're doing in the name of the law, is nothing more than torture."

And in a recent sermon, here in Providence, The Rev. Stephen Arlebetta said: "In the film 'Twelve Angry Men', Henry Fonda plays the lone dissenting voice in a room full of competing interests. One by one, by force of argument, and moral persuasion, he appeals to the suppressed morals of the other eleven jurors, who finally realize that they were all too willing to execute an innocent boy."

The question is – why?

Why, do we hate, fear and cast out?

Maybe because it's about…. **them**: those who prey on our fears simply to win elections, justify paychecks, and create jobs.

Today's crime rate isn't much different from what it was in the 70s. Is it possible, then, that, this recent crime wave monopolizing the airwaves, is nothing more than a well-thought-out, media construct? That, perhaps, politicians, looking to justify exorbitant salaries, have seized on the tough-on-crime rhetoric, as a way of perpetuating those salaries?

Is it possible, for example, that, the vast majority of men and women on parole, act in accordance with the rules of their supervision, and pose no threat to the welfare of society? Is it possible, that, the media focuses on the exception, rather than the rule, and sensationalizes it to the point where our lawmakers are forced to respond?

In several surveys, notably in a 2010 "Justice Policy Institute Report", most legislators admit that, they make laws based on media coverage, on the public pressure such coverage causes, and not on reality. While such a mindset may very well win elections, it also costs billions this country can no longer afford, because it forces judges to hand out sentences that are unwarranted as well as unnecessary.

In "Moral Man and Immoral Society", theologian Reinhold Niebuhr, reflected, that, as individuals, we are all perfectly capable of living moral lives – but when we take those very same individuals and put them in a group (what communications experts call "Group Think")….an interesting phenomenon occurs – competing interests, like

Judgment Day

justifying jobs and winning elections, transform otherwise moral human beings into an immoral lynch mob.

One very well-known example of this phenomenon of self-advancement vs. justice is a now-famous sports case. The prosecution in this case tried to convict the defendants who were, apparently, innocent, allegedly to win an upcoming election.

Another famous example is the curious case of Mr. Kirk Bloodsworth, the first man in the United States to be cleared on DNA evidence.

He was sentenced to death, but later exonerated. The prosecution in this case allegedly seemed more motivated by securing a conviction than at getting to the truth.

The message is well understood – convictions at any cost, above truth, above justice, not for any reason approaching public safety, but to win elections.

The reason? An out-of-control media that has constructed a crime wave that doesn't really exist. A media more concerned with creating news, rather than reporting it, a media more interested in selling ad-copy – commercial time, than it is in the truth. A media who has decided, that, the "news" equals a daily-parade-of-crime.

The pressure from a frightened, nearly panic-stricken voting base then becomes so great, that elected officials act immorally, sometimes even illegally, to remove that pressure.

This country now (vindictively) warehouses thousands of innocent, wrongly-convicted men and women, at a staggering cost this nation can no longer afford, not to keep us safe, but to simply justify a legislature being in session twelve months a year…

It went on…and on…but I'm sure you get the point—Samantha was right, the note Clair had received could very well have been written by Sam, herself, because her own published articles reflected the very same sentiment.

Of course, being a fierce advocate of the Constitution didn't make anyone a killer.

At least I hope it didn't.

I'm not ashamed to tell you—even if I should be—that I was starting to fall in love with Sam, but not for the first time I wondered: just who *was* she, really?

CHAPTER FIVE—December

The First of December dawned bright and clear and dry; it was a cool day, but I welcomed it after the humidity of the summer and early Fall. I got to the office by nine, finding Sam already at work, and after some small talk and a cup of coffee, I sat down to write out a "To-Do" list.

The first thing we needed to do was approach all the judges with a last name beginning with the letter "S"—as I told you earlier, there were only three, because Rhode Island is such a small state. I called Spinelli and told him to put guards on Simpson, Sanders and Siebert. If Sam and I were right, and the word the killers were spelling out *was* JUDGES, then it was the only logical thing to do. It made sense, but to assure myself, I wrote out the previous five names: Jordan, Unger, Donato, Gregory and Edwards.

No, I was *sure* we were right—and so I turned to the next thing: taking in Jason Donnelly.

After discovering that the months involved in the killings spelled out JASON—July, August, September, October, and November, and since it was now December, Spinelli had done a search of any ex-con with a last name beginning in D. There was only one, as it turned out, the aforementioned Jason Donnelly, a fairly vocal, very militant type, who was always shooting his mouth off about getting back at the system that had "screwed him". Donnelly had successfully completed his five years' probation—without incident, I might add—and was now almost constantly "holding court", as it were, in a dive down on Atwell's Avenue in Providence, a biker joint called, "*Clyde's*". And since we were working on the assumption that we only had until the 19th of the month—you'll remember that our working theory was that the date corresponded with the first letter of each victim's last name: Jordan on the 10th; Unger on the 21st—and so on, we had no choice but to take him down as soon as possible…just in case we were wrong. Spinelli was working on a warrant, and we planned to take him down before the week was out. It was a good plan, but as I later learned, having the phone on speaker hadn't been such a good idea, because Spinelli didn't want Sam in the field. Truth was—neither did I.

"All right, *Dad*," I told Spinner, rolling my eyes at Sam. "I heard you the first time—no license, no field. Go take a chill pill and get back to me when you have the warrant for Donnelly, ok?"

Sam and I had been sharing long stares and lingering looks ever since she had hugged me that day in her home, and she had told me repeatedly how sick she was of her husband spending all of his free time, and weekends, too, on the ball field. We hadn't made any moves on each other, though—I was leaving that up to her—but the tension was sometimes so strong it was almost as if there were an electromagnetic field between us, and once, when we were both looking down at paperwork and inadvertently bumped into each other, our eyes met, and…nothing had happened, although, God help me, I had *really* wanted to kiss her! Now she was just making a face at me. Sam is a beautiful woman, as I have said, and very mature-looking, but when she doesn't get her way she does this pouty-lip thing that just about drives me out of my mind. How her father didn't spoil her rotten is a mystery to me, because, even as a grown woman, I had trouble saying "no" to her.

"What?" I asked, putting my cell phone down.

"Nothing, I guess. I just really wanted to be involved."

"You *are* involved, partner—but like he said, no license, no fieldwork. If you want, we'll go to City Hall first thing Monday morning and pull the paperwork for you."

"After you take in Donnelly."

"After," I agreed.

"Couldn't I just tag along, stay in the car or something?"

"Jesus, woman! Did you *hear* him? You show up, they'll pull *my* ticket. Then where will we be?"

"All right. I'll be a good girl." She lowered her eyes with a sigh and went back to the concordance.

"Let's not get carried away," I said softly, as close to actually flirting as I'd come since we had first kissed.

Sam didn't respond, and the rest of the day dragged.

It was a good thing that I was being paid for this, though, because it was taking up all my time. The newspapers—with the exception of Clair—had been beating the holy living shit out of the cops. The Feds had been brought in as well, gumming up the works, and the whole damn nightmare was now a political fucking football, driving me hard.

I looked over at Sam several times during the course of the day, wanting to comfort her but knowing how she would take it. As I told you earlier when I mentioned disliking labels—Sam is *gorgeous*, but I wanted her because of *who* she was, not *what* she was. It wouldn't have mattered one way or the other if she was a man or a woman, but I wanted her because she and I were so much in tune, so connected, so much alike. I've got gay friends that don't get this, and straight friends who just shake their heads, the same way I have conservative friends who think I'm liberal and vice versa, and I'm only bothering to tell you about this now, so you will understand what came next.

We broke off at five-past-five, and Sam asked me what I had planned for the night.

"Honestly, pal? I need a few hours without thinking about all of this."

"Like *that's* going to happen," she said with a laugh, and tossed back her hair, something that just made me sigh. God, she was pretty!

"Oh, I'll pull it off, all right—I'm on overload and I need some downtime. I've got a nice bottle of white wine, and a shelf full of chick-flicks. I'm going to have a night in, and go to bed early." I put my hands on my hips. "What about you?"

"Mister Coach of the Year has another game. I thought I'd do what *you're* doing, although it will be *The Little Mermaid* with my kids."

"Sounds nice, Sam."

"It is, actually—they're both awesome."

For a fleeting moment I wondered what it would be like to be someone's Mom, but then I let it go—I have too many issues with my own mother, and all I wanted right then was to crash.

I was home a half hour later, having stopped briefly at the convenience store for a pack of *Winston's* and a TV-dinner, and I tossed everything on the table and kicked my shoes off as soon as I came in.

I was wearing a dark blue dress because I guess I just wanted to feel pretty today—told you I'm a girlie girl sometimes, didn't I? But instead of getting changed or making supper I just plopped down on the couch and lit a cigarette, staring at the wall and trying to empty my overworked mind. To no avail.

I put the cigarette out after a few drags, put my head back and must have fallen asleep, because the downstairs buzzer woke me up at six-forty.

"Who is it?" I asked the intercom.

"Sam. Can I come up? I'll only be a minute."

I sighed because I really didn't think it was a good idea. I was tired and felt like crying and I was sure I knew what she wanted—to argue with me about the Donnelly warrant.

But I buzzed her in, unlocked the door and went to the kitchen to wash my face and take a sip from the little bottle of *Scope* I keep near the cookie jar. I was drying myself when there was a knock on the door.

"It's open," I said tiredly.

Sam came in, tossed her keys on the table and put her hands on her hips. She was wearing a really nice tan top with draw strings, jeans and sneakers. Her *Nike* windbreaker was slung over one shoulder, and her little pouch, the one I knew she kept the .38 in, was on her waist.

"Christ," she said, looking me over, "don't tell me I woke you up?"

"I guess. It's ok. What's wrong?"

"Why does something have to be wrong?"

"You're right," I said and laughed lightly. "Seems I'm always expecting trouble of some sort."

"Maybe that's why you always seem to get it," Sam said softly.

"Want some coffee?"

"No, I can't stay. I only wanted to ask you again if there was any way you could see yourself clear to letting me tag along when you take Donnelly in." She held up a hand. "I promise I'll stay in the car."

"I can't do that, Sammy. I'm sorry."

"Look," she said and sighed, 'if it was just Spinelli, I'd be okay with it, but I can't rid myself of the feeling that it's *you* who doesn't want me there."

"You're right. I don't."

"Care to tell me why?" Sam folded her arms across her chest, and I knew I was in for it.

"You mean *aside* from maybe losing my license? Ok, you're not field-trained, for one thing, and you have two little kids at home."

"I can handle myself."

"Never said you couldn't."

"Then what's the big? I thought we were in this together, like partners or something? Can't you stand up to Spinelli? For me?"

"And you'd stay in the car, for real?"

Sam sighed. She was full of shit and knew it; worse, she knew *I* knew it, too.

"Tell me the *real* reason, Lynn."

"The real reason?"

"Yeah." She came close enough to wake me up completely, because she looked mad enough to throw a punch.

She also looked like she wanted to cry and it brought tears to my eyes, as well. I deliberately turned my back on her, put my hands on the countertop, closed my eyes and shook my head. "You want the truth, do you?"

"After everything we've shared. *Everything*," she added meaningfully, "don't I *deserve* the truth, Kaylyn?"

I took a deep breath, looked up at the ceiling without turning around, and spoke without looking at her. "Because I'm falling in love with you, moron, and if you got hurt, I wouldn't be able to live with myself."

Sam was quiet for so long that I actually thought she might have left, but she was still standing there when I turned around, and there were tears on her cheeks, making her beautiful green eyes sparkle like emeralds.

"Did you ever stop to think, Lynn," she whispered, "that maybe I care about *you*, too? That maybe I couldn't take it if something happened to you?" She reached out and touched my cheek, and God, no one has ever touched me like that, before or since. I was crying openly now, my eyes riveted to hers, my hand on top of hers on my face.

"For the love of *God*, Samantha," I whispered, "if you have something to say, just *say* it, or get out and leave me alone! I can't *do* this anymore!"

Sam brought her face to within an inch of mine, still looking in my eyes. "Maybe I'm falling in love with *you*, too, stupid," she said, and kissed me.

We held each other right there in the kitchen, kissing each other tenderly, touching each other, our hands roaming, and so help me God I don't know how it happened but while we were kissing somehow we had undressed each other.

Our hands were in each other's hair and our foreheads were pressed together. I took her hand, led her over to the door, locked it and took her into the bedroom. Our clothes, her sneakers and her jacket were still on the kitchen floor, but neither one of us cared. We were both still crying, at least a bit, as I took her in my arms at the foot of my bed. We stood there holding each other for a moment, and then I got on the bed and pulled her down on top of me. Samantha's hair is like silk, and her skin like satin. Her body is toned and hard, but soft where a woman *should* be. I wish I could tell you about those few hours we shared, I really do—but I just can't; it's too personal. To do so, to give you details, would somehow cheapen the most beautiful and intense experience of my life, and despite what was to come, I have never felt the same way about anyone else—and I doubt I ever will.

• • •

At nine-twenty, we were lying in bed together, utterly spent. Sam's head was on my chest, and her gorgeous, soft, honey-wheat hair was a glorious mess on my bare skin. Samantha picked up her head to look at me, and when our eyes met, I started to cry. Sam wiped my tears away with her thumbs.

"Hey," she whispered. "What's wrong? I didn't hurt you, did I?"

"No, silly—but I hurt *you*. This is the second time I ruined your marriage, and I don't know how you can even *look* at me." I *could* have added that I was also crying because this had been the one and only time someone had said that they loved me in bed—and actually made me believe it. I *could* have said that both of us were so lost and broken that we were pathetic, but all I could do was cling to her and tell her how sorry I was.

"Look at me, Lynn. Please *look* at me!"

I did, but it wasn't easy.

"Now you listen to me. I didn't plan this, and I know you didn't either. My marriage isn't *ruined*, and nothing that's happened, at any time, is your fault. We're complicated human beings, you and I, and so is my husband, by the way. I don't know *where* my marriage is heading, but you have to understand that it has nothing to do with you. Wade and I..." She shook her head, pushed back her hair and sat up, holding herself up on her elbow. "We had problems long before *you* came along, Lynn. I lied to him about my age when we first met, and despite the fact that we didn't *want* anyone to get hurt—people *died*, Lynn. Do you understand that? And then he faked his death and left me here alone with the baby. I fell in love with another woman while he was gone, because I couldn't *stand* the thought of giving myself to another man. If you want the truth, Lynn—I've never even *been* with another man. But while he was away, Wade slept with a nurse in Afghanistan, and when he came home, I just couldn't let Jennifer go. You know the whole story. It's a fucking public record, for Christ's sake, and anyone who has read Clair's *Broken Heroes* series knows it all, too. So if you want to feel guilty about something, feel guilty about something in your own life. And just so you know—if I didn't *want* to go to bed with you, no one could have made me."

Being Kaylyn Vale, I had a lot to say about all of that, but all I could manage at the moment was to hug her—fiercely.

"Okay—but where does that leave us?"

Sam frowned, played with my hair and then looked down. "I don't know, Lynn. I have feelings for you, but I never liked the idea of going behind anyone's back, and I have my kids to consider, too. I'd *like* to make my marriage work, but I don't know if I can." She met my eyes then. "We'll see, ok? In the meantime, let's get this son-of-a-bitch we're hunting so everyone can get on with their lives."

"Speaking of your kids—shouldn't you be getting home?"

Sam looked at her watch—I managed a smile because other than an ankle bracelet, it was the only thing she was wearing.

"Yeah—*he's* good for another half hour, but I best be going."

While Sam went into the kitchen to retrieve her clothes, I lay back on the bed and covered my eyes with my forearm.

"God, are you beautiful," she whispered as she came back into the bedroom and sat down beside me.

I ran a hand along her back while she sorted out her clothes and put on her bra. She spends so much time outdoors that her skin looks like copper. "I could say the same thing, you know."

She kissed me, finished dressing and grabbed her jacket. She stood there looking at me then without saying a word.

"What is it?" I asked.

"I was just thinking…if not for the kids, I would have stayed the night."

"We're ok then, you and me?"

"Friends…*best* friends, with benefits—at least for now, if that's ok with you?"

"More than ok." I sighed. "Are you going to tell him?"

"I don't know. I need to sort this out."

"Me too. This is…complicated. I don't see myself going to sleep anytime soon, though, so if you want to call…"

"Ditto." Sam continued to stand there, though, making no move to leave, so I got up, wrapped my arms around her and kissed her.

"Go home, Sam."

She started to cry, and this time I wiped *her* tears away.

"I don't really want to leave," she said, and sniffed.

"Go home," I repeated—and I'll see you in the morning."

"Ok," she said, and then she was gone.

I locked the door, scooped up my clothes, and headed for the shower, my head spinning and feeling very much like the Michael Douglas character in the film, *Basic Instinct*.

• • •

Sam, of course, got her way in regards to the Donnelly warrant, but I'm sure that doesn't surprise you—some hard-boiled detective *I* am, huh? Overcome by a cute girl with a pouty lip. It happened the next morning, when I was in the office working on the case. It had occurred to me during the night that maybe the killer wasn't spelling out *anything*—and everything up to this point was just to fuck us up. What if, I wondered, we were wrong about Donnelly—and taking him in, was, after all, only a precaution in the first place—what if *nothing* went down on the 19th? What if something happened today? Or tomorrow? Or not until next month—or not at all?

"Damn it," I said under my breath, and threw my pen down on the folding table in disgust just as Sam came in.

"Hey you," I said, getting up nervously. You might think that being who and what I am I'd be better able to cope with an awkward situation like this, but if you've ever slept with a co-worker, and then saw them the very next day, you understand how nerve-wracking it can be.

Sam, however, made it easy, and not for the first time I understood just how manipulative she could be.

"Hey, yourself, Megan Fox," Sam said, and hugged me.

Here we were, in my private investigation office, hugging like school girls. My old handler at "The Company" would have come out of his grave like a scorched cat if he could have. I returned the embrace, but I was frowning and grateful that Sam couldn't see my face. Don't get me wrong—Megan Fox is *gorgeous*. I *wish* I had her lips, her hair, her...never mind, but everyone who knows me says I look like Alexandra Daddario, another absolutely *beautiful* woman; either way, I felt like she was playing me.

"What's wrong?' she asked, gently disentangling herself. Did I ever tell you that her IQ is *north* of 150?

"Just wondering about the dates, here," I told her, and shared what I had thought about them.

Sam shook her head. "Stop second guessing yourself. We've got a solid plan here. Let's stick to it."

We got into a good, working rhythm after that and we were doing pretty well until Spinelli called about the Donnelly thing. Sighing, I put my phone on speaker, not wanting Sam to think I was hiding anything from her. You've got to understand, I didn't know what she wanted from me, or even what she was doing. Was she really interested? Using me for sex? Bored? Trying for equal time, because of Wade, or even setting me up for something? Like The Don suggests in *The Godfather*—I wanted to keep her close.

"Ok, pal," I told Spinelli after I had written everything down. They were going to move on Donnelly at his apartment early Thursday morning, which gave us two solid days, and I just hoped that the cluster-fuck with the Feds didn't gum up the works. "One more thing, though," I added, meeting Sam's eyes, "I've got a blanket ticket," I lied. A "blanket-ticket" is slang for a temporary license used to bring in bounty-hunters, associates and the like. "So Sam Ashbery will be with me." I hurried on before he could interrupt me. "She's been a big part of this, and I want her involved."

Spinelli sighed. "Your call, Lynn," he said finally. "Just remember, if she gets hurt, or if something goes south on us, it's your license, as well as your call."

"I'm a big girl, Spinner, and so is she."

Sam reached across the table and took my hand as I rang off, and as I squeezed her fingers, I remembered why the Spartans had believed in fighting right alongside their lovers—you tend to fight harder when you've got someone to protect.

We worked until four-thirty, and then I called it a day. It was still chilly, but tolerable, and the sky outside was gray, somber and overcast, the kind of evening you'd like to spend curled up with a good book, or in bed with a lover.

"Thanks for the Donnelly thing, Lynn," she said as she gathered her stuff. "I won't let you down and I promise to do exactly what you tell me to do."

Judgment Day

I smiled as I hugged her goodnight, unable to help myself. "You're going to get in trouble saying things like that to *me*, Chicky."

"Don't threaten *me* with a good time," Sam said, and giggled.

"Everything all right at home?"

Sam hiked her shoulder in what passed for a shrug. "I guess."

"Remember," I told her, "if you want to talk, I'm there for you."

"Same goes for me," she said, meeting my eyes.

Sam got in her Jeep and I got in the Mustang. We sat there for a moment as we let the cars warm up, and then I noticed she was just sitting there looking at me. I almost opened my window and asked her to come home with me, but I'd complicated the girl's life enough as it was and if she had really wanted to, she would have asked.

Sam drove off, and I sighed. It was almost dark now—you know how it is in December, dark when you get up and dark when you go home. I hate that, and it made me feel lonelier than I usually do at the end of the day. In a weird way, having been intimate with Sam had only intensified my sense of isolation—the part of you that yearns for that connection feels the aloneness more acutely when that person is away, and I suddenly decided that I just couldn't be by myself at suppertime. I picked up my cellphone and asked David Redman if he wanted to meet me for dinner. As it turned out, that decision very well could have saved my life.

• • •

David and I meet at *The Country Inn* in the town of Warren, a wonderful restaurant specializing in Italian Food, steaks and chops and fresh seafood. The Inn is the kind of place you want to be on a cold winter night, especially if you have a drink in your hand and someone to keep you company. We ate at the bar, and I ordered The Broiled Bay Scallops—delicious; David ordered a big sirloin, telling me that the thing he had missed most in prison, was tying in to a really good steak.

"You missed *food* the most?" I said as I sipped from my glass of white wine. I looked at him sideways as I did so and he laughed.

"Yeah, well, there *is* that," he admitted.

"Mind if I ask you something?" I said, putting down my glass.

We were both picking from the Cold Antipasto we had ordered as an appetizer. David grabbed a piece of cheese and shrugged.

"You can ask me anything, Lynn."

"Was it really bad…I mean…*bad*…behind the wall?"

"Now why would you ask me something like that after all this time?" he wondered, picking up his draft beer.

"I'm trying to get a handle on what would set a guy like Worthington off, and maybe even this Donnelly."

David nodded, as if what I'd said made sense to him. I wasn't sure that it made sense, though, even to me.

"Yeah, it's bad, but not for the reasons you might think."

Our food arrived then, and we waited while the girl, a tall redhead with really pretty blue eyes set everything down. It was early and therefore quiet—not quite the early bird special, but quiet enough to talk privately.

"Care to elaborate?"

"Well, there are the things you see in the movies. The violence, I mean, guys raping each other, fights in the chow hall, that sort of thing. You get to be hyper-vigilant, watching your back all the time. It wears on you." He cut a piece of steak, chewed, and then wiped his mouth on a napkin. "But what really got to me was the isolation, like when my father died. I can't tell you what it's like to be stuck in there when stuff like that goes down out on the street. You miss all the birthdays, graduations, weddings and funerals. After a while you feel like you don't belong anywhere anymore, except maybe for where you are. For a guy like Worthington, though—Lynn, I can't even imagine what it must be like to be stuck in there when you didn't even do anything to deserve it." He ate another piece of meat, dragging it through his mashed potatoes first. "It's hot all the time, and there are bugs…the water stinks—literally—and the medical care is non-existent. The beds, too…in every joint I've ever been in, the mattress is only an inch thick and set on these metal coil springs, World War II surplus beds made for the short term, not years on end. I've got permanent nerve damage in both legs from those beds. And then there's the laundry. Shit comes back looking like it was soaked in a vat of rancid tea."

"Sounds awful," I said, suddenly feeling guilty for sitting here eating one of the most expensive things on the menu.

"It sure is, little lady, and the food...man, you sometimes got rice, potatoes and pasta in the same meal. No meat, no fresh fruit, vegetables that hardly resembled anything you'd see in a garden somewhere. And you know what bothered me the most the first year?"

"No, what?"

"I kept looking at them bars and wondering what would happen if there was a fire."

I nodded. "Was it hard, with no women, I mean?"

"A lot of guys just make an arrangement with other guys, you know, taking care of each other. Me? I always figured that if you went in for that sort of thing, you were probably gay to begin with. I don't care, mind you, but it just isn't me, you know. You a straight man in prison—it's torture."

"So, in your opinion, could it drive a man crazy?"

"No doubt in my mind about that, Lynn. I *know*. I came outta there crazier than a shithouse rat and so damn angry all the time that I never thought I would ever successfully complete my probation without killing someone else. The thing is—I *did* kill someone. Maybe it was justified, but I *did* take a life. Can't even imagine what being in the slam for something you didn't do might do to you soul."

• • •

Talking with David made me realize how awful prison must be, and as I sat there I began to wonder why we call it 'corrections', when it actually seems to *create* more crime. I wondered—and not for the first time—if it was designed that way on purpose...to keep the system going, and then I shook it off. God, I was starting to sound like Samantha!

We finished eating, and then fought over the check.

"Hey, I invited *you*, remember?"

David sighed. "Ok, but I've got the tip—and next time, *I'm* buying."

"You got that," I growled, doing my best to imitate him.

David chuckled, swore under his breath, and shook his head. He followed me out to my car, and gave me a hug. That's the thing I love most about him, by the way. In all the time I've known him, he's never made a pass at me. I think he knows I think of him as a big brother, and he says I'm like a daughter to him, but he's a man, after all, and you never know. Anyway, I was comfortable enough to hug him back, and if he's ever even *thought* about stuff like that, he's kept it to himself.

"Be careful going home, Lynn."

I wanted to tell him that I was probably the most dangerous thing out here, but I smiled like a good little girl and told him I would. I got in the Mustang and loaded Chris Botti's *Italia* into the CD player, and listened to *Venice* as the car warmed up.

The ride home would only take a half hour, but I didn't have any more cash on me so I decided to hit an ATM. I stopped in the little lot on the outskirts of Farmington—you know, that little place with the dry cleaner, the Laundromat and the real estate office? Anyway, the bank was closed, and the lot was almost deserted except for two cars near the laundry place. I parked the Ford and went up to the bank, and as I slid my card into the machine I noticed a car pull in at the far end. Remembering David's admonition to be careful, I turned around as I took my cash, but the car went around back, and I didn't think anything more about it.

It was full dark, and the overcast sky wasn't helping. The nearest streetlight was thirty feet away, and the wind was making a mournful sound as it stirred the leafless tree-limbs. The cold night air felt like snow was on the way. I got nervous all of a sudden, cursing myself for letting David spook me, and as I opened the driver's side door I took a deep breath. The bank was on the corner, near the woods, but there was a little access road used for deliveries and so forth, between the side of the strip mall and the trees, and there was a dumpster there. All I can tell you is that I wasn't myself, and that whoever grabbed me must have been hiding behind that damn dumpster. I had my purse in one hand and my keys in the other, and I was leaning back a bit to get the door open, when an arm went around my neck. I'd been in enough scrapes to know when I'm fighting someone who knows what he's doing, and to tell the difference between being grabbed and being choked out. Whoever held me was good, damn good, and as he dragged me into the alley I began to black out. I assumed it was the cash, or maybe he was going to rape me, but the gun was in my purse and my purse was on the ground and…after a minute I knew the guy was most certainly trying to kill me. I fought as hard as I could, but if you've ever been choked you know it makes you panic. I began to see spots before my eyes—and then I got mad, mostly at myself for being so careless. I had taken that big breath earlier, which probably gave me the strength I needed to fight back, and because I was so angry, I was able to drive my elbows, first the left, then the right, into my attacker's sides. I kept it up, and there was a muffled grunt, so I knew I was doing at least a little damage. I took advantage of it when the arm around my neck slipped a little. I dropped to one knee, and drove my elbow straight back, hitting the guy in the cheek. He let go of me and went down, and then got up in a hurry. He wasn't big—maybe my height, but he was strong and he knew how to fight. He was also wearing a black ski mask. We traded punches and then I decked him with a good one on the chin. I didn't have time to retrieve my purse, so I went to kick him in the head—and that's when he pulled the gun. I couldn't see what it was because it was so dark, but I heard the hammer go back and assumed it was a revolver. I froze, and then headlights splashed onto the wall and the dumpster and into the woods, and whoever it was got up and ran. I went to grab my purse—and the Glock inside—but the headlights came right at me and stopped only a foot or two away. I held my hands out to my sides; blinded by all that light, ready to dive sideways into the woods and start running myself. But then I heard David's voice and I let all the air out of my lungs. I've never been the kind of girl who swoons but I was suddenly exhausted and I just stood there as he hurried over and grabbed both of my shoulders, which kept me from sinking to the ground.

"You ok?" he asked, peering into the woods as if he wanted to go after my attacker.

"Don't," I told him. "He's got a gun."

I went over and picked up my purse and he left his truck and followed me back to my car. I sat on the front seat and took a deep breath, rubbing my throat with one hand and trying to slow down my racing heart.

"Good thing I was behind you," he said. "You ok?"

"Yeah," I croaked, but David wasn't convinced.

"You know who it was?" he asked, looking over his shoulder.

"No," I told him, but that was *all* I said, because I'd learned something during the fight. Whoever had attacked me—was a woman.

• • •

When David Redman had been on probation all those years ago, he had learned to drive slowly; the last thing he had wanted back then was a run in with a traffic cop, and driving within the speed limit had become a habit with him. Because of this, he had only been a half mile or so behind me, and most probably, had saved my life.

David convinced me to spend the night at his place, and because I was so shaken up, I thought it was a good idea. We had checked behind the strip mall, looking for cars, but the rear lot had been empty. As we pulled up at his place, I got out of the Mustang slowly and just stood there holding onto the roof, waiting for my head to stop spinning.

"Yeah, you're ok, all right," he said, coming over and putting an arm across my shoulders.

"I'll be all right, Dave," I assured him. "I just need to sit down for a while."

We went inside, and Dave sat me on the couch. He went into the kitchen and I put my head back. My neck was sore and the muscles in my upper back were on fire, so I gladly accepted the three *Advil* and the glass of water he handed me when he came back in. I downed them, and he went into the kitchen again, coming back with a bottle of brandy and two small glasses. He poured one for me and sat on the other couch with the coffee table between us, looking at me as he poured two fingers for himself.

"You don't have to get me drunk to hit on me," I said, trying to hide my embarrassment with coarse humor.

David sighed. "You know something, kid—if I wasn't about a hundred years older than you, you might have something to worry about." I had hurt his feelings without meaning to.

"Sorry, pal. Just a joke."

"The shit you think is funny, Kaylyn? Most of the time…it isn't."

"Hey, it was a *joke*—ok?"

David looked at me for a very long time. Ever talk to an ex-con? They don't think like we do. Everything with them is about respect, personal space and doing their best to see right through you. You can't bullshit them, and they can tell if you're lying from a mile away. Having known David for so long, I was convinced that he believed that I knew who had jumped me—and wasn't telling him, but again I was wrong.

"I have a daughter," he said at length. "Be about your age now, maybe a year or two younger." I was dying to ask questions, despite my spinning head, but forced myself to listen. "Her mother made her stop talking to me when I went to prison, and all these years later I still have no contact with her."

"I'm sorry, David—I didn't know."

"Not telling you so you can be sorry, Lynn—I'm telling you so you'll understand how I feel about you. I love Wade like he was my own…and Sam…well, she's a hurricane, but she grows on you. You and me? We're a lot alike, and from the start, I thought…well…"

"Well, what?"

"I thought, maybe, with you, I'd have a second chance at having a daughter, so don't fool around like that no more, ok?" There were actually tears in his brown eyes, making me feel more like an ass than I already did.

"She's a grown woman now," I said, knowing he'd get mad if I said I was sorry again. "Have you tried getting in contact with *her?*"

David took a drink, and spread his hands. He lit a cigarette and blew out a plume of smoke. "There was a restraining order…"

"God, that was years ago! It must be expired by now!"

"I'm sure it has."

"Then why don't you have an attorney get in touch with her, break the ice for you?"

"I suppose I could do that, but I'm more concerned with *you* at the moment."

"I'll be all right," I told him, and lit my own cigarette.

"You really don't know who jumped you?" he asked.

"Comes with the license, David—could be anyone."

"Ok," he said, "you'll tell me when you're ready I guess. For now...I'm going to bed. Take the spare bedroom. Wade and Sam used to sleep here, back in the day, so I'm used to having company." He got up and looked at me for a very long time.

"What?" I asked, stabbing out my cigarette.

"I've already lost *one* daughter, Lynn. I don't want to lose, you, too."

He left the room, and I started crying. Some hard-boiled detective I am, huh?

• • •

David was gone when I woke up at seven-thirty the next morning. I went to the bedroom window, thinking he must be in the garage, but his truck was gone. I took a shower and got dressed, and went into the kitchen looking for coffee. On the counter was a mug, a K-cup, a banana and a box of cereal. There was a *Post-It* note on the box: "Milk's in the fridge, kiddo—be careful today."

It had been a very long time since anyone had taken care of me like that, and I ate slowly, thinking how very lucky I was to have 'family'. That might sound funny to you, but I've always believed that family is not necessarily a matter of blood, and I was grateful, to say the least.

As I drove to the office I kept going over the attack in my head. My neck still hurt, and I'd pulled a muscle in my back, but I knew I'd be ok. I also knew that I should file a report, or at least tell Spinner, but something kept me from doing so. I was afraid the cops would pull me off this thing, and even though it made sense that the case and the assault were connected, I didn't know for sure. As I'd told Dave—it comes with the territory.

My desk phone was ringing just as I unlocked the office door, and I got it on the third ring.

"Kaylyn Vale Agency," I said, holding it between my shoulder and my ear as I put down the file folders I had taken from the trunk.

"You're pretty strong for such a skinny little shit," a woman's voice told me. The voice was muffled, as if there was a cloth over the mouthpiece on the other phone, but all the same—the voice sounded familiar. I looked at the phone on my desk—the caller was "unknown", but I still knew who it was—the woman who had jumped me the night before.

"Try coming at me head on next time, bitch."

"Not a problem," the voice said, and chuckled, "but all the same—you did all right."

"What do you want?"

"Aren't you going to ask me who I am?"

"Would there be a point to that?"

"No, and I'm not giving you time to trace this, either. I just wanted to let you know that you can't stop me, and that I'm really very, very disappointed in you. See you around, Lynn."

The caller rang off, and just then, Samantha Ashbery came in—sporting a bruise on her cheek.

• • •

Being paranoid does funny things to you. Makes you think odd thoughts. Even when they don't make sense. I hadn't even *thought* about Sam as a possibility in the attack, but that bruise on her face threw me, and for a moment, I wanted to ring her neck.

"Hey," she said. "You ok? Must have been *some* call."

That gave me a moment to regain my composure, and since she had literally been coming in the door while I was taking the call, it couldn't possibly have been Sam on the phone.

"What happened to your cheek?" I asked, putting the phone back in the cradle.

Sam laughed, and put a hand self-consciously to her face. "Oh, that bad, huh? My son did this last night with a baseball. Mr. Wonderful gave it to him. Nice, huh?"

I was still tense enough to throw myself at her, but I took a deep breath, and promised myself I'd check her phone, first chance I got. Sam was wearing jeans, sneakers and that denim jacket she favors, and the little pouch was on her waist.

"Lynn?" she said. "What's wrong?"

"I got jumped last night, Sam," I decided to tell her, looking directly into her eyes, "and whoever it was, just called me."

"Oh, my God! Who was it?" she asked, taking off her jacket and coming over to hug me.

I wanted to hold her off, and I wanted to punch her in the face, but it *couldn't* be her, I thought, it just *couldn't* be! I was falling in love with this woman, and I felt so stupid and so vulnerable and so angry, that I simply didn't know which way to turn, so I ended up just standing there, letting her hold me, as she rubbed my back with both hands like I was a child.

"Are you ok?" she whispered.

"Yeah," I managed, "nothing's damaged but my pride."

Sam pushed me to arm's length and drilled me with her gorgeous green eyes. "Are you *sure* you're ok?"

I nodded and touched her cheek. "You're hurt worse than I am." If she was playing me, she was very, very good at it.

"And they *called* you?"

"I'm not sure, Sam, because it *could* just be someone messing with us, but I'm willing to bet a saw-buck against a C-note that the guy who jumped me has something to do with our killer." I had deliberately lied about the caller's gender, just to gauge her reaction, but, again, I got nothing.

"What did he say?"

I frowned. "Mind if I wait and tell you and Spinelli at the same time?" I had no intention of telling the police, not now, at any rate, and I was just trying to put her off. The look on her face was one of pure concern, and I suddenly felt very foolish about suspecting her.

"I guess not," she said, although she made no attempt to hide her disappointment.

"We're taking Donnelly in tomorrow, and I don't want to complicate things with something that could very well turn out to be a hoax. Now, let's get to work."

To refresh your memory, we were working on the assumption that the killer—or killers—were spelling out that word, "JUDGES"— J for Jordan; U for Unger; D for Donato; G for Gregory and E for Edwards.

It could also be possible, we had decided, that the killer wasn't spelling *anything*, but I didn't buy that. And then there was the matter of the months spelling out the name "JASON"—J for July; A for August: S for September; O for October and N for November. Now that we were into December, Jason Donnelly fit the profile very well. The Feds that had been called in said this was a classic sort of telegraphing a punch so to speak, the killer giving us a clue to his identity as it were, but again I didn't buy it. I knew now that the killer was a woman, and worse, I knew that I knew her, and just couldn't place her. Maybe Donnelly *was* involved, but if he was, she was using him as a decoy... either that, or the whole damn thing with the name J-A-S-O-N was just an unhappy co-incidence.

I come on like I know what I'm doing, but the identity of the killer was right under my nose and I was too smitten with Sam, too stressed out and too exhausted to see it. The knowledge nagged at me, but I shook it off and concentrated on the task at hand—it was all I had at the moment and it all seemed to fit.

"Ok," I told her, sitting down and grabbing my pen. "The Feds are going to watch Simpson, Sanders and Siebert from now until the end of the month." If you recall, the three of them were the only active judges whose last names ended in "S", and if our theory was correct, killing one of them would nicely finish the word, JUDGES, and on the 19th of December, since S was the 19th letter of the alphabet. "That leaves us free to take down Donnelly."

"You don't seem too happy about that," Sam told me.

"That's because I'm not. I'm convinced that Donnelly's not our guy. It's why I insisted that we keep a guard on these three until *well* past the 19th."

"If you're that sure about Donnelly...why are we bothering with him at all?"

"Because I *could* be wrong," I told her in a quiet little voice. "And because—I've been wrong about people before."

• • •

I'm sure you read about the Donnelly debacle in the papers. I hate being right all the time, but the Feds gummed up the works just as I knew they would, and two police officers, as *well* as Jason Donnelly, were killed. It went down like this. We assembled out team on the corner of the Avenue, and went in heavily armed. Spinelli was punishing me for bringing in Sam, so we were on the outside, and it's a good thing we were, because the kid was armed to the teeth.

They kicked down his door and found him lying in bed with some skinny little hooker he'd picked up the night before, but instead of going quietly, Donnelly grabbed an old Navy .45 that he had under the bed and shot the first cop that came through the door in the face. So much for Kevlar vests, eh? They returned fire, and hit Donnelly once in the shoulder, but he rolled out of bed and grabbed a modified M16 that we later learned had been stolen from an Army base, and shot up two other cops, killing one by hitting him in the back of the head.

That pretty much squashed any chance of taking him alive and questioning him, but when you have two groups—well, three counting Sam and me—all trying to get the credit, things don't tend to go well.

The press conference later focused on the two "Heroic Officers" who had been killed in the line of duty, and the Feds leaked some information that they were sure that Donnelly was our killer, but I knew he wasn't...whether I hate being right most of the time or not.

• • •

I know it seems like I'm glossing over all of the action, but trust me when I tell you the *real* action hadn't even begun. This thing was far from over, and once again we got it wrong. Badly.

On the following Saturday night I was home alone, watching television when the phone rang. I don't know how to explain how I knew who the caller was—but I did.

I picked up on the second ring.

"I was expecting you to call *last* night," I said.

"Well, hello to you, too!"

The woman's voice was still muffled, and it was driving me crazy, because I knew her, or *thought* I did.

"What do you want?"

"Nothing—not a thing. Just two old friends, catching up."

"So, this whole thing? It's about me?"

"Wow—what an ego! No, Kaylyn, I know you don't believe in them but you being involved…it's just a co-incidence. Incidentally, why aren't you having your calls traced?"

"How do you know I'm not?"

"If you could get your head out from between your girlfriend's legs for five seconds maybe you'd figure it out. Not that I blame you, Lynn. If I was going to switch teams, it would be for a girl like her."

I wasn't going to play games with her regarding Sam, so I tried something else. "Are you ever going to tell me why you're disappointed in me?"

"VERY disappointed, actually. But, no…I'm not going to tell you until you explain why you're not having our calls monitored."

"Maybe I just want to keep this between us. Why don't you tell me who you are, if we're such good friends?"

"Really, Lynn—I've taken it easy on you for the first five rounds of our fight, but I'm not going to *throw* it for you, either."

"That what this is, a prize fight?"

"No, Lynn, but let me tell you a story. A while back, there was this police chief in Farmington. Most everyone knew he was dirty, and had ordered his men to take out Sam Ashbery and maybe that reporter she was hanging with. They were doing so because the girl's stepfather was paying them off, and suddenly, the chief just happens to commit suicide. Lot of folks in the business figured you had something to do with that."

Remember I told you about the Ashbery trial? Wade and Sam had been forced to flee because the Farmington Police had released her step-father without even informing the District Attorney about the assault on her. All the deaths that occurred after that—it was all because of that one guy. And my caller was right—some people in the know believed I *had* been the one to silence him—but then again, I didn't understand the connection between that and what was now taking place with all these judges…and I told her so.

"Seriously, Lynn? The note he left, the way in which he was killed, no sign of forced entry, and absolutely no evidence at the scene? That's *classic* 'Company', honey."

"I still don't see what that has to do with this."

"Because you of all people should understand how utterly unfair our system is, Lynn! That innocent people are railroaded just to perpetuate the damn system! That it's all a game, and has nothing whatsoever to do with justice!"

"So all these dead judges—they've harmed you in some way?" I asked, stalling for time.

The caller was silent for a long while, and then sighed. "I expected more from you, Lynn—I really did. Stay out of this—or I'll *take* you out."

The line went dead, and I just sat there, trying to figure it all out. Now more than ever—and for obvious reasons—I knew I couldn't tell the police about this, that I was in this for keeps, but I still couldn't rid myself of the feeling that I was missing something that was right under my nose.

• • •

Most everyone involved was breathing easier as we got closer to the 19th—most everyone that is, except me, so I wasn't really surprised when Spinelli called me on the morning of December 13th. I wish I could explain why I'm like that, but I can't. I just know things that I can't explain, and those nagging feelings I always tell you about never seem to let me down.

Sam and I were both in the office that morning. I had actually given her some work on another case while we were waiting this out, and I was paying some bills when the phone rang.

"Kaylyn Vale," I said.

"We've got another one, Lynn," he sighed, sounding old and beaten.

I knew what he was talking about, but some part of me simply needed to hear it.

"Another what, Spinner?"

"You familiar with downtown Providence?"

"Like the back of my hand, why?"

"Meet me at the Barlow Tower as soon as you can get here. Judge Elizabeth Mahoney was shot and killed only an hour ago—and this time, somebody actually saw the killer."

• • •

The Barlow Tower is named for the famous Civil War Era painter, John Noble Barlow, and overlooks the river downtown. The waiting list to get into that place is two years, and if you have to ask how much the rent is you probably can't afford it.

It was raining that morning, a cold and dreary day, and I wasn't about to walk all the way from the lot on Commercial Street. Sam and I drove over there in my Mustang, and I actually pulled into the parking garage under the Barlow. I flashed my I.D. at the young cop on duty, told him that Lieutenant Spinelli was expecting us and we went straight to the elevators.

Judge Mahoney had lived in a pent-house apartment, so I knew she was well off. Big surprise, huh? There were 26 floors in the building, and I could tell all the way up that Sam was nervous. As beautiful and capable as she is, there's a lot of the little girl in her, and she gives herself away when she's stressed: little things like biting the inside of her lips, twisting her hair and blinking a lot.

Despite the situation, I really wanted to just grab her and kiss her—hard. "You ok?" I asked.

"No, not really," she admitted. "I thought we had this figured out…but the letter 'M'? What the hell are we dealing with here, Lynn?"

"I was wondering that myself, actually. At first I thought that maybe we were wrong about the word, JUDGES—and I guess we were, but then I thought that maybe the killer was spelling out JUDGMENT…but that's no good, see? Because there's an 'E' after the 'G', for Edwards. Or maybe he isn't really spelling anything."

"He *could* be spelling out JUDGEMENT, Lynn. It's a disputed spelling. In law we spell it with no 'E', but the *Bible* frequently spells it J-U-D-G-*E*-M-E-N-T. See what I mean?"

"You sure?"

Sam hitched up her shoulders in what passed for a shrug. "I'm a writer, remember?"

The doors opened just then and we found ourselves looking at two more uniformed cops. I asked for Spinelli and they led us down the hall.

Judge Elizabeth Mahoney was probably sixty years old, and lived alone except for a housekeeper who came in three days a week and sometimes made her meals. The apartment was gorgeous, with several original paintings, hand-made tapestries and selected prints by Winslow Homer adorning the walls. She seemed to have preferred seascapes. There was Berber Carpet on the floors, and the bathroom looked like something out of an episode of *Dynasty*.

The victim was lying naked on the tile near the bathtub in a pool of blood, shot once in the forehead. She'd been reaching for a towel at the time and had fallen out of the tub when she'd been shot. I tried to keep Sam out in the living room, but she looked in, made a face, and went back out. To her credit—she kept her breakfast down.

I squatted to examine the body and got back up on knees that creaked—I really *had* to get more consistent with my running schedule.

"Thirty-two caliber?" I asked.

Spinelli nodded. "That would be my guess, Lynn—we'll find out after the autopsy, but what the hell are we *dealing* with here? Her last name is *Mahoney*, for Christ's sake!" He bit his lower lip and shook his head. "The Feds are going to *fry* me for this letter 'S' thing, wasting all that time watching Simpson and the other two!"

I gave him Sam's take on the disputed spelling, and he swore.

"For God's sake, Lynn! So what are you telling me now? That we're back to watching judges with a last name ending in E!" He had raised his voice and I didn't like it so I gave it right back to him.

"You know what, Bobby? I was perfectly happy minding my own damn business! You want me out, just say so!"

Spinelli sighed, and his shoulders dropped. "No, Lynn, and I'm sorry. Truth is, I'd be lost without you on this one. If you say this is the way to go, I'll run it by the Captain."

I was too angry at being yelled at to accept his apology, but I wasn't about to walk away from this case, either. "Was there a note?"

"Yeah...in the bedroom, and you won't like it."

There was a quote from Matthew Chapter 7 written on the dresser mirror...in blood: *"Why do you look at the mote in your brother's eye and ignore the plank in your own?"*

I looked at that for a long, long time, thinking about the woman who had called me, and sure that this clue was specifically for me. I don't know why, but I did. Part of me was thinking about how badly I had injured my own step-brother, and part of me was thinking about the caller being a woman—and did *she* have a brother? And then I thought: *she thinks* I *killed that Police Chief—is she saying* I'm *a hypocrite?* Or was it just another Bible quote being used to highlight what the killer was trying to say? That no one has the right to judge another?

"You're wondering why he switched it up," Spinner said, misreading me, because this hadn't been left in a *Word* document.

I looked around the room. "No, not really—there's no computer in here. Is there one in another room?"

Spinelli shook his head.

"Where's your witness?" I asked, noting with some satisfaction that my voice was still quite terse.

"In here," he said, and left the room.

I followed him, grabbing Sam's arm as we left the living room and entered the kitchen, where a pretty, young Hispanic girl with long dark hair was sitting at the table with a glass of water before her, giving her statement to some other detective. She was wearing a brown and tan maid's uniform.

"Hey, LT," he said, addressing Spinelli. "We're just about finished here." The other detective was around forty, and well built, and had eyes only for Samantha, which pissed me off. "Did you want to talk to her?"

"Can we have a moment alone?" I asked Spinner, ignoring the guy completely.

Bobby tilted his head at the door, and the guy left. "All yours," he said to me as he folded his arms and leaned against the counter.

"I'm Detective Vale," I told the girl. "Can you describe the man you saw?"

I was having a hard time keeping the gender of my own suspect out of my sentences, and it was beginning to wear on me. I knew Sam was expecting me to tell her and Spinner about the person who had jumped me and I hoped she could keep her mouth shut.

As it turned out, the girl spoke only in broken English, but did a pretty good job of describing the build of my own attacker.

"And you didn't see his face?"

"No, Ma'am—it was covered with one of those hat masks."

I pushed her a little bit more, and came away with the fact that the perpetrator had been wearing a black ski mask...the same kind the woman who jumped *me* had been wearing. "Thank you," I said, and turned to Spinelli.

"You get what you needed?" he asked.

"Not yet—but I'm working on it."

Back in the elevator Sam asked me exactly what I was looking for. I could tell that she was dying to know the whole story I had promised to give, but she held her tongue.

I could also tell that the sight of all that blood had shaken her. "Why don't you come home with me," I said, touching her hair, "and I'll tell you everything?"

"You don't want to go back to the office?" Sam inquired, and swallowed nervously.

"What do *you* want right now, Samantha?" I asked quietly.

"I think I want to come home with you," she admitted.

"Then come with me," I told her in a husky voice.

Samantha smiled. "That's the plan," she said.

CHAPTER SIX—January

The rest of the month passed quickly, and before I knew it New Year's Eve had come and gone. I was on edge, and seeking redemption for all I'd done wrong. No one is perfect; I know *I'm* not—but I haven't lived a good life and I was anxious to make up for at least some of it by stopping the killer before she could get to anyone else.

You probably think I'm crazy for getting so involved with Sam, but because she was still a suspect, at least in in *my* mind, I wanted to keep her close, and taking her home with me on that dreary December day had been a big part of that. I was also in love with her at the time and I'm not going to apologize for that. Sam and Wade threw a Christmas Party that year—it wasn't as festive as it should have been, not with the newspapers hounding and criticizing our efforts, but this had become a national story, and people were scared.

Wade Ashbery all but ignored me at their little party, but who could blame him? I had seduced him in Afghanistan, and he probably suspected that I was sleeping with his wife. I could tell right off that things were not going well for them, and I left early. Sam walked me to my car, and wanted to know what we were going to do next.

"Well, if we're going with your theory on the word, JUDGEMENT, Sam, then we only have five days to work with once the new month starts." As E was the 5th letter of the alphabet, our killer would strike again on the 5th of January, which didn't leave us much time. "But this time—it's going to be different."

"What are you thinking?"

"You hanging in there with me on this?"

"All the way," she assured me, meeting my eyes.

"Ok then, here's what we're going to do. Starting tomorrow, you and I are going to go through every single case in the past five years of every judge whose last name begins with E. The judge who seems to be the harshest is going to be *ours*, Sam."

"What do you mean—ours?"

"Whoever we agree upon, you and I are going to stake him out, and this time, we're going to catch the killer before he strikes."

I still hadn't told her about the woman who had tried to kill me. I hadn't even told Bobby, let alone Clair, but I wanted to keep Sam close, especially while we were keeping our target under surveillance, if only to eliminate Sam as a suspect. I knew I was risking an obstruction of justice charge by keeping this to myself, but this was personal with me now, and I wanted to deal with it on my own.

"You mean—try to be there before it happens?"

"That's exactly what I mean, Sam—assuming we pick the right judge. I'm going to have the State Police and the Feds watch the other potential targets, but we're not going to tell anyone else what we're doing."

"That's something I've been meaning to ask you," she said. "There are no interstate incidents in this whole thing. Why are the Feds involved in the first place?"

"Some of that's political," I told her, "but some of these judges have issued decisions on the Federal level, and that got their foot in the door, so to speak."

"I'd feel better about this if I was fully licensed," she said.

"We'll take care of that first thing." I opened my car door, and met her eyes. "You and Wade—not good?"

"Is it that obvious?"

I shrugged.

Sam sighed. "I guess I've never forgiven him for faking his death, Lynn, and he's never forgiven me for being with Jenn. I honestly don't know if we're going to make it." She brushed back her beautiful straight hair, and God help me, I almost said "I love you", right then and there.

"I'm here for you, either way," I told her, and gave her a kiss on the cheek. As I drove off, something she had said bothered me. Wade, had, indeed, faked his death. What kind of a man would do that to the woman he loved?

As the days and weeks passed, that simple fact would weigh heavily on my thinking, but at that moment, I was too angry at myself for letting these killings go on for so long with nothing to show for it, and too smitten with Sam to think clearly. That would change, but not until we were on the edge—a place I've stood for most of my life.

• • •

Ashley Vaughn, my old Agency contact, was in town over the New Year's weekend. Ashley is a cute blonde and has a *fantastic* little body… and if she was any straighter you could use her for a ruler. Because of that, our New Year's Eve together consisted of visiting her ailing mother and then ordering Chinese Food. What can I say? It was better than spending the night alone, and she gave me her personal cell phone number, in case I needed any more help with the case. As it would turn out, that would eventually become extremely useful.

I was in the office by myself at eight o'clock in the morning on January 2nd. Since the Christmas Party, Sam and I had gone through all of the cases, and ended up picking Superior Court Judge Richard Evans as out "target". Our reasoning went like this: in over 90% of his cases, Judge Evans had gone several times over the sentencing guidelines. Once, he had even overturned the Not Guilty verdict handed down by the jury. He was notorious for bending the law to ensure a conviction, and instead of abiding by the Due Process Clause of the U.S. Constitution, seemed to delight in abrogating Constitutional Safeguards; the law, it seemed, didn't apply to defendants if he, personally, thought they were guilty. His personal profile clearly showed that God, Himself, gave him the right to harm other human beings, and he did not restrain himself from speaking to defense attorneys as if they were red-headed step-children. Sam pointed out that, if the law didn't apply fairly to everyone, then it meant nothing, but that obviously didn't matter to Richie Evans—who appeared to believe that the law was his to bend to his own whims. He routinely denied motions for new trials, even when he clearly knew he was wrong, and secretly had stock options in at least two private prisons. His only daughter had run away from home when she was only fifteen, and his ex-wife didn't talk to him. All in all, not a good guy to draw for a criminal case. The ACLU actually referred to this guy as "The Hanging Judge", but regardless of what anyone thought of him, I was going to do my best to keep him alive.

I had no way of knowing if he *would* be the killer's next victim, but he looked like the most obvious choice.

Next I turned my attention to the Donato case—the one where Kyle Worthington had been caught red-handed and later found hanging in his cell. That case in particular disturbed me, because it was so very different from all the others. I told you before that all of the murders up to this point had been committed up close and personal, with a .32 caliber revolver as the weapon of choice. Each murder had been meticulously planned and carried out, but Worthington had been sloppy, rushed the whole matter, and killed from a distance—with a scoped rifle. It lead to one of two conclusions: either he had been a copy-cat, or there was more than one killer.

Sam came in at nine-thirty, and asked me what I was working on. Her hair was in a pony-tail and she was wearing a gray sweat suit and her padded denim jacket; I could tell right away that she hadn't slept well. I didn't say anything about it. When you've been to bed with another woman it is never a good idea to tell her she looks like shit.

I keep a geological survey map in my office, and I reached behind me to answer her question. "Evans lives in a rambling old farm house up near the Smith and Sayles Reservoir." I pointed to the spot on the map with a pinky.

"That's the town of Chepachet, up by the Branch River."

"You know the area?' I asked.

Sam nodded. "The Branch flows north towards North Smithfield, and eventually to the Blackstone River; in the 19th Century, it provided energy for all the textile mills." She smiled wistfully. "Wade and I used to take a canoe up there, once upon a time."

"Any river traffic?"

"Yeah, lots of people keep boats on docks behind their houses. And there's a ton of little fish sheds and boat houses." Sam was standing behind me, and leaned closer. As usual she smelled like vanilla. "Why?"

"I'm thinking we can rent a rowboat up at the reservoir. Lot of fishing up there, as I understand it."

"You want to row down by his house and watch it from the woods?"

"Something like that, yeah. I was actually thinking about taking a ride out there today to scope it out." I peered at the map. "Right here," I told her, tapping the map, "there's a hill overlooking the Evans place. We can go down there and find out how to keep an eye on the place."

"You don't plan on telling him he's being watched?"

"He already knows…but not about *us*."

"Got the picture," Sam said and nodded.

"We'll have to be there for the whole day, Sammy, from twelve-oh-one the night before, until eleven-fifty-nine the next day. All we know is that the murder will be attempted on the 5th, but we don't know *when*." I turned to her and was almost overwhelmed by how *good* she smelled. "You up for that?"

"Yeah, but are you sure we won't be bumping heads with the team that's officially watching him?"

"We'll make sure of it, partner. They'll be *watching* the house… you and I…we'll be *in* the house."

Sam pursed her lips, started to say something, and then changed her mind.

"What?" I pressed.

"This seems awful personal with you, Lynn…and I not sure why."

I had thought and thought about what I wanted to do, and *struggled* with it for days, and at that moment couldn't let the opportunity slip by. I got up, wrapped my arms around her and hugged her. Sam looked surprised when I released her, but she smiled. I looked straight in her eyes and let it fly.

"That's because it is—and I'm not going to let this bitch make a fool out of me again."

Sam's brow furrowed, and her face crinkled up the way it does when she's not sure she understands something. "What do you mean—*bitch?* What haven't you told me, Kaylyn?"

"The night I got jumped…it was a woman, and she's called me twice since then, taunting me." I was looking directly into her eyes as I said it, and if she was playing me she was better than anyone else I've ever known.

"And you didn't *tell* me?"

"I didn't tell *anyone*, Sam. Not a soul."

For a brief moment, tears sprang to her eyes, and then her look hardened. "I thought…"

"You thought what?"

Sam blinked. "I thought, you and I…I thought we…*had* something together. Why would you keep something like this from me?"

"What exactly do we have, Samantha?"

"Do I have to draw you a picture, Lynn?"

"You're a married woman, Sam—yeah, draw me a picture."

Sam opened her mouth, pressed her lips together and looked like she was going to cry. And then she closed her eyes and kissed me tenderly. I slipped my hands up and under her sweatshirt and cupped her big, beautiful breasts in my hands, returning the kiss ardently. Sam made a little sound in the back of her throat and then pulled me over to the couch.

"Say it," I demanded, as she pushed me down and got on top of me. "*Say* it!"

"I love you, stupid," she said. "I've tried hard not to—but I do."

"I love you, too," I sighed, and figured we could spare an hour or so before heading out.

• • •

If you've seen the film, *Basic Instinct,* you'll understand what I'm about to tell you. In the movie, the Michael Douglas character is almost *certain* that Sharon Stone is the killer, but he's so attracted to her that it clouds his judgment. I wasn't that far gone—even though I *was* in love with her—but I wanted her close…just in case she kept an icepick under her bed…

• • •

Sam drove her Jeep, and we got to the reservoir around noon. We rented a rowboat and headed out. When we were a mile or so from the Evans place, we tied the boat off and started out on foot. An hour later we found what we were looking for—that little hill with a vantage point on the house. Evans lived alone, and was in court that morning, and I wanted to see what kind of security he had in place. As it turned out—he had none…I wasn't surprised: he was an arrogant bastard and probably didn't go anywhere unarmed. There was actually a little plaque on the front door, with an etching of a Colt .45. The caption read: "*I do NOT dial 911.*"

It only took a minute to get in, and we made our way upstairs, assuming his bedroom would be on the second floor. The house smelled disused, musty and damp, but the upstairs windows were all open a crack, and the heat was set at sixty.

Sam hadn't touched a thing, but I told her to put on the rubber gloves I had given her, and she did so now, making a face.

"What's wrong?" I asked.

"Are you shitting me? We just broke into a judge's *house*, Lynn!"

"We didn't *break* anything," I told her and chuckled.

"Funny. Remind me I'm not talking to you!"

I took her gloved hand and lead her downstairs. The back door led to a screened-in porch, and there was an old-style barrel-bolt on the door to the house. I opened the door, went out to undo the latch on the screen door, and went back to the lock. It was a simple matter to tape the bolt so I could just turn the knob when I had to three days from now.

"Now, what?" Sam asked.

"Now we go back upstairs and find a place to hide."

I found what we were looking for right away: a spare bedroom at the end of his hallway—with a view of the stairs leading up from his living room. Unless the killer climbed in an upstairs window, which wasn't likely since the house was built on a hill, whoever wanted to get to Evans would have to walk right by where Sam and I would be hiding. I unslung my gym bag and quickly installed a tiny camera in the old-style wall lamp. I clicked it to the 'on' position, and then checked the feed on my receiver.

"Excellent," I said. "Come on, let's get out of here."

"I heard that," Sam said.

We were just starting down the stairs, when we heard a car come up the dirt road outside. I briefly considered using the back door, but by then there were already footsteps on the front porch and I had no way of knowing who might be around back. I had taken the time to lock the front door behind us, but there wasn't anywhere to go now but back upstairs.

"Come on," I hissed, grabbing Sam's hand.

We got into the spare bedroom just as I heard a key in the lock downstairs, but I didn't have time to shut the door. We heard male voices, but couldn't tell what was being said. I went to the window while Sam stood there biting her lower lip, and looked out. I had been right about no one being able to use an upstairs window—the hill slopped away from the house and the nearest tree was fifty feet away. The only way out was though that window and into the tree, but since neither of us are exactly like Sylvester Stallone in *First Blood*, I didn't relish the idea of throwing ourselves at a tree limb.

There was a closet, and I pulled Sam inside just as the men started up the stairs. I wanted to look at my receiver, but it was already in my bag. Sam's eyes were wide in the near gloom as I put a finger to her beautiful full lips, and she nodded once, indicating that she was ok.

I closed the closet door until only a crack was showing, and pulled out my Glock.

The men continued talking in gruff tones, but I still couldn't make out what was being said. Had I been right about the killer having an accomplice, or was this something else? Were they ripping the place off? And if so—how did they have a key? What would they do if they found us? And what if Evans had hired private security that might shoot first and ask questions later?

The men were at the top of the stairs now, and I clearly heard Spinelli's voice, talking to another man. I relaxed, until I realized that we were far from all right. If Spinelli had been alone I could have openly approached him—but if the other guy was his captain…or a Federal Agent, we were in trouble. I didn't think this would get us any jail time, not since we were involved in the case, but the Feds can be pissy and I knew they'd yank my license as soon as look at me.

They walked down the hall to the main bedroom and continued talking, and then came back. I still couldn't make out what was being said, but then they opened the door to the spare room and came in.

"Is this guy serious?" the other man asked Spinelli, and I risked a peek through the little space where the door and the hinges met the frame. I'd been right—the other man was a Federal Supervisor, and he looked pissed.

"We tried to get him to stay in another location, Agent Tanner, but no doing. Evans is an ex-Marine, and old school. When I told him his life was in danger he actually laughed at me."

"Yeah, well, he'll be laughing out the other side of his face if our *perp* gets in here. Just *look* at this place! Like a fucking sieve!"

"All we can do is watch the house and hope for the best. We told him we wanted men inside, but he laughed *that* off, too."

"Christ! What an asshole!"

"I told you, this guy is Old Testament, and no joke. I honestly think the fucker is *hoping* for a confrontation." Spinelli frowned. "Did you see the sign on his fucking door?"

"Okay, okay!" the other man said, and threw up his hands. "We don't know who the target is anyway. Maybe we'll get lucky. I'll put some guys with scopes on that hill over there the night before, and another man to patrol the grounds. Come on; let's get to the next one. We're running out of time here."

"That would be Everly, Phillip F.," Spinner said, looking at his notebook.

"You're shitting me? Like the fucking Everly Brothers?"

"That's what it says."

"Jesus!"

"Yeah, I guess that's what the *F* is for," Spinner told him and both of them laughed.

The Federal Agent came over to the window and looked out. "Well, no one's getting up *this* way, not without a ladder, anyway." He actually grabbed the edge of the door and for a second we thought he would pull it open. "Come on, Spinelli. You said there was a coffee shop around here?"

"Back at the reservoir."

They walked out, still talking, and started down the stairs. Sam and I were still holding our breath when the front door closed, but we didn't move until we heard the car pull away. Then we started giggling, and I ended up kissing her.

"Fun, huh?" I asked her.

Her eyes were wide as we stood up. "Yeah," Sam quipped. "I never had it so good!"

"Really?" I made a pout. "In that case, I'd better ramp up my game."

"Honey," she said, and kissed me. "You ramp your game up any more and we'll never get off the couch!"

"My kind of girl," I said with a huge grin.

We waited out back for a full fifteen minutes, and started down the old logging trail leading to the water. The woods were thick down here, so I was hoping we'd have plenty of cover. Sam asked me what I was looking at as we got back in the boat.

"That Fed told Spinner he was going to have guys with scopes on that hill." I pointed. "And a man patrolling the ground." I shook my head. "We're probably going to have to get here earlier than I thought we'd have to, Sammy, and we'll have to wear dark clothes." A thought suddenly occurred to me. "Hey, how are you going to get away for that long?"

"I don't know, Sam admitted, "but I've got a couple of days—I'll think of something."

"Can you row?"

"Sure. You want to head back?"

"No—row a mile upstream. I want to see what we've got."

"What are we looking for?"

"Docks, abandoned houses, fishing sheds and shacks. Everything. Nothing. I won't know until I see it. You ok with that? I'll row back to the reservoir."

There were at least a dozen places along the way where we could hide out, and by extension, just as many for our enemy. We turned around, and I took the oars. "You know, I was just thinking."

"I thought I smelled wood burning," Sam said as she leaned back and lit a cigarette. God, her hair looked so beautiful in the sunlight!

I flipped her 'the bird', but couldn't help but chuckle. She had handled herself well. "Our killer's got to be local. No way she could have done all this without being right here under our noses. Fact is, she might have already scoped out the terrain just as we have."

"You really think it's a woman?"

"I *know* it is, Sam," I said, and drilled her with my eyes.

We stopped in a little restaurant on the way home that specialized in seafood and shared a late lunch. Sam had crab-cakes and I got fish and chips, and we talked about our game plan. Over coffee I told her to go home and get plenty of rest.

"We'll need to get here around ten o'clock on the night of the fourth," I told her, "so rest up for the next couple of days and try to come up with a plausible reason for getting away."

"I've got a girlfriend up in Attleboro who just had breast cancer surgery," Sam said. "Wade hates her. I'm sure if I told him I was staying with her, he wouldn't even *question* it. My mother-in-law will watch the kids—especially for something like that."

"All right. I'll call you tomorrow afternoon, after I go over my maps again."

"What are you going to do tonight?"

"Sleep. And so are you."

"What about this afternoon?" Sam said, looking at her watch. I knew what she was thinking. It would only be four or so when we got back.

"What have you got in mind?" I asked, in my best, soft girly-girl-voice. That's what I loved best about her—we took turns seducing each other.

"You'll just have to wait and see."

"I don't have a problem with that," I told her, and thought to myself—*if she is the one…at least I'll go out with a smile on my face!*

• • •

Sam and I met at my office a nine-o'clock on the night of the 4th. I had taken out two of my old commando uniforms, in flat black, and we managed to get dressed without being silly. I had rented a car for the trip, because I didn't want anyone to see either of ours, and we parked both cars around back, where no one could see them.

We stopped for iced coffee, and hit the road in the rental.

"*Ice* coffee?" she asked. "In January?"

"Keeps you energized, Babe. Something hot would only slow us down."

"Makes sense," she said, and lit a cigarette to go with it.

I pulled my straw out of the cup, and placed a napkin over the top to shake it up. The sugar never really melts with all that ice, and if you like it sweet, as I do, you've got to move it around.

"How'd your story go over?"

"He actually grunted once, while he was going over his wrestling schedule for the month." She shook her head and sighed.

"I'm sorry, Sam," I said, and meant it." I looked sideways at her as I drove. "You still love him, don't you?"

"I seem to be able to love two people at the same time, Lynn. Do it all the time."

For a moment I actually thought she was going to cry, but then she got control of herself and we made the rest of the trip in relative silence.

We parked at the reservoir, and got in the little row boat I had rented earlier in the day.

The river was dark, like an ebony ribbon under that cloud-covered January moon. It was a cold night but there was hardly any breeze. The water made little rings while I rowed, and I looked around. With all these trees no one would be able to see us approach—but then again, the killer, if she had had similar thoughts, would have the same cover.

Have you ever been on a river in the dark? If there's anything more romantic I'm sure I don't know what it is. The breeze stirs the trees gently, and even in the winter you can hear a frog or two—at least, I *hoped* they were frogs. The water is still, like a dark mirror, and you can almost touch the sky. For a fleeting moment I wondered what it would be like to make a life with the girl behind me, and then I shook it off—there was work to do, and no room for woolgathering.

I've told you before—if you're living your life alone, I understand you; if you have somebody, you're luckier than most.

The clouds looked like swirls of our ice coffee in the water by the time we got to the little inlet we'd used two days before, and the ground was cold and hard, so our boots left no prints. We got onto the old logging road, and started up to the house. I had been hoping to get some kind of *Intel* on the patrol, but Spinner had been unusually uncooperative. In the end I had decided that it really didn't matter, because a guy walking around in the woods at night is free to go where he chooses.

I just hoped we didn't run in to him.

The trees were dark and skeletal, except for the evergreens. Ever read a Ray Bradbury novel? *The Halloween Tree* or, perhaps, *Something Wicked This Way Comes*? No other writer, EVER, described the woods at night better than Bradbury; he can actually make you *feel* the cold and the wind or hear train whistles in the distance; he makes you *feel*... what you're feeling.

I guess, at that moment, Kaylyn Vale was having her own peak experience, because I grabbed Sam's hand—in love with her; afraid of her...afraid *for* her, and not willing to trade a moment of it. This was certainly not the time or the place for declarations of true love, but something compelled me to stop, and take her in my arms for a kiss.

She looked dazed when I let her go, but smiled gently.

"What was that for?'

"I just wanted you to know that I love you, Samantha."

"Jesus, don't scare me like that, Kaylyn! I love *you*, too! Tell me later when we're *out* of this, ok?"

"Ok," I agreed, and looked ahead into the night.

It was ten-twenty when we reached the edge of the trees. We stood there in the dark, dressed all in black, looking at the Evans house, which looked like something out of a Stephen King novel under all those clouds. I knew from talking to Spinner that Judge Evans was already home, and that the State Police, as well as the Feds, were already watching.

"Now what?" Sam whispered to me.

"We need to get inside," I whispered back, "but I want to wait a few minutes, to see if a patrol comes by."

Ten minutes must have gone by, and then we saw movement on the north side of the house, facing the river. The wind had picked up, and it was awful just standing there. A lone man was walking along the access road by the water, going away from us. We couldn't see details, but I've seen enough soldiers on guard duty to recognize one when I saw one. I didn't know how wide a perimeter he had set, and I was gambling that he was alone, but I was confident enough to believe we had at least enough time to make a dash for the back door.

"Come on," I told Sam. "It's now or never."

Samantha grabbed my arm. "Wait! Aren't there men on the hill?"

"Yeah, but the house is between us and their position. Let's move!"

I went first, running in a crouch. It took only seconds, but being exposed like that made it seem a lot longer than it was. I flattened myself against the side of the house near the door, and Sam became part of the wall right beside me; I had been right about her—she was a natural. I listened for a moment, but the only sound inside or out was the wind sighing through the fir trees. I opened the screen door gently, and gave the inside door a slight push. It slipped open without a sound, and we were in. I paused to put that little strip of tape in my pocket, and turned to Sam, with a finger to my lips.

The heat was still on low—I guessed no higher than sixty-five, but we were wearing black ski masks and after being outside for so long the place felt like a sauna. Sweat began to trickle down the back of my neck, but some of that was from nerves, too. I took the receiver from another pocket and checked the feed with Sam looking over my shoulder. The camera showed the stairs leading up from the dining room, and the hall leading to the bedroom. I looked away from the camera and towards the hallway. The bedroom door was slightly ajar, and I could see the television flickering. I pointed up, indicating we would head for the spare room, as previously arranged, hoping that Evans didn't come out and shoot at us, or that we'd be forced to shoot *him*.

The irony of that thought actually made me smile under my mask—I *told* you I was nuts, didn't I?

We crept up the stairs, got into the spare room without incident, and left the door open a crack—exactly as we'd found it. I quietly pulled two chairs over, and we sat down with the live feed before us, watching both the stairway and the hall leading to the bedroom.

An hour went by, then two. It was edging towards one o'clock in the morning and I was beginning to get sleepy. Sam was sitting beside me with her back ramrod straight. I knew she was wound as tightly as a Swiss watch, and would be ready at a moment's notice. I was sweating like a pig, and fighting off the fatigue that was threatening to overwhelm me. Another hour passed. It was now almost two. Evans shut the television, and we were suddenly in almost total darkness, except for the cloudy moonlight coming through the skylights. At two-twelve, there was a noise downstairs; it was a soft noise, as if someone had quietly opened a door and just as quietly, shut it.

The cellar, I thought, and turned towards Sam. Her beautiful green eyes were wide under her mask, and I knew she had heard it too. I swore under my breath. None of Spinner's men, or the Feds, for that matter, would have taken up position inside—not after getting laughed at by Judge Evans. That meant only one thing—the killer had done the same thing we had done: she was already in the Evans home, and had probably been here longer than we had. I was holding my breath without realizing it, and almost sprang out of the chair when a dark figure appeared at the bottom of the stairs. I couldn't tell if it was a man or a woman, but the live feed showed someone approximately my own height and weight—the same size as the woman who had jumped me. I debated pulling my weapon, but suddenly thought better of it. The intruder was dressed all in black, with her face covered, and I didn't want to shoot anyone until I knew exactly what we were dealing with. At the same time, I wasn't about to let the killer make it to the bedroom, and decided, right there on the spot, to tackle whoever it as soon as she reached the top of the stairs.

I stood up, and handed the live feed receiver to Sam. We had discussed just this scenario, among others, and she knew enough to cover me when I made my move. As quietly as I could, I pulled the door back an inch or so. Now I could see the staircase without the camera. I had the element of surprise on my side, but I was dealing with a consummate professional if it was, indeed, the person I had tangled with at the bank, and knew I would have my hands full. There was also the possibility that Evans would hear the commotion and investigate with his own weapon in his hand, so I knew I was going to have to take the intruder down, and take her down hard and fast, to get out of the line of fire. I had to assume that Evans was armed, and I suddenly regretted my hard-headedness in not confiding in Bobby, but I've done things a certain way all my life, and they usually serve me well.

Usually.

The intruder was three quarters of the way up the stairs when I saw her take a weapon from a side holster, and that's when sudden inspiration struck.

Sam and I had to get the killer back down the stairs, and under the overhang of the hallway above. If we did it fast enough, Evans wouldn't have anything to shoot at, even if he did come out on the landing with his own weapon.

I looked at Sam and held up two fingers—the prearranged hand signal for taking the killer together. Based on our practice sessions, I would employ the same sort of coke hold the killer had used on me. Sam would secure the gun, and, once we had her in tow, Sam would quickly understand the direction I was taking.

At least, I hoped she would.

The only other alternative was to shoot the bitch first and ask questions second.

When the intruder reached the landing I crept from the room with Sam right behind me. I only needed four or five steps, but as I told you, our killer was a professional. She turned and pointed the gun at me when I was still two feet away, and I ended up decking her with a right cross. She landed on her ass and the gun flew out of her hand. Sam picked it up while I was wrestling with the suspect, and just then the bedroom door opened.

"Police! Freeze!" I clearly heard Spinelli yell, and as he walked under one of the skylights I could see that his sidearm was aimed directly at my head.

"Bobby! It's Kaylyn!" I cried, and got a punch in the jaw from the killer for my trouble. The killer got up, grabbed for the gun Sam was holding and it went off, taking Spinelli in the calf. He dropped to one knee, and, while I was still holding on to our suspect, I had the presence of mind to pull Sam's ski mask from her head. Spinelli fired once, hitting the intruder in the right shoulder. She lunged for the stairs, still holding her revolver, and I grabbed her, and, before I knew what was happening, we were tumbling down the carpeted stairs all the way to the bottom, trading punches and holding on to each other as we went.

We spilled onto the floor, and despite the bullet in her shoulder, she got up first, shoved me hard and broke for the back door. I stumbled, regained my footing and started after her.

"Help Bobby!" I yelled at Sam, and the next thing I knew I was running through the woods chasing my suspect.

• • •

If you've ever been in combat, you know how it affects you. If you haven't, I can assure you that it is the ultimate stimulant. If you don't believe me, just ask any adrenaline junkie. All of my fatigue was suddenly burned away, and I was filled with energy I didn't even know I had. I was pretty sure that she still had her revolver or maybe even a backup weapon, but was opting for speed at the moment, rather than turning and risking a shot at me. I know you see that a lot in the movies, but people who know what they're doing don't take potshots like that. It was possible that she'd take cover and try a shot, but I was right on her heels, no more than thirty feet behind her, and she was bleeding—a lot. I poured it on and closed the gap. Twenty-five.

Twenty. Fifteen. I could hear her labored breathing, and suddenly I was right behind her. I threw myself forward and took her down hard, right on her injured shoulder. She cried out and turned and kicked my leg, causing me to slip as I was trying to get back up. She was reaching into a side pocket when I got back on top of her, and suddenly we were rolling down the embankment and landed in the water. Cold like that constricts all of your blood vessels, making your arms and legs feel like lead. She came up with the gun in her hand but I punched her in the face and took it away from her. She went down, and came up a few seconds later ten feet away, climbing back to the bank. I swore, shoved her gun in my belt, and swam after her.

My quarry ran west along the steep embankment, but she was limping, and I knew I'd done some damage when I tackled her. I climbed out, got my feet under me, took a deep breath and pulled out my 9mm.

"Freeze!" I yelled, but of course, she kept running. "Bitch!" I snarled and fired a warning shot into the dirt between her feet, but it didn't even slow her down. She wasn't stupid, and if she knew who I was, then she also knew that if I shot an unarmed suspect in the back, we'd be sharing a jail cell. Cops can bring down a fleeing suspect, but if you're a P.I. and don't want to lose your license, who'll opt for knocking her out, if you can.

Shoving the weapon back in my holster, I ran after her. She veered to the left, and disappeared into the woods, but came out a few feet later near a dock. I looked ahead, and in the moonlight I saw the boat.

"Son-of-a-bitch!" I growled, knowing, that, if she got the motor started, I'd lose her for sure. So I ran for all I was worth, and got to the dock just as she was pulling the cord on the outboard. It coughed, died, and then started, but I threw myself at her just as the motor caught, and standing in the rocking boat as the big outboard purred, I lost my balance and went over the side. She started to sit down so she could open it up, but I grabbed the gunwale, pulled myself back up by the right rear pocket of her black denim pants, and heard the pocket rip at the same time that she pitched over my head and into the water. Like the moron I am, I dove back in after her, and treading water, traded a few more punches with her. During the struggle I managed to pull her ski mask off, revealing a very pretty woman around my age, with lustrous brown hair. I should have recognized her right then and there, but when she turned her head I saw that the other side of her face was horribly burned and disfigured, and instead of coming up with a name, all I could do was stare at that only pretty thing on that side of her face—a malevolent blue eye that blazed hatred at me under the cloud-filled winter sky.

She spit at me, took a deep breath and went under. I wanted to go after her but I was spent and my back and both legs were killing me from falling down all those stairs, so I swam back to the boat.

I climbed in, and used the spotlight on the front of the boat to scour the dark water, but all I got for my trouble was some bubbles ten feet away, and then nothing. I spent ten more minutes searching, and then turned the boat around and headed back to the inlet Sam and I had used.

Whoever she was, the bitch had slipped through my fingers again. I pulled off my mask, swore, and winced at the pain in my lower back. I shivered, and rubbed the back of my neck.

That's when I noticed the notepaper lying in the bottom of the boat, a little wet square that must have fallen out when her pants ripped. It was too soaking wet to even *try* to open, and I wanted some leverage with Spinelli because I knew I was *really* in the shit now, so I slipped it into the shirt pocket under my commando sweater and promised to look at it later.

• • •

Having heard the boat they were all waiting for me when I pulled in. The big Federal agent that had been with Bobby the other day reached down and pulled me up on the bank. Sam was standing right beside him, looking scared; I could only imagine what they'd said to her. Bobby came limping over with his right pant leg rolled up, but even in the gloom I could tell he had only been grazed.

"You really fucked up *this* time, Vale," he said, taking my hand and helping me out of the boat.

"Did I?" I asked sweetly, and tossed a wink at Sam. I pulled the revolver out of my belt slowly and handed it to him by the barrel. I had never taken my gloves off, so I wasn't worried about prints. "Here," I said, "I retrieved the murder weapon for you!"

• • •

We spent the rest of the night and some of the next morning, Sam and I, being debriefed at the State Police Barracks in Providence. We gave our statements once, twice and then a third time, while they fished for lies and inconsistencies. When they knew they weren't getting anywhere, the big guy who had pulled the boat in threw up his hands and stormed out of the room. I could only smile, wink at Samantha, and wrap the green army blanket tighter around my shoulders. The Feds were *royally* pissed off, but I'd come up with the only solid evidence they had so far—the .32 caliber revolver that I fervently prayed was the weapon that had been used to murder the other judges. It made sense that it was, but I was still concerned that it was only a backup piece. The gun went immediately to the forensics lab, and I knew I'd have a bad night or two while I sweated it out.

Evans, it seems, wasn't as dumb as he came on, and had finally relented and gone to a safe house. It was Bobby himself that had impersonated him, dressing like him and even driving his car. It had fooled me, so it had most certainly fooled my suspect. They let us go around eight o'clock, and Bobby offered to drive us home.

He started laughing as soon as the doors were closed.

"You are the *craziest* woman I have ever known, Kaylyn Vale!"

"Flattery will get you nowhere, big boy," I replied.

Sam sat in the back seat, her hair a mess and looking gorgeous, if exhausted. She'd have to come clean to her husband for sure now, and I didn't envy her.

"You really didn't even get a look at the suspect?" Bobby wanted to know, looking sideways at me.

"Guy was wearing a ski mask," I said, wondering why I wanted to keep the killer's gender to myself.

"Skinny little bastard," Bobby said with a grunt.

I shrugged, not wanting to get into it. "How much trouble are we in?"

"Well, Tanner wants you guys pulled off the case, but my Captain will squash that."

I assumed that Tanner was the big Fed. "You sure about that?"

"Like you said, Lynn—you *did* retrieve the murder weapon."

"I *hope*."

We were coming down through the College Hill section of Providence by this time, and got stuck at the lights near The Bank of America Building—nicknamed "The Superman" building for its resemblance to the *Daily Planet*. Bobby turned his head and glared at me.

"What the hell is *that* supposed to mean?"

The Bank was blocking the sun, so we were all in shadows. I was still soaked, and I shivered a little.

"I'm just saying that the suspect *could* have had a backup piece, Bobby." I turned the heat up a notch.

Bobby grunted. "I suppose we shouldn't be taking *anything* for granted at this point," he agreed as the light changed. "Incidentally, where do you two want to go?"

"My office. Both cars are there."

Bobby raised an eyebrow. "Really? I didn't see any cars when I drove by last night."

"That's because they're out back."

"Devious little thing, aren't you, Vale?"

"You forgot to mention *gorgeous*, big guy—but I *am* a gumshoe, after all."

Spinelli chuckled, and looked in the rearview mirror. "How are you doing back there, Mrs. Ashbery?"

"Sam. Mrs. Ashbery is my mother-in-law."

"She's charming," Bobby said, glancing at me as we drove through Barrington and entered Farmington. "You've taught her well."

"I do my best," I told him.

Bobby let us out twenty minutes later and Sam and I went in through the back door.

"I'm seriously going to get divorced after this," Sam said, frowning. "I really should call him, but I'm too tired to care. Mind if I take a shower?"

"Want some company?" I asked, "I mean, since you're getting divorced and all."

"Fuck you, Lynn," Sam said and giggled.

"That's the plan," I told her, and took her in my arms.

We got dressed an hour later, and Sam promised to call me later in the day and let me know how things had gone with Wade. I nodded, and yawned, and lay back down on the couch. I fell asleep instantly, and didn't wake up until almost five o'clock. I sat up and swore, knowing I'd have trouble sleeping tonight because I'd been sawing wood all day, and decided, against my better *judgment*, if you'll pardon the expression, to make another appointment with Doctor Brown. I got her just as she was leaving the office, and she told me he could squeeze me in tomorrow at four, so I hung up and just sat there, all juiced up and with no place to go.

My cell phone rang while I was sitting there yawning, and, thinking it was Sam, answered it without even looking at the screen.

"Hey, babe."

"Well, hey there, sexy," the voice of my killer said.

"How's your shoulder?" I asked, switching gears without missing a beat.

"I've had worse. By the way, you fell pretty hard when I kicked you. How's your ass?"

"Curvy, or so I've been told."

The voice chuckled. "I'm not into that sort of thing, but you *are* put together pretty well, I must admit. Always were."

"Hey, how about you cut the shit and tell me who you are if we're such old pals?"

"You must have gotten a pretty good look at me. Who do you *think* I am?"

"It was dark," I mumbled. "I couldn't see very well."

"You saw well enough to almost puke when you saw my face, Kaylyn. Now, who needs to cut the shit?"

"Look—this is between you and me. I think you've figured that out for yourself by now, so how about coming clean on why you're doing this, if you don't have the balls to tell me who you are?"

"You're a detective—I have no doubt that you'll figure it out... eventually. As for the why...I already told you—I'm doing this because our prison system is a business and our courts are a joke. All they're interested in is getting re-elected, and looking tough-on-crime. By doing what I'm doing, I'm hoping to shake them up, Lynn. Either we have a Constitution that applies fairly to everyone, or we don't. You, above all people should see that."

"That's the second time you've said that to me—why?"

"Ask your mother."

"My mother's dead, you sick bitch!" She had scored a touchdown there, and I vowed to regain control of myself.

"Is she?"

"Please," I heard myself saying, and hating myself for it. "What do you know about her?"

"She's like us, Lynn—didn't you know that? That's why she left you. Not because she didn't *want* you, but to protect you."

"WHO THE FUCK *ARE* YOU?" I heard myself scream.

"I'll be in touch," she said, and hung up.

"Fucking witch!" I snarled and flung the cell phone at the wall. I wanted to cry, but I didn't want this sick bitch getting *complete* control of me, so I took a deep breath, counted to ten, and went to pick up the pieces of my shattered cell phone.

Fortunately for me, the SIM card was undamaged, and I simply snapped it into the backup phone I keep in my desk and turned it on. Everything seemed to work and I set it down on the desk, lit a cigarette and closed my eyes, going over the conversation in my head.

"*Just like us*," she had said.

I started pacing, and suddenly had to pee. I was sitting on the toilet, smoking and tapping the ashes into the sink and looking at the pile of wet clothes I had left on the floor. I finished what I was doing and went to drop the bundle of clothes into the tub, when I heard something *crinkle*, and remembered the notepaper.

Turns out it wasn't a note at all, but a print-out of an on-line *Providence Times* article, by, of all people, Clair Sacchetti. The paper was still wet, though, so I didn't unfold it all the way because I didn't want to rip it. When I had the title and the date, I brought the paper over to the baseboard heater and put it on the floor to dry. I went to the computer armed with the little bit of information I had gathered, and looked up the article, knowing I'd be able to confirm it when the paper was all dried out.

The article was about Kyle Worthington, and demanded an investigation into his alleged suicide—right up Clair's alley, as this sort of thing had happened before. (Clair talks all about that in her *Broken Heroes* series), but it threw me for a loop. Why would the killer be carrying around an article about a dead man, and what connection did she have to him in the first place? Kyle Worthington had had only one sibling, a sister, Rebekka, deceased, and both of his parents were also dead. Not for the first time I wondered about the connection between my caller and Kyle, but none of it made any sense. I was exhausted by this time, physically and emotionally. My face felt flushed and I had a head-ache and my back hurt. I knew I should have gone home, but I felt safe here and decided to take a bath. I shut down the computer, threw the wet clothes into a plastic garbage bag to take home and wash, and filled the tub with the hottest water I could stand—hoping to get that awful chill out of my bones. I actually sighed when I laid back and rested my head, but my thoughts were swirling like a sandstorm—the killer, my Mother and Sam. The killer, my Mother and Sam. The killer, my Mother and Sam.

And suddenly, something Sam had said about her husband caused me to sit straight up in the tub as if I'd been pulled up by strings.

Sam had told me that a big part of their marital problems was that Wade had faked his death, and while he'd been in Afghanistan she had fallen in love with Jennifer.

Faked his death.

Was it possible that someone in Kyle Worthington's family was really still alive?

I thought about his sister, supposedly killed in a bombing—and suddenly the image of the burned face of my killer flashed into my head.

Were the two connected? Or was I grasping at straws?

My new cell phone was on the sink, so I reached out, grabbed it and sunk back down in the steaming water. I dialed Ashley Vaughn's number and she picked up immediately.

"Hey, Pal, what's up?"

"Nothing really," I said carefully, knowing how paranoid she was, "I just wanted to thank you again for New Year's Eve."

"My pleasure! Mum was *so* happy to see you!"

"About that," I said, "I'm taking a few days off and I'd like to fly down to D.C. day after tomorrow so we can go over that probate issue for your Mother." Ashley knew damn well that there wasn't any probate issue, but I had caught her off guard and it took her a minute to get back on her feet.

"Uh, sure, Kaylyn. Any time. Just call me when you get here and I'll pick you up."

"Great. Thanks. See in a couple of days."

"Uh, Kaylyn...is everything all right?"

"Couldn't be better!" I said cheerfully. "Talk to you soon!"

I hung up before she could press me, got out and wrapped myself in a towel. I sat on the couch, thinking about it all, and despite the fact that I'd been worried about being able to sleep, went out like a light and didn't wake up until five-thirty the next morning.

The first thing I thought of was the note on the floor, and when I unfolded it I was rewarded with the fact that it, was, indeed, the same as the article I'd read on-line. I had nothing to do until four when I had my appointment with Erica Brown, and I wanted to call Sam, but I decided to go for a run and see if she called me, instead.

The morning was crisp and clear and cold, but there was no wind whatsoever. Perfect for a good run. I fell into a steady rhythm, and as I ran, went over everything that was bothering me. On a previous call, the killer had said something about my alleged actions being "Classic Company"—and the only way she could know that was if she, herself, had been a Company operative.

But even with the image of her burned face fresh in my mind, I still had no clue as to who she might be.

Then I started worrying about the gun and if it really was the murder weapon. I knew I should call Spinelli, because I was also wondering about the DNA analysis on the blood the killer had left at the scene, but I decided to let sleeping dogs lie and before I knew it I was running up Sam's driveway. I hadn't consciously thought of coming here, especially since it was so early, but as I stood on her back steps, trying to decide if I should knock on the door, Sam opened it and took me in a bear hug without a word. I held her and she started crying, but she didn't say a word and neither did I. Finally, knowing that she was probably freezing, I disentangled myself.

"Let's go inside, Sam, you're shivering."

I closed the door behind us and grabbed her by the shoulders. Her beautiful green eyes were red-rimmed and swollen, and I knew she'd been up for at least a long as I had been.

"I saw you coming up the driveway," she said needlessly. "What are you doing here?"

"I'm going to D.C. tomorrow, to follow up on something, and I'll be busy tonight, so I just wanted to check on you."

"D.C.? What for?"

I told her about the article and who I'd be seeing, and Sam frowned.

"You really think that someone in Worthington's family is involved in this?" she asked.

"To tell you the truth, Sam, I don't know what to think—but my God, woman, why would our suspect be carrying something like that?"

"I don't know," she admitted, and turned away.

"Sam—what's wrong?"

"Wade slept at his Mother's last night, Lynn. He wants a separation."

"Because of us?"

Sam turned around. "I haven't even told him that part of it. He's just pissed because I'm working with you. He's says I'm being irresponsible, putting myself in danger like that."

"I'm sorry, Sam—I really am." I wanted to tell her that part of me agreed with her husband's assessment, but I didn't dare. "Look," I said instead, "why don't you take today off, and get some rest? Tomorrow, while I'm away, you have the key to the office if you want to get away for a while."

"Ok," she said, and started to cry again.

I took her in my arms and comforted her as best I could, but my head was spinning with everything I was dealing with, and I simply couldn't take on anything more at the moment.

"Listen to me," I said, pushing her to arm's length. I tucked a lock of her hair behind one ear and smiled at her. "I love what we have together—but you have children to think about and I want you to try to make your marriage work. Besides," I added, trying a bit of humor, "what are you doing messing around with an old broad like me?"

Sam laughed, sniffed, and grabbed a tissue to blow her nose. "Wade's almost nine year's older than me, too, Lynn." She tried a smile of her own that almost worked. "Maybe I *like* old people."

"Well, you *are* a weirdo," I told her with a smirk. "A pretty one, though, but seriously, honey, I'm no good for you. I'm more messed up than you'll ever be, and I don't want you throwing your marriage away over me."

"We had problems long before *you* came along, Lynn—just tell me you'll be there if I need you."

I wanted to tell her to forget about me and get on with her life, but God help me I just couldn't do it—even though I knew it would be the best thing she could do.

"Always," I heard myself saying. "No matter what."

• • •

Dr. Erica Brown shook my hand warmly and smiled as I came in.

"Sit down, Kaylyn, please."

"Thanks for seeing me on such short notice, Doc," I told her, taking my usual chair.

"My pleasure, Lynn, especially since, after our last session, I was convinced you weren't going to follow up on what we talked about."

"That obvious, huh?"

"I've been doing this a long time. In fact, I'm surprised to see you here at all."

"I actually *wasn't* going to come back, Erica."

"Care to tell me why?"

"I think you know why," I said, and looked over my shoulder.

"What's wrong?"

"I'm, uh, just wondering if we could sit on the couch today."

"If you like."

We got up and sat down again. Me on one end, her on the other.

"Being in front of the window is a problem?" she asked softly.

"I feel better with my back against the wall, Erica. There's a lot going on, and I'm not at liberty to tell you most of it, but all of that…" I shook my head. "That really isn't why I'm here."

"Ok, but before I ask what brought you back—I want you to tell me why you were willing to drop our sessions all together."

"Because most of what's bothering me is classified—but you already knew that. The other part is what's going on now with the case I'm on, which, I am also not at liberty to discuss. So you see, I wasn't going to come back because I can't talk about the things that are bothering me and I'm not willing to stop doing what I'm doing. Truth is, what I do is who I am."

"Then why *are* you here, Lynn?"

"Because I've come to the realization that it's the underlying issues that are the problem."

"Sounds like you've had an epiphany."

I ignored that. Erica is awesome, but I hate phony, bullshit, ten-dollar words. "It has to do with my Mother."

Erica Brown raised an eyebrow. "Your Mother's deceased, if I remember correctly?"

"She is—but maybe she's not."

"I'm afraid I don't understand."

I couldn't tell her that the killer was calling me, but I had to tell her *something*. "I told you when we first started, that I was recruited by 'The Company' right out of High School. Now, someone, uh, connected to the case, tells me that the same thing happened to her, my Mum, that is, and that she might very well be alive."

Erica sighed. "This is all very frustrating for me, Kaylyn. You're not the only person I've ever treated who has to deal with classified information, and I simply don't see how I can help you if I'm not getting the whole picture."

"Forgive me, Doc—but I don't think you need it. You see, I've hated my Mother for most of my life, and now, well, if she left to protect me and not because she didn't want me, well, it gives me hope. It explains why she wasn't there, and now I may be able to put the accountability on what happened to me back then where it belongs, and not on her."

"Wow. I'm impressed. That's really a very healthy attitude, Kaylyn, good for you."

I studied her for a long moment, looking for condescension in her eyes and finding none. "My question is—should I even be entertaining such hope?"

"Of course. Hope is a *good* thing, Lynn."

"*The Shawshank Redemption*," I said and laughed.

"I'm sorry?"

"It's a game I play with an associate of mine. One of us mentions a line from a movie and the other one has to guess the title. In *Redemption*, the Morgan Freeman character tells Tim Robbins that to hope is dangerous…Tim Robbins tells him something like hope is a *good* thing. I guess that's where I'm stuck."

"I see. This information about your Mother? How reliable is it?"

"That," I said, "is what I plan to find out."

We talked for a while more, and near the end of the hour I brought up something I'd been struggling with.

"I've also been having these dreams."

"Can you tell me about them?"

I shrugged. "No details, really. I just see myself in the past, historically speaking. I'm still me, still doing what I do, but I'm on horseback, carrying a sword, that sort of thing."

"I'd say that's pretty easy to figure out, Lynn."

"How so?"

"To me, and this is only my opinion, it says clearly that you're not happy with the life you're currently leading."

"Really?" I said. "To me, it means, that—no matter what, no matter where—I was somehow meant to do what I'm doing."

And that, I realized, was the answer to all of my questions.

• • •

The plane to D.C. was right on schedule and I moved through the check-points without incident, even though I felt positively *naked* without a weapon on me. I met Ashley in a little coffee shop near super time, and, after we had ordered, she slid closer to me in the curved booth.

"Probate issue, honey? Seriously!"

"Yeah, well, sorry about that. The truth is, and this is confidential, I found an article about Kyle Worthington on the suspect." I told her the whole story and Ashley frowned.

"Please don't tell me you want access to our computers, Lynn!"

I calmly finished chewing my turkey-club sandwich, having known ahead of time that this would be a sticking point for her. "No, but how hard would it be for you to dig up everything you have on any relatives, living or dead? Worthington's, I mean—especially his sister, Rebekka…any aliases she might have used, other assignments she may have been on, that sort of thing?"

"Not too difficult, but for real, Lynn, you're *best* suspect is a woman who was killed five years ago?"

"I'm not saying she's a suspect, Ash, all I'm saying is that the killer had an article about Kyle Worthington on her. It's a lead, and you're the only one I can trust with this."

"I'll do what I can, Kaylyn, but it's going to *cost* you," she told me with a smirk.

"Don't tease me like that, cutie. You know I'm a switch hitter and if you gave me half a chance I'd spin you like a top."

"Don't threaten *me* with a good time she said, and we both laughed.

• • •

I got a call as soon as I got home, and I grabbed the phone quickly because I was waiting for information on so many different things. I glanced at the screen, saw that the caller was "unknown", and braced myself.

Judgment Day

"We really do have to stop meeting like this," I said as I picked up.

"We'll meet in person again, soon enough."

"I can't wait," I said. "What do you want?"

"I just wanted you to know, that, despite how much I respect you, you're not going to stop me."

"You don't mind if I try, though, do you?"

"Not at all, I love a good game."

"That what this is—a game?"

"You *know* what this is, Kaylyn, and what kills me is that you know I'm right. This country is more like Nazi Germany now than the United States of America, and all I'm doing is bringing people's attention to that."

"So what's next? You going to try for Evans again—or someone else?"

"Didn't I already tell you? I'll get around to him eventually."

"Are you planning on keeping this up forever?"

"Nope—I'm thinking an even dozen should do nicely."

"What the hell are you spelling, anyway? Is it JUDGEMENT?"

She laughed. "You're a bright girl; you'll figure it out…eventually."

"You don't have to do this, you know."

"I guess that's the difference between us, Lynn—we both know it has to be done, but I'm the only one doing it."

She hung up without another word, and I never got a chance to ask her about my Mother.

I didn't know whether that was good or bad, but in the end, I was going to get what I wanted.

That's who I am.

That's what I do.

H.A. Peine District Library
202 N. Main
P.O. Box 19
Minier, IL 61759-0019

CHAPTER SEVEN—February

The rest of January was pretty uneventful. I didn't see much of Sam, because I was pushing her to fix things between her and her husband, and things seemed to be going well for them—at least at the moment. So I worked out, handled another case, and worked out some more. I was also trying to decide if I was really in love with Sam, or just being a needy little bitch, and I didn't want to see her again until I was sure—if such a thing is even possible.

The .32 caliber revolver I had taken from the suspect turned out to be the same gun that was used on all the other murders—except, of course, for the rifle Kyle Worthington had used.

That kept me solidly on the case, but didn't point us in any particular direction, because there were no prints on it—big surprise, that.

The DNA evidence on the blood came back like this: *no known match on file*, which threw me, but didn't really surprise me all that much when I thought about it if I was really dealing with someone with deep-cover experience.

In my old business, someone like that is called a *Legend*—someone who actually *becomes* their cover story. Someone like Dr. Brown would call that a *psychosis*, I suppose, but that level of obsession is necessary if you're going to kill people for a living on a regular business.

At "The Company", someone like that is all but untraceable, and any clue leading to their true identity is layered with so many twists and turns that it is almost impossible to find out who they really are. I mean, seriously—most of the so-called *assets* are people like me, and maybe my Mother…people who have no one, people no one will miss. Who better to kill on assignment?

Hey, I never said it was a *good* business—but it *is* a business.

February First was a cold, dreary, rainy day, about forty degrees, for which I was grateful. If it had been any colder, all that rain would have turned the streets into solid sheets of ice. As it was, the power lines and tree limbs near my office were covered in sheaths of ice, and there were patches of black ice on the road that made driving precarious, at best, because they weren't consistent, and you couldn't tell where they were. I decided to stay in the office all day, and work out what to do next.

I turned up the heat, pulled down the shades, locked the door and made coffee. I was even planning on having take-out delivered for lunch, because I really wanted to stay off the roads. I wasn't hungry at the moment, but I made myself eat a cup of yogurt, which I keep in my little refrigerator here, simply because I knew I worked better with something in my stomach.

I looked at my watch as I sat down (a lifetime habit), and saw that it was only nine-ten in the morning. That meant I had the whole day to myself, so I got out all of my handmade charts and graphs and lists, and got to work.

I was convinced now that the whole scripture thing was a smokescreen, so I didn't even bother looking at that stuff, but if Sam was right, and our killer *was* spelling, JUDGEMENT, then it meant that the next letter would be N, and that also meant that I had until the 14th. I was taking a chance, however, in assuming this, because I had no reason to believe that the killer wouldn't stick to her schedule, and go for Evans again, but there was nothing I could do about it and the Feds had talked him into taking some time off at any rate—last I heard, he was happily shacked up with a couple of Federal Agents in a really plush safe-house somewhere.

My phone beeped while I was pouring over all that information, and it made me jump. It was a text from Ashley, and simply said: *call me.*

So I dialed her number and she promptly hung up.

And then I got it and called back on the secure line.

"Good job, dummy," she said.

"Hey," I told her, "I never said I was *smart*, only pretty. What's up?"

"Well, I got the information you wanted, but there isn't much. A lot of it was listed as *Need-To-Know*, and I don't have the clearance to get into those particular data bases. I probably got flagged just doing this, but I *am* a researcher, after all, so I should be able to handle any questions."

"Shit, Ashley—I didn't want you putting your job on the line over this!'

"No, it's ok, really. We've been consolidating a lot of old Intel. Trust me, I wouldn't have done it if I thought it would cost me my job, pal. I like you, but I don't like you *that* much."

"Give me what you've got then," I said, and picked up a pen.

"Ok. Rebekka Worthington and that's her real name, by the way, was killed, *confirmed*, five years ago at the embassy in Beirut while she was working there undercover as a staff member."

"What was she *really* doing there?"

"*Need-To-Know*, honey."

"Silly me. What else you got?"

"She was killed by a car bomb, leaving her brother, Kyle, as her only surviving relative. Parents, Joseph and Ruth, were killed years before in an auto accident. She and her brother were very close, but then she came on board with us, and if she kept in touch with him she kept it to herself. Before coming to work here, she was something of a radical: peace marches, protests, always criticizing the government, that sort of thing." I heard paper rustling. "After that she was recruited, as you know, and went immediately into The Factory."

That made me sit up and take a deep breath. *The Factory* was a code name for an unusual project where the recruits were given the same kind of training as the Special Forces Branches of our armed forces. They did commando work, conducted raids...and assassinated high level targets. All and all, a serious kind of girl, and no one you'd want mad at you. I know because I was in the same program.

"Was there a psych eval?"

"Classified—above *my* pay-grade, sweetie."

"Figures. Any aliases?"

"Only one—Rhonda Witherspoon. Ring a bell?"

"Nope."

"Anything else you want?"

"How about a physical description?"

"At the time of her recruitment, Worthington was five foot seven, and weighed a hundred and twenty pounds. Brown, blue; fair complexion. Pretty."

"Got a picture?"

"Yup."

"Can you email it?"

"It's an old hard copy, Lynn, and I'd rather not compromise my own email. Can I fax it?"

"Sure," I said and gave her the number.

"Anything else?"

"Not unless you're switching teams and want me to take you for a walk on the wild side."

Just then I heard my old fax machine start up.

"Don't tempt me, girlfriend. I'm on my third boyfriend in two years and I'm growing sour on men."

"Ok, but you don't know what you're missing."

Ashley laughed. "Tell you what—you still owe me, and big time, but I'll have to think a little bit before I put myself in *your* clutches."

We both laughed, and I rang off.

I got up on stiff legs—my back was still killing me, too—and walked over to get the fax out of the machine.

I almost had a heart attack when I pulled it out. Staring up at me was the pretty face of the woman I had fought with, minus the burns.

Worse than that, I had known her, a long, long time ago.

• • •

Do you remember when I told you about that mission to Rwanda? It was my first ground mission, with the exception of my first hit, and I told you then that "other stuff happened" and that I would tell you about it later.

I had been in a bad way after empting my .45 into that big guy, not so much for taking *him* out, but because of what had happened to that poor girl. I was an abused child myself, so I'm extremely sensitive to the suffering of others, and as I was lying there in the dark, crying, the brother of the man I had killed—and two of his friends—somehow got through the perimeter and into my tent.

Two of them had machetes and one of them a knife, and I woke up as soon as they came in. I remember screaming, but one of them clamped his hand over my mouth and I honestly didn't think anyone had heard me. I was lying down on my cot, wearing only a tee shirt and panties, and they stripped me in seconds, beating me as I fought them. The biggest one got on top of me (I found out later that it was his brother I had killed), and the other two held my arms and legs. They were laughing and drooling and spitting on me, speaking in guttural broken English, saying how, after they had all *fucked* me, they were going to cut me into little pieces. The one on top of me was biting my neck and trying to pull his pants down at the same time. The guy holding my arms was trying…I'm sorry, it's still so hard to talk about…trying to…put *himself* into my mouth, so I gritted my teeth, and refused to scream, thrashing and bucking and actually managing to kick the one holding my legs in the mouth.

"Bitch," he snarled, and spit his own blood into my face. "I will cut you for so long that you will *beg* for death!"

"Not yet, not yet!" the one on top of me panted, and then his head exploded.

He fell on top of me, and all the air went out of my lungs. I was still using every ounce of strength I had to keep my legs pressed together, and when he collapsed I almost passed out.

There was a second shot, and the one who had spit the blood at me was thrown back against the side of the tent. I saw a shadow then, standing there in the dark holding a handgun, and then the third one ran for the tent flap and the shadow took *him* down with three shots in the back.

I turned sideways in disgust, and rolled the big guy off of me, and then I promptly heaved my guts up. I heard shouts outside and booted feet running towards the tent, but then gentle hands were on me, helping me to sit up with my back against the side of my cot. The shadow squatted down, and that's when I saw it was one of the other women, one of the other *girls*, on my extraction team.

Her name was Rachel Stark—and she was the woman in the photo I was now looking at.

• • •

"Oh my God," I heard myself saying as I held the fax and leaned against the wall. I don't remember how I got there, but I was suddenly on the floor, the photo in my lap, my legs bent and bunched, crying my eyes out as I curled up on my carpet.

Rachel Stark had been a very pretty girl, a lot like me, same height, same build, with soft blue eyes and light brown hair. The woman I had seen in the water was so horribly disfigured that I simply hadn't recognized her, but if the photo *was* a picture of Rebekka Worthington, aka, Rhonda Witherspoon, then she was also Rachel Stark—the woman who had saved me from being raped and murdered in Rwanda.

The same woman I was now hunting.

• • •

My cell phone rang just then, bringing me out of the fugue I was slipping into. I picked it up numbly, looked at the screen, saw that it was Sam, and put it down again. A half hour later I heard a key in the door. Sam came in, saw me on the floor, and pulled her weapon out of the little pouch she always wears. She took a good look at me, went to the bathroom, checked the back door, and then returned to me, squatting down before me and putting her gun away, touching my hair, telling me it was ok—exactly as Rachel had all those years before.

"I'm ok, Sammy," I said, and slipped my arms around her neck.

"The *hell* you are," Samantha said. "What happened?"

"Just hold me, Sammy," I begged, looking up at her and unable to hide my tears. "Please—just *hold* me."

Sam did as I asked, whispering in my ear, rocking me back and forth in her strong arms as if I were a child. I was reminded again of what a good mother she must be, and vowed on the spot, to make sure she stayed with her husband, and then I told her that I loved her.

"I love you, too, Lynn," she whispered, "so help me, God, I *do*. Can you sit up now?"

I looked into her eyes, and saw the truth of what she had said, and as I told her that I could, in fact, sit up, I collapsed into her arms and started sobbing again. When the worst of it was over, and I was able to look at her again, I saw that she had been crying the whole time, and had never made a sound.

• • •

People tell me that I have beautiful eyes. I've been hearing it all my life. But if anyone has eyes that are more beautiful than Samantha Marie Ashbery, sea green soft and intense—all at the same time—I'd like to know who it might be.

Sam got me to the couch, went to get me a bottle of spring water from the little fridge, and lit a cigarette. She took a hit and passed it to me as soon as I had taken a sip of water.

"Got a bottle of Valium in the desk, Sam. Get it for me?"

Sam nodded, brought it to me, and lit another cigarette. She was leaning forward, looking at me, as I popped five milligrams and washed it down. I leaned my head back and sighed.

"Thank you."

Sam put the ashtray in my lap and lifted my chin with a gentle finger.

"What happened, Lynn?"

"See that fax on the floor? Get it for me, please."

Sam did, and sat back down.

"She's pretty," she said. "Who is it?"

"Rachel Stark. She saved my life in Rwanda."

It took the better part of twenty minutes, but I told her everything I just told you.

"Lynn, I'm sorry, but I don't understand why you're falling apart on me. Did something happen to Rachel?"

"I guess you could say that, Sam."

"For Christ's sake, Kaylyn!"

"She saved me from being raped and murdered, Sammy—she's also the woman we've been hunting."

"Oh, my God, Lynn! Are you sure?"

"I had a friend at the agency, someone I trust, pull Rebekka Worthington's file and photo; it's the same girl."

"And you didn't recognize her at the river?"

I shook my head—no. "She's been horribly burned, Samantha. One whole side of her face." I handed her the photo. "Look how pretty she was—how could I have known?"

"And now she's calling you. Is she doing this *because* of you?"

"No, she's doing this for her brother, I'm sure of it, and I'm also sure she's going to *keep* doing it, Sam, unless we can stop her. She's always been into criticizing the government, and after she was injured, it must have put her over the top."

"How do you *know* she won't stop? Maybe now she feels she's made her point?"

"No way," I said, shaking my head while she was still talking.

"How do you know?"

"Because she told me so. She said: 'an even dozen should do nicely'. That's a quote."

"An even dozen," Sam repeated, and her eyes seemed to glaze over. "A dozen, huh?"

"Yeah, why? What is it?"

"Give me a minute, Babe—I'm thinking!"

Sam got up so fast that it made me dizzy, and went over to the folding table. She rummaged through the papers until she came up with what she was looking for, and then sat down, grabbing a legal pad and knocking over the empty *Skippy* jar with all my pencils in it. As they rolled to the floor, Sam took a pen and started scribbling. I got up and stood behind her.

Sam was writing: JORDAN; UNGER; DONATO; GREGORY; EDWARDS; MAHONEY; EVANS…then she wrote the numeral "7", and scribbled some more. She wrote the numeral "12", and circled it.

"Twelve from seven leaves five," she mumbled, and started writing again.

JUDGE. JUDGES. JUDGMENT. JUDGEMENT.

Sam crossed out the first three words, and then wrote JUDGEMENT again.

"Judgement is nine letters," she mumbled, and tapped her pen on the pad. And then she sat bolt upright as if she'd been hit by lightning. "That leaves only three more." She frowned, stared at the paper and then nodded.

"What is it?" I asked.

"Son of a *bitch*," she hissed between her teeth. "I don't know why I didn't see this before, but your pal Rachel, if she told you the truth about an 'even dozen'—she's spelling J-U-D-G-E-M-E-N-T… D-A-Y!"

"Sam! Are you sure?" I sat down beside her and looked at the pad.

"You tell *me*."

"It makes sense!" I said and kissed her cheek. "So the next letter IS an N!"

"Not only that, but the next one after that will be a T! Because then we need three more. I'm SURE of it!"

"We've *got* her, Sammy! Son of a bitch! We've GOT her!"

After what I had just gone through, I could believe how much better I was feeling, and just sat there, looking foolish.

Didn't I *tell* you that her I.Q. was *north* of 150?

• • •

Samantha and I made love all afternoon. It was more than just physical; we needed the release, the closeness and the intimacy desperately. And, again, I'm sorry for not describing it to you. I'm sure that at least *some* of you would like a graphic picture of two beautiful and healthy young women pleasing each other, but what we had, despite what was still lying ahead of us like a bulldozer sitting in the middle of the highway and unseen around a curve, my time with Sam was the most intensely private and most beautiful experience of my life…and this is the best that I can do.

We both went home at five, joking that our poor couch was taking a battering, and when I got back to my apartment the horror of all those old memories of Rwanda had faded away, replaced with a certain sadness about Rachel. I made myself something to eat: two scrambled eggs, toast, and a few pieces of bacon, and sat down on the sofa with the plate in my lap, watching an ancient episode of *M*A*S*H*, that somehow seemed appropriate, considering the whole Rwandan thing.

While *Hawkeye* was crying to *Henry* about some poor soldier he couldn't save, I got up and poured myself a glass of white wine and went back to my chair. I lit a cigarette to go with it, knowing that I'd be in bed early, and leaned my head back, allowing the day to wash away.

My phone rang at a quarter past eight, and when I saw looked at the screen I was suddenly wide awake.

UNKNOWN.

It was almost as if I had *conjured* her just by *thinking* of her.

I snapped off the lamp, shut the television, and picked up.

"I was just thinking about you, Rachel," I said gently.

The silence lasted for so long that I thought she had hung up, and then I heard her sigh.

"*Brava*," she whispered.

"Thank you," I managed in a gentle voice.

"Took you long enough, though."

"I just told a friend, I never said I was *smart*."

"You are, though—you're the only one in the game at the moment worthy of my attention."

"So—I'm Holmes, and you're, what—Moriarty?"

"Something like that."

"I owe you my life, Rachel, and so much more, and I don't *want* to hurt you. Can I talk you out of going any further with this? I can help you, you know."

"Help me with what, Kaylyn? Help me into the electric chair, the injection chamber, a 9x12 for the rest of my life?"

"I know what you're doing, you know."

"Do you now?"

"You gave it away on your last phone call."

"How so?"

I was so desperate to stop her and help her at the same time that I blurted out what I was thinking before I had time to consider it. I'd come to regret doing that, but, looking back, I really don't think it would have made a difference.

"Let's just say that *Judgement Day* comes for all of us, eventually."

"Clever, girl," she said and laughed. "But you were in *The Factory* with me, honey—you know what I'm capable of, what we're BOTH capable of. That training they gave us, it's the same thing they teach the SEALS, and The Green Berets, and Force Recon Marines—adapt and overcome, remember?"

I could have bitten my tongue off. "What's *that* supposed to mean?"

"You'll find out…in good time."

"Can I ask why you keep calling me?" I said, just to get her off the subject.

"Sure—as soon as you tell me why you aren't tracing these calls. And by the way, if you do, you'll wind up looking at a whore house in Madrid."

"For the same reason I think you are," I said, "because you've made this about you and me."

"You're right—it's the same reason. Maybe I should recruit you, like *they* recruited us, like they recruited your Mum."

"What do you know about her, Rachel?"

"Just two girls chatting, are we?"

"Please."

"Your Mother was my *handler*, Lynn. She was only sixteen when she had you and got pulled into this shit only two years later. Join me, and I'll tell you how to find her."

"You're lying," I said as tears sprang to my eyes.

"You know better than that."

"All of this," I tried, "is it because of your brother?"

"Of course it is. That slut he was married to and that skank that worked for them. Hell, Babe, what young guy *wouldn't* do two women at the same time? I'm sure *you've* done stuff like that yourself. How would *you* like to be labelled a sex offender?"

"I can help you get your life back, Rachel," I promised her, simply to keep her off balance.

"Sure, and then I can have Sunday dinner with my family and get lots of dates with my pretty face."

"You're *still* pretty—you always were."

"On one side, maybe."

"That night...when I saw your face in Rwanda...you were the most beautiful thing I had even seen."

"Don't try to kid me, Kaylyn—I invented it."

I laughed. I just couldn't help it.

"What's so funny?"

"A friend of mine, an ex con, recently said the same thing to me."

"The black guy?"

"How do you know about him?"

"I know everything about you, Lynn, including your hot little girlfriend."

"Leave her out of this!"

"She put *herself* into the mix, honey, and as for your ex con—that's only one more reason you should be on my side."

"So we can kill people together?"

"Let me tell you something, since we're just chatting. Do you know, do you *understand*, that this country makes NOTHING anymore? That the prison system is the third largest industry in the U.S.? Do you know that, over the past twenty years or so, the so-called authorities have made more than a quarter of a *billion* arrests? That almost 80 *million* people have records? That 12,000 more are added every day? That's one out of every three adults." She paused. Do you know what it *is* to be labeled a sex offender, Lynn?"

"I imagine it's awful."

"Awful? How's *this* for awful, because my brother went through it. It means, that, AFTER you serve your sentence, and if they DON'T civilly commit you for the rest of your life, you are then sentenced to a life with no employment, no housing and no relationships. It means you have to pay for probation, for parole, for *counselling*, for those damn bracelets. It means they are *making* more crime, Lynn, not preventing it, to keep the jails full, to win elections, get reappointed, and to sell newspapers. It's not crime control, it's a *business*! And my brother was innocent! The Constitution expressly **forbids** *ex* *post facto* punishment, Lynn, and cruel and unusual punishment as well. But they call it public safety! What happened to our Due Process? The Equal Protection clause of the 14th Amendment? We here in the United States, comprise less than 5% of the world's population, Lynn—and yet we 'house' almost 35% of the globe's known prisoners. They *want* more crime, because it's how they make their money—and I'm going to stop it."

"By taking lives?"

"Yes, Lynn—just like they took my brother's, and mine, and yours...and your Mum's. She was as pretty as you are, by the way."

I knew I was dealing with a crazy person; just by the way she was bouncing around. A crazy person that had saved *me* from being ripped apart.

"Do you think what you're doing will *make* them listen?"

"Either we have a Constitution, and it applies equally to all of us, or we don't. Those sacred words must apply to everyone, Kaylyn, or they mean nothing! Don't you *see* that? Those suits, those nice people—they're the ones who made killers out of us. Yes—if I make enough noise—they'll listen."

"They'll *kill* you, Rachel."

"Last thing *I'm* afraid of, Babe. But don't you mean—*you'll* kill me?"

"I want to help you." I paused. "But I know how to stop you, too."

"Do you now? You always *were* arrogant, Kaylyn—that's what almost got you killed in Africa. You think you've got me figured out? Go for it! We'll see who comes out on top!"

She hung up, and I wanted to punch something, because I had just thrown down the gauntlet, and if she deviated from her plan, I'd have no one to blame but myself.

• • •

Turns out Rachel stayed right on track. Judge Evans was shot and killed by a high-powered rifle on the 5th...not the month she *wanted* to do it in...but he was just as dead, sitting in the back yard of the safe house. No one saw it coming and no one saw who did it. A quote from

Scripture—James 2:13, was mailed to the State Police Headquarters in Providence:

"*For Judgment will be merciless to one who has shown no mercy.*"

That meant that Rachel would strike twice in one month, with the letter N coming next and on the 14th of February. I was sure of it.

This was all my fault, and I *should* have given her name to the authorities right then and there, but has anybody ever saved *you* from being gang raped and cut to bloody pieces?

• • •

Sam and I were all business and back in the office on February 7th. The cops were absolutely *beside* themselves over this, and the newspapers were having a *field* day with them. Judges were actually taking early retirement, and a lot of them were taking *serious* vacation time as well. If Rachel had wanted to bog down the court system and draw attention to what she was doing—it was working quite well for her. This was National news and the Feds were feeling the heat, too, and Spinelli asked me to work with Sam to find out who might be the next most likely target. Knowing Rachel—or *thinking* I did—I was inclined to believe she'd stick to her original plan now…just to rub our noses in it.

Sam thought so, too.

"Right now," she said, rubbing her nose with the tip of a pencil eraser, "we've only got four active judges with the last name beginning in N. One is on the probate bench, but the other three: Navaro, Nailor and Norton are all currently assigned to the Superior Court. Of the three…" She flipped a page on her notepad, "Norton is our best bet. He's a hard-case by almost anyone's standards, and a mean son-of-a-bitch as well. He's been sanctioned twice by the Judicial Review Board for his disrespectful manner, and has been the subject of at least five cases where Judicial Misconduct was alleged. He yells in the courtroom, has absolutely no manners and five years ago—get this—he actually shot a jogger who he says was *trespassing*." Sam looked at the notebook beside her, studied it for a moment and looked up. "I'm sure of it, Lynn…if Rachel's going forward with this—and we'll find out for sure on the 14th—then Donald J. Norton is our guy." She held up a newspaper clipping from the shooting five years back. "Look at this! Guy looks like a bulldog!"

I put down the piece of *KFC* chicken I'd been picking on and wiped my mouth with a napkin. "What's his track record?"

Sam was eating coleslaw from one of those little cups they give you, and paused for a moment while she took a sip of bottled water.

"Ah…the trials he presides over have an almost 90% conviction rate."

"What a country," I mumbled. "I guess he never heard of innocent until proven guilty."

"This guy? No way. He's about as impartial as a Soviet judge at the Olympics."

I cracked up. How could you not love a chick who says things like that? "Russian, honey, Russian."

"Whatever." She tapped the picture with a pinky. "But based on what Rachel is doing…and why—he's our best bet." She frowned.

"What is it?" I asked.

Sam was looking through a rather sizable printout of all the cases that Norton had presided over. We'd been going back only five years up to this point, because doing otherwise was so cumbersome, but after Evans had been murdered—and while being guarded—Sam had insisted that we go all out.

"I don't know. Something caught my eye earlier and…"

"And what?" I asked impatiently.

"Just a sec."

Sam made a face, picked up her glasses and wiped her fingers on a napkin. Her hair was in a ponytail and at the moment she looked like a college girl. She flipped pages and then flipped back, grabbing a ruler and sliding it down the page.

"Oh my God," she whispered, and looked up. "Christ, Lynn! I was in such a hurry the first time that I didn't even catch it!"

"Catch *what*, Sam?"

Sam didn't answer. Without a word, she highlighted the line she was looking at with a yellow marker and turned the sheaf of papers so I could see it.

"Son of a bitch!" I mumbled, as soon as I saw what she had found. "I've got to call Spinelli right away." I picked up the phone, and he picked up on the second ring.

"Hi, Lynn. What have you got?"

"The next target is Judge Donald J. Norton. Put everything—and I mean *everything*—you've got on him, as soon as you can. Yesterday, in fact."

"*Everything* entails quite a bit, Vale—why are you so sure?"

"Because he was the Judge that presided over the Kyle Worthington case, Bobby—that's why!"

• • •

Earlier in the week, and after struggling with myself, I had given Bobby the article on Worthington that I had taken from Rachel. I told Bobby that I had simply found it in the boat, but the cops were convinced that Worthington's family was a dead end, if you'll pardon the pun, but this—this was too huge to ignore…even for them.

"Holy shit!" he hissed. "Are you sure?"

I sighed. "Would it help if I faxed the damn data over to Headquarters, Bobby? Of *course* we're sure."

I looked at Sam, who nodded, and tore the page off. She threw it on the copy machine, made a dark copy on regular paper, and slid it into the fax machine.

"Sam just sent the page over to you, Bobby," I told him, suddenly feeling very tired.

"It's coming out now. Holy shit," he repeated.

"Ok, now I'm going to ask you something you're not gonna like."

"I don't like *any* of this, Lynn—shoot."

"Whether Worthington has any living relatives or not is no longer the issue, Bobby. Fact Number One is that Kyle Worthington shot Judge Donato. Fact Number Two is that we found an article about Kyle Worthington at the scene. I want your permission to approach Judge Norton and tell him all of this."

"My Captain won't like it, Kaylyn. Norton's been quite clear about not wanting to be baby-sat—his words—especially after Evans—also his own words."

"Would your Captain like it better if we had *another* dead judge on our hands, Spinner?"

"Hang tight," he said. "I'll call you right back."

"Good boy," I told him, and hung up.

"*Men*," Sam and I said at the exact same time, and then cracked up.

• • •

Bobby was as good as his word, and fifteen minutes later Sam and I were on our way to Superior Court, where Norton had a light caseload this morning. Sam was driving her Jeep, and despite the cold, the sun was brutal, and we were both wearing sunglasses. Mine are round and remind me of the kind Jean Reno wore in the *Professional*. Sam favors small, aviator-style sunglasses that make her look like a cop. We had gone out so fast that neither of us had bothered putting our jackets on, and despite the fact that she was well-dressed this morning, Sam was still wearing a short-sleeve shirt and I couldn't help but notice, as she drove, how toned and muscular her arms were.

Or how her breasts literally *defy* gravity.

"Why do you keep staring at me?" she asked after a while and without turning her head.

"If you have to ask, Honey—I must be doing something wrong."

Sam giggled, reached over and slid a hand up and down my left thigh.

"You're not doing a *thing* wrong," she said quietly.

I knew I had to throw a bucket of cold water over the both of us—or we'd be useless by the time we got to the courthouse, so I asked her how things were going at home.

Sam sighed. "Good days and bad days. God, Lynn—I'm a mess."

"Join the club," I told her.

We arrived at the courthouse, and, after going through the metal detector, were ushered into the waiting area adjacent to Judge Norton's chambers. The clerk asked if we had an appointment, and I told him we didn't, but after showing our identification we were told that

Norton would see us in about half an hour. Forty-five minutes later the clerk came back and told us that the Judge would see us now.

We went in and found him sitting behind his desk. Donald J. Norton was exactly what I expected, a cave man with a bulldog face and a blustery manner. He was around fifty years old, and in excellent shape. I disliked him immediately.

"Two private detectives," he said, "and pretty ones at that, coming to see me. My God, ladies, I feel like I'm an extra on an old episode of *Perry Mason*—what can I do for you?"

"Thank you for seeing us, Your Honor," I said and offered my hand. He stood up, and shook hands. "I'm Kaylyn Vale, and this is my associate, Samantha Ashbery. Lieutenant Spinelli of the Rhode Island State Police suggested we talk to you about the murder of Judge Evans and the others."

Norton laughed, and I knew right off that this wasn't going to be easy.

"Why? Am I a suspect?"

Sam and I just looked at each other.

"Sit down, ladies, please," he said. When we were all settled I waited for him to speak first. "Let me guess. Old Spinner and the Feds want me to go into hiding? Put my tail between my legs, that sort of thing? Am I right?"

"New information has come to light, Sir, which suggests you will almost certainly be the next target."

If I had gotten to him, he didn't show it. He leaned back in his chair and laced his fingers behind his head.

"And why is that?"

"A newspaper article concerning Kyle Worthington, who actually killed Judge Donato, was found at the scene, Your Honor, and since you presided over his trial…"

"I see." Norton took his hands down and folded them on the desk in front of him. "So you think—what? That someone associated with him will try to kill me? I'm curious as to how you arrived at that conclusion. Seems to me, that, if Mr. Worthington hated me so badly, why was I not the first person on his list?"

"Sam?" I said, deferring to her.

Judgment Day

Sam explained all about the spelling of the word, JUDGEMENT, and then sat back. "So you see, Sir, we believe your life is in danger, and that the killer will attempt to assassinate you on the 14th of this month."

"Ashbery, Ashbery," he said, instead of addressing what Sam had just told him. "*Wade* Ashbery's…wife?"

The way in which he said *wife*, and the look on his face when he *said* it, suggested strongly that Sam was certainly something *other* than a wife. In a couple of minutes, I was going to shoot this SOB myself.

"Yes, Sir," Sam said in a tone that brought the temperature in the room down at least thirty degrees. "But what you think of me doesn't change the fact that you are in danger."

"You want to know what I think, young lady? I think that you and your husband should be in jail, and if you had drawn any judge other than Christina Haggerty—you *would* be. I also think that the State Police, as well as the Federal Agents involved, couldn't find their own asses with two hands and a flashlight. Seven people—seven *good* people, people who dedicated their lives to ridding the streets of vermin, are dead, and you two prance in here and tell me I'm in danger! Really? Richie Evans was murdered while under guard, for Christ's sake! And now you two want me to, what? Hide somewhere? Get out of here! The both of you! And tell Spinelli—the next time he has something to tell me, he can knock on my door like a man and tell me himself!"

Out in the hallway, Sam turned to me with a grin.

"I thought that went well," she said, "didn't you?"

"You think this is funny, Sam? I don't know how you kept from telling that smarmy son-of-a-bitch to go and *fuck* himself!"

Sam shrugged. I'm used to it, Lynn, and if he wants to ride this out—let him."

I admired her resiliency, but I was still pissed.

I took a deep breath, and as soon as we were outside I called Bobby and told him that Norton wanted nothing to do with any of us.

Bobby, as it turned out, was as complacent on the matter as Sam had been. "Doesn't surprise me, Lynn. He pretty much said the same thing to Captain Simmons."

"So that's it?" I asked as we climbed back into the Jeep. "That's all you have to say?"

"I'll ask the Cap if he wants the Governor to call him, Lynn, but the man is a sitting Superior Court Judge, for Christ's sake. Yeah, that's all I have to say."

"Your funeral," I said, totally exasperated, and promptly hung up on him.

"Where to?" Sam wanted to know.

"Back to the office, I guess. If I know Spinner, he's already got a contingency plan in place. God Almighty! What a fucking cluster fuck!"

We stopped at *Dunkie's* for some coffee, and we hadn't been back in the office for twenty minutes when my desk phone rang.

I got up, looked at the screen and sighed. "It's her," I said to Sam, and picked it up, putting it on Speaker. "Kaylyn Vale Agency."

"How'd it go with Norton?"

"What are you doing, Rachel—watching me?"

"I've always been watching out for you, Lynn, starting back in Rwanda. Haven't you figured that out yet?"

"You can keep throwing that it my face, Rachel, but what you're doing is still wrong."

"Then why haven't you turned me in yet?"

"You know why," I said in a tiny little voice.

"Am I good for a question then?"

"What do you want to know?"

"I'm just curious. How'd you know I'd hit Evans?"

I looked at Sam and she shrugged. It didn't matter at this point. "His track record."

"I think they *all* have a poor track record, Lynn. Maybe you just got lucky."

I knew I was talking to a crazy person. Worse—Sam knew it too. But Rachel had made this personal, and I was playing the cards I'd been dealt.

"I've got a question too."

"Shoot," she said and giggled, "if you'll pardon the expression."

"If you're always watching out for me—why'd you try to kill me that night in the parking lot?"

"God, girl! You thought I was trying to *kill* you?"

"Sure felt like that, Rach."

"You must be getting soft in your old age, Kaylyn, but then again, I've been in a choke hold myself, and on more than one occasion. I guess it *feels* that way, but, no, all I wanted to do was *scare* you. If I had wanted you dead, I could have taken you out with a scope. Could have done it this morning, in fact, when you and your gal-pal went out."

"I told you to leave her out of this."

"She took *herself* off the bench, Lynn. Those are the rules."

Sam walked over to the desk, and lit a cigarette. "I'm standing right here. You got something to say—say it to *me*."

"As a matter of fact, I do. I've read all of your articles, Sam, and I was delighted when you came on board with Lynn. Seems to me, you're on the wrong team though."

"You think so?"

"I know so. For example: That last article you published in *Reason Magazine*. The one about the Prison Industrial Complex?"

"What about it?"

"I'm paraphrasing, but didn't you quote Professor Nils Christie? That crime control in the United States is simply a business? It was well researched, that article. I particularly liked the part about how this so-called War on Crime has been funded by an unprecedented amount of federal money to local police departments. According to you, we've hit a quarter of a *trillion* dollars on this crap in just this year alone, most of it to pay for the arrests in even the smallest of offenses. And we have—what? Six…seven…hundred *thousand* cops in this country? You're right, Sam…we're living in a police state. And the impact of so many arrests has been catastrophic on the economy, because most of those people can't get a job once they get out. Millions of people are being stigmatized by this growing obsession with background checks, internet dissemination and the commercial exploitation of arrest records, too. This makes it all but impossible for anyone with an arrest record to secure employment or even decent housing, which causes even *more* crime—but then again they *know* that. It's their bread and butter, after all. I mean, seriously? Without crime, they're out of business, so if they have to *make* crime, they will. And everyone's getting in on the act. We have for-profit websites now that are in business for the sole purpose of making sure that anyone with a conviction is sentenced to a lifetime of no relationships, no housing and no employment, AFTER they have served their sentence. Just like they did to my brother. So, yeah, Sam, you're on the wrong team."

Sam crushed her cigarette out in the ashtray. "Maybe I'm just not a psycho."

"Meaning *I* am? Why don't you ask your girlfriend about Chief Keating?"

"What about him?"

"*Ask* her! And then tell *me* who the psycho is!"

Police Chief Brian Keating of the Farmington Police had actually ordered his men to shoot Sam the night her step-father had killed her mother. He had done so because, after arresting her step-father for attempting to rape Sam, they had also accepted payoffs for letting him walk. Chief Keating had also been responsible for ordering his men to run Clair and Sam off the road, and for the fire-bombing of Clair's house. A lot of people in the "industry" thought that *I* had killed him, but the truth was—he *had* committed suicide.

This had gone far enough, and I knew I had to regain control of the situation.

"If you're so dedicated to this, Rachel?" I asked just to sidetrack her, "why'd you let your brother handle the Donato hit? That was sloppy, by the way."

"Kyle did the first three all by himself, Lynn. I only came on board when they killed him, and don't tell me *he* committed suicide, too."

Sam was glaring at me, but I didn't know if she was upset with me, the call—or both.

"Then why was the third one so different from the first two?"

"I honestly don't know. Maybe he got impatient. But he apparently had the right idea. Those *good* people you're helping, *they're* the ones who murdered him."

I sighed, and leaned on the desk, speaking directly into the phone, suddenly feeling tired and drained.

"Rachel—listen to me, please. Please stop this. They'll *kill* you eventually—you know that, don't you?"

"Someone has to stand up to them, Kaylyn—someone has to expose what they're doing. They've criminalized normal human behavior, and like Sam says in all her published work, this isn't about protecting true criminals…it's about exposing the ones no one *sees* as criminals."

"Please let this go, Rachel—I owe you my life…I know that… and so much more, but I'm begging you!"

"Ok—I let this go…and what? You'll just let me walk away?"

"I can't turn you in if I don't know where to find you."

"Clever, girl—but what do I have to live for, me and my pretty face?"

"Did that happen in the bombing?"

"God, you're just like Sherlock Holmes, aren't you, Lynn?"

"Just hang up, Kaylyn!" Sam exploded. "Why are you even *talking* to her?"

"Because she's smarter than you, apparently, *Mrs.* Ashbery. After what happened to you and your husband, I really thought you'd be intelligent enough to see this for what it is."

"I see fine, Rachel!" Sam snapped. "I see that you like to *kill* people!"

"And you *don't*, Sammy? I'll be in touch, Lynn," she added, and hung up.

Sam kicked the side of the desk and then swore. I just stood there, watching her, and then, with her hands on the desktop, she met my eyes.

"You have to tell them who she is, Lynn. And you have to do it now!"

"I don't think I can do that, Samantha," I admitted and sat down.

"Look, you owe her—I get that. Totally. But I also get that she's crazier than a shithouse rat! Turn her the fuck in before we both end up in prison!"

"You want out, Sam, just say so," I told her wearily.

Sam was on me in an instant, grabbing the chair in both hands, spinning me around, her green eyes on fire.

"I'm in *love* with you, you crazy bitch!" She shook the chair. "Don't you *get* that? I fucked up my marriage for you. MY decision, not YOURS! But I will *not* just sit her and watch you destroy yourself just because she helped you, once, a very long time ago!" I started crying, and so did Sam. "Use your fucking *head*, Kaylyn! Even if the calls are blocked, they'll be records. I don't care *what* kind of *Spy vs. Spy* crap she knows—the cops'll find out. Is that what you want? For both of us to be indicted for this? Is *that* your idea of loving me?"

Sam pulled me out of the chair and shook me until I looked at her. "Is that what you want for me?"

"No, Sam," I said, sobbing. "I'll tell them, Samantha. I swear I will!"

We held each other, both of us crying, and when it eventually stopped, Sam tilted my chin up with one gentle finger. Her eyes were red-rimmed and full of tears, but the color was more intense than anything I have ever seen. Greener than green; her eyes were liquid emeralds.

"*Did* you kill the police chief?" she asked quietly. "Did you do that for me?"

"If I said yes—would you turn *me* in, Sam?"

She kissed me, and again I thought: *her lips are as soft as they look.* "You know me better than that."

"No, I didn't," I said, and hugged her again, digging my chin into her back and blinking tears as I stared at the wall, wondering if she believed me.

• • •

"Bobby, it's Kaylyn. Can you stop by the office later today? Ok...no, that's fine. We'll see you at three."

I put the phone down and looked at Sam. "Ok?"

"Ok," she agreed, and came over to hold me.

"I feel like my head is going to explode, Sam. I've got to sit down for a while."

I disentangled myself and went to the couch, putting my head back and closing my eyes.

"You got any booze around here?" Sam asked.

"In the desk. Bottom drawer. Left side."

I wasn't looking at her, but I heard her open the desk and pour the bourbon. She came over to the couch with about two fingers of whiskey in our coffee cups, and sat down.

"Drink this," she ordered.

I did as I was told, and downed it in one gulp. It felt like fire going down, and then it warmed my belly and relaxed the back of my neck. I sighed.

"Better?" she asked.

"Yeah. Thanks."

Sam lit a cigarette and passed it to me; then she lit one for herself and sat back, sipping her whiskey.

"You pissed at me?" she asked after a long while.

"No, Sam." I squeezed her hand. "You were right. It had to be done."

"I'm sorry, Kaylyn. I know how hard that was for you."

No you don't, I thought. *You haven't got a clue.* Out loud I said: "It's ok."

We just sat there, holding hands, talking in whispers, until a quarter of three. And then Sam got up and limped into the bathroom, rubbing the back of her thigh as she went. I heard the water running, and then she came back with a wash cloth. Her face was wet, but she looked a little better.

"Here," she said, handing me the cloth. It was hot, and felt good in my hand. "Fix your face."

I scrubbed my face and the back of my neck, folded the cloth and put it over my eyes for a moment.

"Thank you," I mumbled.

"It's only a face cloth, Lynn."

"I meant about making me do this."

"Oh."

"Make sure the door's unlocked will you?"

Sam nodded and I got up and went to the folding table, sighing as I sat down. "Might as well make it look like we're working," I told her.

She made a face, and sat down across from me. "How do you think he'll take this?"

"I know how to handle Bobby," I told her.

I had my chance to prove just that only fifteen minutes later, as Spinner knocked and then came in.

"Wow—you two look like you had a rough night."

"Always know exactly what to say, don't you Spinelli. Sit down, why don't you?"

"Oh-oh," he said, looking back and forth at us. "This can't be good."

"It isn't. And it's complicated."

"Jesus, Lynn—how can it *get* any more complicated?"

"Because some of what I suspect will be classified."

"I'm listening."

"Kyle Worthington had a sister if you remember?"

"Sure—she was killed in an embassy...she worked for the agency," he said, interrupting his own sentence.

"That's what we've been led to believe, but I've been getting these calls, and because I though it was a hoax, I didn't even tell Sam," I lied. "I figured I could tell you both at the same time."

"Tell us what?"

"That I believe Rebekka Worthington is still alive, and that all of this...is her doing."

"How the hell could you...wait a minute...did you get Intel from 'The Company' on this?" His eyes were wide and he looked angry.

"You know I can't give up a source, Bobby—any more than *you* could. This is *dangerous*, and yet, you can come out with that promotion you want, smelling like a rose, if you play this right."

"And just how am I supposed to pull *that* off?"

"Go through official channels. You've got all the political firepower you need right now. Make some inquiries. She's avenging her brother's death, and an article about him was found at the scene. Get the picture? You'll be a hero."

"Yeah, but how did you figure..."

I was already shaking my head—*NO*. "You want that promotion or not?"

Bobby sighed. He was pissed, but he was far from stupid. He glanced at Sam. "And you knew nothing about this?"

Sam shook her head. "I'm hearing this for the first time myself."

"Uh-huh," Spinelli said. "Sure you are." He looked at Sam for a long time, and then back at me. "Whatever else you are, Kaylyn, you've never fucked me over. I'll run with this, but if I get burned, if you make me look like a fool…"

"After all we've been through together, Spinelli—do you *really* think I'd screw you?"

He sighed. "No, I don't."

"Then check it out. Do it quietly. I'm telling you—it's her, and she's very, very good."

"Nuts, too," Sam added.

"But you knew nothing about this, right?"

Sam gave him a look that was a cross between Lauren Bacall and Scarlett Johansson—a look that actually made him blush.

"A girl's entitled to an opinion, isn't she?" she asked sweetly.

• • •

"What do you think he'll do?" Sam asked, watching from the window as he drove away.

"He's a bright boy, Sam—this is his ticket out of this mess."

"You ok?"

"No, Sam—and I don't think I'll ever be ok again. Come on, though—let's get to work. We've got less than a week to get ready for her."

• • •

Sam and I met at my apartment at eleven o'clock on the night of the 13th. That gave us an hour before midnight, and we were planning on staking out Norton's home in Barrington, and, if need be, follow him around the next day.

Norton lived on a Private Way just off Nayatt Road behind the Barrington Country Club, which gave him a magnificent view of the course, as well as a breathtaking vista of Narragansett Bay. The course itself boasted Parkland, Wooded and Seaside Holes, and was designed in 1911 by Donald Ross, who is something of a legend in golf course design—it also gave Rachel a hundred different places to lie in wait with a rifle and high-powered scope.

Years ago I had briefly dated the Golf Pro at the club, and he still had a thing for me. He had agreed to let Sam and I have one of those little carts they use on the course, which make absolutely no noise by the way, and so we left Sam's Jeep in my parking garage and set out in the nondescript, dark blue Honda Civic I had rented for our expedition.

We got to the club at a quarter of twelve, and parked in the employees' lot. Gerry was there to meet us, and told me as we got out that security had been alerted to our presence.

"I should also tell you," he added, "that the cops have been all over this place for the last two days—drove my boss crazy." He smiled then. "You look *good*, Kaylyn."

"So do you," I said sweetly, which was a lie, and then introduced him to Samantha. As I have told you, Samantha is by far the most beautiful woman I have ever seen, but Gerry hardly even looked at her as he shook hands. What can I say? I'm good at what I'm good at.

Gerry Gordon was ten years older than me, and in incredible shape, but he is anything but handsome and can best be described as 'plain'. Ashley had met him once during that summer when I decided that golf would be a good way to meet prospective clients, and had described him as 'ugly'. He, however, is also good at what he's good at.

"Did the police set up on your property?" I rightly guessed.

"Yeah—they're using the clubhouse as a command post."

I made a mental note to steer clear of that area. Spinner had told me that they were actually going to use the house across the street from Norton to set up their own snipers, and, even though Judge Norton had protested, they were going to have a marked State Police cruiser parked in front of his house as well.

None of that bothered me, though, because I knew that Rachel wouldn't have to go anywhere near the house to shoot the bastard, so I planned on using the hill behind his house, which overlooked his backyard and, in my mind, at least, afforded the best vantage point for a rifle. There was a little coffee shop there, and plenty of huge granite rocks that had probably gotten pushed up out of the ocean by Continental Drift eons ago. I planned on watching—not the house itself—but where anyone *else* might be watching the house.

"Is there anything else I can do?" Gerry asked hopefully.

"No, Gerry. I owe you one, though."

"Maybe you'll make it up to me by letting me take you to dinner?"

"That's sweet, Ger—but I'm actually seeing someone," I said, and glanced at Sam—just to needle him a bit.

"Oh," he said, and then, for the first time, felt Sam up with his eyes. "*Oh*," he said again.

"See ya, Gerry," I said, and Sam and I got in the little Yamaha cart and started up the hill.

"You *dated* that guy?" Sam asked, looking back over her shoulder.

"Wouldn't exactly call it *dating*, honey—we spent all of our time that summer in his bedroom."

"Yuck, Kaylyn! He's gross!"

"He's also hung like a bull, sweetie, and I mean a *big* bull!"

"God, girl—you're a slut! Anyone ever tell you that?"

I slipped my arm around her shoulder and fondled one of her boobs. "You mean—*other* than you?"

"Fuck you, Kaylyn!" Sam laughed, and took my hand off her boob.

"Not right now," I told her with a smirk. "We've got work to do."

We drove for a bit and then Sam asked: "Why'd you break up with him?"

I sighed. It was a good question. "Well, he's really very sweet, and awesome and *very* unselfish in bed…but, all my life, I've been looking for something in a relationship, and Gerry just didn't have it."

"What have you been looking for, exactly?" Sam asked in her best, flirty Scarlett Johansson voice. Sam is a natural-born seductress, and the tone of her voice made me laugh. "I'm serious, Lynn—what have you been looking for?"

"Someone I can be myself with; someone I can *connect* with. I can't explain it any better than that."

"Do you think you'll ever find it?" she asked if a very soft voice.

"I already *have*, stupid," I told her, and looked at her.

"Oh," she said, and touched the back of my neck, sending shivers down my spine.

"Stop that!" I said. "We've got work to do!"

We drove around the course, skirting the trees, and came to the little coffee shop, which was closed at this time of night. I parked near that cluster of rocks I told you about, and we got out. The sky was clear and the ocean was a dark green ribbon of beauty on the horizon.

We could hear the waves hitting the shore, and the air was clean and salty. Sam sighed.

"What's wrong?"

Sam shrugged. "Wade used to take me up here all the time when we first started dating."

I took her in my arms for a moment. "Sammy—I love you…and I love what we have…but you're obviously still very much in love with *him*, too, and I want what's best for you—even if it isn't me, ok?"

Sam shrugged me off—gently—and looked in my eyes. "I want what's best for *you*, too."

"Even if it isn't you?"

She nodded, and tears filled her beautiful green eyes. "Yeah."

I touched her cheek. "Enough, now—ok?"

"Ok."

We got up on the rocks and I took out my spy-glasses. Sam had the pair of binoculars she uses at Fenway Park, as she favors the *bleachers* there, and we settled in. Spinner knew where we were, so I wasn't worried about trouble with the cops, but I didn't like the way they were handling this and I knew Rachel well enough to understand that she wouldn't make this easy for us. Rachel Stark was a highly-trained infiltrator and could take Norton out from almost anywhere, and since Norton was such an arrogant bastard, I worried that he'd show his face and promptly get his head blown off.

Not that he didn't deserve it.

Sam was watching the hills to the east, and I had my glasses on the tall pines overlooking Norton's house. I knew it was going to be a long night and was glad we had both slept late.

"Is Wade still at his Mum's?"

"No—but he's sleeping in the spare bedroom."

"Has he touched you?"

"For Christ's sake, Lynn! What a question!"

I suppose it was—they were both so good-looking that the idea of the two of them together was a turn on, and at the same time, made me jealous. "*Has* he?"

"No," she admitted, "and I don't want to talk about it."

"Just remember what I told you."

Judgment Day

"Ditto," she said, which somehow made me angry.

To take my mind off of it, I scanned the yard below. Norton's house was a rambling old Victorian, with a beautifully landscaped yard. It was well lit, and there was no way that anyone could approach from that direction without being seen.

"I'm sorry," I mumbled.

Sam took my hand and put down her binoculars, meeting my eyes. "Me too."

"Tomorrow—when this is over—we'll talk, ok?"

"I want you in my life, Lynn, no matter what. I miss Jenn terribly, and I hate the fact, that, just because we're not sleeping together anymore, she doesn't even want to talk to me. I don't want to go through that again."

"You won't," I said, but I knew it was a lie. I've seen more of the world than Sam has—and being friends with an *ex* never works. Ever. I loved her, but I vowed then and there to break this off as soon as the case was over. Sam had her own license now, but she was an awesome writer and a great lover…and she was still in love with her husband. There's an old saying: no matter how much you tell yourself you're still a kid, when you're over thirty—you know you're *not*.

Well, I was thirty-*four*, but I was mature enough to know that, to Sam, I was nothing more than a pleasant distraction—and I didn't want those children of hers growing up without a father.

And it was time for me to grow up and let this kid get on with her life.

"Can I ask you a question?" Sam asked abruptly.

"Sure."

"What did you mean, when you said you'd never be 'ok' again?"

"I broke the code, turning Rachel's name over to the authorities, Sam. I know it had to be done, but it's taboo, and goes against what I stand for."

"You're against turning psychopaths over to the cops?"

"It's not about what *she* is, Sam—it's about who I am."

"I'm not sure I get that."

My elbows were killing me because I had been holding the spy glass in one position for so long, so I put them down and turned to her.

"Let me explain it like this: I have a history with her. She's nuts, but she's also family, so to speak. She was my partner, like you're my partner, and you don't let your partner down—no matter what. You can't go through the kind of things we went through together, and not be…connected. It's like combat veterans and what they feel about each other. The SEALS have a code, or so I've been told: No one gets left behind. And this is no different. Rachel is crazy, there's no question of that, but I wanted to handle this my own way and in my own time. Doesn't matter what she's done or even what she *might* do—she's family, and if someone needed to put her down…it should have been *me*."

"And you blame me for that, don't you?"

"I wish I could, Samantha—I wish I *could* blame someone else, but this was my decision and I guess I'll have to live with it. Sometimes…the line between right and wrong gets blurry, and I'm just having trouble with that. See what I mean?"

"As long as you and I are ok," she said after searching my eyes.

"We'll always be ok," I assured her, knowing that I really didn't mean it.

We sat on that rock until four o'clock in the morning, and that's when the wind picked up. We were well-dressed for the occasion, and both of us were wearing thermals, but that wind was cruel, and it started to wear on us. I took the little Thermos out of my ruck-sack and poured us both some coffee. It was still piping hot, and did us both a world of good. By five I was thinking that Rachel would hit him as he came out in the morning, and by six I was sure of it. Despite the rest we had gotten the day before, both of us were sleepy and cold and annoyed. When seven o'clock rolled around, I started to panic.

"What's his schedule for the day, Sam?"

Samantha consulted the little notebook we had put together, and looked up at me. "He's got an evidentiary hearing at nine."

The sun was up by this time and the reflection off the water was brutal. If Rachel was going to hit him using a scope, it made sense to me that she'd be to our east, facing *away* from the sun. But none of the angles from that direction offered any vantage point, and then it suddenly occurred to me that Rachel might be out on the water. I turned my head and scanned the bay for boats, but there was nothing in sight. I put my spy glass down and took out my sunglasses. At eight o'clock Norton came out the front door, and paused, looking up at the hill, as if he was defying whoever might be watching.

"Asshole," Sam murmured, and I silently agreed.

Norton continued to stand there, taking big gulps of fresh morning air and most likely sending the cops into apoplectic fits. Then he walked calmly to the driveway and got in his Lexus. I half expected it to explode when he stated it, but nothing happened. He backed out, and headed towards Nayatt Road. The cruiser waited a moment and then followed.

"Come on," I told Sam and scrambled for the golf cart.

We got back to the Honda ten minutes later, and I went west, confusing Sam.

"Aren't you going to follow him?"

"No, she's going to hit him at the courthouse—I'm sure of it."

"How do you know?"

"Because none of us thought of it, and because she's been watching us all along. I know some back roads," I added, "I want to be at the courthouse when he gets there."

The Honda was fast, and I pushed it, running lights when I had to and drawing more than one angry blare of a horn. On Tri-Town Highway I opened it all the way up, hoping that I didn't run across a speed trap. I didn't, and we arrived at the courthouse before he did, going straight to his assigned parking space out back and parking across the street where we could watch as he drove in.

"We've probably got five minutes, Sammy. Let's get out." I handed her one of my walkie-talkies and clipped the other to my belt. "I'll take the back steps to the courthouse. You go over to that little coffee shop over there." I pointed. "And check the rooftop on the Probate Court. She might be up there."

Sam smirked. "Ok if I go in and get warm?"

"Long as you can see the roof, Baby."

Sam got out and immediately crossed the street, nonchalantly looking up as she did so. She was a natural, and I felt a pang of remorse at the thought of losing her.

There was a 'roach-coach' on my side of the street, and I walked over and got some coffee, standing in line with a bunch of early court staffers. When a small group of four or five women met on the steps with their coffee and all lit up, I joined them, lighting my own and sipping from my cup.

Despite the cold I was sweating and wondering what I had missed. As long as I've been doing this I always know when I screw up, even if I don't know what I've done. I felt like that now, and I didn't like it.

Ten minutes later Norton's car drove into the lot. I could see now that his car had tinted windows, and I didn't like *that*, either. He parked in his assigned spot—and then just sat there. Just then there was a loud *crack* down the block and closer to where Sam was, and the cops that had been following Norton flipped their lights on and pulled over. The noise could have been a gunshot or a cherry-bomb or a firecracker for all I knew, but as the Troopers pulled their weapons and approached the dumpster where the sound had come from, I heard a car door slam and looked back at Norton's Lexus, expecting him to be heading up the steps…or slumped over the wheel with the window blown out.

I got neither. He was still just sitting there.

I had only turned my head for a second when I had heard the shot, but I somehow knew that Rachel had beaten me again. An arrogant sitting Superior Court Judge didn't sit in his car when he had a hearing to prepare for, and as I sprinted for the Lexus I knew that I had blown it.

The two Troopers who were by the dumpster saw me, and I thought I recognized one of them, which was good, because neither one of them shot me, and I reached Norton's car a moment before they did, pulling the door open and finding him sitting there was his throat cut from ear to ear.

There was a note stuffed in his top left suit coat pocket. I would find out later that it was another quote from Scripture, this time from Isaiah:

"*Woe to you that call evil good, and good evil.*"

"Out of the way, Vale," the Trooper said, shoving me roughly aside.

Just then my phone chirped. There was a text. Two words only. Both in caps.

"GOT YA!"

• • •

Sam and I were told by the Trooper that Captain Simmons wanted to see us down at Headquarters, and I knew we were in trouble.

"You want to bring us in, big guy," I asked, "or can I drive over there myself?"

Sam was standing beside me, looking scared and very, very young.

"If it was up to *me*, Sweetheart, you and your little playmate here would both be in cuffs right now."

"Figures," I said. "Tying girls up is the only way you probably ever get any."

"Just get your Private *Ass* out of here, Vale, or I'll charge you with interfering in a police investigation!"

"Investigate *this*, Motherfucker," I said, and flipped him the 'bird' as I grabbed Sam's arm and hauled her off.

As soon as we were in the Honda, Sam started giggling. Nothing was funny, and I knew that it was only the release of nervous tension, but I cracked up just the same and kissed her full on the lips.

"What was *that* for?" she asked, blinking.

"I got all squishy thinking about you in handcuffs, that's all."

"Your *brain* is squishy, Kaylyn! You know that? You are—by far—the *craziest* bitch I have ever known!"

"Yeah, but I'm good in bed."

Sam laughed even harder. "God help me—you certainly are!"

The cop at the desk put us in an 'interview' room as soon as we arrived, but a uniformed police woman brought us coffee and smiled at us, which seemed to make Sam breathe easier. Ten minutes later Bobby came in and sat down.

"You two ok?"

"Yeah," I said. "Where's your Captain?"

"Down at the scene. Feds have the whole damn block cordoned off. Courthouse is closed, too."

"How much trouble are we in?"

"None, actually," Bobby said, surprising me. "Fact is, they need a scapegoat, but you're the one who got there first. We *all* have egg on our faces, and the Cap just wanted me to tell you to lie low for a while, and not to talk to any reporters. He, uh, also wants you off the case. Too much heat from the Feds."

"You know what, Bobby? Good. Just have that fat fuck cut me a check and I'm out, ok? Fuck him and while we're at it, fuck *you*, too!"

"Jesus H. Christ, K! Calm the fuck down! I said he *wants* you off the case, but he isn't going to get his way. Fact is, the Governor does *not* want you off the case. See what I mean?"

"I don't understand," Sam said.

"I do," I snapped. "Politics!" I said it like it was a dirty word, and I guess it is.

"I still don't get it," Sam confessed.

"The cops are going to work us and take all the credit because, officially—we're out. Screw you, Bobby!" I got up, and Sam did too.

"Aw, com'on, Lynn! Be reasonable!" Bobby whined.

"Listen to me, Spinner, and I'm only telling you this because we go back a ways. That bitch is not—repeat—NOT—going to stop, and the only way I can nab her is if I'm on my own, without you yahoos gumming up the works. Have the check sent to my office." I made it as far as the door and then he stopped me.

"Don't you even want to know what we found at the scene?"

I paused with my hand on the doorknob. "Let me guess: someone lit a firecracker and threw it in the dumpster."

"It was a cherry-bomb, actually. How do you think she did the rest of it?"

I sat back down, fuming, and drummed my fingers on the table. "I *know* how she did it."

"Care to share it?"

I sighed. "She was already *in* the damn car, Spinner. Probably got in it yesterday down at the courthouse. Where none of us were watching. And I'll bet you'll find out that the surveillance camera that was on the row where Norton's car is assigned was out of service or realigned."

"And the fireworks?"

I shrugged. "She paid some *bay-zo* or some kid to do it. When the diversion took hold of us and we all looked away from the car, she rolled out and simply walked away."

"How can you be so sure?"

"Because that's how I would have done it."

CHAPTER EIGHT—March

I knew someone was in my apartment as soon as I opened the door, and when I snapped on the light I saw Rachel sitting in my favorite chair, pointing a gun at me.

I held my hands out at my sides and just froze.

"Smart girl, Kaylyn. Sit down."

I came in, dropped my bag on the floor and went for the couch, wondering if I could get to the gun on my hip as I sat down.

"Don't even *think* about it," she said. "I've got a man with a rifle on Sam and if I don't call him in exactly fifteen minutes—she's dead."

"Mind if I smoke?" I said.

Rachel laughed. "Like I smoked *you* today?"

I just looked at her and lit a cigarette.

"What do you want, Rach?"

"That's an interesting question: what do I want? Let's see. I want my brother back, my life back and my face back…and I want the girl back whose life I saved."

Rachel was sitting so that her good side was towards me, but even like that I could see the edge of the damage on the other side of her face. I can't even imagine what burns like that would feel like, or what they might do to the psyche of a pretty young woman that hadn't had much self-esteem to begin with.

"I'm right here."

"Are you? The girl *I* knew never would have ratted me out. I thought we had an agreement? I thought this was just between you and me?"

"I already told you, Rachel—I'm going to stop you."

"By telling the *cops* about me? What's the matter, couldn't take me on one-on-one?"

Rachel was pointing a 9mm pistol at my stomach, but that didn't stop me from losing my temper. "You've been *calling* me, shithead! They'll be records! I don't plan on doing prison time as an accomplice for this. This is your game, Rachel, not mine!"

"Just what *is* your game, Kaylyn?"

That was an interesting question, as well. "I honestly don't know anymore, Rach. I really don't."

"Want me to tell you?"

"Sure."

"You're off your game because you've lost yourself, Lynn. You don't even know who you *are* anymore let alone what you *stand* for. You're not even really alive. You're just existing, getting from day to day the best way you can—even if it means feeling nothing."

"You've just described about half the people on the planet, Rachel."

"Do you see their faces, Lynn? Do you see their faces at night?"

"Who are you talking about?"

"The faces of the people you've killed, the faces of the people they *made* us kill."

"I don't think much about it anymore, Rachel. I'm numb."

Rachel reached into a pocket and took out a silencer and fitted it to the barrel of the gun. The movement gave me a good look at the left side of her face and it made me shudder.

"Maybe I should just kill you then and put you out of your misery?"

I had left a little Dixie Cup on the end table beside the sofa. There was a half inch of water in it and as I dropped my cigarette into it there was a quick sizzle.

"Go ahead. You'd be doing me a favor."

Rachel shook her head. "No, I don't think so. You live with it, with all you've done and all you *didn't* do."

"And what about you?"

"I finish the game. But I'll make a deal with you. You stay out of this, for good, and I'll tell you where to find your Mother."

"And if I don't?"

"I'll kill you *and* your little playmate." She stood up and put the gun in her pocket, daring me with her eyes to do something. "Go ahead. Go for it. See what happens to Sam. I might just go ahead and kill her anyway, because the girl I knew in Rwanda never would have sold anyone out. You sold yourself out, too—and for what? A romp in the hay with some slut who's just using you?"

Rachel took a kerchief out of her jacket pocket and covered her head. She pulled up her collar and put one hand on the doorknob.

"Remember what I told you," she said, and then she was gone.

There wasn't a sound out there in the hallway, because the floor is carpeted, but I went to the door anyway and listened, crouching low with my gun in my hand. I heard the distinct *ding* of the bell on the elevator, and then nothing—so I stood up and gazed out through the peephole: there was no one in sight.

I was still wearing my jacket so I didn't need to get dressed, but before I opened the door I put my gun in my pocket and crept out, hurrying down the hallway opposite the elevator, taking the EXIT stairs two at a time all the way to the bottom. I knew I should be taking the time to call Sam and warn her, but I truly didn't think Rachel would do anything tonight, and this was my one and only chance to follow her to see where she went.

As a detective, you follow up on leads, but this game with Rachel had left me with none to follow. She would call, I would answer, and then she would hang up. Even if I *could* have traced the calls, she was most likely using a 'burner' phone and it wouldn't have led me to an address. I knew she had to be local, but where? And as I got to the bottom of the stairwell I paused, thinking about what I would have done had I been in her shoes. Rachel would almost certainly have used the parking lot behind the building rather than risk the security cameras in the garage, so that meant I had a minute or two until she got to the back lot.

The garage under my building is open at the front entrance where the gate is, and at the back end near the lot, where the building itself sits on huge concrete columns. I took a deep breath, cracked the door and stepped out, crouching near an SUV where I had a good view of the lot.

A moment later I was rewarded for my presence of mind when I saw her walking across the lot, kerchief and all, towards a late model compact car. I couldn't see the color because that end of the lot isn't well lit, but I was pretty sure that it was a Ford.

Now, what to drive?

Rachel knew I owned a Mustang, but she also knew I'd been driving the Honda. The latter was out in the side lot, and my Pony was sitting not ten feet away. It's black and it's fast and it was right here, and I'm pretty good at tailing people, so I opted for the Mustang and quickly got in, starting the engine as soon as I saw Rachel get in the car, which I could now see was a Ford Escort.

I left the lights off and waited.

Rachel pulled out a minute later, got on the access road near the hiking trails, and pulled over.

I was still sitting in the garage.

Nice try, bitch, I thought.

A good five minutes went by, but then her tail-lights flashed as she stepped on the brake, put the car in DRIVE and pulled away from the curb. The access road was almost a quarter of a mile long and leads to Nicholas Cooke Parkway, named for the first governor of Rhode Island, and runs from the Farmington Town Line to the Barrington Town Line for half a mile in either direction, so I knew I could afford to sit here for another minute.

Rachel's claim of a gun on Sam advised me to use extreme caution here, but it was only ten past nine, and if I waited long enough she couldn't possibly think that every car she saw behind her was a tail.

On the other hand, I couldn't afford to lose her, either.

I waited until her brake lights flashed again at the end of the access road, and then she put her right blinker on. I came out of the garage at a crawl, but as soon as she took the turn, heading towards Farmington, I hit the gas and roared down to the crossroad. I stopped at the corner, and saw her a few hundred yards away, and as luck would have it a car pulled out of a driveway just as she passed it, and I knew I was good to go.

Now there was a vehicle between us, but I still held back, still running with my lights off, maybe a dozen car lengths behind the car that had come out of the driveway. There was a set of lights ahead at the intersection, and both of the cars in front of me where already slowing down, so I took the opportunity to swing into the same lot where Rachel had jumped me—still with my lights off—swung around, flipped the lights on, and put my right directional on as I pulled out of the empty lot, making it appear as if I had been in there when they passed it.

"Fuck you, honey," I actually mumbled out loud.

Now there were *two* cars between us, and I was almost giddy with excitement. I punched in the cigarette lighter—a special order, by the way—and pulled a smoke from my pocket without taking my eyes from the cars in front of me. The lighter *popped* and I lit up, drawing deeply and hoping to get my hands to quit shaking. Rachel turned right at the lights, headed towards Farmington Wharf, and I hung in there at the light as the other two cars went straight, waiting for the woman across from me to take her left and take up a position between Rachel and me. Now there was nowhere to go but the waterfront, and there was no other way out of there unless she drove into the water, so I pulled into the lot where the original Clam Shack is—best crab cakes on the planet, by the way—and shut my lights. The other car turned off at that little apartment building down there, but Rachel went all the way to the end near the wharf, and pulled into the little lot where the shuttle commuters park during the day. She got out of the Escort, and started walking down towards the docks.

Please, God, I thought, *don't let her get in another boat!*

I don't know how I feel about God anymore—there's simply too much chaos, pain and destruction in the world for me to believe in a supposedly-loving Father, and the planet itself seems to thrive on entropy, violence and decay, but for once my prayer was answered, and

Rachel walked past the long line of boats, and tuned right at the end, where there was a long row of old buildings on the same side where I was parked. I got out and started running, and got to the edge of the building where she was walking just as she went up the front steps.

I had never been down on this side before, so I had never noticed the weather-beaten sign above *Eva's Boarding House*, advertising: ROOMS FOR RENT.

I waited in the shadows, grateful that there was only the one little light across the street on a telephone pole, and a moment later a light went on in the third window on the first floor, where the building was practically hanging out over the water.

I waited for over an hour, but that light never went out.

• • •

When I got back in the Mustang I looked up the number for the boarding house on my phone and called it. A woman answered on the third ring, sounding as ancient as the building looked.

"Eva's Boarding House."

"Uh, hi—uh, I just got to town, and another girl told me you might have a room available."

"Sorry, dear, just rented the last one out to an elderly gent only this morning. Poor old thing. On a fixed income, and his own daughter threw him out. Can you imagine such a thing?"

Thank you, God—a talker! Maybe He *was* listening after all!

"Oh, that's so disappointing! I've come to care for my mother—she's not well, you see—and my sister, well, she must be related to the woman who threw out her own father because she won't let me stay at the house! I was *so* hoping you'd have something!"

"Well now—don't you worry, dear. We rent by the week and by the month, no leases; people come and go all the time. Can you leave a number? I'll call you as soon as I have a vacancy."

"Are you Miss Eva?" I asked to give myself time to think.

"Why, yes, hon, I am."

"No wonder you're so nice. The girl *said* you were!"

"What girl, dearie?"

"Why, the one who told me about the rooms for rent. I met her at the hospital when I went in to see Mother," I added, congratulating myself on how manipulative I could be. "Poor thing," I mumbled after pausing a moment.

I could have been talking about my 'mother' *or* the other girl, but old Eva—she took the bait.

"I know!" Her voice dropped to a conspiratorial whisper. "Those burns are just awful!"

"Poor thing," I repeated.

"So nice, though, isn't she?"

"Yes, but shy. She *did* tell me, though, that you run a very nice place."

"That was sweet of her, and trying to drum up business for me! Been here for almost a year now, pays by the month, and never late, either. And I do run a clean house, too, except for that one time when that man brought those roaches in. The building inspector said it was because the house is so old, but I know a filthy person when I see one and I know he brought those things in here with him. Took care of *that* though—are you a friend of Debbie's?"

"Debbie?"

"The burned girl," she whispered. "And, God, she'd be so pretty…if not for, well you know."

"Oh, no, and please don't tell her I called. She must be so self-conscious! No, I just bumped into her while I was visiting Mother. She must go there for treatment. Poor thing."

"Isn't she though? She's an author, by the way! Bet you didn't know that! Sits in there all day, writing and writing. Stories for kids. I think she must be lonely—all those burns."

"And I'll bet no one comes to see her, either."

"Well, there *was* one man—she said it was her brother, but he didn't look anything like her. He came by a few times back in—oh let me see—was it late August or early September?"

"What did he look like, Eva?"

"Oh, tall, skinny, brown hair a little younger than she is. He stopped coming after a while. People thought he was, you know, paying her for, you know, but I never believed it. All those burns."

Eva had just described Kyle Worthington, and the time frame was right, too.

"I'm *sure* she's a good girl, being a children's author and all, Eva."

"That's what I think, too! Well, my show's about to come on now, Sweetie, so give me your number and I'll call you when someone moves out."

"Great!" I said and gave her the number of one of the four different 'burner' phones I keep in my glove compartment just for such purposes. "And thank you so much!"

"And thank you for calling and for being so nice to poor Debbie."

"Oh, not at all, and as I said, please *don't* tell her I called. She'll be self conscious, and think we were talking about her, because if I *do* move in, I'm *sure* we can be friends!"

"Sure wish I had a vacancy! You sound *so* nice! What's *your* name, by the way, honey?"

"Me? Why, *my* name is Debbee, too. Only I spell it, with two B's and two E's—Debbee Morgan." I had just given her the name of my third grade teacher.

"Ok, Debbee, and please *do* call soon!'

"Oh, I *will*, Eva. And thanks again!"

I hung up, not feeling guilty in the least for deceiving the old lady. Now I had a line on Rachel, and could stake her out whenever I wished.

The *next* part of my night wouldn't be as easy though—because now I had to go and convince Sam to leave town before Debbie-the-children's-author *killed* her!

• • •

It was almost eleven o'clock, but this was something I couldn't put off—not with Sam in danger like this—and I shook my head as I headed towards her place, knowing I was opening a can of worms and still seeing no way out of it. I felt guilty, too, now that I knew where Rachel was. I *should* have been calling Spinner right this second and telling him where she was—but I just couldn't. I know you probably think I'm a monster for letting her stay on the street—and as it would turn out, Sam would eventually think so too—but this was something I just *had* to do on my own, and I vowed right then and there to keep her whereabouts to myself…at least until I had a chance to think this through.

I just hoped she didn't kill anyone else in the meantime.

Rachel had accused me of being arrogant, and I guess I am, but she was all of that and more, herself, and if she stuck to her game plan that meant I had until the 20th of March, because, as Sam and I had guessed, the next letter would be a 'T'.

Still, I wondered, why was I dragging my feet? Deep down I knew the answer: she had saved me from being savagely tortured and ripped apart, but at the end of the day, was that really any reason to chance another victim?

I've been told that I'm my worst enemy, and I suppose that's true, but when you've been through the sausage grinder with someone it creates a bond that is not easily or quickly broken. Later, when the worst was over, I'd come to realize that my reasoning was pure bullshit and that this was really about clinging to the desperate hope of finding my mother, but I was so fucked up at that moment because I was worried about Sam, that I simply couldn't think straight.

When I was five minutes from Sam's place I pulled out my phone and called her. It rang four times and went into voicemail. I swore and kept driving. I was turning onto her street when she called me back, and I answered before the second ring.

"Hey, Kiddo."

"Kaylyn, it's eleven o'clock! What's wrong?"

"A lot. I'll be in your driveway in a minute."

"Jesus, Lynn! Wade's on the couch! He fell asleep watching the damn Bruins game!"

"Good," I told her, "because what I have to say concerns you both. I'll be up in a minute," I added, and hung up.

Wade answered the door when I got there, wearing a wife-beater Tee and sweatpants. He looks a lot like the actor, Zac Efron, but he's built like Vin Diesel and, at the moment he didn't seem too happy to see me.

"Why is my wife crying, Kaylyn?" he said by way of saying 'hello'.

"Let me in, Wade. The both of you are in danger."

Wade had been, and I suppose always would be, a Force Recon Marine. Their training is similar to the Navy SEALS, but they have a reputation for being the guys you call when the other Special Forces need help. Force Reconnaissance Marines are a specialized, elite, operations-capable unit, and are among the deadliest and most highly-trained combat troops the world has ever seen. Historically, Force Recon Marines have been specialists in unconventional special operations, like the mission Wade and I shared in Afghanistan, and all of them are experts at hand-to-hand combat; if there's a weapon on the planet they don't know how to use better than anyone else, I've never seen it. All in all they are not people you want mad at you—like he was mad at me right now.

"What the fuck are you talking about?"

Sam came in just then, her eyes brimming with tears, which probably kept me from saying something stupid.

"Look," I said, "I know it's awful coming here like this." If you've ever been in the same room with a married couple—and you've slept with both of them—you know what an understatement that is. "But Rachel came to my apartment tonight, and she threatened you, Sam. I want you and Wade and the children to get out of here, now, tonight—before it's too late."

"Who the fuck is Rachel?" Wade demanded, folding his arms across his chest.

Sam met my eyes. "Let me tell him," she said, and ten minutes later he knew all of it—except for the fact that I knew where she was.

"Why didn't you take her out when you had the chance, Lynn?"

Gone was the gentle man who had comforted—and slept with me, overseas; Wade was only concerned about his family at the moment, and I didn't blame him.

"Weren't you *listening*, Wade? She said she had a gun on her!"

"You're a fucking hurricane! You know that, Lynn? Everywhere you go you fuck up people's life's and—"

"Wade!" Sam snapped. "You're not helping!"

"You just *had* to get mixed up with her, Sammy? Didn't you?"

"Listen to your wife!" I hissed, "And think about her and the kids! You want to take my head off, do it *after* I bring this psycho in. But right now, get Sam out of here!"

"I'm not going anywhere," Sam said quietly.

"Be reasonable," I begged, "and think of your children."

Everyone was quiet for a moment, and then Wade sighed. "How good is she?"

"The best."

"As good as you are?"

"Maybe even a little better…and she's as good as *you* are, too, Wade. Look, I'm sorry!" Tears leaked out of my eyes, and I felt like I was in a bad movie, but I just couldn't keep my mouth shut, not with so much at stake. "You were there for me in Afghanistan, Wade. And Sam's been there for me right *here*. I'm sorry, I'm sorry, I'm sorry! But I didn't force either *one* of you to sleep with me, and we have to get past that if we're going to protect the kids!"

"Would she 'hit' a child?" Wade asked, the Marine re-asserting itself.

"I don't know. But why take the chance?"

"You go, Sam. I'll stay here with Lynn and—"

"NO!" I hissed. "You're *both* going! Sam, *you're* going to protect your kids! And Wade—*you* protect your wife! This woman is highly trained and she's *insane*! She's killed *eight* people that we know of, or at least had something to do with all eight, most of them while under surveillance. That sound like someone you want to play with? Now do as I say and get going!"

"She'll *kill* you, Lynn," Sam whispered. "You know that, don't you?"

"I really don't even care anymore, Samantha. This is my mess, and *I'll* deal with it, whatever comes of it. I just hope the two of you can forgive me for being such a screw up, because the truth is, I never meant to hurt either one of you."

Neither of them said a word, so I guess I got my answer right then and there.

• • •

The rest of February blew by in a flash, and it was March before I could blink. Sam and Wade had reluctantly done as I'd asked, and I hadn't even asked where they were going. I knew Wade wouldn't be able to stay away forever, not with his job at the school, but I hoped and prayed that whatever came, Sam would stay in hiding until this was over.

I only had until the 20th of the month to figure out who the next target might be, but I was working on a plan to confront Rachel *before* she struck again…now that I knew where she was…and so with some effort, I pushed both Sam and Wade from my mind, knowing that, in all probably, I'd lost any hope of ever having either of them in my life again.

Turns out I was right about everything that had happened that day at the courthouse. For one thing, the security camera that was dedicated to that section of the parking lot had somehow been re-aligned, and the State Police ended up relying on the cameras from the coffee shop across the street, which clearly showed a woman wearing a kerchief getting out of the back seat of Judge Norton's car; but you couldn't see her face as she hurried to the sidewalk, and grabbed a man's arm. He looked startled when she linked her arm through his, and the Feds were currently looking for him, but the end result was the same: Norton was dead, and Rachel had beaten us again.

A teenage girl confessed to throwing the cherry-bomb in the dumpster. She'd been skipping school and said a lady with a "burned-up face" had given her a twenty dollar bill to do so, adding that she wanted to "play a joke" on someone. The girl had been questioned and released to her parents. This information gave my statement about a "dead woman" being a possible suspect a little more credibility, and no one was laughing at me anymore—at least not to my face—but as Bobby told me one night over coffee: "Where do we look for a dead woman?"

"I don't know," I told him, wondering once more why I didn't just go ahead and send them down to the boarding house. I also couldn't figure out how Rachel had known that I had given her up as a suspect, so I assumed she had a few contacts of her own, or maybe she was watching me more frequently than I'd care to admit.

I'm telling you this story by relying on my own case notes, and after consulting them I can tell you for a fact that the conversation I was having with Spinelli occurred on the 8th. If Rachel was sticking to her game-plan, that gave me twelve full days until the 20th, when her next victim would be someone whose last name began with the letter "T"—but I planned on taking her down before we even got *close* to that, and if you want the *truth* as to why I didn't let the cops handle this, I was afraid that Rachel might have a contingency plan in place to harm Sam and the kids. That meant, that, when I did take her down—I was going to have to take her down *permanently*. *Something* had to be done, and I was damned if I was going to be coerced. It's possible that Rachel could have had some kind of "Doomsday" failsafe in effect as well, but there was nothing I could do about that and all I could do was pray that Sam stayed in hiding until I'd dealt with Rachel. I was also thinking that it was better to take a chance on my own than trust that she wasn't tapping into any communications from the Feds.

I was also scared that if I sent Bobby and his crew down there, she'd blow the place up or something. You might think you know about people like Rachel and me from watching the movies, but trust me when I tell you that you have no idea what we're capable of. More than one assassination, for example, has been accomplished by blowing up an entire jet-liner, so I knew I had to do this on my own.

And since I'm being so honest, it's not just that I owed Rachel so much that made me hesitate…it was because what happened to her could surely happen to me. When you live in this awful world of kill-or-be-killed, you're always an inch away from snapping and going off the deep-end yourself.

Of course, I didn't share any of that with Bobby.

"So what are you thinking?" Bobby asked when I was quiet for longer than was comfortable for him.

"Well," I began and took out my notebook, "if Sam is right, and the killer IS spelling out JUDGEMENT DAY, then the next target will almost certainly be a judge whose last name ends in a T."

Bobby made a notation in his own notebook, and promised to get his people working on it. I hardly paid attention, since I had no intention of letting it get that far.

"I also wanted to ask you," he said without looking up, "about the manifesto the killer sent to Clair Sacchetti."

"What about it?"

"In your opinion, is it authentic?"

"Look, Spinner." I closed my mouth, and looked around the parking lot. We were sitting in his car at *Honey Dew Donuts*, and I was more than a little bit paranoid. "You wouldn't tap me, would you?"

"Go to bed with you in a New York minute," he answered with a smirk.

Normally, that sort of thing would make me giggle, but with everything that had happened I simply wasn't in the mood. "I'm serious—you're not wearing a wire or anything?"

"That's a hell of a thing for you to say to me, Vale," he snapped, looking angry.

"I'm sorry, but I had to ask. Someone at The Agency put her job on the line for this, and I can't give her up." Some of that was a lie. *I'm* the one who figured out it was Rachel, but I couldn't very well tell him that without telling him everything else. And as I've already said, this was *my* mess, and Rach had made it personal. "I'm telling you that Rebekka Worthington is alive, and if you check the records and see what they did to her brother, you'll see for yourself that the note is authentic."

"And I get the Feds to go along with your instincts—how?"

"Because an article written by Clair was found at the scene, Spinner! It's a fucking lead, damn it, and if they don't follow it they'll end up chasing their tails!"

Bobby held up his hands. "Okay, okay! Just asking!"

"Look," I said, "I've got something to do…please just get on those 'T's' and get me some names, okay? We're running out of time here!"

"I'm on it. Incidentally—I haven't seen much of Sam lately. Everything ok?"

"No, not really. Her husband's royally pissed because she's been working with me. I don't think she'll be back."

"That's a shame. Kid does nice work."

"That's just it, Spinner," I said as I got out, "she *is* a kid."

I drove home slowly, thinking I should just go back and tell him everything, but I was in this up to my ears now and if they ever took Rachel alive I couldn't be sure that she wouldn't implicate me. I *had* to do this on my own, whether I liked it or not, and after sending that manifesto to Clair, God alone knew what else she may have written.

I wasn't in the damn apartment ten minutes when my phone rang: *unknown caller.*

"Gonna put you on speaker while I pour a glass of wine for myself, Rach."

"Maybe I should come over and join you."

"Whatever," I said, and downed half a glass. I refilled it, added an ice cube and sat down on the couch. I put my phone on the armrest and lit a cigarette.

"You don't sound too happy to hear from me."

"What do you want, Rachel?" I said, and closed my eyes

"Nothing really. I'm just bored."

"Really? Go blow something up, why don't you?"

"Wow…you really don't get this, *do* you?"

"Yeah, I get it, Rachel—you got fucked, your brother got fucked. Join the club."

Rachel was silent for a moment, but I could hear her breathing. When she spoke again it was the voice I remembered from Africa, warm and caring and compassionate: the voice she had used right after I was attacked.

"*You've* been fucked over, too, Kaylyn—and more than once."

I leaned my head back and sighed. "Yeah, but that's no excuse for blaming the whole world for it, Rachel. The fucking system sinks, but if we all went around killing people every time something went wrong, we'd never solve anything."

"Ever wonder why you're such an angry person, Kaylyn?" she asked in a sweet, soft voice.

"What are you—my therapist?"

"No…*I'd* never lie to you."

"No, *you'll* just threaten the people I love, right?"

"Believe it or not, Kaylyn," she answered in that same gentle tone, "I *never* would have hurt Samantha. I just wanted this between you and me—even though you *did* rat me out."

"Well, I'm alone now and you got what you wanted, and all I told the cops was that I thought you were still alive, Rachel—you did that to yourself by carrying that damn article around with you." I had to pause because I was on the verge of tears. "Mind telling me how you found that out, though?"

There was the sound of movement, and in my mind I saw her shrug. "If the public knew how easy it is to tap into official communications, we'd have a panic on our hands, don't you think?"

"I suppose." I should have known I wasn't going to get a straight answer.

"How did you feel that night, Kaylyn?" she asked in that same, infuriatingly tender voice. "How did you feel when they beat you and ripped your clothes off?"

"I was scared," I answered as tears ran down my cheeks.

"And who stopped them?"

"You did!" I screamed. "*You* did! Is *that* what you wanted to hear?"

"Yes, but not for the reason you think. They were animals, Kaylyn, and I put them down. I put them down and now they can never hurt anyone else again. I'm just trying to get you to see that this is no different. And while I'm at it, let me tell you a story. While my brother was in prison, banned from his own life, he met a man who was doing time for raping and killing a child. There was no motive, no means and no opportunity, as there must be to obtain a conviction, no witnesses, no DNA, not a *shred* of evidence—and yet this innocent man got life without the possibility of parole. Meanwhile, the *real* killer took out six more kids while the innocent man was repeatedly raped in prison and eventually died of AIDS. Turns out the District Attorney KNEW he was innocent, too—but he had his win, and the public was satisfied. Doesn't that put that DA—as well as all those judges—on the same level as the monsters who tried to rape *you*, Kaylyn? Don't you see that I'm doing the same thing for my brother that I did for you? These people *make* crime, Lynn! It's their bread and butter. I believe the Supreme Court calls such things 'a moral hazard', because while they *pretend* to make the streets safe, without victims they'd all be out of a job. Don't you see that, honey? Don't you see how evil they are? They KNEW the real killer was still out there in that case I just shared with you—and they didn't care! The media feeds them, and they all share the wealth! And my poor brother. They called *him* a sex offender? For having a *threesome*? He couldn't find a job, or a girlfriend or even a place to live when he got out. How is *that* supposed to *prevent* crime, Lynn? We have a Constitution, Kaylyn—it prohibits *ex post facto* punishment! It *prohibits* cruel and unusual punishment. It *guarantees* equal protection under the law. But you know what? It's all a lie. If I did nothing for my brother…it would be the same as if I had left you to those animals. And you want to *stop* me—why, Kaylyn, why?"

"Two wrongs don't make a right," was all I could manage with a sob.

"Yeah, but I *got* to you. At least a little? Didn't I? My brother was banned from his own life, Kaylyn! Do you understand what that means? He *did* find an old girlfriend, at least for a while, someone who knew his *ex* and the truth about her, but then the woman's landlord banned my brother from the apartment. Everywhere he looked for a job he was turned down, and no one would rent to him. If it hadn't been for me—he would have been homeless. They *wanted* him to explode, Lynn—don't you *see* that? Well, I'm simply giving them what they wanted."

"You're killing people, Rachel."

"There are causalities in every war, Kaylyn. This is no different. They are going to start abiding by the law, or I will simply keep on killing them until they manage to stop me. Whichever comes first."

I was exhausted, and I couldn't take anymore, so I said something that I thought would make her hang up on me.

"I feel sorry for you, Rachel. The way you think—it's pitiful."

Rachel sighed. "You're the one who's pitiful, Kaylyn, and you know what? I don't think I'll call you anymore."

She hung up, and without understanding exactly why—I cried my eyes out.

. . .

Bobby called me the next morning with the list of "T's", and as it turned out, there were seven of them. I wrote them all down, but it really didn't matter. I was planning on dealing with Rachel Stark *long* before the 20th, and then it hit me: was I really planning on killing—

in cold blood—the woman who had saved my life? Was I really that far gone? I could try and tell myself that I was going to take her in, and doing it on my own because this was just between the two of us, but I knew that I was lying to myself because there was no way in hell that Rachel would ever come quietly unless I got to her when she wasn't looking.

And then it hit me: I was a detective, wasn't I? I was being paid by the state—and paid well, I might add—for my time, so why didn't I take a little bit of that time to keep an eye on her? I could stake her out if I was careful about it, follow her around and see what she was up to. There was no way in hell that she was just sitting in that boarding house all day every day, despite what old Eva said, and if I managed to tail Rachel without blowing my cover, I might actually be able to find out who her next target was instead of guessing. And without Sam's help—that's all I'd be doing: guessing.

Time was on my side, I told myself, just like in the old song. If I didn't get anywhere with this, I still had until the evening of the 20th to confront her directly. I was pretty sure that only one of us would leave that boarding house alive if I did that, so "sitting" on her for a few days seemed like a very good idea indeed. Again, I thought of just turning her location over to the Feds, but I just couldn't do it. In addition to the awful guilt of betraying someone who I had once been quite close to—someone who had literally saved me from a decidedly gruesome death, there was the notion that, if anyone else got killed because of my cowardice, I'd never be able to live with myself. In Clair Sacchetti's *Broken Heroes* series, I come across like a cold-blooded killer, but the truth of the matter is that *I'm* as broken as Wade and Sam ever were, and if I've killed, and actually been good at it, it's only because I've been well-trained. If I had to live my life over again I would be exceedingly happy being an ordinary, everyday wife and mother. I know that might piss off some of you feminist types, but trust me when I tell you there is absolutely nothing glamorous about the work I do, and anyone who tells you that there is glory in combat has simply never *been* in combat—bet your liver on *that* one. War is an ugly, disgusting business, and unless you're a psychopath, taking a human life won't ever do anything but fill you with guilt and self-loathing—no matter *how* necessary it might seem at the time.

Judgment Day

So, where to begin? I asked myself as I put my jacket on and left the office. I got in my car and checked the date on my phone.

March 9th.

That meant I had exactly eleven days until Rachel struck again; eleven days to figure out what to do. It never occurred to me that she might deviate from her plan, because she had been so consistent all this time, but there was, in the back of my head, the nagging doubt that maybe Sam and I had had it wrong all along, or that, to employ even more prison lingo—she might "switch it up".

The car was warm by this time, but I shut it down and just sat there. I use a P.O. Box on my business cards, and since the Post Office is right next door, I decided to get my mail before I did anything else. There was not much of interest: bills, three checks, a couple of flyers—and a post card.

From Sam.

All it said was: *there's nothing to forgive.*

I almost lost it right then and there, and turned my back and leaned against the self-serve counter so that the elderly couple at the window wouldn't see my tears. Do you remember the night I told Sam and Wade to leave? I had asked their forgiveness for being such a screw up—I mean, have you ever even *heard* of someone dumb enough to have affairs with *both* members of a married couple, and at different times?

Neither of them had said a word, so I had thought that I was on my own.

Now, to get this note from Sam, well, it almost overwhelmed me and I pretended to read one of the flyers while I regained my composure.

The elderly couple was waiting for the clerk to tell them how much their package would cost, First Class, and I caught part of their conversation.

"How can you say there's no God?" the woman asked, showing her husband the tigers on some wildlife association brochure she was holding. "Aren't they beautiful?"

"And deadly," the husband told her.

"You always bring everything down to that level," the wife scolded.

"Me?" said the husband. "Just remember that this god of yours creates some of us to be *food*. How beautiful would that tiger seem to you if you were a water buffalo?"

"They're still beautiful," the wife tried.

The husband sighed. "Do you ever stop to think, Maggie, that something, some*one*, can actually be beautiful, and *still* be a killer?"

Just like Rachel, I thought as I shoved the door open with my shoulder. *Or Sam. Or me.*

And right then and there I knew how I was going to play this.

• • •

The wind whipped around the corner of the strip mall as I hurried to my car, making think of something Wade had once told me: that there's an old Italian saying—March is crazy…and that wind made my eyes water. I got in the car, slammed the door and started it up. I have an on-going deal of sorts with the local branch of *Rentals America*, but I wanted something different for the first part of my stake out. I called a friend who owns a delivery service, someone who owed me a favor, and asked if I could borrow a van for the day. And then, before I even gave myself a chance to even *think* about it, I called Samantha on her cell phone.

She picked up on the third ring.

"Hey!" she said. "You ok?"

"I'm fine, Sam. I just got your post card."

"Yeah, well—I figured you'd call if you wanted to talk."

"I miss you," I heard myself saying before I could stop it.

"Me too."

"Kids ok?"

"Uh-huh."

"Wade?"

"He's home already, Lynn. He only took an extra week to add it to the February vacation, and then he went back. We're staying at—"

"Don't!" I snapped. "Not over the phone." I knew from the post mark that she was in Tampa, and I guess I was more than a little paranoid. "Son-of-a-bitch! He went *home?*"

"I told him to, Lynn. I won't tell you where we are, not if you don't think it's safe, but trust me we're ok."

I would find out later that Wade had used his State Department contacts to find Sam and the kids a safe place to stay, but at the moment I didn't know *what* to think about it. "Ok. Long as you're sure."

"You'll laugh when you find out where we are."

"I doubt that, but ok."

"Any movement?"

"I'm handling it, Sam."

She sighed. "But you'll call me if you need help?"

"I promise."

"We talked about you, Kaylyn. Wade and I."

"Oh?"

"I'll tell you all about it when I get back, but we're ok—all three of us. I promise you, we worked it out."

"I'd better go."

"Oh, all right. Uh, how long do you—"

"Sam, as God is my witness, I'll wrap this up by the 20th—or die trying."

"Hey, c'mon, Lynn!"

"Sorry. It'll all work out…and then we'll talk."

"Take care of yourself, Kaylyn."

"Not a problem," I told her. "It seems to be what I do best."

• • •

I got the van at quarter past ten, and drove to the boarding house, parking at the loading dock on the warehouse across the lot. I was wearing jeans and a hoodie, and had actually dropped off a couple of crates for my friend, and as I was sitting there it occurred to me that Rachel might already be out for the day.

I debated calling Eva, but suddenly realized that I was tempting fate asking the old girl to keep quiet about "Debbie" on two separate occasions, and so I ended up going back into the warehouse with the paperwork from the crates on a clipboard my friend had given me, resigned to the fact that I was going to have to find a place to hang around. Then I decided to call my friend and have *him* call the warehouse manager with some bullshit story about needing to have the van towed, just to give me an excuse to sit there a while longer, but as luck would have it I saw a woman come out of the boarding house wearing a windbreaker over a hooded sweatshirt, and pulling the collar of the jacket up to cover her face from the wind. I couldn't see any details, but I knew it was Rachel just from the way in which she carried herself. She walked down to the street—I was on the same side of that access road, on the corner of the loading dock—and saw her pause there, and look at her watch.

She lit a cigarette and just stayed there, pacing back and forth, and after a while I began to get nervous. Clouds rolled in while I was standing there, and son-of-a-bitch if it didn't feel like snow was in the air, and then a cab came down the street and Rachel got in.

I waited a minute or two and then followed.

The cab headed back to the main street and turned left. I took my time at the lights, and then took the turn myself. It would be a little easier to tail her since she wasn't driving, but I still wasn't taking any chances. A few big, lazy flakes began to fall, and then the wind picked up, scudding across the water, and for a while there it looked as if we might actually get a few inches. But it quieted down after ten minutes or so, and I began to realize that Rachel was most probably heading into town.

The cabbie went through downtown Providence and finally worked his way to Highland Avenue. I kept three car lengths between us, and kept on going when the cab took another left onto a side street known for the seedier things in life: namely, drugs and prostitution. That section of town is actually pretty upscale now, especially up by Federal Hill, but until just a few years back, they had some problems similar to what Boston had once experienced in the so-called "Combat Zone" off lower Washington Street, with strip clubs and the like.

I stopped the van near an alley that I knew connected the cross-street with the street the cab was on, and saw it pull over hallway down the block. I pulled over near the loading dock of an abandoned Chinese import warehouse, and ran the length of the alley.

By now you know that I can hold my own in a sprint, but the ground was slippery and Rachel was already going into a building on the opposite side of the street just as I got to the end of the alley. I waited a minute, pulled my hood tighter, and started walking.

Rachel had gone into the *Premier Hotel*, a dive that was once pretty upscale. They've since torn it down and revamped that whole neighborhood, but when all of his was happening the *Premier* was the sort of place used by hookers and drug dealers.

I hesitated out front and it didn't take long for someone to approach me. There was a young woman, maybe in her early twenties, hanging in the doorway of an abandoned building right across the street. She was smoking a cigarette while I stood there looking around, and pitched the butt into the slush at the curb before crossing the street.

"You looking for someone, honey?" she asked me.

She was white, abnormally skinny, and had watery blue eyes. The way her hands shook screamed *user*, but the way in which she was dressed—mini-skirt, boots and imitation rabbit fur jacket—also told me that she was a hooker. It bothered me that she could have been quite pretty—if she hadn't needed a *Care Package*.

"I was thinking about going out," I said, using the old-time slang *Johns* once used when on the prowl for a *hook-up*.

"Going out, huh?" She laughed and looked me up and down. "You a cop, Sweetie?"

"Do I *look* like a cop?" I asked with a smile, knowing quite well that I did; I have *The Look*, or so I've been told, but most street people usually mark me as ex-military. I also knew that if I lied to her she'd spread the word that *narcs* or something were working the block. Either way she knew damn right well that I didn't belong down here.

"As a matter of fact, yeah," she told me, her eyes growing hard.

I sighed, knowing that I had to tell her the truth, or at least some plausible version of it. "Ok, Cutie—no, I'm not a cop, but I'm a P.I., and the girl who just went inside is my sister, and she's been running around with some creeps and I think she's using again. All I want to know is who she's with, and what she's doing. I'll *straighten* her later," I added, employing even more prison lingo, "but I'm not looking to jam anyone. Can you help me?"

"You still look like a cop to me, Sister. Take a hike." She turned and went to step off the curb, and I knew I needed to act fast.

"Wait—what if I paid you? That way it'd be entrapment if I'm lying to you."

"Paid me for what, Hottie?"

"To go to bed with you, stupid—what did you think?"

"You into chicks?" she asked, looking me up and down once more.

"You wouldn't believe what I'm into, Kid, but, no, all I want is for you to take me upstairs and sit in the damn room for a half hour. I'll tip you half-a-yard over your usual price."

"Fifty bucks, huh? Just for *sitting* with you?"

"Yeah, and another fifty if you keep your mouth shut."

Her little blue weasel's eyes narrowed. "Why don't you just get a room on your own?"

"Seriously, Babe—what is this, *Motel 6?* Do business travelers come here, for Christ's sake? I go in there alone and the joint'll be empty five minutes later." I let my eyes tear up, something I'm actually pretty good at. "Help me. It's my *sister*."

"You gotta tell me what you're going to do first," she told me, shaking her head.

That was actually a pretty good question. What *was* I going to do? Spy on her? Collect a little information? *Confront* her? That last one decided me. "All I want is to find out who she's with. What if you check around, and *I'll* sit in the room?"

"No way, Chicky! I'm no rat."

"Not even for *another* hundred?"

The girl blew out a breath. "You for real?"

"What's your name, Kiddo?" I asked.

"They call me Dusty."

"Look, Dusty—two hundred dollars over your usual price—in YOUR pocket—just for helping me out. What do you say?"

Dusty looked at her boots, dug her toe in the slush, looked up and down the street. "Hand me half the money when we get in the lobby, so it looks like were really doing business."

"That's my girl!" I said and smiled.

"You *wish*," said Dusty.

• • •

We took the stairs to the fourth floor, and as soon as we got in the hallway I started wondering if I'd bitten off more than I could chew. If I trusted this kid and she screwed me, I'd be sitting alone with my thumb up my ass when some goon the size of Montana kicked the door open and held me out the window by the ankles. Dusty unlocked the door, and we went inside. I was scared now, but didn't want to let her know I was carrying, so I did the only thing I could think of. I touched the side of her face tenderly and looked into her eyes. Hookers don't kiss their "dates", but when you want to be intimate with someone, you look them in the eyes.

"Hey," she said, drawing out the word, "you *are* into chicks, aren't you?"

"Sometimes," I said, and let all of the emotion I was feeling about Sam and Rachel flood my eyes. I could feel the tears stinging my cheeks, and I could tell that she was buying it. "But it's my sister—she's OD'd *twice*, Dusty! Please, *please* help me!" I added in a whisper.

"Ok, ok," she said. "I'll do it, but I just wanted you to know, for later—I can be real nice to you, if you want. You'd be surprised."

"Pretty girl like you," I said, "wouldn't surprise me a bit, but right now…"

"I'm on it," she said. "Stay put!"

"Dusty," I hissed when her hand was on the doorknob.

"On the level," she promised, and stepped out into the hall.

• • •

After a minute or two I had the gun in my hand. After five, I cocked it and stood beside the door. After ten I was sweating and unbuttoning some of the buttons on the heavy shirt I was wearing under the hoodie, and after fifteen I made up my mind to leave.

I was reaching for the door when it opened and I hastily put the gun in my pocket—my finger still on the trigger.

"*Son-of-a-bitch!*" Dusty hissed, her eyes wide, when she saw my hand in my pocket. "You *are* a—"

I closed the door with my foot and clamped my left hand over her mouth and shook my head, meeting her eyes. "No, I'm not. But I *am* a P.I.—and you scared the *shit* outta me taking so long!"

"Ok, ok! Chill! There's a lot of girls…and guys, working this joint. Took me a while to find out who she was with. Relax, will ya?"

"Who is she with? Is she using?"

"Those burns on her face—how'd she get 'em?"

"Drove her car into a telephone pole once when she was high."

"Man, no *wonder* she's buying."

"Buying *what?*"

"Guy she's with goes by the name of Gem—he's a hooker."

The tears that sprang to my eyes then were real, and I actually had to sit down. Out of all the things Dusty could have told me—that was the furthest thing from my mind.

"Hey, calm down. How else she gonna get laid—all them burns?"

"How much longer will she be?" I asked, sick to my stomach at the thought of what Rachel was doing and how utterly lonely she must be.

Dusty looked at her watch. "Another twenty minutes. She paid for a full hour. The girl who gave me the 411 says she comes here all the time. Far as she knows—your sister ain't using. Not with Gem, anyway." She looked me over again. "You gonna wait here?"

"No, I'm going to go downstairs and wait for her outside."

"You sure, Honey? I'd do you for short money, after what you're paying me for this."

"Speaking of that," I said, and gave her the rest of the cash. "Here."

"You sure I can't do nothing else for you?"

"Yeah, I'm sure."

Dusty put the money in her pocket. "Ok, but you know where to find me if you change your mind."

• • •

Rachel came out of the hotel twenty-five minutes later. I had pulled the van into the alley and I was just sitting there, hoping that she didn't come this way, but five minutes later another cab pulled up and Rachel got in. She leaned over the back of the front seat, talking to the cabbie for a moment, and then he pulled away from the curb. I waited until they reached the end of the block, and then I pulled out of the mouth of the alley and followed. There were still a few big, lazy March snowflakes in the air, and the sky was alabaster and charcoal gray. I put on the defroster and kept two car lengths between us, as the cabbie went all the way to the end of Atwells Avenue and got on the highway. He took the 195 interchange and I let some distance grow between us. The cab was in the middle lane, but I stayed to the far right so he wouldn't see me in his rearview mirror.

They got off at Route 114, heading towards Riverside, which is sometimes called East Providence, because it is separated from the downtown area by the Providence River. There used to be a famous amusement park there, right on Crescent Beach and just off of Bullocks Point Avenue.

Crescent Park had been built in 1886 and didn't close until 1979. It's all condos and low-income housing now, but when I was a kid, maybe six or seven years old, my Mom and Dad used to take us there a lot. The food was awesome and there was even a Dance Hall and a Riverboat Ride. All that's left now is the Carrousel from the early days, and just driving by that area made me sad. Some of my best memories come from that time, and I usually try to avoid the place to keep from feeling what I'm feeling. I don't know why, but I suspect it has a lot to do with my Mother...and a lot to do with why I hadn't simply turned Rachel's location over to the Feds.

The people who know me best think I'm tough as nails, but since this whole thing started, I was acting more like a whiny, needy little bitch than a tough guy, and if I didn't straighten my ass out soon, this was all going to blow up in my face.

"Focus, Vale," I whispered, and lit a cigarette.

The cabbie kept going and eventually worked his way to Wampanoag Trail, and turned into the Gate of Heaven Cemetery.

"Shit!" I hissed. There weren't a whole lot of deliveries being made to graveyards, at least not by delivery vans, and I ground my teeth and kept on going as the cab pulled in the front entrance and made its way inside. There was a secondary entrance around the other side, and I made for that, glad for the hedges and all those tombstones between my van and Rachel's cab.

On the other side of the cemetery there was a little convenience store, and I parked by the dumpster in the corner of their parking lot so it couldn't be seen from Rachel's vantage point, and hurried across the street, almost getting hit by some in-a-hurry soccer mom in an SUV. She gave me the finger, but, hey, it's what they do—entitled, you know? And in a hurry to get nowhere.

I jogged along the hedges, found a little gate, and went in.

The cab had parked at the west end of the cemetery, near a tiny chapel of sorts, and I watched from the cover of a huge oak tree as Rachel got out and walked to the edge of the newest section of that particular lot.

The cabbie was reading the paper.

What the hell? I thought. Was she *meeting* someone here?

And then she actually kneeled down by a relatively new grave, and hung her head.

Rachel stayed that way for a good five minutes, and then got up and just stood there looking down with her hands folded before her while the snow collected on her shoulders and on her kerchief. It didn't take a genius to know that she had come here to see her brother.

Kaylyn Vale had learned early in life that nothing in this crazy world of ours is ever black and white, and as I stood there behind that tree I realized, that, despite what Rachel Stark was doing, she was lonely and grief-stricken and just as much a part of the human race as the rest of us. She was grieving for her brother, and truly believed he had been wronged and then murdered. The world at large would dehumanize and dismiss her as something less-than-human, but as I watched her wipe the tears from her eyes and return to the cab, I was forced to ask myself what I'd be doing in *her* shoes. Not for the first time—and certainly not for the last—I became painfully aware of just how alike we really were, and just how little separated us. Not to put too fine a point on it, but I felt bad for her, and realized that she also had a lot in common with Sam. Both of them hated the system and understood that our courts no longer functioned as intended, both of them raged at the machine—if in very different ways—and both of them viewed the total abrogation of Constitutional protection as an act of aggression towards the United States of America.

"Can I help you?" someone said in a nasty tone right behind me, and I actually jumped and went for my handgun as I turned around, stopping short of actually pulling it when I saw the uniform of a Cemetery Division groundskeeper.

"Shhhhh!" I told him, which caused him to raise an eyebrow at me. "And show some respect!" I've always been quick on my feet, and the lies I told to little Dusty were still fresh in my mind. "That's my sister over there, and just because we're not talking doesn't mean I want to bother her!"

Rachel was in the cab by this point, but I was still talking in hushed tones.

"Oh, sorry," he said, "I didn't realize." He was about fifty, overweight, and, I gathered, not exactly the brightest bulb on the circuit. He was carrying a broom over his right shoulder, which I assumed he was using to dust off the paths between the rows of headstones, but he just continued to stand there, looking at me.

"Do you mind giving me a little privacy?" I snapped as the cab went out the front gate. There was no way I could run to the van and follow Rachel now, and I was pissed. She'd be on Route 114 again before I even got across the street. The guy made a face, looked me up and down, and turned away. With nothing else to do now other than confirm my suspicions, I walked over to where Rachel had stood, locating the exact spot by her footprints.

I looked at the grave where she'd been kneeling, and all the emotion I'd been struggling to hold in bubbled to the surface. The tombstone read:

KYLE L. WORTHINGTON
Beloved Brother

There were the dates, and below them an inscription in Latin:

LEX TALIONIS

My Latin is mostly limited to phrases of the law, so I had no trouble with the translation: "The Law of Retaliation." You probably know it better as: "An Eye for an Eye".

• • •

The snow was falling even heavier as I returned the van and got back in my Mustang, but there was still less than two inches on the ground and the roads were relatively clear. I turned on WBZ out of Boston on my AM band, and got the extended forecast—according to them, the snow was supposed to taper off just in time for rush hour. As I sat there letting the car warm up, I popped The John Coltrane Quartet into the CD player and selected *My Favorite Things*, a rambling thirteen minute version of the old song with Trane on soprano sax, McCoy Tyner on piano, Stevie Davis on bass and the mighty Elvin Jones on drums—just the four of them turning the familiar, happy pop classic from *The Sound of Music* into a moody, hypnotic, almost eastern-sounding fugue.

I love Coltrane, and I believe that he, along with fellow jazz great Miles Davis, are among the most under-appreciated and most-misunderstood musicians of the 20th Century, with the atmospheric emphasis being almost as heavy on what they *weren't* stating, as on what they *were*…and listening to either one of them always helps me to think.

It was well past time for lunch, and I don't like to eat supper *too* late because it takes me forever to fall asleep, so I decided to combine them.

There was only one problem: I am sick and tired of eating most of my meals alone.

Thinking about Miles and Trane got me thinking about Dave Redman, because we've literally spent hours listening to and arguing about jazz, but I was still working this thing and I wasn't ready to pack it in for the day.

Judgment Day

In a sudden fit of inspiration I headed back downtown and towards the *Premier Hotel*. The snow was *really* coming down as I got there, and I hoped that Dusty would be freezing her little ass off and maybe even be a little bit hungry.

I cruised by where she had picked me up earlier in the day, and sure enough there she was hanging in the same doorway. Looking at the poor kid, I realized that she was a lot younger than I had at first thought. I pulled in at the curb, and put down my tinted windows. Dusty squinted, frowned until she recognized me, and then hurried down the stairs, leaning in my open right passenger-side window.

"Hey, Good-Looking," she said with a smile that almost bowled me over with the sweet scent of *Juicy Fruit* gum, "you have a change of heart?"

"I actually have something else in mind."

"Hey! I'm not into letting chicks watch while guys do me hard or any weird stuff like that, you know."

For about the tenth time that day I almost couldn't control that awful feeling of wanting to cry. I smiled and shook my head.

"You hungry?"

"*Huh?*" she said, as if I were speaking Chinese.

"I was wondering if you'd like to get a late lunch with me—my treat."

"Are you for real, lady?"

"Why? You *eat*, don't you?"

Dusty licked her lips, straightened up and looked down the street. For a second there I thought maybe a cruiser had turned out of the alley behind me or something—but there was nothing there.

"I, uh…I don't know."

"Your boss doesn't like you off your spot?" I asked. "Is that it?"

"You can say, 'pimp', honey, I've heard it before."

"Will he hit you or something?"

"Nah." Dusty laughed. A genuine, hearty little giggle that made me realize that she was a whole lot closer to twenty than she was to thirty.

"What's so funny?"

"Because I work for my brother. He'd *never* hurt me. Ever. We're all we got."

"Gem," I said, understanding—the hooker that Rachel had earlier spent time with.

"Hey—how'd you know that?"

"Maybe I'm psychic."

"Maybe you're just a flake, too."

"I've been called worse," I said and sighed. "Here."

"What's this?" she asked, resting both arms on the window frame again.

"It's my business card." I had wrapped another fifty-dollar-bill around it.

"What's this for?"

"I'd appreciate it if you called me if you ever see my sister again—that's all."

Dusty studied the card: dark blue, with KAYLYN VALE, PRIVATE INVESTIGATOR on it. "Hey, you *are* legit!"

"I've been called worse," I repeated, and smiled.

"Hey, you're all right." She looked up and down the street again. "Lunch, huh? Like a date?"

"More like you're my little sister, knucklehead. You coming or not?"

"What the hell," she said, and got in.

• • •

You've heard me use the term, *asset*, more than once now, referring to people used by The Company to carry out what we call, "wet work", but the term is also applied to someone you can *work*, like I was working Dusty. I felt bad about it at first, but I was paying the kid with the expense money I was being paid by the state, and I wasn't looking to hurt her, just use her as one more connection to Rachel's activities.

The snow was finally tapering off, but I still drove slowly, using the time to get her to talk. If I made a good impression on her, she was someone I could use well beyond the affair with Rachel Stark—assuming I lived that long, but there was also a little voice in the back of my head telling me, that, with just a little effort, I might be able to get her off the street. Truth is, I liked her. She was quick and smart and tough, and best of all—she had a heart, despite how streetwise she seemed to be.

Now, I thought—*where to go?*

The kid was pretty, but way too thin, and the way in which she was dressed ruled out any of the restaurants on Federal Hill, so I settled on a little diner I like down off of Allens Ave, by all those oil refineries on the waterfront, and as we pulled into the parking lot of *The Wheelhouse*, Dusty frowned.

"What's wrong?" I asked her.

"Nothing, I just—"

"You just what?"

For a brief moment I thought I saw tears in her eyes, but she bit her lip and the moisture was gone as quickly as it had appeared.

"Well, I look kind of...well, you know."

My heart went out to her, and I almost hugged her. Almost.

"Take that off," I told her, tugging on the collar of her bunny-jacket. I reached into the back seat where I keep a nice white sweater with a hood, and slipped it off the hanger over the left rear passenger door.

"Here, put this on."

"Yeah?" she asked, taking it in both hands like I had just handed her a piece of silver.

"Yeah."

She wrestled herself out of her jacket and into my sweater, and except for the boots, she didn't look too bad.

"It's a little big on me."

"That's ok. It fits well enough." And it was long enough to cover her mini skirt, too, but I kept my mouth shut about that.

We went inside and took a booth on the east end of the diner, and the waitress came right away with our menus.

"Hey, Lady Vale," the waitress said. "Haven't seen you in here in a while. Everything ok?"

"Been doing a lot of road work these days, Gwen," I lied smoothly. When you've been doing this as long as I have you're always ready with something that keeps people from knowing what you've really been up to.

"Like running?" she asked, because we were both joggers.

"No," I said and laughed. "Like being ON the road."

"And who's this?" she asked, smiling at Dusty.

"This is my niece, Dusty," I said, hoping that Gwen didn't ask if that was a nickname. "From Boston."

"Dusty," Gwen said, just like I knew she would. "That a nickname?"

"It's short for 'Drusilla'," Dusty said quickly, "believe it or not."

"Pretty. Can I start you two off with something to drink?"

"I'd love a cup of coffee," I said, and looked at Dusty.

"Uh, me, too," she said in an uncertain little voice.

"Cream and sugar?"

"Please," I said, "and two glasses of water."

Gwen scribbled on her pad. "Be right back."

Dusty was staring at me over the top of her menu. Ever see *Girlfight*, with Michelle Rodriguez? Dusty was white, and had blue eyes, but the look was exactly the same—the way Michelle Rodriguez looks when peering over the top of her boxing gloves.

"What?"

"Your *niece?*"

I shrugged.

"Just what are you doing messin' with me like this, lady?"

"First of all, call me 'Lynn'. Secondly, I'm buying you lunch, or supper, if you prefer."

Dusty shifted her eyes back to the menu. "What can I get?" she asked without looking up.

"Whatever you want."

"What are *you* getting?"

"Same thing I get every time I come here—bacon-burger with cheese and all the fries I can get."

"Is it good?"

I reached over and flicked her menu with my finger, hard enough to get her attention but not hard enough to piss her off.

"Now why would I get it every time if it wasn't good?" I asked with a smile.

It killed her, but she actually smiled back.

"What else do you want from me?" she asked a few minutes later, again without looking up.

"Just call me if you see my sister."

"First of all, *Lynn*, just because I make my living on my back doesn't mean I'm *stupid*. That chick is your sister like I'm really your niece."

"Ok, she's not my sister—happy?"

Dusty put her menu down. "No, Lynn, I'm not. Someone comes to slap the cuffs on her I'll burn you with everyone on that street."

"Fair enough," I answered pleasantly.

"So you're *not* trying to jam her?"

"No, I'm not," I answered softly. "Matter of fact, she saved my life once."

"For real?"

"For real."

Gwen came back and took our order, and later, while we were eating, Dusty asked me why I was so interested in Rachel.

Of course, she didn't know her real name.

I sighed. "Someone hired me to try and help her, if you want the truth."

"Oh, yeah, who?"

"Me," I said and held her gaze until she started eating again.

• • •

It was well after six when I drove Dusty back, because we had spent an hour talking, or, rather, she had talked and I had listened. Dusty was a smart girl, and wanted desperately to be "legit", as she put it. I told her I would help her, and only asked that, in the meantime, she tell me whenever Rachel came around.

Her street was a mess when I got there, with ambulances and cop cars outside near the hotel.

"Shit!" she snarled. "Not again!"

"What is it?" I asked, cruising on by.

"Every so often some John cuts up a chick, or someone bangs out on a bad load of heroin. Fuck! Now I can't go back there!"

For a brief…a very brief moment…I thought of bringing her home with me. Then I thought of bringing her to my office, but there was only the couch and I wasn't going to leave her there alone. So I went up the hill and turned right, back towards the highway.

"Where you taking me?"

"Going to get you a hotel room for the night at the *Courtyard*. Just for you. One night, see? Stay in, take a nice shower, and watch TV. By yourself. I'll give you money for cab fare so you can get back home in the morning."

I could see that she wanted to argue with me, but the idea of spending the whole night, alone, and in comfort, got to her, and she shut her mouth. I told her to stay in the car when I got to the *Courtyard*, and when I came out with the card-key I told her to go straight up to her room.

Tears filled her eyes, and then she nodded and started to take off the sweater.

"No, you keep it."

"Why are you *doing* this for me?" she said, burst into tears and threw her arms around me.

I spoke while I held her, looking out the window and into the past.

"Because someone did it for me."

Dusty sniffed.

"Oh, yeah—who?"

"The woman I'm asking you to keep an eye on," I told her softly, telling the absolute Gospel truth for the first time that day.

• • •

The snow started up again as soon as I got into the parking garage under my building, and, as it turned out, would add another inch or so before morning. The apartment seemed cold and dark, and all of a sudden I was paranoid. I checked the whole place with my gun in my hand, turned on at least one light in every room, and turned up the heat.

Then I sat down with a bottle of vitamin water and, after fighting with myself, called Sam, and told her everything that Rachel had done that day. I purposely left out the parts about Dusty without quite understanding why, but some little part of me had already begun to think of Dusty as a kid sister, and I wanted to keep that for myself. Sam listened, and then spoke sharply.

"Now you listen to me."

Christ, I thought, *why did I call her?*

"Rachel's *insane*, Lynn, and I seriously don't give a *fuck* about what she did for you or any of that shit! Take her down or turn her in but *deal* with this bitch before she kills you! Fuck!" she added, "I'm coming back there!"

"Sam, don't, please—I'll deal with it...I swear!"

We talked—or rather, I got bitched at by Samantha, and even though I knew she was right, there was so much she didn't understand. The truth is—I hadn't lied to Dusty. If it hadn't been for Rachel, I'd still be on the streets myself—or dead.

"Are you sure, Lynn?"

"Sam, the kids—please don't do this!"

"All right." She was silent for a moment and I knew she was biting the inside of her lip. "You mean something to me, you know," she added at length.

"Ditto," I said.

"*Ghost*," she answered, playing our old game.

"Demi Moore, Patrick Swayze."

"Stay out of trouble, Kaylyn, and if you don't do something *soon* I'm leaving the kids here and coming back there to help you."

"You can't just *leave* the kids!"

"The *fuck* I can't! I'm on a god damn *Army* base with Ross's daughter, Lynn!"

Ross was the State Department guy—and billionaire—whose daughter—the same one Sam was now staying with, had been rescued by Wade and me in Afghanistan.

"Stay put. I'll take care of it."

"Just remember what I said," Sam said, and after some unnecessary—or necessary, depending on your point of view—small talk. We hung up.

Tomorrow would be the tenth day of March and I was running out of time. I vowed to take Rachel on before the 20th, but needed a few more days to set my plans in motion. I stayed up well past midnight working it all out, and settled on the 15th, simply because I couldn't resist the date: the ides of March and all that.

The only problem was—Rachel had apparently had the exact same idea.

CHAPTER NINE—April

It's been said that, what goes around, comes around, and I guess I got back what I put out. Rachel Stark struck again on the exact date I was planning on confronting *her*: March 15th, taking out a Superior Court Judge by the name of O'Hara with a high-powered rifle as he left his car and was walking up the courthouse steps that morning.

O'Hara—the letter, "O". The 15th letter of the alphabet.

So much for our theory that she was spelling out "Judgement Day".

The quote from Scripture was sent to the State Police:

"*An eye for an eye…*"

Matthew 5:38

It was written in BLOCK letters, with a short message under the quote—"*do you* **really** *think you have the right to judge* **me**?"

Spinelli called me right after it happened, and as I was already on my way to the office it only took me five minutes to get to him.

The place was a *zoo*, with cops and television crews running around, and dozens of people being held back by police tape and some huge cops right out of the goon squad. There were so many helicopters in the air that you couldn't even hear what was being said to you.

Car horns were blaring and everyone had a look on their face like those photos of the spectators after 9/11.

The traffic in front of the courthouse was backed up for five miles in either direction.

Spinner looked like shit, and it was more than obvious that the stress was getting to him. He took me by the elbow as soon as I got there, and walked me down the block. It was actually kind of warm that morning—March *is* crazy, you know—so I sat him down on a bench in that little common there and lit a cigarette. Spinelli stood back up and began to pace.

"Sit down," I told him.

"I don't feel much like sitting, *Nancy*."

"Can the *Nancy Drew* shit and sit down before you *fall* down, Bobby!"

He did so and asked me for a cigarette.

"Seriously, Mr. *Runner's World?*"

"Seems like a good time to start up again, Lynn—they just took me off the case…you, too, by the way."

"Fuck 'em," I said.

"They *suspended* me, too."

"Are you *shitting* me?"

"I wish I were—I just got bitch-slapped by Captain Simmons and Agent-fucking-Tanner, too."

"Christ, Bobby, they can't blame *you* for this shit!"

Spinner took a deep drag and blew out a plume of smoke. To his credit he only coughed a little. "*Can't* they, though? This is—was—my case. They're actually talking about shutting down the courts, Lynn! They do that—it'll be the first time in U.S. history."

"It'll also encourage all the other wingnuts to do something like this! God, what the fuck's *wrong* with them?"

"Lynn, do you have any idea how *huge* this is? The pressure is enormous. The fucking *President* called the Governor this morning, for God's sake!" He threw up his hands. "Fuck it…let *them* deal with it."

"Ok, take a deep breath," I told him as I took out my notebook.

"Easy for *you* to say."

"Fuck you, Bobby," I hissed, dropping the notebook into my lap and glaring at him.

"Sorry, pal. I'm not myself." When I didn't reply he held my eyes and added: "For real."

"Forget it," I mumbled and flipped open the book. I pitched my butt into the street and got out my pen. There was no traffic, and no one around us. "This judge—full name?"

"O'Hara, Robert—no middle initial."

I wrote out—J-U-D-G-E-M-E-N-O. "What the fuck? It's gibberish…"

"Will you *stop* with that shit? No one's trying to *spell* anything!"

I shook my head, trying to block him out, and kept writing.

Jordan

Unger

Donato

Gregory

Edwards

Mahoney

Evans

Norton

O'Hara

Nine people. Nine people dead because I didn't have the balls to take Rachel down. *Christ*, I though, *how do I **live** with this?*

"You're right," I admitted. "It doesn't make sense."

"Doesn't matter, Lynn. I'll be lucky if they don't fucking *fire* me now."

"They aren't going to *fire* you, Robert, trust me. This'll blow over."

"Sure it will."

"What? You really think anyone *else* is going to figure this out? How do you fight a ghost?"

"I need a drink." He stood up. "Or three." He paced a bit. "You coming?"

"No," I told him, standing up and looking him in the eyes, "I'm going to go and *get* this bitch."

"Good luck," he said, and walked away.

• • •

My first instinct was to call Sam and ask her what she made of this, but then I thought better of it. Trying to figure out *spelling* wasn't getting us anywhere, and since I knew where Rachel was, my second instinct was to fly down there and blow her head off. I punched the steering wheel *hard* as I sat there in my car, half expecting the damn airbag to go off, and then I swore, because I knew that Rachel wouldn't have gone right back to the boarding house.

I got out my phone and called Dusty—of course it went right into voice mail.

"Can you call me please?" I asked, impatiently waiting for the bullshit about leaving a call-back-number to be over so I could leave my damn message in the first place.

My phone beeped—a text from "unknown": "*how you doing?*" There was a smiley face beside it and I hit REPLY without taking time to think about it and sent: "*Fuck you, Rachel!*"

Then my phone rang: Dusty.

I took a deep breath and forced myself to stay calm.

"Hey, you. You ok?"

"Never been better! Thanks to you—what's up?"

"Just wondering how you were doing and also wondering if you've seen you-know-who."

"I'm good, Lynn, and, no, I haven't seen her since that last time."

"Ok. Uh, thanks. Can we do lunch again soon?"

"You need me—for *anything*...just call and I'll *be* there."

"All right, Kiddo, talk to you soon."

I hung up and the phone rang again as soon as I put it in the cup-holder.

It was Sam.

"Kaylyn—what the *fuck?*"

"All over the news, huh?"

"Duh."

"I'm taking care of it, Sam."

"Sure you are."

"Listen," I said carefully, "I think I know where she is."

"I'm coming back there—today!"

"No you're not!"

Sam swore, took a deep breath and then said: "I can *help* you, Lynn—I think I know what she's spelling."

"Doesn't matter anymore."

"Why not?"

"I already told you—I know where she is."

"You said you *thought* you knew, Kaylyn!"

"Same thing."

"Christ! Are you *lying* to me, Kaylyn?"

"Look, I gotta go."

"Wait! She's spelling: JUDGE ME NOT! I'm sure of it!"

"Doesn't matter—I'm not waiting for her to kill anyone else. Take care, Sam."

"I'm coming *up* there!" she screamed at me, and then I hung up.

• • •

My only ace-in-the-hole was that Rachel didn't realize that I knew where she was. I decided to go back to my office, arm myself to the teeth, give her another hour or so to go home, and go down to the boarding house.

Sam's husband, Wade, was waiting for me in his Ford pickup when I got there.

I sighed, got out, and walked into my office without even looking at him. Wade followed me in and shut the door behind him. It didn't take an IQ of 150 to know that Samantha had called him.

"I'm coming with you," he said.

"No, you're not," I snarled, as I went to my closet and got out my Kevlar vest.

Wade came over and took it away from me, holding on to my collar with his other hand.

"Let-fucking-GO-of me!" I hissed.

Wade held the vest behind his back, glaring at me. Wade stands six-foot-one-or-two, and as I told you he's built like Vin Diesel. He's also a very handsome man, but at the moment all I wanted to do was punch him in the face.

"Not until you hear me out."

I thrashed about, but he was simply way too strong for me. I only had two options: shoot him or listen.

"Go ahead." I shook him off and plopped my ass down on my desk.

Wade looked up at the ceiling and blew out a breath. Then he threw the vest back at me. I caught it with one hand and held it down at my side.

"Look, like it or not...Sam and me...we're your friends."

"You mean you both *did* me, don't you, Wade?"

He moved quickly for such a big man, and grabbing me by the shirt he actually pulled me to my feet. I have to admit it—he scared me, and I simply looked up at him.

"Life is messy, Kaylyn, and my life with Sam, more so than anyone else I've ever even *heard* of, but the three of us, this is what we do, this is what we are, and I am *not* letting you face this fucking witch alone. Got it?" He shook me and pushed me back into the desk.

Wade had been through hell. All you have to do is read *Broken Heroes* to know just how badly messed up he was. But so was his wife and so was I, and...he was right: this is who we are, and the three of us, whatever else you wanted to call it, we cared about each other, and the plain unvarnished truth was that I did need his help. I sighed, shook my head, bit my lower lip and turned my back on him, going to the closet.

"You're not going anywhere without a vest," I told him.

Wade actually laughed. "If you can find one in there to fit me," he said.

• • •

I never planned on sleeping with anyone else's husband when I was in Afghanistan or at any other time, for that matter. I'm simply *broken*, and Wade was there for me. I guess the things that were going on in his own life at the time made him just as vulnerable, and what happened between us happened. Still, I don't like a cheater and don't like the fact that the label, in this case, at least, applies to me. But it is what it is, and this thing with Samantha was just as wrong, but like he said, Life is Messy, and you either pack it in or move on. Assuming that I lived through this thing with Rachel, I was going to make certain changes in my life. I was going to get Dusty off the street, and I wasn't going to go behind anyone's back ever again, but right now we needed to focus on the task at hand, so I promised myself that I wouldn't even talk about that other stuff.

It was just so…uncomfortable being with him…because of Sam.

We had taken Wade's pickup because my jet-black Mustang was so well known, and Wade drove on the way to the boardinghouse, asking me all the right questions about bringing Rachel down. I couldn't see his eyes because of his sunglasses, and I was having trouble reading him, but I was glad that he was here just the same.

When we were almost there, he turned to me and looked over the top of his shades.

"I have one question before we go in."

I raised my eyebrows at him, waiting.

"Do you love my wife?"

"You know—I promised myself that I wouldn't get in to all that with you."

"We talked about you, you know, and we've made a commitment to make our marriage work," he added, as if he hadn't even heard what I had said, "but I want you to know that we both still care about you."

"I'm not Jennifer," I said, misreading him.

"I'm not suggesting you are, or anything like that, Lynn. I just want you to know that we're cool, you and I. Now, do you love her?"

"If you two are all set, what difference does it make what I feel?"

"Do you love her?" he insisted.

"Yeah," I said, drilling him with my eyes, "but I had already made up my mind to break it off with her before I even went to your house that night."

"I'm curious—why?"

"Because there are different kinds of love, Wade, and because you and Sam belong together without any more complications from me or anyone else. Now, you say the three of us are cool, so let's just keep it that way and concentrate on what we have to do, ok?"

He was silent a while with his hand on the wheel, and lit a cigarette with his free hand. "Got a plan once we get in there?" he asked, and I knew that he finally understood me.

That was another good question. I had originally thought to bring Dusty with me as a decoy, to keep Eva busy at the front desk while I went to Rachel's room, but I couldn't stomach the thought of putting the kid in danger and had decided to use the "Debbee" thing to get Eva to let us "visit" Rachel. I told Wade about my phone call to Eva, and he nodded.

"That'll work."

We talked a little bit about how to handle it once we got to her door, and before I knew it we were on her street. Wade parked on the edge of the same warehouse lot I had used when I had had the van, and we just sat there for a few minutes, waiting.

"Look," he said at length, "either she's here or she's not."

I heard what he said quite clearly, and I understood those words as well, but what they *meant* to me was that I was acting like a coward sitting here pretending I was waiting for her to show up, and instead of answering him I just popped the door and got out.

Both of us were well-armed, and wearing bullet-proof vests, but there was no need to check our weapons or put this off any longer. Either I was a professional or I wasn't, and if I wasn't, it was time for me to start waiting tables.

"Follow my lead," I told him, took a deep breath and headed towards the front door.

"Yes, *Ma'am*," he said. There was a smirk in his tone, but this was the second time we had worked together, and without looking around to let him know that he had relaxed me a bit by goofing on me, I simply smiled and kept my eyes on the boardinghouse.

"Good boy," I said, and we went in.

Eva looked exactly like I thought she would. Overweight, gray-haired, pushing seventy or maybe even already there. I walked up to the desk and smiled.

"Hi, I'm Debbee Morgan. Are you Eva?"

"Do I know you, Miss Morgan?" Eva asked, tearing her eyes from some retro channel where the men of *Bonanza* were engaged in a cattle drive.

"We've never actually met, but I called the other night about the *other* Debbie? The children's author? And about maybe getting a room here myself?"

"Oh, yes! Now, I remember! How nice to meet you in person!" I was finally more interesting than Michael Landon, but for how long was anybody's guess.

"And this is my brother, Sean," I added.

Wade stepped around me and offered his hand. "Pleased to meet you, Miss Eva."

"Oh, aren't you *both* so nice. Your mother must be *so* proud!" She apparently remembered that 'Mum' was dying and in the hospital, and a cloud of concern crossed her face as she dropped her voice. "How *is* she, by the way?"

"Oh, pretty much the same, I'm afraid, but that's actually why I'm here."

"Then you must be psychic," Eva said, and a chill ran through me, "because I have a note here to call you as soon as I had a vacancy, and now I do. Where *is* that thing, anyway?"

"Someone moved out?" I asked sweetly, already having guessed.

"Just last night, in fact. That girl Debbie, you know, with the burns? Well, she came to the desk around nine o'clock and said she had to fly right home. Some kind of family emergency, poor thing, as if she already didn't have enough troubles." The cloud covering her face was a full-blown thunderstorm now. "But I'm confused."

"Confused about what, Eva?"

"Because I thought you two really didn't know each other?"

"We didn't—we only met that one time, that day at the hospital when she told me about you."

The sweat was trickling down my back now, and it had nothing to do with the vest or the fact that the heat in here was up around 72 and the sunshine was reflecting off the water and pouring through the dusty windows.

"Well, isn't that odd?"

"I'm sorry, Eva, now *I'm* confused."

"Oh, don't be, dear." Eva looked right, left, frowned, grabbed the remote, muted *Hoss Cartwright*, and pulled a small envelope out from under a newspaper. "Ah, here it is! Debbie said to give it to you."

"But she couldn't have known I was coming!"

"She must have, dear. She said: if a pretty girl with big blue eyes and dark hair comes in here tomorrow or the next day looking for me, she's a friend of mine and would I please give her this note."

I took the envelope when she held it out, half expecting it to explode in my hand.

I was having trouble thinking on my feet, couldn't imagine what to say, and thank God for Wade because he rescued me.

"Well, Eva, could my sister look at the room, then, as long as we're here?"

"Why of course, Sweetie," she said and handed him a key. "And take your time!"

• • •

Wade unlocked the door, pushed me to the other side of the door frame with his eyes, took the key out and pocketed it before shoving the door open with his foot and plastering himself against the wall with his weapon already in his hand. The door swung open, hit the wall, shuddered, and came halfway back on squeaky hinges.

This was exactly how we had planned to enter the room, if Rachel had still been here, him high, me low, and considering whom we were dealing with it didn't hurt to exercise a little extra caution.

We waited a second or two and then barged in, Wade going to his left, me to my right.

There was only the one room, clean as a whistle, but Wade checked the small bathroom while I took the closet.

"Clear," he said.

"Same here."

He put his gun back in its holster under his jacket and shook his head.

"What's the note say?"

"Christ, I'm afraid to open it."

"Baby," Wade said, and reached for it.

"Fuck you, Wade," I said, and pulled it away from him.

"Not unless Sam gets to watch."

I just shook my head, not in the mood for jokes or for anything other than what Rachel had left for me. Not at the moment, anyway.

I used a thumbnail to open the envelope. There was just one line, again with a smiley face.

The note said: "*Seriously, Kaylyn?*"

• • •

We searched the room, thoroughly, I might add, but came up with absolutely nothing. We were about to leave when I noticed something hanging from the desk drawer Wade had hastily closed after finding it empty.

"Hang on a sec," I said, cocking my head. "What's this?"

Have you ever shut a drawer and caught a piece of paper at the back? It hangs down if it gets pushed into the frame, and that's what I thought I had here.

"It's empty. Lynn."

Instead of answering, I pulled the drawer out and tugged gently on the paper, not wanting to rip it. Then I smiled at him.

"Son of a *bitch*," Wade said softly, as I unfolded it.

"Watch your mouth."

The paper was crinkled like an accordion; the print was light but still legible: a receipt from *Discount Rentals*, a car rental outlet at Green Airport in Warwick.

Wade was standing over my shoulder, reading the print-out.

"She blow town?"

"No way, pal…she's in for the full ride."

"How do you know?"

"Well, for one thing, I know her quite well; also, your wife is not only *gorgeous*—she's a freaking *genius*. She figured out what Rachel is spelling, and there's one more letter on her hit list. She ditched this place, because she obviously knew I tailed her here, but that only means she's hiding somewhere else." I frowned as I studied the rental agreement. "It's not the car she was using when I tailed her…oh, wait, here it is. This isn't a return receipt—it's for a pickup. Honda Civic, red, New Hampshire plates."

"So what do we do now?"

"You feel like taking a ride?"

"Sam would kill me if I didn't, Lynn, but what good is going all the way down there going to do?" He leaned over my shoulder, his chest on my back, and pointed at the paper. His pecs felt like iron and he smelled delicious, a mixture of *Safeguard Soap, Canoe,* and **man**. I closed my eyes and for a moment there I almost turned around and kissed him, remembering how awesome it had been the last time, but then I sighed, took a deep breath, and focused—it might not be easy being who and what I am, but once I promise myself that I'll do something the way in which it should be done, I'm like the Rock of Gibraltar. "See right there?" he added. "She was supposed to pick it up this morning."

If Wade Ashbery had any idea of the effect he was having on me, alone in that little room with a very convenient bed right there for the asking, he didn't show it.

"I don't *know* if it'll do us any good, but if she left us a lead to follow, I'll get the manager to give it up, I can promise you *that* much."

"How can you be so sure?"

"Because I have a way with people."

"And then what?"

"And then we take her down."

"You always *were* a little too sure of yourself, Lynn," Wade said and shook his head. "You think you can just waltz right in there and get these people to cough up confidential information, really?"

"It's what I do," I told him, turning around and meeting his eyes. "That's who I am."

• • •

We grabbed some coffee at *Honey Dew Donuts,* and took Route 1 all the way to Warwick. On the way down, I filled him in on everything about Rachel that I thought he should know, and, not for the first time I realized that he was actually a pretty good listener—for a man.

"Jesus, Lynn."

"What?"

"The way you talk about that shit in Rwanda." He bit his lower lip and shook his head. "I would have liked a piece of those guys myself."

"Rachel didn't leave much, I'm afraid."

"I can see why you're having such a hard time with this," he said at length. "And I'm sorry I was so short with you the night you came to the house."

I shrugged. "She was awesome, Wade, and I loved her like a sister. The woman who's doing this…it's not the same girl I once knew."

"I've got a friend like that, too."

"Homer?"

Wade nodded, and glanced at me with one hand on the wheel. "Yeah, Homer."

Homer was Bobby Simpson, aka, Jennifer's husband. He'd been on the rescue mission in Afghanistan with us, and I knew he was the kind of guy you'd want beside you when the shit hit the fan.

"I can't imagine what I'd do if *he* went south on me, Lynn."

"You'd do just what *I'm* going to do, Wade."

He looked at me again, with one eyebrow raised.

"Take him out?" Wade asked after a long moment.

"Take him out," I agreed.

"You ever wonder what did this to her?"

"I don't have to wonder about it. That training they gave us—if fucks you up. Ever see *The Bourne Identity?*"

"Got the picture."

I frowned. "And getting burned like that, not to mention her brother." I shook my head. "Man, I can't even *imagine.*"

We drove in silence for a while, and then Wade lit a cigarette. We'd gone through at least five a piece. Ever wonder why you smoke more when you're riding with another smoker?

"What did you mean when you said she got you off the street?"

"I really can't talk about that, Wade, I'm sorry, but she was already in the program when we met and…she helped me out."

"How come you never told me any of this before?"

"When the hell was I supposed to do that?"

He smiled, not unkindly. "Want me to draw you a picture?"

I returned his smile, because our time together in Afghanistan had, after all, involved more than a little pillow talk.

"I'm actually pretty happy with what we *did* discuss, aren't you?"

He blushed, believe it or not, and instead of answering me he picked up his empty cup and shook it at me as we passed a *Dunkin Donuts* drive-through.

"Want another traveler?"

"Maybe on the way back."

When we got to the airport we had to look around a little before we found the rental place, but ten minutes later we were parked out front.

"Mind a question before we go in?"

"Shoot."

"For a minute there, back at Eva's—were you thinking about hitting on me?"

"I *thought* about it," I said coyly as I opened my door.

"Why didn't you?"

"Why? Would you have gone for it?"

"I asked you first! Come on, why didn't you?"

"Because Sam wasn't there to watch," I told him and got out.

• • •

The rental manager was an officious little prick by the name of Davenport. Fortyish, balding, suffering from a *severe* case of "Little Man Syndrome", he was also very happy in his own little dictatorship and obviously enjoying our exasperation.

"Forget it, Lynn," Wade said, "we'll call the head office."

"Please feel free to do so," Davenport told us. "They'll probably give me a raise for adhering to policy. Who do you think you are, anyway, barging in here and demanding to see the manager?"

"Look, you—"

I grabbed Wade's arm before he could say any more.

"We're just looking for a little help here, Mr. Davenport," I said as sweetly as my growing temper would allow. "Where's the harm in that?"

"Well, how would you like it if someone just came in here and demanded information about *you?*"

"First of all," Wade said, his temper growing even shorter than mine was at the moment, "we didn't *demand* anything—we asked you nicely."

"I'll handle this!" I said to Wade, glaring at him.

"I'm afraid there's nothing to *handle*, Ma'am," Davenport assured me. "We simply can't give out personal information unless it's an official request from the police or something like that."

"Then I'll *make* it one," I told him.

"Beg pardon?"

"My name is Kaylyn Vale, and—"

"You already told me that," Davenport interrupted.

"…and I'm a Private Investigator working with the police." I fished out my I.D. and showed it to him. Davenport looked at it, coughed, and turned to the pretty black girl who had been working the counter when we came in.

"Daphne, please see to the other customers. Follow me," he added to us.

A good-looking young couple carrying a baby had just come in the front door, and Davenport took us over to a small metal desk by the plate glass windows.

"I'm afraid private detectives aren't exactly the police," Davenport told us in hushed tones so that the young couple wouldn't hear him. "And I'm afraid you'll have to leave now."

I could see that Wade was getting ready to grab the guy by the neck, but I beat him to the punch. Literally.

"Look, you little *shit!*" I snarled, grabbing his sports coat by the label. "You've heard about all those judges being killed, haven't you?" Davenport turned all red and looked like he wanted to puke, but he nodded. "Well, we're *working* that case, and this woman is a suspect! I swear, Davenport, I swear to fucking *God*, you take us into your office right now and show us her goddamn paperwork or I'll have more cops and more state auditors in here going through you *and* your fucking books than you can possibly imagine!"

"All right, all right!" he squeaked, looking nervously at the couple on the counter. "All you had to do was *explain* it to me!"

I turned to Wade Ashbery with a huge smile on my face. "*Told* you I have a way with people, *didn't* I?"

• • •

Rachel Stark had used the name, "Rhonda Witherspoon", one of her aliases, and when asked to describe her Davenport confirmed the horrible burns on her face. Rachel had given her address as, *Hotel Central*, Providence, and as we got back in the Ford, Wade sighed.

"You *know* she's not there, don't you?"

"Only one way to find out, isn't there?"

Wade looked at his watch and started the pickup. "Alright, I'm in."

"You *wish*," I said and gave him a smile.

"Fuck you, Vale," he said, and grinned.

"Not unless Sam gets to watch!" we both said at the same time, and then we cracked up.

We got back on Route 1, stopped for coffee, and were on the way back five minutes after that. We drank our coffee, smoked, and then I turned on the radio.

"Think she'd really go for that?" I asked, after ten minutes of listening to some music.

"Go for what?"

"Watching," I said without looking at him.

Wade chuckled. "Oh, I thought you were talking about Rachel!" He shook his head, flicked ashes out the window, and cracked up again. "Only one way to find out, isn't there?" he asked, mocking the phrase I had used earlier.

All of a sudden, and without quite knowing why, I felt like I wanted to cry again and turned my head to look out the window. Wade caught it, though—if there's *one* thing he knows about it's women—and he touched my arm with his free hand.

Now—you men out there will probably be thinking that you understand how I felt, and if you *do*, you're a real man...but the *women* reading this, will most likely think that I'm a manipulative little slut, because I was crying the night that Wade and I ended up in bed...but the truth is, I was legitimately fucked up at that moment, wondering just what the hell kind of a person I was. I'm sorry if I've offended anyone reading this, but women always think that they know what another woman is thinking, and usually put a negative spin on it. Maybe they're right, too—in most cases, or maybe they just project what *they* would do onto another girl— but the tears were genuine, and I really *wasn't* trying to pull anything.

"Hey, *hey*," he said softly, "what's wrong? Want me to pull over?"

I shook my head—no. "Just keep driving, Wade. I'll be all right in a minute."

"You sure?"

"Yeah, I'm sure." And I was. If he pulled over and put his arms around me, we'd end up in bed again—I can almost guarantee it.

I rubbed my eyes on my shoulders—right, then left, and then lit a cigarette.

"Sorry about that," I said after a few more minutes.

"Was it something I said? Something we were talking about?"

"Nope. You didn't have anything to do with it. I just can't believe what a screw-up I am, falling for both of you like this. Christ, what a loser!"

Wade kept driving and only spoke after thinking about it for a while. It's one of the things I admire most about him. It's why I consider Sam such a lucky girl.

"I think you're being too hard on yourself."

"Do you, now?"

"Yeah, I do."

"This kind of life…the kind of life I lead…it's hard to get close to anyone, you know?" I turned my head to look over at him. "If there's anything worse than being lonely, I'd like to know what it is."

"I know about being lonely," he admitted.

"Yeah, well, it's no excuse for screwing both your lives up."

"Hey, c'mon, Lynn! You didn't exactly twist our arms you know, either of us. We're very…complicated…the three of us, and well, let it go now, will you? We did."

"I'd tell you how sorry I am, but as my Dad used to say: 'that dog won't hunt'."

"No need for 'sorry', Kaylyn. Sam and me…we've got it good. We went through a bad stretch there, lying to each other the way we did, me about faking my death to protect her, and what she did with you, and some other things if you want the truth, but we've agreed that sex is just something we're both really into, and nothing's off the table from now on except for going behind each other's backs. People like us?" he added after a second or two. "We know what's important. We know how to be alive…and how that could change at any moment."

I just looked at him. "I just wish I had someone of my own, you know?"

"Why do you think I teach school now, Lynn? The life you lead; the life *I* led…" He shook his head. "There's no *way* to get close to anyone."

"I've actually been thinking about that a lot."

"You know, after Janice died…" Jan had been his first wife, before he met Samantha—she'd been killed by a drunk-driver, and the poor girl had been pregnant at the time. "Well, after that, I thought I'd be alone for the rest of my life." He shrugged. "And then Sam came along." He laughed. "Brought a hurricane with her, but, what the hell, the storm's over and we're still here. You wouldn't *believe* the kind of stuff I got into before Sam, and to tell you the truth, I never gave a *shit* about what anyone thought of me, either, especially since most people are such hypocrites. Anyway. Please don't beat yourself up for being lonely—you didn't make either one of us do anything that we didn't *want* to do."

"You actually make me seem like a decent person," I said, and laughed.

"You're awesome, Lynn. You're pretty, *really* pretty, very smart, and you've got a big heart. When the time's right, when the right person comes along…you'll know it."

"That simple, huh?"

"No," he added as he slowed down for a light, and turned to look at me, "you have to *believe* in yourself, too."

• • •

Rachel of course, was not at the *Hotel Central*, but I thought I knew where I could find her, especially with a little help from Dusty Anderson; still, it was time to cut Wade loose. I wanted him to go home. It's as simple as that: first of all because I'd never forgive myself if anything happened to him, but also because I fully intended to keep my promise to myself. I was *done* being a cheater—especially with the hus-

Judgment Day

band of someone I'd come to care for very much, and I wanted to go and scope out the *Premier Hotel*, alone, and maybe the whole neighborhood where Dusty worked.

"Where to now?" Wade asked when we got back in the truck.

"My office, if you don't mind." I purposely looked at my watch, hoping he'd infer that I had something to do.

We didn't talk on the way over—I think we were both starting to look at each other a little too much, and when we got there he got out when I did and I knew I was in trouble.

"I, uh, have something to do," I told him as I dug out my keys.

"I figured that out for myself, actually. You've looked at your watch half a hundred times. Why do you wear it with the face on the *inside* of your wrist, by the way?"

"Ever see *The Omega Man*?"

"Charlton Heston, 1971," he said with a smirk—our old game again. "Incidentally, it's one of my favorite movies."

I smiled in spite of myself. "That scene where he's siphoning off his own blood to make the serum? He was wearing *his* watch like this, and I copied it. I was just a kid when I saw that movie, but it stuck with me. Well, I'll say good-night now."

"Aren't you going to invite me in?"

I put my hands on my hips. "No, Mr. Ashbery, I don't believe I am. I have someplace to be and I want you to go home and call your wife."

"So, you want me to, what? Take the flak vest off out here?"

"Oopps!"

We went in and he took off the vest while I made a K-cup for myself.

"Here."

I took it from him and sighed. It had been a long time since I'd been with a man, and I *wanted* him, but I also wanted to become the person I *could* be, the person I was *trying* to be—even if it hurt a little to get there.

He hugged me and I almost—*almost* gave in to it, and him, while he pulled me close.

"Go home now, dummy, and call your wife. She's a lot prettier than I am anyway."

"Sam thinks you're hot, and *I've* never been one to compare apples to oranges."

"Go!"

Wade held up his hands. "Ok, I'm going. I'm going!"

"And *call* her!" I added with one hand on the door frame.

"Yes, Ma'am." He paused on my doorstep. "And by the way—yeah, I think she'd go for it—definitely."

"Go!" I hissed at him, and shut the door while he was still laughing at me.

Then I put my feet up on a chair and did a few dozen pushups.

· · ·

The couch looked very inviting after all of that, and I sat down with my head back and closed my eyes. I wanted to do something, *needed* to do something, but there was nowhere to go and nothing to do and so I just sat there, feeling lonely and defeated. None of this was really my fault, I tried to tell myself, but if I had simply given Rachel's location to the authorities this would have been over by now.

You may be reading this and wondering just what kind of a monster I am—I was actually thinking the same thing myself, but dwelling on all of my wrong decisions wasn't going to change a thing. It is also quite true that if I *had* told the Feds where to find her, Rachel would have taken more than a few of them with her.

A no-win situation no matter *how* you looked at it.

I've been through a lot of storms in my life and survived them all—I'd lost my mother, and then my Dad, and there was a bad stretch of road before Rachel found me, too, which is why I felt so close to Dusty, but looking back on it all, even if you throw in all the terrible things I did as an operative for "The Company", even if you throw in Afghanistan, I knew that, given the same set of circumstances I would have done everything up to this point exactly as I had done it.

Sometimes, all you have in this life is the moment you're in, and at that moment, the moment in which I had decided to deal with Rachel on my own, I had made the right decision. I've had to kill people in my life, and no matter the need or the cause, it hurts—it takes something from you, *does* something to do, but you either let it get the better of you or you move on. This thing with Rachel was exactly the same thing, if not in form than at least in substance—if I had given her location to anyone else even more people would have died, so despite how much this sucked, and despite the guilt that was gnawing at me, I knew that I had done the right thing—even if it didn't always feel that way.

I sat up, rubbed my face, and got to my feet.

The clothes I was wearing were sweat-drenched, and so I locked the door, got a clean shirt and some nice jeans out of my closet, got undressed and took a shower before I changed.

It was time to focus on what I had to do…not on what I thought I *should* have done.

"All right, time to figure this out," I mumbled out loud, as if saying it would somehow make it come true.

Rachel had given the car rental people the *Hotel Central* as her current address; Wade and I checked it out, and of course she hadn't been there, but I knew in the deepest part of my heart that she wasn't done with this awful thing yet, and it had nothing whatsoever to do with what Samantha thought she might be spelling out. I was done playing games with Rachel, and I was going to find her. I was a private investigator, for Christ's sake, and that's what we do, isn't it?

The shirt was a nice tan color with a neat little collar, and the jeans were brand new. I tucked in my shirt, pulled a sturdy black belt from a coat-hanger, and changed my shoes, opting for an old pair of ankle-high *Reebok Ex-O-Fits* that matched nicely. The older version of this shoe actually takes a good shine and makes it look like you're wearing shoes instead of sneakers. They're comfortable, give you decent support—and you can run in them if you have to. I went back to the closet, and took out a brown suede jacket with a decent lining, and draped it over a chair. The 9mm I usually carry was heavy by comparison, so I took a .25 Caliber *Raven* automatic from my safe and put two spare clips in my pocket. The .25 has been called a "lady's" gun, but if you shoot someone in the head with one of those things the slug just runs around and around the skull, chewing up everything in its path. It doesn't have the stopping power of the heavier calibers, but if you know what you're doing it gets the job done all the same and it's as light as a feather. I clipped the holster onto my belt, threw the jacket over my shoulder and took a last look in the mirror as I dabbed on a little *White Diamonds* perfume.

People tell me that I look a lot like the actress Alexandra Daddario, and I suppose that's true all the way around, and I'm flattered that people think I'm that attractive, but it's mostly my eyes that match hers almost exactly; they're a *startling* blue, and somehow reflect the fact that I am haunted by the things I've seen and the things that I have done. As I put on my ear-rings—two simple gold circles—I studied those eyes and vowed to somehow get past those things that were haunting me. It was well past time to exorcise the demons in my past, and I thought I could do so, beginning with my next stop.

The phone rang while I was putting on my jacket.

"Hey, Sam," I said and tried very hard not to sigh.

"You two have fun today?"

"What part of 'I care deeply about you' don't you *get*, Samantha?"

"Chill, Dollface! It was only a joke! He told me about your whole day together, and I wanted to run something by you."

Our "whole day together", including some of the things we had talked about, encompassed quite a bit, but I simply wasn't feeling like dealing with anything but finding Rachel.

Not at the moment, anyway.

"Shoot."

"Well, what if I come back there and we work the neighborhood near the *Hotel Central?* Rachel's sort of been telegraphing her punches all along, and if she gave that address she's somewhere close. I'd bet money on it."

"Sam. Will you listen to me for a moment?"

"Huh? Oh, sure."

"I don't *want* you here. I grew up without a mother, and it's not just about the *kids* being safe, it's about you being safe for *them*. Please say away until I finish this, ok?"

Samantha was silent for a long moment, and I knew a fight was coming, but then she surprised me.

"You're your own worst enemy, Kaylyn Vale—anyone ever tell you that?"

She hung up before I could tell her that I'd been hearing that, from just about everyone, all my life.

• • •

Goodbye Pork Pie Hat was playing on my stereo when I started the car, and I picked up the jewel case from the passenger seat, having forgotten I'd bought the Charlie Mingus CD, *Ah Um*, the day before at lunch time. I'd always been a fan of Mingus, but the liner notes said that he had once been referred to as "The Angry Man of Jazz", and, in my opinion at least, you can hear that in his music. Mingus had had a troubled youth, and didn't even know who his real father had been, and, although it wasn't exactly the situation I dealt with concerning my own parents, it made me feel a kinship with the bassist. More than that, I liked his face—he was someone I would have liked to have known.

As I sat there listening to the music, I could still hear the *throb* and *gurgle* of that beautiful, balanced and blueprinted engine as it ran through the dual exhaust. Being an old-school "gearhead" (my first real boyfriend was a mechanic, not to mention my friendship with David Redman), I may have already mentioned that my Mustang is not-exactly street-legal. In *simple* terms, to balance and blueprint an engine basically means that the mechanic/engineer literally weighs and balances all of the rotating mass of the motor, and that all of the manufacturers' specifications are double and triple checked. The *blueprint* ensures getting more power out of any given engine design than you can possibly imagine, and by *balancing* all of the reciprocating parts and rotating assemblies, it vastly reduces vibrations that, in standard engines, cause the engine to operate at far below what it is capable of putting out in horsepower—in street terms: it makes the fucker a monster.

I lowered the volume on the stereo, and took out my phone.

"Hey!" Dusty said picking up on the third ring. "What's shaking, Valegirl?"

I rolled my eyes. "Valegirl" was apparently her new nickname for me. I took a quick glance at the dashboard clock before I answered.

"Got a business proposition for you."

"Oh, I *knew* you'd change your mind!"

"Not *that*, knucklehead! I mean a *real* business—you free for supper?"

"My business *is* real enough, honey—trust me, and as for supper, since I turned down the invitation I got to the Governor's Ball tonight, sure. A girl's got to eat. One thing, though—*my* treat this time. Had a good week."

"How 'bout we argue about that *after* we get the check?" I said, gritting my teeth—I knew from personal experience what it took to have a "good" week in *her* business.

"Sounds like a plan."

"You free now?"

"I make my own hours, dolly-face."

"Where should I pick you up?"

"You know where my office is…I'll be here."

"Fifteen minutes work for you?"

"Fifteen works like a charm."

I hung up, and headed out, knowing I was *using* the kid but also knowing that, unless she told me to go and *fuck* myself, I was also going to get her off the street or die trying. You'll understand why in just a minute, but this was two "birds" I could kill with one stone.

It took me better than twenty-five minutes because of the traffic, but Dusty was on the corner near the main street when I got there, well away from the hotel, and she was wearing my sweater and a nice pair of jeans. Seeing her dressed that way made me want to smile and cry at the same time, and as she got in the car, I looked at her, really *looked* at her, and realized just how *pretty* she could be if I got her clean and healthy.

"Hey!" she said, and then: "What's the matter?"

"Huh? Oh, nothing."

"You were looking at me kind of funny."

"Hard to believe there was a real woman under all that manikin makeup you were wearing last time I saw you—pretty one, too."

"Wow, honey—you could just about charm the pants off a broad!"

"I've actually done that!" I said with a genuine laugh that felt really good. I glanced sideways at her. "Once or twice."

"For real?"

"Yeah, I've been known to date a girl or two in my day."

"So you really *are* a switch-hitter!"

I laughed again. "I don't see it that way—I go to bed with *who* the person is, Dusty, not *what* they are. If I feel…connected…I'm good to go."

"Wow, that's cool."

"Glad you approve."

"So, I got changed and all cleaned up. Where do you want to go?"

"You like Italian?" I asked after thinking for a moment.

"Who doesn't?"

"Then why don't we head on up to Federal Hill and eat at *Venda Ravioli?*"

"Are we dressed for that? I heard it's kind of ritzy."

"It's nice, honey, but we look ok."

"Is it expensive?"

"Not too bad, but you don't need to worry about that."

"Kaylyn, listen, we're kinda becoming friends here, aren't we?"

"I thought we already were," I said with a smile as I pulled out.

"Me too, but if we are, I don't want you paying for me all the time. I've got money."

"I know you do, Dusty, and that's part of what I wanted to talk to you about."

"You mean your business proposition?"

I laughed. She was so cute I simply couldn't stand it. "Yeah, that."

Dusty looked at me for a long time. I could feel her pale blue eyes on me, measuring me as I drove.

"What did you have in mind?"

"I was wondering if you'd like to come and work for me," I asked, turning to her at the lights.

"Seriously? What would I do?"

"Well, you'd be my assistant for starters—you know, receptionist, researcher, that kind of thing. Later, if it works out, we'd see about getting you your own license."

"I already *have* a license, Lynn. I can drive."

"No," I said and laughed. "I meant an investigator's license."

"Me, a P.I.? Are you for real? I'm a hooker, for Christ's sake."

"So was I," I admitted as the light changed.

"God, you're serious, aren't you?" she asked as she studied me.

I nodded. "Yeah, for about a year when I was eighteen." I pursed my lips. "You don't have a record, do you?"

"Well, I got picked up once—for loitering, but no, other than that I'm clean, why?"

"Just be easier to get you established if you don't have any convictions. How old are you, by the way?"

"Twenty one."

"How long you been using?"

"You can tell?"

"I've known a heroin user or two in my life."

"About a year—not too much."

"Then it shouldn't be that hard to get you off of the shit."

"You ever use?"

I shook my head. "No, always been too much of an athlete for that."

"Then how do you know it wouldn't be that hard?"

"I said, *too* hard—there'll be withdrawal, but I'll be there for you. I know because I got someone else off of it—once upon a time."

We were in the parking lot by that time, and it was a good thing, because she stared to cry. I reached over, which wasn't easy because of the bucket seats, but I got my arm around her and just held her. I could have been Rachel at that moment, and Dusty could have been me, or the other way around for that matter—it's funny how life moves in circles.

"Why?" she sniffed, when the worst of it was over. "Why do you care so much about someone like me?"

"You're no different than I am, Drusilla. Why *shouldn't* I want to help you?"

"You're *nothing* like me."

"Why? Because I have a business and drive a nice car? Those things don't really mean much at the end of the day, my girl. What matters is believing in yourself."

"The person you helped—it's that chick with the burns, isn't it?"

"Yup. She helped me, I helped her—that's how friendships works...when it works."

Dusty unbuckled her seatbelt. "You ever going to tell me the truth about her?"

"I'd actually like to do that tonight, because it's part of the whole package, but if I do, you can't tell a soul, ever, not even your brother."

"If there's one thing I can do, Lynn," she said as she opened her door, "it's keep a secret."

• • •

We got a nice little corner booth where it was noisy enough to cover our conversation, but not noisy enough to make talking difficult. I ended up ordering *Veal Piccata* for both of us, because Dusty was frustrated by so many choices, and I asked our server, a cute young guy who flirted mildly with my "niece", to bring us a small carafe of white wine. We *both* ended up getting "carded", which made me giggle, and when the dishes arrived—swimming in lemon, wine and capers, with side orders of perfectly-cooked pasta—we dug in.

While we ate, I told her my story—pretty much as you, yourself, have heard it, and Dusty listened with rapt attention, her eyes filling with tears once or twice. She seemed particularly interested in how Rachel found me on the street after I had run away from my foster family at eighteen, and nodded to herself as if she understood the difficulty I was having and my mixed emotions for someone who had literally saved my life. I sat back when I was done, and wiped my mouth with a napkin. I had eaten more than was good for me, but I didn't care; the meal had been delicious, and as I have told you, I thoroughly enjoy having company at dinner.

"So what do you want me to do?" Dusty asked when I was through.

"That mean you're in?"

"Yeah, I'm in."

"For the full ride?"

"You mean the part about drying me out?"

"Can't do any of this until you're clean, babe."

"I've got to talk to my brother...I mean, I can't just *leave* him, you know, but how are we going to get me straight if we're out chasing down Rachel?"

I sighed. I'd been wondering that myself. I couldn't very well sit with Dusty while she went through withdrawal—not and find Rach at the same time.

"We're not, honey, and I'm sorry for that, but the quicker I find *her*..."

"Got the picture. So what do you want me to do in the meantime?"

"Starting right this minute, you're on my payroll...and off the street. Tonight, after we leave here, we'll call your brother and tell him. I don't suppose we could talk *him* out of the life he's leading?"

Dusty was already shaking her head. "We won't have to. He's been talking about hooking up with this chick he knows, and doing the carnival circuit down south. He's only stayed in this because of me, and because we've had no other options up to this point. If he knows I'm going in with you—he pull the plug here."

"You sure?"

"Yeah, I'm sure." She frowned and teared up again. "So, you haven't answered my question: what do we do in the meantime? What do *I* do?"

"My first instinct is to take you home with me, honey, but I can't have you there while you're cleaning up. But I've got a nice big couch at my office, pulls out into a bed, and there's a shower and a refrigerator. Starting tonight I want you staying there, and helping me find Rachel before she slips away from us."

"Or kills someone else?"

"Yeah," I said. "There *is* that."

• • •

Two hours later we were in my office. I locked the door, pulled the shades, and turned up the heat.

"Do you need anything from your room back at the *Premier?*"

"Nah, got everything I need in my bag."

She held up the little gym-bag she had brought after talking to her brother while I had waited in the car.

"What about clothes?"

"I'm wearing them, Lynn, except for my, you know, work clothes." She shrugged. "I left them behind."

Her earnestness touched me so deeply that I went to her and hugged her, not even bothering to hide my tears. In seconds we were both crying, and then I held her at arm's length and found a smile for her.

"Tomorrow, we'll go shopping, first thing."

"Whatever you say, boss."

"You need a fix?"

"I'm a little jittery, but, no, I'm good right now. I brought a little if I need a touch to stop the shakes."

"It won't be easy, but I know you can do it."

"One thing you should know about me, Lynn? When I make up my mind to do something, nothing in the world can stop me. Hey, you're looking at me funny again!"

"Am I? I guess I'm just proud of you, that's all."

Dusty started sobbing and again I hugged her. "No one's ever said that to me before."

"Well, get used to it."

"One thing, though?"

"What is it?"

"Well, we're never going to get a *thing* done if we keep crying like this, so stop being so nice to me!"

"Sorry, baby—but you'd better get used to *that*, too!"

· · ·

We hit the ground running first thing in the morning…literally, as you'll see.

I got to the office around nine o'clock, fully expecting to find Dusty sprawled out on the couch and high as a kite. Instead, I found her showered and dressed and vacuuming the rug. The folding table had been straightened out, the pencils Sam and I had knocked over picked up, the print-outs in neat piles, the blanket she had used the night before folded neatly and put back in the closet.

"Hey," she said as I came in, shutting down my little *Dirt Devil*. "I was just going to do the front windows." She frowned. "They're kind of yucky, no offense." There on the desk was the large bottle of *Windex* I had bought at *Ocean State Job Lot*, with an unopened roll of paper towels beside it.

"Wow," I said, putting my hands on my hips and looking around. "Girl could get used to this."

Dusty shrugged, and I couldn't help myself. I went over, hugged her and said: "Leave the windows for now. Let's go shopping!"

• • •

I had been waiting for her to tell me her story, and she did it that morning, without any prompting from me, as we drove to the store. I listened as patiently as I could, because it was painful to listen to, but she got through it while I forced myself to keep my mouth shut, and by the time we got to the mall I realized we actually *did* have a lot in common.

"So you see?" she said. "Other than my brother, I have no one."

"Well, you've got me now," I told her as we found a parking space, "you know, if you want me."

A dark green Camaro pulled in a few spaces up, but that wouldn't make an impression on me until later

"Oh, I don't know," she said. "You're ok, for an old broad," she added, "so I think I'll keep you!"

"Nice of you to let me hang around!" as said as I got out.

Dusty did something then that almost brought me to tears as we walked to the store—she grabbed my hand like a little girl and smiled hugely at me.

"Now I know what it's like to have a sister!"

"Me, too," Kiddo."

We walked for a while, holding hands, just as you sometimes see sisters doing, or mothers and daughters.

"You're alone, too, aren't you, Lynn?"

"Umm-hmm. Got a *few* good friends, though."

"It sucks being lonely. Not having a family."

"I've got a friend. He used to be a Marine…"

"A *good* friend?" Dusty asked with her eyes sparkling.

"Good enough, Gertrude! And cool your jets, *chica*—he's married!"

"Never stopped *me*."

"That's because you're a slut."

Dusty was laughing at me. "Actually, the correct term is 'professional'. Go on—I'm just breaking them on you!"

"Anyway, this friend, he always says that family isn't necessarily a matter of blood."

"Oh, cool—I totally get that!" She nodded to emphasize that she did, in fact, *get* it. "Long as people are willing to have your back, you can make your own family, right?"

"Right," I said as we went in.

"Just like you and me, right?"

"Right again," I told her, thinking how strange life is, how it can turn on a dime for better or for worse, that meeting one single person, can make your whole life…or break it.

We ended up getting her four new outfits; slacks and jeans and some nice tops, along with some decent, *functional* bras, socks and some panties. I bought her two pairs of shoes and a nice spring jacket from the ladies' section of *Eddie Bauer*, and then we headed to the car. She had wanted to stop for lunch at the mall, but I wanted to get her stuff back and start canvasing the neighborhood around the *Hotel Central* before it got any later, so I told her we'd grab a *snack* now and have a nice dinner together later.

Dusty seemed ok with that, so I thought I'd stop at the gas station right outside the mall and grab us some coffee and donuts just to hold us over.

The day had been overcast to begin with, but now it was actually starting to sprinkle, and the clouds coming in were dark and ominous. I got under the overhang at the gas station just as it started to pour, and got out, figuring I might as well fill up while we were here.

"I've got the coffee!" Dusty said, a little *too* loud, and ran in. Her hands had been shaking for the better part of an hour and I knew she was getting near her time. I knew I was out of my mind, taking her on like this, but I was still afraid that Rachel actually *would* kill Sam, and I needed help in that neighborhood if I was going to find out where Rachel was holed up. I sighed, resigning myself to the fact that I was just going to have to stand for the kid taking a fix, and then I noticed that the car that had pulled out of the parking lot at the mall at the exact same time as we had, that same dark green Camaro with tinted windows, was in line at the next set of pumps.

Now, it was the only gas station near the mall, so it was convenient—for anyone—but I don't like co-incidences, especially when I'm working a case, and I just had a feeling as I stood there topping off the tank, that something wasn't right.

When you've been doing this as long as I have you develop a sixth sense that alerts you to possible danger and mine was on high alert at the moment; I have never ignored it, and it has never let me down.

I turned around and watched the Camaro surreptitiously in the big overhead convex mirror, put back the pump, got in the car and waited for Drusilla.

She got in the car smelling like rain and I didn't even wait for her to buckle in or even to take anything out of the bag. I pulled out as fast as I could, floored the Mustang, cut across three lanes of traffic leading to the highway ramp, and watched in the rearview mirror as the Camaro pulled out of line and came after us.

"Hey! What gives?"

"You're about to find out why I want to take Rachel down so bad."

"She following us?" Dusty turned in her seat. I didn't complain. Whoever it was *knew* that I knew.

"Rachel, or someone she hired. Camaro, dark green. And they're not tailing us honey—they're coming after us."

"Shit! You serious?" She wisely put the bag with the coffee on the floor.

"Serious as a heart attack, pal." I checked the rear view mirror again, just to see if they had made it across all three lanes, and as I was roaring up the ramp and onto Interstate 95 I saw that they were less than a quarter of a mile behind. "Still want to be an investigator?"

Dusty turned in her seat again, watching as the Camaro gained on us. She gave them the finger and then turned around.

"Fucking right, I do."

"Then buckle your seatbelt and I'll show you what I've got under the hood."

The Camaro was gaining on us, but it was the middle of the day and the traffic was light. I floored the Mustang and it surged ahead—70, 80, 90, 100, 110…they started to fall behind but I kept my foot on the floor and glanced at the speedometer as it inched towards 120 miles an hour.

"Shit, Lynn!" Dusty said excitedly. "You're a beast!"

The guardrail seemed to be one, long white blur, and I hoped to God—if *she* was listening and truly *not* insane—not to let me blow by any State Troopers. The pavement was slick, but this section of the highway had just been re-done, and those big *Cooper* tires stuck to the road like glue.

I held it there for a while, staying in the far left lane, and when the traffic thinned out I crossed all the way over to the far right.

The Camaro was now at least a mile back, and as we came into a section of the road that curved gently as we entered Massachusetts, I slowed down, taking my foot completely off the gas, and took an off ramp in North Attleboro at better than 70 miles per hour. I went under the overpass, swung around, and pulled into the parking lot of an empty-looking industrial park, parking the car behind a row of truck-trailers that were lined up and blocking the view from the highway overhead. It looked as if they had been there for a while.

I didn't *think* the Camaro had seen us get off the highway because of that bend in the road, but I wasn't taking any chances. I took my Glock from my hip, cocked it and opened the door.

"What the hell are you *doing*, Kaylyn?" Dusty demanded.

"Stay put," I told her, "and lay on that horn if anyone pulls up behind us," I added and walked to the end of the row, stopping by the second to last empty trailer, so I could peer between them. I had the gun at my side, against the trailer, but the place was deserted and I wasn't really worried about anyone seeing me.

It took five minutes, but that damn Camaro came flying into the parking lot and started around the back end of that row of trailers. Dusty saw me turn, her eyes wide, but I shook my head as I started back towards the Mustang, and she laid off the horn. I pulled open the driver's door just as that Camaro came into view again. I rested my arms on the top of the door-frame, and squeezed off one round that ricocheted off their hood, and cracked the windshield.

I couldn't see who was driving, or how many people were in the car, because of the rain and those damn tinted windows, but whoever it was threw the Camaro into reverse, spun around, and took off. I fired two more shots, one taking out the right-side rear-view mirror, and my second shot, aimed at the right-rear tire, missed by inches. I swore and got back into the car.

"Holy shit!" Dusty exclaimed.

"Hang on, kid—I'm going after them."

I spun the Mustang in a short arc, and floored it, catching them just as they hit the on-ramp and started back into Rhode Island on I-95.

The Camaro was fast, but it was no match for my Pony, and I tapped the rear bumper as I caught up, causing them to skid a little. The Camaro sped up, and I followed, chasing them onto the highway. There were no other cars nearby, so I squeezed off one more shot with my left hand out the window, blowing out the rear window. I could see now that there was only one person in the car, but the rain was coming at me in sheets and even with the wipers on HIGH I couldn't tell who it was.

We came into the Pawtucket S-Curves a little too fast, and the Camaro skidded all over the place, and hit the guardrail with his front left fender. Sparks flew, but the Camaro didn't slow down, and I was right on his tail in seconds. The traffic was heavier here, but I did the best I could, chasing the son-of-a-bitch as the Camaro weaved in and out of traffic. I tried to pass, but I saw the driver lift his hand—and at that moment saw that it was a man. He squeezed off one round just as I backed off the gas, and the shot hit the side of a tractor-trailer truck. I fell behind and stayed on his tail, tapping his bumper as often as I dared to.

To Dusty's credit, she stayed calm, and when I risked a glance at her, her pretty face was white, but she was in control of herself.

I hit the gas again, turned the wheel, and tapped the right-rear quarter panel, like a wolf nipping at a stag. The Camaro slid sideways, and I did it again, putting the bastard into the guardrail. He spun around, doing a complete 360, careened into a bus, and went sideways across all three lanes. By this time most of the other drivers around us had grown a brain, and had backed off, and it was a good thing, too, because the Camaro got side-swiped by a delivery truck, hit the guardrail on the other side of the highway—and went right over. I hit the brakes and slid across, getting into the breakdown lane just as the Camaro landed on its roof and got slammed by a semi on the opposite side of the highway. I stopped in the breakdown lane, and got out, peering through the rain and the mist and the fog. The semi slowed down and stopped, and now the traffic on both sides of 95 was at a dead standstill.

I told Dusty to stay put, ran across the road, hopped the divider and went to the Camaro with my gun drawn.

The passenger-side door was open, and there was a lot of blood, but the Camaro was empty.

I holstered the weapon, took out my phone and called the State Police, knowing that Dusty and I could forget about dinner.

CHAPTER TEN—May

They put us in the very same interview room we had used the last time, and just left us sitting there. It was a good hour before the locked door clicked open, and Spinelli came in looking haggard and drawn. He was carrying two manila folders.

"Thought you were suspended?" I asked.

"I was—until about an hour ago. They brought me in to get a statement from you, but they're going to pull your ticket, Nancy."

"Who's 'Nancy'?" Dusty asked.

"Who the hell is this?" Spinelli asked.

"Drusilla Anderson," I replied. "An operative in my employ."

"Oh, yeah? Since when?"

"Since yesterday, and they can *shove* my damn license, Spinner."

Spinelli made a face, and I kept quiet, just looking at him. Bobby is tall, maybe six-foot-one, and in great shape. He's got brown eyes with a reddish tint to them that usually look like rusty nails in an old wooden door. He's actually quite handsome, and has never lost the bearing of his Navy days. He had been a SEAL, and he was a good man to have in your corner. I liked him a lot, but at the moment I wasn't sure where he stood.

He opened one of the files and studied it before looking back up at me.

"An operative, huh? Says she's a hooker."

"Read on, big guy—she doesn't even have a conviction."

Spinner looked down again. "One arrest, for *loitering*. Is *that* what they're calling it these days?"

Drusilla's hands were shaking, and, well, Bobby's a cop. There was no way that he wouldn't pick up on the fact that she was a *hype*—and I wondered how he'd play it. I held one of her hands and squeezed it, giving her a wink.

Spinelli picked up the other file and threw it down in front of me. "What do you know about your little playmate?"

I opened the file and found myself looking at the photo of a guy who could have been the driver of the Camaro. He was about forty, and looked like a thug.

"Who is he?" I asked instead of reading it for myself.

"Was. We found him in the grass further down the median strip. The shoulder harness on the seat belt cut his jugular vein when the car flipped over, and he bled out."

I looked at the file again. "This is an FBI file, Bobby." I looked up. "This guy was a hit man?" My voice went up an octave on the last two words.

"Suspected. He's been picked up half a dozen times, but they've never been able to pin anything on him." Spinelli pursed his lips. "You might find it interesting to know that he was an associate of Rebekka Worthington's while she was in Lebanon."

"Son of a bitch," I whispered, and just then Captain Simmons came in followed by Agent Tanner. Dusty drew in a breath, and I squeezed her hand again.

Simmons was a barrel-chested man in his early fifties that remind me of the actor Claude Akins. He put one foot on a chair and rested his arm on his knee while he studied me. Tanner, the ugly fuck, went to the corner and sat down, looking smug.

"You'll be lucky not to do time for this, Vale," Simons said at length. "In fact, the only thing keeping you out of a jail cell right now is this guy's record."

I laughed, sat back, and took out my cigarettes, just to piss him off.

Judgment Day

"You watch too many old movies, Cap," I said, "and that's *not* the only thing keeping me out of a jail cell right now," I added as I lit up.

"What the hell is *that* supposed to mean?"

"I know where she is." I blew smoke out in a long stream. Rarely had a cigarette tasted so good.

"Where *who* is?" Tanner asked, sitting up quickly.

"Your shooter," I said. "I walk, and keep my license, *and* draw all my back pay…and I'll tell you were to find her."

"You'll tell us or get charged with an obstruction of justice charge!" Tanner sputtered as he got to his feet.

"In that case," I said, "it was only a joke."

Tanner's mouth fell open, but Simmons actually laughed.

"All right, Miss Vale, you win, back pay and all, but don't ever expect to work with us again."

"I can live with that," I told him, "but I'm here right now because the god damned State Department *wanted* me here, and if it wasn't for *me*, you'd all still be chasing your tails, so cut the bullshit and let me the fuck out of here and I'll tell you exactly where to find this crazy bitch."

Tanner frowned, swore under his breath and stormed out.

"You win, Kaylyn," Captain Simmons said, "but you haven't exactly made any friends today."

"I always win, Cap—that's who I am…that's what I do." I crushed the cigarette butt under my shoe. "As for not making any friends—I can live with *that*, too."

• • •

Dusty and I weren't part of the meeting they put together, but Spinner called me two hours later while she and I were having a late supper and told me that they were going to cordon off the whole neighborhood near the *Hotel Central* at five A. M. the next morning. They were going to use tactical teams, door-to-door searches, dogs, helicopters, roadblocks—the works.

I thanked him for keeping me in the loop, and told him to keep me posted.

"Will do, Lynn…and by the way: you are one *crazy* bitch! I *do* believe you've ruined me for any other woman!"

"Don't let your wife hear you talking like that, Bobby," I said and laughed, unable to help myself.

"Screw *her*," he said. "She moved in with her sister the day they suspended me. Said she wants a divorce."

"*Did* she now?" I purred.

As I told you earlier—it had been a long time since I'd been with a man.

• • •

"What are *we* going to do?" Dusty asked after I hung up and told her about the conversation. She was already starting to know me quite well, and I smiled.

"We're going hunting, Dusty."

"When?"

"Right now, as soon as I pay the check." I craned my neck, looking for our waitress.

"You *ever* going to let me pay for supper?' Dusty said with a sigh.

"Yeah, as soon as we dry you out." I studied her. "How you doing, by the way?"

"I, uh, took a little when I went to the ladies' room—just a little."

"Okay," I said and sighed, "but as soon as this is over…"

"I can do it," she assured me. "I just can't go cold-turkey while we're still working this thing."

I've never been addicted to drugs, but I understood quite well what it was like, so I kept my mouth shut and ten minutes later we were in the car.

"We've got plenty of time before they set up," I said, looking at my watch.

"You want to chance being in that neighborhood? What if they come early?"

"They can go right now, if they want, Kiddo—we won't be there."

"The *Premier*," she said, and nodded.

As I told you, she was getting to know me quite well.

"The *Premier*," I confirmed and started the engine.

I had checked the body damage on my Mustang before we had eaten, and it was minor stuff. I knew I'd have to give the car to David for a week or so to whip it back into shape, but that could wait.

"You really think she'll be there?"

"You know that place better than I do, Dusty—it's only two blocks away from the address she gave to the rental people, and everyone there keeps their mouth shut. Yeah, I think she's there." I pulled out of the parking lot and headed back to the office.

"Where are you going?"

"Back to Farmington, first—I want to change, grab another gun, and put on my Kevlar vest." The police had confiscated my Glock, pending an investigation into the shooting on 95, but I keep half a dozen large caliber weapons in my safe.

We got down there in no time, and I changed my clothes, opting for the black shirt, black running shoes and black jeans that I favor for night work. I added the vest, covered it with a black leather jacket, and took down a *Colt Python* .357 Magnum with a four inch barrel and walnut grips. Most detectives these days favor automatics—mostly because of the larger clip-capacity, but revolvers don't jam and nothing puts a person down like a magnum. The *Python* was heavy, but it could stop a truck, and I wasn't taking any chances. I added three speed-loaders just in case I got into a fire fight, and slipped them into the left hand pocket of my jacket. I paused for a moment, and then added a nice little .380 automatic as a back-up, and slipped it into the right hand pocket.

Both guns were loaded with jacketed-hollow-point bullets, quite capable of piercing body armor.

Dusty had stood there the whole time, watching me.

"What?" I said when I was finished.

"I, uh, never realized how…you're *hot*, Kaylyn. God, I wish *I* had a figure like yours! You're curvy, but you're *solid*, too. Your arms look like *steel*, for Christ's sake!"

She wasn't hitting on me, I decided after searching her eyes, and for that I was glad. You might think that I don't have any boundaries, and it's true that I'm hornier than an alley cat in heat, but she was just a kid and I really *had* come to think of her as a little sister.

"You want a body like *this*, Kiddo? Get off that shit you're on and I'll train you myself."

"For real?"

"For real. But you won't *look* good until you *are* good, and that means keeping that damn needle out of your arm."

"I can do it, Kaylyn, I promise!"

"Don't promise *me*, baby—promise yourself." I turned back to the closet and took out another vest. "Here, put this on."

"Yeah?"

"You aren't going without it, Baby Sister."

Dusty took off her shirt and took the vest from me. She *could* have had a nice body—she had the build for it and perky little boobs, too—but she was as skinny as a rail and I knew I'd have to make her health a priority…if I lived that long. When she had it on and had covered it with her shirt, I touched her hair. She was so adorable, big blue eyes and all that I swore right then and there to be everything to her…that Rachel had been to me.

"Here," I said, turning back to the safe and handing her the .25. "Put this in your pocket, and *keep* it there, unless you absolutely *have* to defend yourself." She hesitated, and I added: "You know how to use that?"

Instead of answering, and without taking her eyes from mine, she cocked the weapon, un-cocked it, slipped the safety back on and grinned at me.

"I'm a fast learner," she quipped, with a huge grin.

"Yeah, well, let's just hope you don't have to use the damn thing. Come on."

We were back in her old neighborhood fifteen minutes later, and I parked on a side street behind the hotel.

"You ready?"

"I won't let you down, Lynn—how do you want to work this?"

"First things first. Let's talk to your brother, and go from there. I don't know for sure that she's even *here*, Dusty, but maybe he's seen her again. We have to start *someplace*, and since she's been here before it's as good a place as any to start. If we don't have any luck with your brother, we'll check out this neighborhood tomorrow while the cops are checking the block around the *Central*. I mean, she has to be staying *someplace*."

We got out and started walking. It was dark, a little *too* dark, because every other street light seemed to be out, but that worked to *our* advantage, too.

At least, I *hoped* it did.

I thought I heard someone close a car door down the block behind us, but when I turned to look there was nothing moving in the shadows. A few moments later I thought I heard someone scuff a shoe on the pavement—again, behind us—but when I turned around and stopped to listen, the sidewalk behind us was empty all the way back to the main street, and it was so quiet you could have heard a pin drop. I grabbed Dusty's hand, and walked a little faster. I ducked into a doorway a minute later, pulling the girl with me, and peered out just in time to see someone enter a building down the block. I took a deep breath, and stepped out again, feeling better, and happy to know that I *hadn't* been imagining things.

"Come on," I said, "show me where the back door is."

The street smelled like urine and rust and decay, mixed with the faint stench of some dumpster somewhere close that was overdue to be emptied. I suppose every city has streets like that, but I also don't know why it seems to be so prevalent.

From time to time I wonder: is there really any hope for us as a society?

Dusty took the lead, and all but dragged me along. She may have been a skinny little B-cup, that girl, but she was as strong as an ox. From far off—there was the lonely wail of a train whistle.

"That's it just up ahead."

The place she was pointing at was a loading dock with a steel fire door beside it.

"Is it locked?" I whispered.

"Yeah, but that's not where we're going. Come on—I'll show you."

Dusty passed the loading dock and turned right down an alley that ran along the west side of the *Premier Hotel*. The thing that hit me the most was that we hadn't run into a single, solitary person, except for whoever lived in that other building. Either the neighborhood was full of working people, who went to bed shortly after work, or it was dangerous, and folks stayed indoors at night. I suspected it was the latter.

"There's a service door halfway down," Dusty told me, "you know, for working girls." She grinned, and her teeth were very white in the gloom. "It's locked, but I have a key."

We were inside in seconds, and the door locked behind us automatically.

The sound it made seemed ominous—at least to my ears.

There was another metal door, and it opened to a stairwell that didn't smell any better than the dumpster. Dusty was in front of me, and seemed to know where she was going, but since there was only one 40-watt bulb on each landing, it was pretty dark working our way up.

The landing on the fifth floor was completely dark, and I grabbed Dusty's hand hard to stop her.

"The light's out," I hissed.

"*Fuck*, Kaylyn! It's always out! You almost made me fall down the stairs!"

The *Premier* had ten stories, and I didn't relish the thought of going all the way up in the dark.

"What floor's your brother on?"

"Here! Right here, Kaylyn! Let go, so I can open the damn door!"

It hit me then that this was *her* world, the world she knew all too well, and was comfortable in; again I vowed to take her away from all of this. I didn't know why, exactly, my feelings for this girl were so strong, but, looking back, and after several painful sessions to come with Doctor Brown, I suspect it had a lot to do with what Rachel had done for *me*...and my guilt at what had to be done to *her*. The door was open now and Dusty was putting her keys back in her purse.

"Come on—he's right down the hall."

I was already holding the *Python* in my right hand, but I tightened my grip when Dusty knocked on the door: once, twice more, a pause, and then again.

There was the unmistakable sound of a dead-bolt being thrown, and then the door opened a crack, held by a chain.

"Hey," she said.

"Hey," a male voice said; I assumed it was her brother, 'Gem'.

I heard the chain being slid along its track, and then the door was opened all the way. I remembered the revolver at the last moment and put it away just in time to walk in.

"What's up?' the young man said, looking in the hallway, both ways, before closing the door and locking it.

"What? No hug?" Dusty asked.

"Sorry, Drue—Mary and I were sleeping." He hugged her and turned to me. "Oh, is this the chick you told me about?"

"Yeah. Gem, Kaylyn. Kaylyn, this is my brother, Gerald."

"Please, call me 'Gem'," he said and actually offered his hand.

"Kaylyn Vale," I said, taking his hand.

Gerald was a male version of Drusilla, maybe three or four inches taller, and had the same, pale blue eyes. He was thin, but he didn't look emaciated, and I remembered that he didn't use.

"It going down tonight?" he asked, and swiped a shock of unruly light brown hair out of his eyes.

I knew that Dusty had told him what was going to happen—if leaving out most of the details—which was why he and Mary were heading down to Florida to join her Uncle's Carnival.

All I could think of at that moment, with the thought of them going south to join a travelling carnival, was *Twilight Eyes*, by Dean Koontz.

See what happens when you're lonely? You think life is a novel.

"No, not tonight, tomorrow; what time are you leaving, anyway?"

"Our flight's at six, which is why we were already in bed, Drue."

I did the math—they'd be long gone before our friends tore up the neighborhood two blocks down looking for Rachel.

"Yeah, sorry about that," I said. "We won't keep you. I just wanted to know if you've seen the woman with the burns on her face."

Gem's eyes grew wide—he had, after all, *serviced* Rachel, and more than once, I'd guess—for money.

"Wow, is she—"

"She's a part of it," I interrupted, not willing to give him any more details than he already had. "But she's in danger, and I need to find her."

"Shit!"

"What?" Dusty asked.

"Well, she's *here*! Took a room just tonight, on the eighth floor. I was up there earlier…well, you know, but she looked like something the cat dragged in, and I don't mean those burns. Haggard—looks like she hasn't slept."

"Give me the room number."

"Eight-o-eight."

"Ok, I guess we're out of here," Dusty said, glancing at my eyes. She turned to her brother and hugged him fiercely. "Be careful, and call me as soon as you get off the plane."

"Not to worry, Drue-Blood. It ain't like we're moving to Australia." He grabbed her shoulders and looked in her eyes. "This chick you're with," he said, as if I wasn't there, "she seems all right to me. If she wants to help you get off that shit—*let* her!" He kissed her and looked up at me, standing up straight. "Take care of her. She's all I got."

"Like she was my own," I said, and meant it, shaking his hand again.

• • •

We crept up those back stairs like creeping tactical soldiers in a movie, not making a sound, and went down the hall to Room 808.

The door was open a crack, and there was a light on inside.

I was ahead of Dusty, and I put my left hand out behind me to slow her down as I pulled the *Python* and cocked it. The big *Colt* felt good in my hand, real and solid enough to take away the jitters.

I risked a glance behind me and put a finger to my lips.

When I got to the door I flattened myself against the wall and just stood that way, wondering what to do. No one in their right mind would leave their door open at night in a place like this and I wondered what Rachel was up to…or if she was even in there at all. She may have been crazy, but she was far from stupid and I wasn't going to underestimate her.

The *Colt* was in my right hand, and I used it to wave Dusty against the wall on my side, and with my free left hand made a patting motion so that she would get up against the wall like I was.

There was so much I didn't know! And I silently berated myself for not asking Dusty if Gem had ever told Rachel that he had a sister. The guy in the Camaro had had a cell phone, or so I'd been told, so had he called Rachel? Did she know about Drusilla? And if Gem had seen Rachel earlier, was she now baiting me, setting a trap?

The window at the end of the hall—ahead of me—was open, and the dusty old drapes moved slightly as the wind sighed into the building. The drapes weren't long enough to hide a person, so there was no way that anyone could be under them, so I turned my attention to the other doors around me to see if any were open, even a crack. When I was satisfied that they weren't, I decided that I couldn't very well stand here forever, and so, taking a deep breath, I inched forward, and pushed the door all the way open with my left hand, fully expecting to hear a shot as I pulled my hand back.

With the door open I walked backwards towards Drusilla, never taking my eyes from that long rectangle of light that was the door-way. The light seemed yellow on the old carpeted hallway, and the rectangle of light that covered the floor was slanted and ominous. I grabbed Dusty's little purse without even looking at her, and she didn't protest. I was still looking at the door, so I didn't know if she had armed herself as I felt around in her purse until I found what I was looking for.

A compact.

Now, if the *Premier* was like most places, the rooms would all be in the same configuration; I'd been in two—the room I had shared with Dusty and just now at Gerald's, so I was hoping that Room 808 would be the same. I inched forward, keeping low, and squatted down, using the mirror to look inside.

Nothing—except that one of the windows was open with the curtains blowing softly into the living room. The rain had stopped, but there was moisture in the air, and the breeze felt damp and cold. I moved the mirror around, hoping I wouldn't take a bullet in my hand, and when I was satisfied that the room was exactly the same as the other two I stood up, pocketed the compact and looked back at Dusty.

Stay put! I said silently and clearly, just as I'd been taught in my lip-reading class back in my "Company" days.

I entered the room with the revolver held before me in a two-handed combat grip, and swung it first left, then right, noticing that the bedroom door was closed. Creeping further into the room I checked behind the couch and then peeked in the bathroom. The wind was making a curious, eerie, sighing noise, but other than that the apartment was as silent as a tomb.

That left the bedroom.

Somewhere far below, someone yelled: a woman, followed by a man's angry voice—an argument.

All of my senses were on full alert, and again I heard that lonely train whistle, far off in the distance.

My whole body was shaking as I headed towards the bedroom, shaking from the tension and the strain of being hyper-vigilant for so long.

I don't know why, but it made me angry so I threw caution to the wind, strode to the bedroom and kicked the door open, covering the room from left to right.

Like the rest of the apartment the room was empty.

"Clear," I said loud enough for Dusty to hear me, and as I was starting to put the gun back in my holster Dusty appeared in the doorway, white-faced with her eyes big and round because of the knife Rachel was holding to her throat.

The analytical part of me tried to figure out what kind of knife she was holding against this girl that I loved—a Navy MK-2 or a Special Forces *Randall*—either way, it looked as sharp as a razor and reflected the light like a mirror. I raised the gun and pointed it at Rachel's head. Rachel knew me, and knew I wouldn't miss at this distance—not with a four inch barrel.

"Uh-uh," Rachel said as she entered the room with Dusty before her; she kicked the door shut with her foot, but because the bolt was drawn it hit the jam and remained open a crack. I thought I heard a noise in the hallway, as if someone had drawn a deep breath, but then I decided it had been the wind. "Don't even *think* about it, Lynn."

I kept the magnum pointed at her face—or what was left of it. "Nice knife, Rach," I said. "What's the matter—they yank your gun permit?"

"Smartass," she sneered. "No, Kaylyn, I didn't have time to get to it. I barely beat you two up the stairs."

"Let me guess: you were out on the ledge the whole time." I was thinking about both open windows—one here, one in the hallway.

"What different does it make, you little shit? Put the gun down or I'll slit her throat."

"Go ahead," I said, unable to even *look* at Dusty's eyes. "She doesn't mean a *thing* to me."

It was obvious now that Rachel had been on her way to Gerald's apartment when she heard us inside, and had run back up the stairs. If she was using a knife instead of a gun, it also meant that she had one close by—and would ty to get to it using Drusilla as a shield. She moved deeper into the room, dragging poor Dusty with her, edging towards the desk by the window, confirming my suspicions.

"Who the *fuck* do you think you're talking to, you little leezie? At least the other bitch had a set of *tits* on her—this one needs a *Care Package!*"

"Put the fucking knife down, you coward!"

"Coward?" Rachel moved the blade, ever so slightly, drawing a thin bead of blood out of the side of Drue's neck. She cried out, but Rachel held her firm. "You're the fucking coward, Kaylyn! You're a needy, whiney little bitch—and you always were! Now put down the fucking gun!"

"No," I said and took a deep breath. "The only way you're leaving this room is in a body-bag, Rachel. This has gone far enough."

"Oh, I'm just getting *started*, honey—now put the gun on the desk or I swear to fucking *God* I'll kill her! I won't ask you again!"

There are moments in your life that define you—and I was about to experience two of them—when you find out who you are. I loved Dusty—she was the little sister I never had, and I would *die* to protect her, but I had made my mind up: Rachel was NOT getting out of the room alive…no matter what.

"You won't have to," I said calmly, meeting Drusilla's eyes, and just then Dusty threw her head back, catching Rachel full in the face. The knife slid down to Drue's shoulder as Rachel stumbled back, digging a long furrow over the bony part of her upper arm, and then fell to the floor as Rachel clutched at her broken nose; just as she was lunging for the desk I leveled the magnum at her again—just as she pulled the drawer open.

"Rachel, don't!"

Rachel Stark—the woman who had saved my life, *twice*, my friend and comrade—froze...and then looked up at me with a smile.

"Can't do it, Kaylyn, can you?"

The weapon was already cocked, but I tightened my grip, hating myself for the tears I felt welling up.

"Please, Rachel—don't *do* this!"

"You'd *shoot* me, Lynn? Me? After everything I've done for you?"

"The girl I loved, Rachel, is long gone. I don't even know who you are anymore."

"Fine, but what about your mother? You shoot me, you'll *never* find her."

"I can live with that, Rachel—now *please*, get away from the desk!"

"You can't *do* it, *can* you, Lynn?" Rachel said and lunged for the inside of the drawer.

I heard a sound behind me: the unmistakable *click-click-click* as a revolver was thumbed back to full-cock; three crisp clicks as the sear-pin dropped into the hammer notches.

"No, but *I* can," a woman said from behind me—and blew Rachel's head off.

Rachel flew into the wall, slid down with half her head blown away, and I turned around to find Samantha Ashbery standing there with a .38 in her hand. Sam came forward, apparently undaunted by the red smear on the wall and seeping into the carpet, and fired a second shot into Rachel's head—just as a professional would have.

Then she turned to me with a look of derision on her face.

"You *weren't* going to do it, Kaylyn." She shook her head. "But *someone* had to."

"Sam, I—"

"What the *fuck* were you doing, Lynn?" she asked in disgust, "*talking* her to death?" Sam bit her lip, sighed, and handed me the gun with one gloved hand. "It's untraceable. Tell them you took it from her, tell them whatever the fuck you want, and see if the kid's all right. I'm outta here."

"Sam, how did you know w—?"
"I *followed* you, stupid. See you around."
"Sam, please—"
"Have a nice life, Kaylyn," Sam said—and then she was gone.

• • •

There are moments in life that define you, and I had just had two of them; two moments during which I found out who I really am.

Have you ever read *The Lord of The Rings?* Like *Frodo Baggins* on that cliff at *Mount Doom*, I found that, when the time came—I just couldn't throw the "ring of power" into the fire…

But then again…

You might not be able to understand this, but until that moment I really *had* been broken, as broken as Wade and Sam have ever been. Still, I knew without a doubt, that, despite my resolve, I really *wouldn't* have let Rachel hurt Drusilla, and that, all by itself, was a *good* thing. Until that moment, I thought I was just like Rachel—a more *controlled* Rachel, but Rachel just the same. Until that moment I thought I was a cold-blooded killer, but in that moment I learned that my compassion was stronger than my anger, and that my reason outweighed my rage…and that, *too*, was a good thing.

If *Sméagol* hadn't intervened, there isn't a *doubt* in anyone's mind that *Frodo* wouldn't have been able to destroy the *ring*, but would *I* have been able to kill Rachel?

We'll never know, not for sure, anyway, but if *Sam* hadn't been there, if *Sam* hadn't intervened, there *is* one thing I was certain of—no matter what, I wouldn't have let Rachel get her hand on that gun—if for no other reason than, I would have done whatever I had to do—to protect my "little sister".

And I could live with *that*, too.

Nothing in this life is ever black and white, and as I told you earlier, I had learned who I am—not a killer, but a caring, compassionate woman, who, in the final analysis, had been able to overcome the bitterness of an entire lifetime.

And *that* was a good thing, too—maybe the *best* of things.

• • •

Kaylyn Vale stood there watching Samantha Ashbery walk away…and then I fairly flew to where Dusty was crouching, holding a bloody hand over the deep gash in her shoulder.

"*Told* you I was a fast leaner," she said.

"*Jesus*, girl!"

I drew her to me, hugging her, kissing the top of her head, saying over and over and over again, that I was sorry.

"It's ok, Lynn. *I'm* ok. I *know* you really wouldn't have let her kill me." And, no matter what—*that* much was the truth.

"Come on," I said, "Let's get you patched up."

I got her to her feet, put my arm around her waist and her good arm around my shoulder, and walked her to the door. I dialed 911 with my free hand…and then, using the Number "3" on my speed-dial, I called Spinelli.

• • •

A rainy April sloughed into a very hot May, and I spent most of that time getting Drusilla healthy. We had a bad couple of weeks, getting her dried out, but it passed, and I never left her side. I can't even *imagine* my life without her, and every single day I remember what Wade told me that night in Afghanistan—that family isn't necessarily a matter of blood.

Dusty was right—once in a while, you simply have to *make* your own family.

• • •

The *Pulitzer Prize* winning editor, Clair Sacchetti, got her exclusive in the matter of The *Judgment Day Killer*, and Sam has published a book, *Injustice: A Constitutional Crisis*, doing for all of us what Rachel *should* have done, fighting our broken justice system with reason and compassion and logic. Sam actually dedicated one chapter of her book to Kyle Worthington, and caught some serious flak for it, but, what the hell, that's just who Sam is.

Lieutenant Robert L. Spinelli of the Rhode Island State Police is now *Captain* Spinelli, and he and I…well, for lack of a better term—we're friends…with benefits; one of these days I really *do* have to ask him what the "L" stands for.

Rachel Stark—also known as Rebekka Worthington—was buried without fanfare on a rainy day late in April, right beside her brother, with only me, Dusty, and Sam in attendance—Sam didn't talk to us, and we didn't talk to her.

Wade Ashbery is once again spending most of his time teaching and coaching and helping his brother run *Ashbery's Dairy Farm*, a Rhode Island treasure, and ex-con David Redman, one of the best friends I have ever had, is once again dividing his time between his duties on the Becker Ranch, and his volunteer work at *Second Starts*, a re-entry center for men and woman on parole who want to do the right thing.

Drusilla Anderson, aka "Dusty"…she's now an indispensable part of my life, as well as my business, and is actually taking night courses in Criminal Justice and Business Law at the University of Rhode Island.

And as for Kaylyn Vale—I really *don't* have many friends anymore, but the ones I *do* have are loving and loyal and true, and I *like* the girl I see in the mirror when I put on my ear-rings in the morning.

I'm thinking—*everyone* should be so lucky.

CHAPTER ELEVEN—Six Months Later

"I'm sorry, Kaylyn" Doctor Erica Brown said, "I really, really am, but none of this is a secret, and it's certainly *not* classified, and yet—you've glossed over what happened after Sam left the *Premier Hotel*. After she barged in and startled Rachel Stark and you were able to get the gun away from her. I'm curious: why are you *doing* that? Is it something you're having trouble dealing with?"

That was putting it mildly, wasn't it? The story Dusty and I came up with is that Sam was behind us and startled Rachel, allowing me to get the gun away from her; I would have left Sam out of the picture completely, but as she was leaving the *Premier* she walked right into the first two cops who had responded to the gunshots, cops who knew me and knew that Sam was on my payroll. Sam told them she had come outside to wait for them, and that she really hadn't seen anything.

I simply ran with what she had told them and concocted my own scenario.

Now, no law enforcement professional on the planet would have believed that I had wrestled the gun away from Rachel and *then* shot her in the head with the exact same gun from six or seven feet away—let alone a point-blank *second* shot to the head, but Rebekka Worthington had been the most wanted criminal in the country, the most wanted in decades, and we had killed her, and to tell you the truth—that's the sort of thing careers are made on.

Police Departments, politicians, and to be fair, the FBI, are simply not into giving themselves a black eye. This had been an extremely public case, a case in which the local authorities as well as The Feds proved to be woefully inadequate, and if they moved against me in any way whatsoever they ran the risk that the truth of their incompetence would get out—either that or they'd have to kill me to keep me quiet.

Putting aside the fact that they never would have found Rachel without Sam and I, the authorities also knew damn right well that someone in that room had mowed Rachel down in cold blood and then capped her a second time for good measure.

Here were their choices, then: press charges against me, or take credit for bringing down one of the most dangerous home-grown terrorists in U. S. history.

It didn't take a genius to figure out what they'd end up doing, and after some grumbling and posturing, they let me walk and simply told the media that Rachel had been killed in a struggle with police officers and federal agents.

Even Erica didn't know the real story, and it was obviously getting to her…if only because she believed that I needed to get it out.

"I don't know, Doc. I guess I haven't figured it out myself. All I can tell you is that it all happened so fast, and killing a person is something that damages you. You'd have to know Rachel to understand that, but I believe she viewed herself as a patriot, someone like the Founding Fathers at war with an oppressive government. She was trying to get us to see that sentencing a person to no job, no housing and no relationships—after they have already served their sentence, doesn't *prevent* crime, it *causes* it. If only she had done what Sam has done in her book—exposing the hypocrisy of the system—she may have even been viewed as some kind of social engineer. As it is, all she'll be remembered for are the murders, and it's hard to acknowledge that and reconcile all that violence with a person who was truly once a very loving and compassionate person. I just felt like, I don't know…I felt like I simply needed to let it go."

Doctor Brown nodded as if she understood, but I wasn't sure that I did.

"What I'm hearing is that you believe you're responsible for Rachel's death."

"That's putting it mildly,"

"Only one person was responsible for Rachel's death, Kaylyn, and that person was Rachel herself."

"I don't even care about any of that, Erica! God!"

"What? What's frustrating you?"

"You always accuse me of going to some novel or some movie for an answer, but all I can think of now is the Clint Eastwood film, *Unforgiven*."

"Tell me how that applies. I'm interested."

"I'm paraphrasing, because it's been so long since I've see it, but the Eastwood character says something like: *it's a terrible thing to kill someone—you take away everything they have... and everything they're ever going to have*." I looked at her, because until then I had been staring out the window. "Regardless of the cause, Erica—it's awful and I just want to be rid of it."

Erica Brown sat back, sighed, and folded her hands. "Under the circumstances, Kaylyn, I'd say that's a healthy decision."

"I'm glad you think so. I just can't take being responsible for the death of someone I loved, someone who had done so much for me."

"You're *not* responsible, Lynn; as I've already told you, that responsibility lies solely on Rachel Stark, because it was her own actions that eventually led to her death. Most of the time, all I hear in this room are people trying to shirk their responsibility—*you* seem to take more of it on, even when it isn't yours, and it's something we need to work on if we're even going to get to the underlying issue."

"Back to my mother again."

"Yes, it seems to be your focal point."

"Rachel taunted me; told me that she knew where my mother was."

"Do you believe that?"

"Yeah, I guess I do."

"Alright, we'll come back to that." She looked at her watch. I knew we only had fifteen minutes left. "What became of this thing with Wade and Sam? After you reconciled with them, you told me that there was an interesting, uh, compromise proposed to the complications the three of you had created. Did the three of you ever, um…get together?"

"I don't kiss and tell, Doc," I said with a smirk.

"Understand now, this isn't idle curiosity. I truly believe that you gravitate to situations like that simply because you've made yourself unable to commit fully to one person, and it's the reason, I fear, why you've never had a lasting relationship." She paused and smiled. "And by the way, I'll take that as a 'yes'."

"What about my relationship with Drusilla?" I asked, side-stepping her question.

"Are you sleeping with her?"

"No, of course not. She's like my little sister."

"Then it's not the same thing, is it?"

I sighed. "I'm in a relationship right now."

"With a married man, I'm forced to point out."

"He's separated," I said somewhat lamely, waiting for her to say that I was "minimizing" my own actions.

Erica sighed. "All right, let's get back to your mother for a moment, because it's obvious that you don't want to deal with your inability to relate to anybody one-on-one. Do you really think you can find her, now that Rachel's dead?"

I didn't know how to answer that, not out loud, anyway, but in my heart of hearts I knew the answer. I would find my mother, because, I'm Kaylyn Vale—that's who I am; that's what I do.

AUTHOR'S NOTE

People familiar with my work will no doubt notice that a version of Kaylyn Vale appears in several of my novels. Kaylyn was originally intended as a "throw-away" in the novel, *Warrior*, where she was only supposed to appear as "the raven-haired beauty" who trained the character, Kalina Zamonar.

Kaylyn, however, had other ideas. In my mind, Kaylyn resembles the wonderful actress, Alexandra Daddario, with her gorgeous, long dark hair, incredible blue eyes and breathtaking figure. Still, what *became* the character of Kaylyn Vale went far beyond mere physical attributes. Kaylyn somehow became *real* to me: loyal, brave and possessed of a most unusual integrity. By the time the novel *Nomad* was written, Kaylyn had become an integral part of the story, and also figures prominently in the follow-up, *Assassin*.

In the *Broken Heroes* series, I found I needed a counter-point to the heroine of the story, Samantha Ashbery; a darker, more worldly version of Sam, if you will. By the time *Forever Means Forever* and *It's Later Than It Seems* were written, Kaylyn was once again a very vital and indispensable part of the plot.

Her appearance in my work seems to coincide with a very special woman who came into my life and remained there during times when most others certainly would have fled. As Kaylyn herself is fond of saying, "A friend is the one running *into* the burning building to get you, while everyone else is running *away*."

When you have a friend, a *lover* like that, you can do anything, even serve a tour in Hell, as Kazeem of Zambooria and Wade Ashbery, along with yours truly, know all too well.

The idea for *Judgment Day* stems from engaging in several conversations with college professors and folks in the legal profession on how oppressive our government has become; how the laws of this once great land no longer seem to matter, and how those of us who believe that The Bill of Rights was divinely inspired know that we have to hold our elected officials legally accountable for their actions, instead of allowing them to legislate only in direct response to the media and in the interests of their own careers.

Once again I needed a strong female lead, and once again, Kaylyn was there. I am unashamedly smitten with her, essentially since the *core* of her character resembles someone I love—even if both of them *are* more than a little bit crazy, and while the antagonist in this story goes far beyond the confines of law and morality to make *her* presence known, only Kaylyn Vale was strong enough, smart enough, and compassionate enough to bring her to Justice.

For Kaylyn—and despite the methods she sometimes employs—it is essential not to become the thing you are fighting; to paraphrase Nietzsche, it is important not to stare into the darkness for long periods of time—if you do, you might begin to resemble the very thing you loath.

A *fine* line, perhaps, but there nonetheless.

In my opinion, other authors have also become enamored with their characters: Anne Rice and *Lestat* come to mind first, as does Dorothy L. Sayers, and her character, *Lord Peter Wimsey*…still, I have no way of knowing if either of those two were inspired by real life people, and I suppose it doesn't matter—it is enough for *me* to know who Kaylyn Vale is and what she means to me, and I can only hope that my work lets "Kaylyn" know it, too—despite how utterly *insane* she must be to have marched into Hell to drag this writer out by his feet.

Please enjoy the book—the adventures of Kaylyn Vale *will* continue…

—Jaysen Christopher

H.A. Peine District Library
202 N. Main
P.O. Box 19
Minier, IL 61759-0019